Spy Dragon

By John Fullerton

The second in the Brodick Cold War thriller series.

Burning Chair Limited, Trading as Burning Chair Publishing
61 Bridge Street, Kington HR5 3DJ
www.burningchairpublishing.com

By John Fullerton
Edited by Simon Finnie and Peter Oxley
Book cover design by Burning Chair Publishing

First published by Burning Chair Publishing, 2021

ISBN: 978-1-912946-18-1

By the Same Author:

Spy Game (Brodick Cold War Thriller Series: 1)
The Soviet Occupation of Afghanistan
The Monkey House
Clap (writing as JW Diaz)
A Hostile Place
This Green Land
White Boys Don't Cry
The Reticent Executioner

Kill the chicken to scare the monkey
殺鷄嚇猴 (*shaji xiahou*)

Beirut. Friday, March 16, 1984

A tall Westerner with a lined face and greying hair emerges from an apartment block onto a one-way street still in shadow. He wears a suit and carries a Samsonite briefcase. Shoulders back, he marches rather than strolls to a Renault 5 Turbo in a nearby parking lot, unlocks it, opens the driver's door and drops the briefcase—containing a 9mm semi-automatic pistol and walkie-talkie—onto the front passenger seat. He settles behind the wheel, turns the ignition, releases the handbrake and reverses out onto the road. At the intersection, a black Mercedes lurches out in from of him. A second Merc screeches up behind, braking hard and cutting off any retreat.

Masked men jump out brandishing handguns and an AK-47.

One smashes the driver's window, which explodes with a popping sound and a cascade of glass; his comrade lunges forward and punches the foreigner twice in the head and opens the door. They drag him to the first Merc, force him into the back, down on the floor. They leave the briefcase.

The first car races away, the second reverses out of sight, burning rubber.

It's all over in under eleven seconds.

Not yet 7am, the morning has that special West Beirut fragrance, a mingling of sea air and cardamom-flavoured Turkish coffee. A woman pegs her family's washing onto a line across her second-floor balcony, an infant wails, the sublime voice of Fairuz drifts from a doorway, at street level a metal shutter clatters up to reveal a bakery; a queue forms in anticipation of breakfast: mouth-watering *ma'noeshe,* hot flat loaves crusty on the outside, drenched in olive oil and *za'atar,* the latter a mixture of dried oregano, salt, sesame, sumac and basil.

The Renault is stranded on the street, the driver's door open.

William Francis Buckley—United States national, veteran special forces officer and the current CIA station chief in the Lebanese capital—has vanished.

1

Scared. A not unfamiliar sensation.

Saying 'yes' to the mission was automatic, thoughtless, a given and a ritual demonstration of loyalty and apparent sense of duty on the part of a servant of the Crown. But moments later and barely out of his Controller's office in Century House, heading back along the corridor and down to his lowly floor, Richard Brodick asked himself that familiar question to which there was never a satisfactory answer.

'What the hell have I done?'

Duty? Loyalty? No, not really. Not anymore. He was no one's servant, least of all that of the British state. He'd finally outgrown his predilection for *Boy's Own* adventures.

As he entered his office—too cramped to be shared comfortably—Brodick consoled himself with the notion that he'd be a fool not to be afraid, and Brodick knew himself to be anything but a fool. It seemed to him that cleverness and fear went hand in hand in his trade; in this instance a role that would shortly deliver him to Damascus via Cyprus in the comfort of a Club Class window seat on an Air France flight.

He sat at his desk under the glare of the overhead strip lights, ignored the curious glances of his three colleagues and drank in—perhaps for the last time—the musty stink of dust, typewriter oil, floor cleaner and ancient files. He would not miss this.

It wasn't a matter of serving his country. He was over that. He wasn't fighting the global scourge of Communism while humming

Land of Hope and Glory under his breath. He didn't see himself as a knight in shining armour either, heroically dismantling crime syndicates in Kiev and St Petersburg. There was no Henry V moment at Agincourt, no stiffening of sinews: or for that matter any other part of his anatomy. He knew himself too well. He loved the promise of secret power; it was a drug to which he could easily become addicted if he wasn't already hooked. His youthful illusions shed, or so he told himself, he felt lighter, freed of the burden of duty, emancipated from the grind of moral scruple to pursue something far higher and more meaningful: his own success.

Within minutes of the plane taking off from Larnaca—on the second leg of his journey and turning southeast to cruising height of 33,000 feet above a placid Mediterranean—the funk evaporated and was replaced by a sensation of serenity. Brodick imagined himself and his fellow passengers penetrating an invisible barrier between the safe certainties of what passed for Western culture to that unknown, turbulent and barbarous airspace labelled *'Here Be Dragons'*. His peculiar calm in the face of heaven-only-knew-what danger was fortified by a complementary aperitif of Veuve Clicquot followed by a half bottle of Meursault with his smoked salmon and, to avoid having to talk to anyone or look them in the eye, the previous day's edition of *L'Orient Le Jour*: a Beirut broadsheet widely judged to be still reliable after nine years of internecine murder. Brodick couldn't judge either way: his schoolboy French wasn't up to it.

The plane began its descent as it approached the Lebanese coast. Smoke spiralled up from Beirut airport, shut down after what the newspaper said was an Israeli air strike that had destroyed or damaged thirteen Middle East Airlines planes. There was still snow on Mount Lebanon. Perhaps he might get a chance to try the slopes, civil war and occupation permitting. The outdated tourist brochure in the seat pocket said a visitor could ski in the morning and swim in the sea the same afternoon: or was it the other way around? And right now, down below, was the Bekaa Valley, glorious in Spring sunshine.

But the worm of terror wasn't done. It returned, twisting and turning in his bowels as he entered the Damascus airport arrivals hall and queued with the foreigners—there were only four business class travellers, two of them obviously Russians, and not many more in tourist class—while a slight, unshaven official with a grubby collar, frayed cuffs, bitten-down nails and a blank expression plucked at the well-thumbed cards of a massive Rolodex. Eventually he took Brodick's fake passport, held it upside down: gingerly at first as if afraid it might explode and contaminate the Syrian Arab Republic with a lethal dose of imperialism. He then thumbed through it from back to front with painful slowness—painful to Brodick, that is—until he came to the bearer's muddy photograph, turned the document the right way up and presumably searched his card files for a *Drew Sullivan*, Brodick's cover name.

It seemed to take forever. Brodick resisted the urge to offer his assistance.

The official handed the passport back.

No welcome to Syria. Nothing, not a word.

Brodick hesitated then stumbled away, disconcerted by the sheer indifference of Ba'ath Party authority, but nonetheless keeping control of his sphincter muscle.

Customs didn't so much as glance at him. Brodick felt almost insulted.

Outside a very tall man with a bloodhound's flabby cheeks and a hangdog expression held up a placard which read in capital letters: *'SULIVAN'*.

'I'm Sullivan.'

'Darwish.'

No smile, no handshake, no change in the Druze driver's deadpan expression.

*

Beautiful. Blue sky, rolling hills scented with wild herbs. At the Syria-Lebanon checkpoint, Darwish followed Brodick into what was little more than a hut, an elongated lean-to plastered with posters of Syrian and Lebanese flags and the grim features of President Hafez al-Assad and his Lebanese counterpart, the baby-faced Maronite Christian mafioso named Amin Gemayal. People queued: well, not so much queued as crowded in, squeezed to the front, planted their elbows on the counter and tried to push their passports at the two officials. Lorry drivers, families, bawling babies. It didn't take long. A few minutes was all, breathing in the stench of dirty feet and smoke from two dozen cigarettes. Here, everyone except the babies smoked. Brodick's passport was snatched from him, the pages ruffled, a clear space found for the stamp. Bang. Exit stamp. Bang. Entry stamp. A handful of banknotes exchanged, the whole process quick and absurdly cheap. A stub of a receipt with an unintelligible scrawl. Again, no one bothered to look at him, except the men in shades lolling around outside in the sunshine, idlers sucking on cigarettes, pistols in their waistbands, noting the Volvo's registration number along with the faces of driver and passenger.

Onwards and then, right in front of them, the vista opened wide between the mountain peaks; a rim of sea at last unrolled along the western horizon like a painted backdrop for a Molière comedy. Brodick tensed. It wasn't far now. No more daydreaming: a thrill of excitement and delicious dread made him sit up straight on the back seat, his serenity forgotten. A convoy of military trucks came up from behind and passed them, vomiting diesel exhaust, a dozen heavily laden machines in drab green with tarpaulins lashed down, heading west, in the same direction. Soviet-built GAZ jeeps sprouting whip aerials like cat's whiskers preceded the column and brought up the rear. Darwish drove onto the verge and waited for them to thunder past, headlights on, taking up the entire road. They waited a while to allow the Syrian leviathan to draw well ahead.

Then they rolled on through a town clinging to the mountain slopes. Cottages, yellow walls, gardens full of flowers. Roses. Geraniums in hanging baskets. Lemon and olive trees, fig and vine. At first glance it could have been Corsica, Sardinia or Sicily.

Something was wrong, though: wrong as in peculiar. Very peculiar. Brodick peered out of the windows, first right, then left, shifting along the rear seat to get a better focus and trying to make sense of it. Beyond the women and children, the goats, the dogs, the old men smoking *shisha* and drinking coffee in courtyards and gardens, the clusters of trees, the tranquil and ageless village life of the Mediterranean littoral, he saw that the place was suffering from some kind of malaise. Brodick would have said it was chickenpox if he hadn't known better.

It was a sickness, all right.

The cottage walls were pockmarked by thousands upon thousands of bullet holes, a rash that covered the whole town of Aley. Some of the roofs were damaged; a few had been torn off, leaving only the ribs of charred roof beams, shattered terracotta roof tiles had then been swept into piles by the residents. Small arms fire, heavy machine guns, the 12.7mm calibre of Soviet origin, and the strange claw marks and swathes of torn-away plaster left by detonations of rocket-propelled grenades were the cause. Yet people were conducting their business, living their lives, as if nothing had happened; was happening.

And there, just below the town, soldiers were sitting in the sun: some shirtless, smoking, washing clothing, playing backgammon or eating. They didn't look at the Volvo. The Syrians had dug into the fields with their charges, like tethered attack dogs: long-barrelled artillery, Soviet-built 105s and 130mm guns, spaced out in long, irregular lines. Sandbags lined the walls of the weapon pits: they'd been there for months, many of the bags rotten and broken, spilling sand. The muzzles of the guns were raised over the city below like admonishing forefingers, warning of calamities yet to come.

Below the guns the road fell away in hairpin bends. Mortars had been dug in to the bends, both medium and heavy batteries, poorly concealed by tattered camouflage nets. The city itself—and at this distance the pox hardly showed itself at all—seemed to glitter on its promontory, squeezed between mountain and sea. It couldn't be the reflection of sunlight on thousands of windows. No, it wasn't that.

It was gunfire winking up at Brodick, all along the so-called Green Line that snaked through the once wealthiest districts and the banking zone, dividing eastern and western sectors, while more necklaces of muzzle flashes winked on and off around the Palestinian refugee camps. Small arms fire.

The pox of war welcomed him with its dancing lights and, as he descended, he heard the sound of the festivities, a popping and rippling of AK-47 bursts, the thud of RPGs and 109mm recoilless anti-tank rifles. Just like fireworks back home, only it wasn't bonfire night. So jolly. And at this range, quite harmless.

Welcome, tourist. Welcome to the fun of someone else's war. You could always head home if you didn't like it. That was a luxury denied to everyone else in the madhouse. They lived here. Most of them didn't have a choice.

*

Brodick checked into his hotel, only yards from the main thoroughfare, what the tourist guide had called Lebanon's Oxford Street: Hamra, in West Beirut. This was Le Commodore, already famous among foreign correspondents as a safe haven because it slotted neatly and unobtrusively among much larger buildings that helped shield it from air and artillery attack. A wooden counter to his right was staffed by two young Lebanese males in immaculate white shirts and dark ties. They smiled and nodded as Brodick entered through the revolving door and approached. He handed over his passport. 'Welcome to Lebanon, Mr Sullivan.'

They were so polite, so deferential. Behind the reception desk on the floor lay assault rifles, rocket launchers, belts of ammunition and the anti-tank rockets themselves. A sign on the counter read—in Arabic, English and French—*"Please leave guns at reception"*. The hardware's owners were over at the circular bar on the left, Amal militiamen in tight jeans, t-shirts, trainers and beards. Secular Shi'ites mostly from the south who were happy to drink something stronger than coke. Or maybe there were leftist fighters of the Druze-led Progressive Socialist Party (PSP) among them, too.

'Sir, would you like your bar bill on your laundry list? Sir?'

'I'm sorry.' Brodick wasn't paying attention. He turned away from his contemplation of the drinkers—there were Westerners among them, he noted, probably journalists—and asked the receptionist to repeat what he'd just said.

The young man spoke slowly in case Mr Sullivan was himself a bit slow. 'Sir. Would you like your bar bill on your laundry? For expenses, yes?'

He got it. 'Oh, right. Yes, thank you.'

The foreign press could charge laundry to expenses, but not their drinks. Spies were no different. The Commodore was experienced in such matters. It might not be luxurious like the nearby Bristol, but the staff had been schooled in the rules of the game. Its millionaire Lebanese leaseholder had ensured his guests had what they needed most: relative safety, ample international telephone and telex lines, and easy access to cash and credit. The loans could always be repaid in any one of several currencies to Le Commodore's overseas bank accounts.

There was no bellboy, or if there was, he didn't appear. Brodick carried his bag to the lift. His room was on the second floor. Ideal in that it wasn't so low that it would take tank fire, but not so high that it would be vulnerable to either fire from right-wing Phalangist 155mm howitzers or Syria's massive 240mm mortars. If it was a matter of an Israeli air strike, then it really wouldn't matter which floor he was on.

He had taken his clothes out of his bag and was stuffing them into the wardrobe drawers. The room was decorated in several shades of brown—brown wallpaper, brown carpet, brown bedcover, beige curtains—the decor looked as if it hadn't changed in thirty years. But then Brodick thought hotel curtains were pretty horrible the world over.

Brodick was carrying his gear—razor, toothbrush and paste—to the bathroom when he was thrown sideways.

'*Shit.*'

Something had punched him, simultaneously lifting him and tossing him against the wall. It hurt. He didn't recall hearing anything at all, but when he picked himself up off the carpet, his ears sang and there was a cloud of dust and smoke beyond his window. He used the bed to push himself upright, grunting at the pain in his shoulder. He started moving to the window with the intention of looking down at the street below to discover the source of the detonation. The toiletries he'd been carrying were scattered across the floor.

Debris pattered against the cracked window like a shower of hail. That stopped him. He'd taken no more than a step when something smacked the pane hard enough to break it in several places, slid down and landed on the windowsill.

It was a head. Unmistakably human. A man's head faced him, lacking one eye. One side of the face seemed to have been burned away. There was a lot of blood on the starred glass, a river of it, globs of it, and the remaining eye looked through the sliding gore at Brodick. The tongue protruded through broken teeth. The head had black, curly hair matted with blood and debris. It still smouldered.

Brodick locked his room and went down to reception.

'Yes, sir, Mr Sullivan. How may I help you?'

Brodick tried to keep his voice steady. He was British, kind of. He was therefore stoical. 'There's a man's head on my windowsill.'

*

Brodick felt better after the second double scotch. It went on his laundry bill.

What had happened now became clear, because everyone was talking about it with Gallic shrugs, shakes of the head and imprecations in three languages. A fuckan car bomb heading for Hamra—right outside the front of the frigging hotel, it was thought—had exploded prematurely in the side street, killing the mother-frigging bomber—*sharmout* was the Arabic term of abuse for the anonymous perpetrator—blowing him to bits, and one large bit—his severed head—had landed on a windowsill. Brodick kept quiet and did not volunteer the fact that it had been *his* windowsill.

After a minute or two, the general talk turned back to matters of importance: what was for lunch and whether the effing Syrians were going to invade Beirut now the Israelis had finally effed off further south. Brodick learned that car bombs were commonplace. Some were detonated with time pencils, others electronically. There were two or three a week, and the barflies maintained that everyone did it: the Saudis and Israeli Mossad, of course, the CIA, the Christian Phalangists, Sunni fundamentalists. Meanwhile that very model of a modern extremist organisation, Islamic Jihad, specialised in a relatively new and efficacious form of attack: suicide bombers. Regardless of the identity of either the culprits or the targets, the drinkers seemed unanimous in their opinion that the losers were always the civilians killed or maimed in the blasts. Women and kids as often as not. Poor sods.

Brodick used one of the hotel's public phones, reasoning that a single landline out of many, involving a brief conversation involving some unknown foreigner named Drew, was unlikely to arouse the attention of the operators of the local KGB residency's SIGINT outpost: although the man Brodick would be calling would almost certainly be of interest. Even so, any reaction on the part of the local KGB *rezidentura* would take time; and by then, hopefully, Brodick would already have concluded his business.

The phones were installed in a line of small cubicles with glass doors at the back of the lobby and just outside the restaurant.

He called the number he'd been given and let it ring three times before he ended the call. Again he called, and again he let it ring three times.

On the third call, Brodick let it ring until it was answered.

'Huh?' A grunt.

'Is that Hasan?'

'Who wants to know?' Spoken in guttural English.

'This is Drew. Drew Sullivan.'

The change in tone was immediate, from aggressive-defensive to mock-respectful. 'Mr Drew? How *are* you, sir?'

'Can we meet?'

'Are you in Beirut, Mr Drew?'

'Yes.'

'Okay. Good. Very good. At Commodore, yes? You know Wimpy Bar?'

'No.'

'On Hamra. Very close to your hotel. Go out, cross the street, take a left. One block. Big red sign. Tomorrow afternoon. Three o'clock. Okay?'

'Great, Hasan. Thanks.'

'You come alone, Mr Drew.'

That was done. He could relax until the next day's meeting. He would catch up on his sleep, maybe swim in the pool, followed by supper on room service. He'd keep a low profile and stay away from the bar and its sweary customers. There was no point in worrying. It wouldn't help. And what was there to worry about? All he had to do was meet the man named Hasan and listen to what he had to say. Hopefully, there would be no more body parts sent to his room. Then he could go home. He hoped he could. That was the plan.

2

Seven Months Earlier

'There were some rough edges, but you'll do.'

The words come back to Brodick as he stands waiting in the Controller's outer office, and for lack of anything better to do, he stares up at one of only two portraits in existence of England's master spy, Sir Francis Walsingham. To counter the tension he feels, he forces himself to recount what he knows; namely, that one picture is in the National Portrait Gallery and that this is the other, in Century House: each no doubt worth a small fortune. The austere face returns Brodick's stare. *Well,* his look seems to say, *are you really up to it?*

Walsingham had long suffered from poor health and died from working too long and hard in the service of Elizabeth I. Personally running agent networks at home and across Europe, he'd followed Spanish preparations for the Armada. He also had had the distinction of being the first English spy chief known to have employed deception: in this case by approving the forging of an addendum to an intercepted letter written by Queen Mary of Scotland. The forged and enciphered postscript almost certainly led her to the block, a cruelty that failed to end the threat of invasion in spite of Walsingham's best hopes.

That there had indeed been some "rough edges" on Brodick's stint as head agent on contract to Britain's Secret Intelligence Service, or SIS, in Afghanistan, of that there is no doubt. That he would "do" had come as a relief and it had made his cheeks burn. These were the only words—the sole comment, in fact, made by Angus MacGregor on Brodick's return from Peshawar—and just a fortnight prior to being packed off as a trainee Intelligence officer on the six-month-long New Intelligence Officers' Course or NIOC at Fort Monckton, Gosport.

To Brodick's relief there was no mention of the murder of Mungoo, Brodick's most important agent, a killing credited—mistakenly—to Brodick himself and for which he had, by failing to tell the truth of it, taken the credit. Had his employers since found out? Presumably not. Would they ever do so? It was possible but unlikely. Brodick had been ordered to terminate Mungoo as a suspected Soviet asset, and it was Brodick's apparent success in having done so that had secured him a place on the course. The reality was that he hadn't had the stomach for it. He couldn't kill his friend, not then and not now, regardless of Mungoo's deviant loyalties and indeed his own. Fate in the form of militant Islamists had intervened and done the job, gunning Mungoo and his wife down on their doorstep on the orders of Pakistan's Inter Services Intelligence or the ghastly Afghan resistance chief Burhanuddin.

To some extent, then, Brodick feels himself to be an imposter, someone who's managed to worm his way into SIS under false pretences. It goes deeper than that, of course, for sensing that he is an outsider—that he doesn't belong in SIS or anywhere else—is something that has dogged him since childhood.

He is at home everywhere, belongs nowhere.

And so here Brodick is, at SIS headquarters, fulfilling his boyhood dream: though dream it is no longer but merely a means of earning a living and getting to the top, or so he tells himself. Gone is the desire to change the world, to make it a better place, to live up to the family tradition of service to God and Country.

Instead, iron self-interest is Brodick's new *weltanschauung*. He's no gentleman, but a Viking in suit and tie, ransacking and pillaging other men's souls and lives.

The first time they'd met, again in MacGregor's office post-

Afghanistan, the boss had looked Brodick up and down. It was not a look of approval and Brodick had felt his employer was distinctly unimpressed.

Eventually McGregor had spoke. 'I get my clothes second-hand. I don't waste my money on such things.' A gruff, not so veiled criticism, then, of Brodick's charcoal suit, his prized possession of fine English wool, handmade—and very well made, too—by a Hong Kong tailor, a garment Brodick had been inordinately proud of until MacGregor had demolished his vanity.

MacGregor had informed Brodick that his own favourite clothing store was the Notting Hill Charitable Trust, next to the Underground station of that name on the Central Line. And it's true: MacGregor does wear Harris, Shetland and Donegal tweeds, the jackets a little too large, the leather patches on the elbows worn, the labels removed, of course, as befits a long-service covert operative. Second-hand green tweed appears to be his favourite.

It seems probable to Brodick that his superior's Calvinist tastes might have less to do with his Scottish origins than the fact that he'd made his reputation as a spy in the impecunious 1970s. Worn linoleum, peeling paint, broken furniture, lousy pay—the twenty-two-storey Century House, believe it or not built right over a petrol station—and its outstations represented a shabby world of Cold War paranoia. This was only partly offset by its successes in leveraging the diminishing British colonial possessions for dollars, giving the Americans the geographical reach they craved as a superpower in return for underwriting the costs courtesy of the unwitting U.S. taxpayer. Britain's subservient role, albeit as a trusted junior partner, had already been established in the fifties and, despite some violent ups and downs, it has lasted decades. For MacGregor personally, though, it must have been a time of counting paperclips, of perpetual cost-cutting while waging the Cold War against the much bigger and well-resourced Soviet juggernaut. First Suez, then the fiasco of Rhodesia's Unilateral Declaration of Independence in 1965, the Soviet invasion of Czechoslovakia three years later and the Falklands crisis of 1982 had exposed the steady decline and neglect of intelligence, the concealed armature of the nation shown up as moth-eaten and as full of holes as Swiss cheese. The oil crisis, a very long recession and the de-industrialisation of Western Europe had helped see to that.

Brodick has heard it said that MacGregor is fluent in Russian, and that he completed a three-year-long Cambridge University course in nine months, coming first in the final exam. Postings are said to have included Moscow, Bonn and Delhi before he was picked for the top floor and what passes in the trade for (invisible) stardom.

Did MacGregor know his father, work with him? Nothing is said.

MacGregor stands next to Brodick now, having emerged unseen and unheard from his office. He is an inch or so shorter than the younger man, his hair white, his skin pale, mouth wide and set in a sardonic half-smile as if mocking the world for its delusions, sartorial and otherwise. So Brodick imagines. MacGregor's glasses perch at the end of a nose that looks as if it had been broken, though not on the playing fields of Eton but more like the wilds of Rannoch Moor during some inclement escape and evasion exercise.

'Thing about Walsingham; two things actually.' MacGregor speaks with a slight Highland lilt, diluted by the many years away from his homeland. 'The first is that he was never afraid to tell truth to power. True then as it is true now: we must be able to tell politicians what they *don't* want to know, whether they like it or not. Something inconceivable in the KGB. Elizabeth is said to have been so angry with Walsingham's advice at one point that she hurled a shoe at him. The other point is that he ran it all himself from his London home with the result that when he died of overwork, the whole edifice—all his precious networks—died with him. We're a team effort, something the Americans haven't yet learned, but which has worked to our benefit on more than occasion.'

Does MacGregor mean to say that intelligence and security

teamwork has worked to Britain's advantage, or is he referring to the notorious U.S. inter-service rivalry? Everyone knows the NSA hates the CIA, the CIA detests USAF intelligence and so on. That surely isn't an advantage but has, on the contrary, made working with the Americans so much harder; and the KGB's job so much easier.

'And who is he?' Brodick has turned to the only other portrait.

They walk over to it.

The plate at the bottom of the frame states: *John Thurloe, Secretary of State. Born 1616. Died 1668.*

'Cromwell's man. In effect, both foreign secretary and his intelligence chief; and highly effective he was, too, regardless of your view of the Dictator. The son of an Essex rector who pioneered mail interception.'

Brodick can't help himself. 'You'd have supported Mary, wouldn't you? As a Scot?'

A grunt is the only response.

Brodick decides to push his luck further, but senses that to ask directly if MacGregor is of Protestant or Roman persuasion would border on insolence. He might as well ask if he's a Celtic or Rangers fan. Slightly more acceptable would be a question about MacGregor's schooling; that usually supplied the answer, albeit indirectly. Certainly Walsingham had been a dedicated Prod. It was a Protestant gale that sank the Armada, too.

'I wouldn't take you for a royalist, though.'

MacGregor turns his head, and his pale blue eyes hold Brodick in their stare as if they see the question behind the question. There's a moment when Brodick thinks he's about to be given a bollocking for his familiarity.

'James VI is probably the last monarch I would have recognised.'

Brodick can't help himself. 'If I remember correctly, he was in favour of the union of the two crowns and entered enthusiastically into the business of empire building.'

'We all make mistakes, laddie, not least anointed monarchs.'

With that, the very republican MacGregor leads the way into

his office and closes the door behind Brodick.

'Take a seat.'

MacGregor is all business and he delivers what is, for him, quite a speech. 'There'll be eleven of you in this NIOC intake. Duration: six months. Well, you know that. Seven males, four females. Six are recent graduates: mostly Oxbridge. Four have been recruited from the armed forces. In that sense, you're the odd man out. You don't belong in either camp. You're neither warrior nor swot. A few are linguists. Three are graduates of the Defence Languages School at Beaconsfield. Others have a gift for numbers because the future is binary and digital, whatever that might mean. Don't let it bother you. Just get on with it and do your best. You have one advantage: you have experience working in the field. The fieldcraft and agent handling should be second nature and you have had a wee bit of firearms and unarmed combat training already. It won't be your first time at Fort Monckton. You've worked solo at the sharp end. Make use of it. Demonstrate your leadership skills.'

They both rise together.

Brodick has his rail warrant for the Portsmouth train in his pocket.

At the door, MacGregor surprises him by offering his hand.

'Welcome to the Service, Richard. You're no longer a contract labourer at the coal face but a fully paid-up member of the club. You're going to do well, laddie.'

Is that an expression of hope or faith? Most likely it's an order, as in "You'd better bloody do well or else!" Brodick has joined MacGregor's expanding circle of boys—and girls—and he knows what the privilege involves. The Controller Middle East picks his people with care. He has the back of his ambitious protégés, and he will protect them from Whitehall politics as well as occasional lapses in personal behaviour. But they have to perform above and beyond what passes for the normal call of duty. Brodick must expect to work as many hours as it takes. Forget weekends, nine-to-five, holidays and the rest of it. In short, membership of this exclusive club-within-a-club stipulates that he has to be both outstandingly successful and outstandingly loyal. The very best of the very best. Screw up, and MacGregor will drop him, won't know him, will never speak to him, will cast him off and he'll end up working in registry or suffer the humiliation of being tossed back on the streets as a civilian. How appalling a disgrace is that?

This loyalty is personal.

It gives Brodick a warm feeling. It's a homecoming of a sort.

3

Two goons sat just inside the glass doors, both in the Amal uniform of jeans and sneakers, handguns under short-sleeved t-shirts. One faced out, his companion surveyed the interior. To Brodick they seemed barely out of their teens. One appeared to be eating ice-cream, or pretended to do so. The place itself was otherwise empty. Why anyone would want to eat American-style junk in a country with its own tasty street food was anyone's guess. Maybe that was why it was empty. Maybe Hasan had chosen the time of day because he knew there were unlikely to be many customers. Brodick walked in, looked around, then turned to look at the gunmen. Gunmen was the right term for these boys: they were gun-dependent. Take their weapons away and they'd be just frightened kids. With them, they felt powerful, significant. They returned his stare with deadpan tough-guy expressions. One of them gesticulated with a stubby forefinger, jabbing it vertically at the ceiling. No, not giving him the finger, Brodick decided, but indicating the first floor.

They didn't search him, something he'd expected. For his part, Brodick had been careful to keep it simple. Chinos, deck shoes, short-sleeved yellow shirt, under it a money belt with a few U.S. dollars and a little, almost worthless, Lebanese cash along with his Sullivan passport. He had already carried out a route reconnaissance, what the Service called *surveillance detection*. The KGB called it *proverka*, the CIA *dry-cleaning*. In this instance, it meant taking an indirect and much longer route to the Wimpy bar, heading off down a side street down towards the Corniche, doubling back, forcing himself to saunter, then approaching the location from the opposite direction, stopping frequently, bending down to tie a loose shoelace, staring into shop windows, entering some of them as the sweat dribbled down his back, inspecting jeans and leather jackets, shoes and shirts, nodding and smiling at the sales staff. Not today. Thanks but no thanks.

Brodick took the stairs two at a time.

Hasan was tall, thin, angular. His hair was cropped close to his skull, and he had a full beard. Brodick instinctively liked him, but wasn't sure why.

The Lebanese had jumped to his feet. 'Mr Drew?'

They shook hands. Hasan's grip was firm, his smile wide.

'Hasan, thank you for agreeing to meet me.'

'You want something? Coke, maybe? Coffee?'

'I'm fine, thanks.'

'Let's talk, Mr Drew.'

'Sure.'

They were alone and from their moulded chairs on either side of a small table they could look down on the street through a window clouded with dirt.

'I know what you want, Mr Drew. You want to know about the American.'

Hasan was clearly not a man to make light conversation. There would be no foreplay.

'I do, yes.'

'Why?'

'I want to help find him if I can.'

'Okay. Listen.' Hasan nodded several times. 'I know where he is, sure. For now. He won't be there long. He's too important to keep him in Beirut. They will have to move him or lose him. He's—what do you call it—a hot property.'

'Who's "they"?'

'The people who have him.'

'Who are they?'

'Shia. Like me. I'm a Shi'ite, from the south.'

'Not Amal, then.'

'No, not Amal. Of course not Amal.' Hasan is serious now, his eyes on Brodick's face, keeping very still, his voice low.

'Not Palestinians.'

'Oh, no.' It was said emphatically with a shake of the head.

'Do they have a name, these people?'

'I think you know this.'

'And I think it's the same people who shot and killed Dr Malcolm Kerr, the president of the American University of Beirut just a month ago. The same people who launched suicide attacks against the U.S. Marines and French paratroopers last October. The same people who blew up the American embassy a year ago with a truck bomb. They now have a newspaper, *Al-Ahed*. Yes?'

'We're at war, Mr Drew. We didn't choose this war. The Israelis still occupy our country: with the support of the Americans.'

'You are, yes. I know.'

'You will also know perhaps that a few weeks ago—in February—the Israeli Mossad murdered Sheikh Ragheb while he was walking home in the village of Jibsheet. He was unarmed. They shot him. Three bullets in the head.' Hasan tapped his forehead with an index finger. 'An important man in Lebanon with close ties to Najaf in Iran.'

'So the kidnapping of Buckley was retaliation?'

'I didn't say that. I said we are at war.'

'So who did it? Who took Buckley?'

Hasan leaned closer across the table, weight on his forearms. 'Islamic Jihad.'

Amal was close to Syria. Islamic Jihad was close to Iran. Very close. Brodick was aware from his briefings in London that Iranian influence in Lebanon had grown sharply since the 1979 revolution in Tehran, especially in the so-called arc of resistance comprising seven southern Lebanese villages that had taken a savage pounding from the invading Israelis. Tehran seemed to have instilled a new strength and sense of purpose into Lebanon's dispossessed, and no community was poorer or more neglected—politically and economically—than the Shia. No community had a greater grudge, no community thirsted more for vengeance and no community was in more in need of resources, from schools and jobs to healthcare.

'And the man who planned the kidnapping?'

Hasan shook his head, breathed out sharply and pushed himself back, looking away.

'It was Imad Mugniyeh. Right?'

Hasan shut his eyes for a moment, lifted up his hands, palms out. Stop, the gesture said. But of course Hasan knew Mugniyeh quite well, had met him on several occasions. It was called coordination. Brodick had been warned Hasan could be a dangle—with Mugniyeh holding the other end of the rope—and no, Brodick was to make no attempt to recruit him.

'Look. Mr Drew. Please listen, okay? The Americans, the Israelis—they are all looking for this Buckley. They have their spies on the street and they are offering big money for information. Their friends in the Deuxième Bureau, also. You know Deuxième Bureau?' Lebanese military intelligence. Also, French DGSE. The Saudis. Everyone—like you, Mr Drew—looking for this American spy. A foolish spy, I think, because he left home at the same time every day, took the same route to work every day, used the same car every day, and moved around with no bodyguard. Stupid or crazy. Or maybe too proud, yes?'

Brodick waited. Would he mention the Centre? They would be watching the watchers, using their SIGINT post in the Soviet embassy. They'd love Buckley to fall into the KGB's lap, of course they would, and they'd be working their contacts hard in the PSP to that end.

He watched Hasan, the movement of his hands, the way his fingers stroked his beard, the way he smiled. He wore black from head to foot. Calvin Klein black polo shirt, black Armani jeans. Lace-up Converse sneakers. In his waistband, against a flat belly, what looked like a 9mm Beretta. Very trendy, very à la mode. He carried a walkie-talkie on his belt. In front of him on the table was a pack of 20 Marlboro Light. A classy young thug on the make, then, probably Syrian-trained, with a love of brand names. Or had he been taken abroad and schooled by the East German HVA? Or Iran's Revolutionary Guards?

If there was a Shia resistance *Vogue* or *GQ*, handsome Hasan would be on the cover.

Brodick thought of Buckley's disappearance. The remarkable aspect to all this was the way the kidnappers had behaved. A lot of planning had been put into it. They would have planned the aftermath, too. Yet through it all there had been nothing. Telephone and radio intercepts had failed to pick up anything. Neither the SIGINT stations in Cyprus nor the Rhyolite satellites. No whispers. No loose talk. No sudden spike in Iranian embassy traffic. Century House was baffled. Were they really that professional? Maybe, fighting Mossad for years, the Shia David against the Zionist Goliath, they'd learned the hard way how to survive.

Whoever they were, they were extremely professional when it came to comms security.

Hasan was talking. 'The Americans get a lot of rubbish information. Too much! They hand out bundles of dollars; and in return they have bought piles of shit.' Hasan's contempt came with a smile. 'It will take them weeks, maybe months, to check the garbage by which time their spy will have gone, vanished.'

'So why don't you tell them what you know and make yourself some money too?'

'I don't like.'

'Who: the Americans?'

'CIA.' Hasan made a face.

Would he prefer the Centre: the KGB's First Chief Directorate?

'So what can you tell me?'

'Buckley is in Basra Prison. You know?'

Brodick didn't respond. He wanted one of the Marlboros though he didn't smoke. He could feel his armpits sweating, the cold drops streaming down his flanks.

It wasn't the heat but adrenalin, telling him to fight or run.

'Southern suburbs. Shi'ite area. Very poor place. Very crowded. Mostly refugees from south. Many fighters. Basra Prison is a basement in apartment building, Mr Drew. Iron doors, cameras, underground cells. They make a special place for prisoners. Foreigners: French, American. And now your Mr Buckley. Guards inside and out. Guards on the roof. Machine guns, RPGs. Rescue impossible, I think impossible: even for Mossad. Even for American Marines.' Hasan snorted at the mention of the U.S. Marine Corps.

'Is there an address? Street name? House number?'

So at least it wasn't the Palestinians. The Popular Front for the Liberation of Palestine, led by George Habash, had close links with the Soviets and more than a decade previously the PFLP's Wadi Haddad had concocted a plan with the KGB's Department V to exchange a boatload of arms for the abduction of a CIA officer working under diplomatic cover in Beirut, a man much like Buckley, only in this case the deputy station chief had taken the trouble to change his times and his routes to and from work. Haddad had underestimated the difficulties and failed to invest sufficient resources into the venture. He should have employed a dozen men, not three. The mission failed: but Haddad did get the arms, ammunition and explosives he'd been promised in a rendezvous off the coast of Yemen. The Centre tried later on to have the same CIA man killed, but that too was unsuccessful.

Hasan looked Brodick in the face as if making up his mind. For some reason Brodick thought it important that he wasn't to be the first to break eye contact.

'I can show you,' Hasan said at last. His fingers—long, white with black hairs on the back of them—drummed on the Formica. The nails were short and neat.

'You'll take me?'

'My people will take you, but you will have to pay.'

'How much?'

Why did Brodick have the sense that he was being led up the

proverbial bloody garden path and fleeced at the same time?

'Ten thousand.'

'Dollars?'

'Dollars. Yes, of course. U.S. dollars.'

'I think you'd better go to the Americans.'

'Too much, Mr Drew?'

'Far too much. Sorry.' He wasn't at all sorry. The fellow had a nerve. 'And for what, Hasan? I see a street, a doorway, some guys with guns? For half a minute? Less? It's not worth it.' He meant not worth the risk: and certainly not worth that much cash. It wasn't a tourist site, and he was no tourist.

Hasan's voice rose an octave, his tone wheedling. 'You will see where Buckley is. You will see for yourself. Very close to the airport. You will see. You will be able to tell your friends, your boss. Show them what their spy satellites don't see. Put a cross on a map and tell them that's where Buckley is.'

So he could lead the "Desert Rats" of the 7th Armoured Brigade to the spot? It wasn't much of a sales pitch.

'I'm sorry, Hasan.' Brodick straightened up, looked around, breathed out slowly. He looked like a man about to leave. 'I don't have that kind of money. I'm grateful for your time and help, really I am. I do appreciate it. Thank you so much.'

'Talk to your people. Maybe they say yes.'

'They won't. I know they won't.'

'So how much can you pay?'

'Maybe two thousand. Maybe. I will also need proof of life.'

For a moment the smiling face turned dark, the smile gave way to a scowl. Hasan's long fingers played with the pack of cigarettes. His voice dropped to an urgent whisper. 'No. No, no. You don't understand. I am not greedy. I have to pay the driver and your escort. Six men. Six. Two cars. It's dangerous. They will want to be paid well to take the risk with a foreigner. If Islamic Jihad finds you, if they stop you and take you, they will try to shoot everyone with you. There will be fighting. Shooting and killing. They won't want witnesses. Understand?'

'It's okay. I understand. Don't worry. It's perfectly all right.' Brodick gave Hasan a broad smile. He hoped his body language indicated the negotiation was over.

'Six thousand.'

'Four.'

Outside car horns blared, people entered the Wimpy Bar downstairs, doors opened and closed, orders were shouted out in Arabic, laughter rang out, plates and cutlery clattered. The newcomers sounded like university students. The juke box started up with Neil Diamond's *Cracklin' Rose*. Hasan looked away, shook his head.

'All right, Mister. Four. Cash up front.'

'Very good, Hasan, thank you. Much appreciated.'

Again, the feeling returned that he, Brodick, was the target. The money was just a diversion. It wasn't serious. That Hasan was prepared to accept less than half the asking price was surely proof that they wanted him in the southern suburbs, and that they'd no intention of bringing him back. If they truly wanted to make money, they wouldn't talk to the penny-pinching British at all. No doubt they had a concrete cell in their Basra Prison ready and waiting. This was bait and he was the fish. Yet on the other hand, there was always a chance… It would be one hell of a thing to be able to signal Century House that he'd already reconnoitred Buckley's location. Quite a coup, though what good it would do anyone—especially Buckley—seemed doubtful. Still, MacGregor would surely be impressed even if the reticent Scot didn't say so.

'Have you met Imad Mugniyeh, Hasan?'

Of course he had. Regularly and often.

'Why you want to know this, Mr Drew? He's a dangerous person. Not good for you or me to talk about him.' Hasan was taken aback by the turn in the conversation.

'I want to know what he's like. As a person. He organised the Buckley kidnapping, after all. It was his project, I think.'

'He's a clever man. Very experienced. Very…' Hasan searched for the word. 'How you say? Determined. Very. Very *strong*. That's what people say about him.'

So it was Mugniyeh.

'Strong?'

'Strong heart.' Hasan put on hand on his own chest. 'Strong mind.' He tapped his temple. 'How do you say in Hollywood movies? One helluva tough guy.'

*

On the circuitous walk back to Le Commodore, Brodick flinched when a sonic boom split the blue sky. If it was any consolation he saw others duck and run. He glimpsed something flash overhead, a metallic glint. It was gone in an instant between the city's battered high-rises. Then another, right behind, a silver needle of reflected sunlight and a second supersonic boom; it was, he realised, the daily visit by the Israeli occupation forces, a reminder by a pair of F-4s or F-16s or whatever they were, a message to Beirut's inhabitants of the overwhelming might of the occupying army in the south. *We're still here!* Brodick forced himself to slow down, to amble in an effort to mirror his progress, using the plate glass windows, but it was almost impossible to spot any watchers. There were just too many people on the move: pedestrians, loiterers, beggars, motorcyclists, shoppers, drivers. From Cairo to Shanghai, static watchers were the general rule in developing states; they might be amateurs, but they were effective, cheap and although the veritable snowstorm of notes took time to gather and correlate, reliable. That wasn't to say there wasn't a mobile team on him, though. It could very well be both.

As he walked into the relative quiet of the hotel lobby, the air-conditioning struck him like an ice shower. Brodick realised he was drenched in sweat. It was tension. It was fear. He could smell it on himself.

That second night, lying in his lumpy hotel bed, he couldn't sleep. Partly it was the gunfire. Brodick told himself it was some way off and no real danger. Automatic fire, the crash of RPG-7 rounds, the hammering of a heavy machine-gun, the odd flash of an artillery shell or mortar bomb flickering in the night sky. The usual skirmishes over turf, he reassured himself. Nothing to worry about. The Commodore was safe. He lay on his back and chewed over his decision to accept Hasan's offer. He knew what he should do, what MacGregor would expect of him. It was the sensible option, the only sensible option and yes, of course, he would do it if only for his own peace of mind. No heroics. He would take a taxi to the embassy the next morning, right after breakfast. He would switch to a service taxi, and switch again. He planned to send a brief encrypted signal seeking authorisation for the trip to the southern suburbs. Then he would wait. Pass the buck upwards; wasn't that the universal rule of all bureaucracies? The Secret Intelligence Service was no exception. If the answer was negative, he'd make his excuses to Hasan. He'd chicken out. Who cared what Hasan would think? Screw him anyway. Didn't Brodick make it his personal mantra to look after Number One? Finally, around 3.30am and reassured by his sensible plan, Brodick slept to the percussive blues of a dying city.

4

He'll never forget his officer training, certain bits of it especially.

Paula keeps her eyes down. Paula Lubnaig, fluent in Spanish and Italian, doesn't want to look anyone in the eye and Brodick thinks he knows why. Paula is as scared as he is: as they all are, surely. Paula is studying Portuguese. Brodick envies her because she's planning her career with SIS in hot climates. Lisbon, Rome, Madrid, Buenos Aires, Sao Paulo, maybe even sparring with Cuba's DGI in Havana. Eminently sensible: why didn't he think of that?

Next to her, Anna. Anna Kingarth, eyes tight shut, keeping the world at bay. Anna is petite, dark, a genius when it comes to cyber warfare, hacking and computing generally, a gift to GCHQ. And if that's not enough, a black belt in Jiu Jitsu and near fluent in Mandarin. Quite a star. Anna and Paula are friends: yet also enemies, or at least competitors. Brodick doesn't really understand their relationship; they seem close at times and at others they bait each other with bitter, sarcastic outbursts. Right now they're sticking together to face a common threat. It's a female thing beyond Brodick's ken.

David is sprawled opposite, grinning, legs splayed, talking, chewing gum, laughing, playing the buffoon, even now in the wee hours he's performing. He has a way of irritating Brodick and just about everyone else on the course. David Sadler, a six-two lout who can't resist sharing his heroics as a former captain of infantry, parachutist, rugby player and general all-rounder who likes to play dumb but certainly isn't anything of the kind but is still a pain with too much testosterone. To an unimpressed Brodick, he's a public school arsehole with a permanent sneer and bad skin, totally convinced of his macho appeal to women: all women. Brodick gets his own back by insisting on calling him *Captain* Sadler at every opportunity.

Harry is curled up on Sadler's left, looking as if he might throw up at any moment. Harry Wood, the scruffy maths boffin with a Scouse accent and that fucked-up nerd look from Cambridge who can't abide all this physical tomfoolery. Hates Sadler's crap. They both do. The others: Claire Harwood, John Foley, Reggie Gill and Andrews, Kevin Andrews. Two missing; no, there they are, right at the end, Olcott and Payne. Good grief. Olcott seems to be sleeping; is he pretending? His mouth hangs open. He's apparently snoring though it can't be heard over the racket.

Payne leans forward against the safety straps, forearms on her knees, alert and watching everyone else. Olcott must have very low blood pressure, or maybe the stress has effectively knocked him out, a switch that just turns everything off when it gets to be too much. Brodick has forgotten the first names of the last two. And there's Brodick himself, of course: the odd man out, wide awake, pulse racing and effing terrified. Not the best time to be a loner. Now he remembers: Cynthia. Cynthia Payne, Classics scholar.

The Westland WS-61 Sea King slows, hovers and without warning, drops with a shriek of metal. The vertiginous plunge is both terrifying and sickening. The aircraft shudders. The Rolls-Royce Gnome engine roars. A crewman tugs open the door. It's black out there. Black and freezing.

Oh God no.

A hand slaps Brodick's shoulder. 'Go!'

For a moment he feels suspended in space, motionless. The English Channel reaches up and hits him hard and pulls him into its embrace. Drags him in and forces him down. He's sucked into the icy depths, struggling and trying to claw his way back to the surface. He gasps with the shock of it and his mouth fills with seawater, half of which he swallows, choking. The rotor blades have flattened the sea but, as he swims out of the downdraft, waves slap him repeatedly in the face, lifting him and dropping him. His orange lifejacket has inflated itself. Thank heaven for small mercies.

He can see nothing. Which way is land?

He's exhausted. His arms and legs are lead and he's only been in the sea a few seconds, surely.

Dear God, I'm going to die here.

But God isn't paying attention to his little drama.

The helicopter has risen, turned for home. Its lights flicker as it recedes, disappearing into cloud or sea mist.

Brodick can hear the roar of surf over to his left and, turning onto his side, he glimpses cliffs and breaking water. That-away. Cumbersome, like a half-drowned, waterlogged creature—a human barrel of self-pity— struggling to stay afloat, he turns, kicking and flailing in what he hopes is the right direction. A wave lifts him, propels him forward, another hits him in the back, pushing him under. He surfaces, goes under again, swallows far too much sea, emerges spluttering, feeling shingle underfoot. He doesn't quite believe it. Yes, thank Christ, he touches solid ground. He's on his hands and knees, trying to crawl up the beach, relieved beyond words. Grateful beyond reasoning.

A wave threatens to drag him back again, sucking at his clothing.

Someone leans down, extends a hand and grabs him under one arm, pulling him up what there is of beach and dropping him like a sack of coal on the stones.

'You're all right, pal.' Question or statement. Brodick isn't sure. He lies on his back, spitting brine and gasping. His hair and clothing are heavy with sand and pebbles. Staring up at clusters of stars through breaks in the mist, he laughs out loud, a crazed cackle. He's alive and that's exhilarating. The best thing in the world.

Over to his right he sees a glow in the sky. The lights of

Portsmouth.

'Okay, gents, on your feet. Come on, let's go! You've got a hot cuppa waiting.'

They're counted—and urged to their feet—by people in wetsuits, goggles, their oxygen tanks discarded in a neat pile. Royal Marines, it seems. Or Special Boat Service. All eleven trainees are present if not entirely correct. Two are crouched on the sand. One retches in the shallows, another sobs. The divers keep a watchful eye on the sorry pair.

Brodick identifies the one crying as David Sadler. *Captain* Sadler.

It's their second night on the training course. Nothing like the surprise of being pushed out of a chopper into the English Channel at 0400 to bond everyone together. One big happy SIS family.

5

Brodick ate and drank in his brown room, an early Lebanese breakfast of *labneh* with olive oil, triangles of warm flat loaves wrapped in a napkin, half a grapefruit and a pot of mint tea. He had to assume he was watched in the room. The mirror in the bathroom, for example, or a listening device in the headboard. It was still safer, more discreet, to stay shuttered from other guests and avoid the temptation of hanging out at the bar. Even on the second floor that night he heard the drinkers' laughter and shouts which finally stopped around midnight. He felt pretty good, all things considered. Gunfire had woken him only a couple of times. More importantly, he was confident that Century House would say no to his reconnaissance mission. They couldn't have a young and relatively inexperienced I.O. prowling around a Shi'ite Lebanese shanty town infested with well-armed militants. He was obviously a foreigner and the risk of being snatched was too great. A newly qualified SIS officer in the hands of Islamic Jihad would represent political embarrassment and reveal London as impotent: quite aside from the beatings and torture Brodick personally would have to endure.

Brodick would stay safe. Sorry, Hasan, better luck next time.

He left his room key at reception—there was nothing incriminating in his room should anyone decide to search it, no documents or equipment—and took the lift down and sauntered outside. He'd left a few receipts in the name of Sullivan in his bags for anyone to find. There were more in his pockets. A doorman in uniform threw him a haphazard salute. It was still cool, and the traffic had yet to clog the city. He breathed in deeply. It felt so good to be outside. Maybe he would have a chance to go for a swim after all once the city warmed up. The taxi he'd ordered from a local firm known to SIS was waiting across the street for his trip to the embassy. He wouldn't take it far: just across the Green Line and then he'd walk a little, change again. He scanned the pavement left and right, something he did automatically, without thinking, and there was nothing to arouse suspicion and no cause for concern. It all looked perfectly normal.

Perhaps someone more experienced and less relaxed would have found that very perfection of normality deeply unsettling, especially in Beirut.

'Hey there! Mister Sullivan. How you doing, man?'

A cheery voice from a big man.

Brodick half turned. Whoever it was had come out of the Commodore after him.

'Long time no see,' said the voice, in American English.

He was indeed large, broad in the shoulders, big bellied, at least a head taller, clean shaven, a grin from ear to ear, of Mediterranean appearance. But other than that, Brodick had no chance to find out any more about the stranger, who grabbed his right hand in both his, pulling him towards him, grin still in place. Brodick tried to pull back, regain possession of his hand. He didn't see the Volvo estate slide up behind him to the entrance of the hotel, nor did he see the two men who opened the boot and came up behind Brodick, pinning his arms behind him and slipping the flexicuffs onto his wrists.

Remember your training!

Brodick lashed out with his feet, ducked and twisted, a well-hooked mackerel.

He had the satisfaction of kicking one his assailants in the balls and hearing him cry out.

Out of the corner of the eye he saw the doorman had been pushed against the hotel wall, a gun to his ear.

Brodick was lifted, feet clear of the ground, and rolled into the boot, which was slammed shut, burying him in darkness. The Volvo moved off.

Of course, no one saw anything. There were no witnesses, which was to be expected.

*

He remembered his last briefing before the Damascus flight.

Imad Mugniyeh. *Feared by his enemies and respected by supporters and allies but little known*, is how Brodick's briefing officer describes him.

Not that Brodick should seek him out or pursue the matter with Hasan. For everyone's sake, most of all Brodick's, Mugniyeh was best left out of it.

Until now, thousands of Lebanese had been kidnapped by one faction or another in the Lebanese civil war. Some for ransom, others out of a desire for vengeance. There were "private" prisons in basements all over the city that held these kidnap victims. Now it was the turn of foreigners and Buckley was the fourth U.S. national taken hostage. No fewer than seventeen groups, sects, factions, or parties were behind the kidnappings, but a name is just a name. It was entirely possible that one single organisation would use a score of different names in different places and at different times. Some would be contractors, paid to snatch foreigners. They were ghosts: not unlike the "brass plate" companies incorporated in the State of Delaware or the British Virgin Islands, spider webs of shell companies and trusts impossible to pin down and beyond the reach of the authorities—each just a sheet of paper in a lawyer's office drawer in any one of a dozen tax havens. The Beirut equivalent being a couple of pimply youths with dirty AK-47s, a heroin habit, a dingy basement and a phone number.

Several names of these phantoms were associated with, or linked to, Islamic Jihad. Brodick had learned the list off-by-heart before departure during his hastily organised briefings: Organisation of the Islamic Dawn, Islamic Jihad for the Liberation of Palestine, the Revolutionary Justice Organisation, Holy Warriors for Freedom, Khaibar Brigade, Organisation of the Oppressed on Earth, Revolutionary Cells.

Islamic Jihad had made itself known by means of phone calls to Western news agencies: the Associated Press, United Press International, Agence France Press and Reuters. To prove it was what it said it was and to distinguish itself from hoax calls, it delivered pictures of hostages to the same agencies, the captives holding up newspapers displaying the date. *An-Nahar* or *as-Safir.*

Proof of life.

Its most notorious and mysterious figure was Mugniyeh himself.

'We don't know nearly as much as we'd like to,' said Brodick's briefing officer the morning of his departure. Mildred Fox-Hilton, a bespectacled woman of indeterminate age with tousled black hair, very glossy red lipstick, a penchant for floral dresses, proud owner of three Bombay cats, fluent in Arabic and a doctorate in Middle East Studies from SOAS, had been summoned at very short notice to help Brodick prepare for his mission. 'That's why we send people like you off on your jollies so you can fill in the blanks for us.'

Fox-Hilton (*'Please call me Mildred'*) explained that, as a member of the PLO's Islamic wing, Mugniyeh had been one of Yassir Arafat's bodyguards in an elite unit known as Force 17. He was thought to have specialised in explosives. His family village in the south of the country was occupied by invading Israeli forces in 1982, and Mugniyeh and his family fled north along with thousands of other Shi'ite refugees into Beirut's overcrowded southern suburbs. He himself was wounded when Israeli-backed Maronite Christian troops and militia, supported by the guns of U.S. warships, unleashed an artillery attack on those same suburbs.

Disillusioned with the departure of the Palestinians from Lebanon and their failure to stand up effectively to the Israeli onslaught, as well as Syria's attempts to maintain a balance of power in Lebanon by abruptly supporting the Maronite Christians when the latter came under threat from a leftist coalition, Mugniyeh turned to Iran's Revolutionary Guards and soon headed Islamic Jihad's security service. He was given the opportunity to wreak vengeance on the aggressors. It was believed that he had planned the bombings of the U.S. embassy during a CIA conference, as well as the headquarters of the Multi-National Force and—from Mugniyeh's point of view and that of his Iranian handlers—the attacks were stunningly successful.

'He isn't just an Iranian supporter or collaborator,' said Fox-Hilton, playing with stray locks of hair. 'He's not merely an agent. He's a fully paid-up member of the Guards. He isn't the only Lebanese recruit. He reports to the Guards, not to Islamic Jihad. He has special privileges. He has a diplomatic passport. We think that by now he may even have Iranian citizenship. He has access to substantial funds and other material resources, such as explosives, vehicles, safe houses. He's really rather special. He's the front man, the name, in these attacks, a kind of terrorist brand if you like. He's a hit man on a vast scale. A star. It's superb counterintelligence on the part of the Revolutionary Guards. You have to admit that the Iranians have played their hand beautifully in Lebanon. Ask the Israelis: Iranian security is so bloody good, too, it's infuriating! Neither we nor the Americans have been able to break their ciphers. And they are very sparing in their communications, so much so that even if we could read them, they probably wouldn't tell us much at all.'

'And how does Buckley fit into all this?'

'We think the data collected from the U.S. embassy in Tehran was crucial. When the embassy was stormed in November, 1979—you'll remember this—a volunteer task force was set up to reconstruct the thousands of documents shredded in the CIA station. It took a while, of course, but that painstaking effort gave them what they needed on Buckley and his career to select him as a target.'

'So this was planned.'

'Indeed. Tehran takes the long view.'

'Then the Iranians must have passed this on to Mugniyeh.'

'What's the use of intelligence unless it's put to good use - in this case, from the Iranian perspective? Maybe your Beirut contact will prove useful and expand on some of the detail.'

*

Of course he was frightened. Bloody petrified. Worse, he was ashamed of himself.

This isn't supposed to happen. Not to me.

It seemed his new career was over in ignominy before it had begun. Compared to this, his Afghanistan adventures had been child's play. He'd made an ass of himself, strolling with such insouciance out of the hotel that morning, not taking sufficient note of his immediate surroundings. He had only himself to blame. He'd been careless. But first, before anything else, he pushed all that blame and guilt aside and dealt with the flexicuffs. His training took hold. The manoeuvre took seconds. They'd practised it at the Fort: in class and yes, in the dark, shut into a coffin-like cupboard to simulate the claustrophobia, the sense of slow suffocation in darkness. It wasn't a matter of pulling, more of a sharp twist of the wrists in opposite directions.

It was done and he felt better, more confident, less helpless.

He had always felt that he wasn't afraid of dying so much as dying badly, of embarrassment, of public shame, of showing weakness.

In his mind he had a street map of the city, and he tried to match it with what he could tell of the car's movements. He tried to time the journey. East and not south—that seemed right—and it was good news because it suggested that he wasn't going to spend the next five years—if he survived the torture and beatings—chained to a radiator in the so-called Basra Prison. Brodick also knew that Volvo estates were a favourite of the Syrian *mouhabarat*. He'd been warned to look out for the secret police, cruising slowly, close to the kerb, rear door slightly open, ready for the snatch. Well, he'd been snatched, and his captors could well be Syrians or their proxies. Which would mean the Bekaa Valley, the mountainous border region or into Syria itself. But to what end?

Was the Centre involved?

With his hands free he could more easily brace himself against the Volvo's movements, though in all fairness it wasn't a violent passage. It seemed to follow what must be the flow of traffic, and taking care not to do anything that would draw the attention of bystanders and other motorists. The Volvo slowed almost to a halt and he heard voices close by, Arabic of course, and laughter, but he couldn't make out the words, while his imagined street map, faulty though it undoubtedly was, told him they'd arrived at a checkpoint: in all likelihood, and Brodick guessed it was the Museum crossing. A Beirut version of a *todesstreifen*, just not as well designed and organised as the East German version. Beyond it lay the Christian-controlled eastern sector: that is to say, territory run by the Lebanese Army, headed by Christian Maronite generals, and its allied Lebanese Forces militia, known as the Phalangists, on the far right of the political spectrum and a proxy of Mossad and CIA.

The Volvo accelerated, throwing Brodick to the rear.

As frantic as a rat in a trap, Brodick tried to claw his way through to the back seat, tearing at the fabric in a mounting frenzy, but only succeeded in ripping out two of his fingernails.

They were climbing as Brodick sweated heavily with his effort to escape.

Tight hairpin bends meant Brodick had to brace himself again because of the rolling motion, and he realised that he was losing his sense of direction, such as it was. He estimated that this phase of the journey lasted about fifteen minutes.

Still no obvious detours to indicate an effort to put him and any followers off the track.

The Maronite heartland.

Why?

Brodick had a searing headache he put down to the lack of

oxygen.

At long last, the route flattened out and the Volvo slowed and stopped. More voices. Footsteps on gravel, coming close. When the lid of the boot opened, the hood was over his head before he had a chance to see anything. In any case the shock of the bright light made him flinch and close his eyes instinctively.

He was grabbed, pulled, lifted, dragged.

Brodick estimated the journey at roughly forty minutes and no obvious detours.

Whoever they were they had him upright, one on each side, propelling him forward so that he tottered on numb legs. The hood stank of sweat. Metal cuffs this time. They didn't beat him, and Brodick was again grateful for small mercies. The softening up would come later.

At the Fort Brodick's cohort had been warned to expect to be raped at some point after being taken in the Middle East, and the males on the course were advised not to feel guilty if the painful and humiliating introduction to sodomy caused an erection and even emission. 'Doesn't mean you're gay,' said the instructor with a smirk. 'It's an automatic physical response connected to your prostate. Not a mental or emotional one, so if it happens, and we hope it never does, do try to keep calm.' Yeah, sure. Sadler had uttered a single bark of laughter, only it wasn't humour. More like embarrassment and fright.

Now a gate, what he guessed was a courtyard, hard under foot, another gate crashing open and shut and then down a corridor with deafening shouts and cries and the sound of innumerable metal doors opening and closing, a cacophony that strongly suggested a prison with cells running down both sides of the building.

They would use plenty of electricity on him.

A flight of steps down, his captors holding him carefully lest he trip.

The manky hood was pulled off, his manacles removed.

The hands holding him let go and a mighty shove in his back sent him sprawling onto a hard floor, cracking his head against it.

The door behind Brodick slammed shut. He was alone and in a cell with a bucket, a mattress. A tiny aperture out of reach and just below the ceiling was barred, allowing just a few millimetres of sky. Brodick shivered and hugged himself. It was cold.

His new lodgings were about two metres wide, four metres long and just under four metres high. He had the place to himself. Both the cell and the metal door were painted battleship grey. The paint on the door was badly chipped and Arabic phrases had been crudely scraped into it, though they seemed, at least to Brodick, to be illegible. The mattress, an inch thick at most, made of rubber and zipped into a green plastic cover, lay on a shelf at the far end. No pillow, no blanket. The cement shelf was a couple of feet off the floor. He saw there was a dried stain of something nasty in the centre of the floor - blood, vomit, piss or shit or all four. He paced, avoiding the dried puddle of whatever, inspecting his new residence. Mice droppings. Half a dozen dead cockroaches.

Above, a single light burned dully behind thick glass.

They'd taken his watch, his cash, his Sullivan passport, his belt, his laces: though he couldn't for the life of him remember them doing so.

His fingers were still painful and sticky with blood from the torn fingernails.

The hatch in the door scraped open and an eye stared him and withdrew. The hatch shut like a pistol shot. He'd have to use the bucket sooner rather than later, an indignity he was not looking forward to, but then he told himself he was no different from anyone else. He would adapt because there wasn't any alternative.

The natural light was fading. He would miss his rendezvous with Hasan.

Try as he might, Brodick couldn't stop himself shivering.

When would they come for him?

6

At Fort Monckton, cryptography is a compulsory subject for all trainee officers.

Unfortunately Brodick has no aptitude for theory or practice, and is thus rescued from a career with Government Communications Headquarters (GCHQ). The course begins with simple substitution, followed by linguistic statistics, then the remarkable Playfair Cipher, used by the Ministry of Defence from 1854 until the early twentieth century. Trainees are marched briskly through polyalphabetic codes and the best known of the manual ciphers, the Vigenere, named after the diplomat of the same name, published in 1586, used by the Confederates in the American Civil War and, amazingly, not broken until the mid-nineteenth century by Babbage and Kasiski, and finally the so-called unbreakable ciphers and 'perfect secrecy' (only possible with hugely burdensome key management), and the famous but very limited one-time pad, still in use.

After a restorative long weekend, Brodick and his companions return to face the thrill—well, to the elect few it *is* thrilling, but to Brodick it's embarrassing incomprehension—of modern algorithms, bit-strings, stream ciphers, block ciphers, hash functions and the new public key systems, leaving him sweaty and confused. Moore's law—that has it that the power of a computer chip doubles around every two years—along with the symmetric block cipher, the Date Encryption Standard or DES, used by banks. All of these cripple Brodick with headaches, while practising attacks in the final month—by targeting the underlying mathematical problems—only provokes a strong desire to throw up his breakfast.

Still, if ciphers don't appeal, the history is inspiring, beginning with the ninth century Baghdad academy of sciences, otherwise known as the House of Wisdom. Here Arabic replaced Greek as the language of knowledge and the most prolific scholar and author of hundreds of works, mostly lost, was Yaqub ibn Ishaq al-Kindi, a polymath known as *Philosopher of the Arabs.* Logic, ethics, political philosophy, a commentary on Aristotle, theology: these were the grist to the mill of his brilliant mind. He was the master of cryptanalysis, that is to say, decrypting enciphered messages without, of course, knowing the cipher: something of immense importance at the time as the Abbasids used to encrypt their official documents. And this is what grabs Brodick's imagination: Kindi discovered the "frequency" principle. That is, some letters are used more often than others in any language. It wasn't just a theory, for it proved vital in the painstaking effort to put together scattered fragments into their final form: the one-hundred-and-fourteen chapters of the Quran. It was this combination of theology and mathematics that gave birth to cryptanalysis.

Code-breaking, in other words.

Much more interesting, at least for Brodick, is a Friday afternoon tour of the Fort Monckton Memory Room. Those scientifically minded members of their cohort are *ooh-ing* and *ah-ing* at the exhibits, starting with original Enigma machines, then the later versions, both the Typex and Sigaba, the U.S. KL-7 and—most exciting of all to these nascent Cold War warriors—a working model of the Soviet *Fialka,* no less. There's also a Russian "*Bexa*" T-205 encryption machine.

A B2 clandestine radio attracts their attention, the best known of its kind in World War Two, which could be carried around in a leather suitcase—a rather battered original in this instance and much repaired—a device especially suitable for agents using public transport in Nazi-occupied Europe, and the recent FS-5000, codename HARPOON: a fully automated, digital radio station.

The complete set, the S4-5000, is new and highly classified: an AEG Telefunken product from West Germany. And here's the RT-3, no less, in current use with the West German intelligence service, the BND, as well as 'stay behind groups', codenamed GLADIO.

'Wow, just wow,' exclaims the ecstatic Anna Kingarth. She's bouncing up and down on the balls of her feet but is told off for touching the RT-3.

Captain Sadler, on the other hand, strolls around, hands in pockets, whistling under his breath. To him they're just metal boxes with dials and plugs and a lot of wiring. He's bored and wants everyone to know it. He thinks all this expensive gear is beneath him. Brodick thinks he's an idiot. In fact, just for a moment, Brodick feels sympathy for the peace-loving peoples of the Soviet Union if and when they're confronted by this relic of empire.

Their instructor gathers them together. He points to the first "ruggedised" PCs, picking out one for special mention, the TCQ-360. It's shielded against electromagnetic leaks, codenamed TEMPEST, subject of a long battle over resources. He explains that when they were discovered, these emanations from otherwise secure devices in Western embassies could be picked up a few hundred metres away by prowling KGB SIGINT cars. Special shields in the form of masking and filters had to be developed and introduced at considerable cost to SIS stations, the Security Service and the Ministry of Defence.

Brodick has a fleeting thought. If *they* can read *our* diplomatic and intelligence traffic, and if *we* can read *theirs*, isn't that all to the good? They'll know we aren't about to launch a first strike, and *we'll* know *they're* not planning to attack us. That would surely produce a certain stability in international affairs. Brodick wonders if he's understood this correctly. The Soviets only trust what they can steal, not what they're given by allies or their socialist friends. But he doesn't give voice to these thoughts for fear of being labelled a lefty, a subversive. Or simply naive.

'Listen up. You've worked really hard this week on cryptography, and we do realise it's not been everyone's cup of tea, so the training staff would like to reward you all with an evening out.'

Desultory cheers greet the statement.

'We're going to split into two groups and head out to a couple of our favourite pubs. Transport will be provided. Drinks are on us.' More cheers. 'Get yourselves sorted and have something to eat and we'll meet again at 2030 sharp. Latecomers will be left behind.'

'Why don't we go in one group?' Harry Wood asks the question.

'Because we don't want to frighten the natives, now do we?'

Brodick is looking forward to this. They all are, even that bampot Sadler, though the twinkle in the instructor's eye and his sardonic grin suggests to Brodick that not all is as it seems. There's something withheld, something not said.

7

Brodick was woken abruptly, alarmed at the cell door unlocked and thrown wide. From his prone position—having curled up, hugging himself on the mattress, something he didn't remember doing—he shot to his feet and backed against the wall, prepared to fight for his life against the threat, whatever it might be. His head rang, his mouth was dry, his heart raced. He felt dizzy. But he extended his arms, hands open, legs apart and slightly bent, right foot extended.

Brodick remembered where he was, or where he thought he was.

He promised himself he would resist.

They could just keep him in there without anything to drink. After a few days he would hallucinate and after a few more days of the same his mind—what was left of it—would turn on itself, and he would answer anything and everything they asked in return for just a spoonful of water.

Or was it going to be simple and quick: electrodes clipped to his foreskin?

'Come, mister, come. Visitor.' The guards watched him with a degree of curiosity and made no effort to approach, but waited for the foreign prisoner with crazed blue eyes. There were two of them, both in uniform: a disrupted pattern design of white, grey and black that might have been designed for Alpine troops. One carried an enormous bunch of keys, no doubt for the prison cells.

'Okay, mister. You come now.' The speaker was the taller of the two and carried a sidearm on his belt. He seemed to be in a hurry.

The uniforms were at least two sizes too big, their boots were dirty, their hair too long for prison warders or military personnel, curling over ears and collars. They looked like film extras. But this was Lebanon, not St Cyr officers' academy.

Brodick hadn't eaten or had anything to drink since the previous morning. He hadn't slept more than a few minutes, at least that's how it felt. He'd been prepared for interrogation and now it was about to start.

He told himself he would be strong. He would stay silent for as long as he could. He would remember his training. He would not give in.

Still his minders made no attempt to use force but stood waiting in the doorway; one in the cell, the other right behind him in the corridor. Brodick was sweating, couldn't help it, wasting what little moisture he still had. His mouth was ashes.

'Don't worry, Mister. Woman. Your friend. She come.'

Woman, what woman? My *friend*? Who could she be? Someone from the consulate, maybe? His hopes rose at once. The tall guard, sporting a full black beard, having delivered this information in heavily accented English, stood aside and made a sweeping movement with his arm, palm up, like a waiter inviting a guest to take his or her place at table. 'Please,' he added.

Brodick told himself he wasn't in the least fooled by this clumsy trick, this lie.

The short, plump uniform with the keys and a prison version of a chatelaine around his waist, showed his teeth through a moustache in an effort to smile.

They were doing their best when they'd have preferred to beat the unholy crap out of him.

Once enticed into the corridor, Brodick was again cuffed. He shuffled along in his deck shoes without laces; Brodick realised that it was still dark outside, but the racket of the prison continued unabated. Metal doors crashed open and slammed shut, steel grills dragged this way and that with metallic squeals, males shouted orders, threats and profanities, mostly profanities. Someone screamed and moaned in a nearby cell as if red hot nails were being driven under his fingernails. Perhaps they were.

Two flights of stairs this time, guided left, then right and shown to a large room. A table, two chairs. His cuffs were removed.

'Sit, mister.'

Brodick did as he was told. There was nothing to look at. The walls were grey here also, paint and plaster peeling, scuffed with dirt with a greasy pattern along the walls where countless people had leaned or moved. The long, horizontal window running the length of the room—or cell—was too high for Brodick to see anything, and in any case it looked dark out there. The light in the centre of the ceiling flickered, fizzed and crackled.

He looked for a camera, for a two-way mirror, but saw none.

It was quiet at last. No shouts and screams, no crash of doors and metal grilles.

He lost all sense time. He sat forward, resting his head on his forearms. It didn't seem cold anymore. Somehow his own body odour was comforting. It might have been twenty minutes or two hours before he heard keys turn in the lock and he turned to see a woman enter. She said something to the guards over her shoulder and the door slammed behind her, the bolts driven home.

Brodick was sure he had never seen her before.

His visitor wasn't from the consulate.

She made quite an impression despite Brodick's exhausted state. She was slim, all in black. She was, Brodick guessed, around five-eight tall, but the heels made her seem much taller. She looked as if she'd just come from a cocktail party or a formal dinner. Her hair, parted in the centre, was also raven black and fell straight to her shoulders. There were no rings, no bracelet or brooch, not so much as a watch - just a single strand of pearls at her throat. In her right hand she carried what appeared to be a shiny black purse or bag. He couldn't tell her age. Thirty? Forty? Forty-five?

The visitor pulled out the chair opposite and sat, knees together, hands in her lap. She looked at him. Stared at would be more accurate, taking stock, assessing. She was very calm and self-assured, or seemed so.

Neither of them spoke. Brodick could hear his own breathing.

Had he passed the examination?

The visitor had a strong face; prominent cheekbones, widely spaced, and a sharp, pointed chin, a high forehead. Her eyes… Well, what could Brodick say about them? They were east Asian. They were epicanthic as one would expect; there was just a dark glitter behind the eyelashes and mascara. Red lipstick, matching her nails, and wide, full lips.

She looked down, opened her purse, extracted something and pushed it across the table towards him. Brodick recognised his Sullivan passport.

'Take it. It's yours.'

'Thank you.' His voice sounded strangled in his own ears.

A faint whiff of expensive scent reached him, a welcome contrast with the prison stench of cigarettes, sweat, dirty feet and shit.

'My pleasure.' She said it with a hint of a smile. Her accent seemed to be American-Chinese. Or maybe American-Korean. Or American-Japanese. It was impossible to tell with just four words. In any case, she—or her family—was originally of Far East or southeast Asian origin, and her English—as was often the case in Asian schools and colleges—of the American variety.

CIA was his immediate thought.

'You missed your appointment with the man you know as Hasan. You can blame me. In fact, you should thank me rather than blame me because if you hadn't been picked up from your hotel yesterday morning and prevented from seeing him again as planned, you would already be an involuntary guest of the Basra Prison and that would have been careless of you. And less than agreeable. Or had you already changed your mind?' She paused, watching him for his reaction, then continued. 'Though I do apologise for the rough way in which you were handled. And also for your uncomfortable overnight accommodation; but then again, it could have been a lot worse.'

Another ironic half-smile that dimpled her right cheek.

'Perhaps I should add that the object of your interest was moved yesterday: Mr Buckley of the CIA is already in the Bekaa and in the custody of the Revolutionary Guards.'

The door opened. The keeper of the keys stepped in, holding a small metal tray.

'You won't have had anything to eat or drink for nearly twenty-four hours, so please… don't mind me. I will talk and you will eat.'

The tray was placed in front of Brodick, the guard retreated with a jangle of keys and the squeak of his rubber-soled boots, the door closing behind him.

On the tray was a half-litre plastic bottle of water—and Brodick started with that for he was desperately thirsty, ripping off the top, tipping his head back and pouring most of the contents down his throat. He paused to look at the woman again, then emptied the bottle. There was a small white cup and saucer with Turkish coffee and next to that a sandwich wrapped in grease-proof paper along with paper napkins; as it turned out, it was grilled chicken with some kind of pickle and very garlicky. Just the smell of it made Brodick salivate. She must have paid one of the guards to fetch all this from a nearby cafe.

He took a bite. His hands were shaking, but he didn't care if she noticed.

He spoke between mouthfuls. 'Where am I? What is this place?'

His visitor ignored the questions as if she hadn't heard them.

She crossed her legs and Brodick heard the provocative sound of her stockings rubbing together. She must have known the effect she was having on him.

'I have a proposal. If you agree and we can work something out to our mutual satisfaction, I will be able to fill you in on more details and you can leave a free man. If not, I will leave and you will stay here until your captors decide what to do with you.'

She shrugged, a gesture that said she didn't really care what that decision would be because it wouldn't be up to her.

Brodick stopped chewing and swallowed. 'Who are they: my captors?'

She didn't answer his question.

'May I call you Richard? I know your name isn't Drew Sullivan. So—Richard—I can have you out of here and back in the western sector at your hotel within the hour and no one will be any the wiser. Certainly not Century House. In return, I need something from you.'

How did she know?

'What? What do you need?'

His heartbeat had increased at the mention of Century House.

She knew far too much. She had to be Agency.

'An undertaking, an entirely voluntary undertaking.'

Brodick leaned forward, looking at the woman as she spoke, using a napkin to wipe mouth and chin. He could have eaten three sandwiches one after the other.

'Undertaking?' He had the urge to pick his teeth but desisted because it wouldn't have created a very favourable impression, and a male as young as Brodick cared what impression he made in front of a strikingly handsome woman, even if she was potentially a rival.

'From time to time I will ask you for a favour, that's all.'

'What kind of favour?'

'A favour that will do you and your career no harm. That much I promise.'

She did not gesticulate. She kept her hands together in her lap.

'Who are you?'

Was he imagining it, or was she really smiling at him?

'It doesn't really matter who I am. You may call me Fang. In Mandarin, Fang means fragrant. I leave you to judge whether I deserve the name.' A real smile this time, but the eyes, so narrow, so dark, remained mysterious. She was flirting with him, he decided.

'Fang is not your real name.'

'Of course not. Your name isn't Drew Sullivan but Richard Brodick. Does it matter? Fang is what you will call me.'

Brodick felt as if he'd been slapped. How did she know?

'So you will secure my release, and in return I agree to the occasional favour.'

'That's it, yes.'

'It's very vague.' Brodick polished off the coffee. He was feeling a lot better, but he noticed his hands were still trembling, so he sat on them.

'You will never be asked to do anything that harms your career with the Secret Intelligence Service. Trust me.'

That word "trust" again.

'You will never be asked to do anything beyond your capacity, or which puts you in any kind of danger. And yes, you will be free to go. And for my part, Richard, I will endeavour to help your career prosper. It's in my interest to help you succeed. I want us to be friends. The very best of friends. We can be a big help to each other.'

She was making a pitch for him.

Knowledge was certainly power and Brodick was conscious of her showing him some of hers, a flexing of psychological muscle. A display of power.

'How could you possibly do that?'

'It will vary. It might be a matter of passing on some useful information. In return it might be access to someone of interest to your employers. Or it might mean making sure you're somewhere which will benefit you—and me.'

He was conscious that by asking the question, he was already halfway there, and that she would know it.

'How many of these favours? And for how long?'

'Until I consider you no longer serve a useful purpose, Richard.'

'So I become your agent. I turn traitor. I betray my people. That's your offer, your deal. It does seem rather one-sided.'

'Oh, no.' She sounded shocked. 'Traitor? Not at all. That sounds *far* too drastic—and formal. We help each other from time to time. An unofficial association of equals. We are both foot soldiers in this racket. We could both do with some help. What do you call it? A quid pro quo?'

'I could agree to your proposal—and then change my mind as

soon as I'm out of here.'

Some foot soldier.

'You could. Yes. Right. I don't deny it. But the next time you find yourself in bad company you might not be so lucky. There won't be a guardian angel waiting with water, coffee, a grilled chicken sandwich and the key to your cell door.'

'Is that what you are? My guardian angel?'

That half-smile again, prompted by his sarcasm.

'Who are you? What are you? Are you working for the Centre? For Langley?'

'Neither, I assure you. Whoever it is I may work for doesn't concern you. Really it doesn't. You'll be helping me. Me, Fang, and no one else. And I'll be helping you, Richard. You're at the very start of your professional career. Your days of playing the amateur as a contract labourer are over. I can be of help to you. You're intelligent, ambitious, capable, and I can help you climb all the way to the top of your organisation. And you will help me. The more success you have, the more success I will enjoy. We help each other. All you have to do is respond to my infrequent requests. One or two a year: something of that order.'

Such flattery! Was he supposed to roll over like a puppy to have his tummy tickled and agree to everything this Fang demanded of him?

Fat chance.

'Is this conversation being recorded?'

'Not that I'm aware of.'

'Why me?'

'Because you show promise. Because you're one of MacGregor's young hawks. Because you're trusted by your own people—so far. Because you're not the usual run-of-the-mill SIS candidate. You're not Eton or Harrow or Winchester with a sense of entitlement. You're not a Balliol PPE or a Trinity Classics scholar. You're not military. You haven't been re-wired by Sandhurst and the Household Cavalry into thinking the way the Anglo-American establishment expects you to think. You're no simplistic patriot bent on spreading liberal democracy—whatever that may be—to the furthest corners of the planet. You're better than that. You're not a class warrior with a chip on his shoulder, either. Like so many British, you're not comfortable with ideology: any ideology. And I know you're not religious. Will that do for now?'

So that was it. She'd picked him because he was seen as a weak link, as an interloper, as someone who didn't fit in.

And she was right.

Brodick made a face, turning down the corners of his mouth. 'You must also know I'm duty-bound to report this meeting and conversation.' He sounded pompous even to himself and not at all convincing, but she knew far too much, and that worried him and his tone betrayed the fear. That was her intention, obviously. What she knew didn't come out of the pages of *The Guardian*, *The Daily Telegraph* or the British Library and she wanted him to know that.

She was getting it from inside Whitehall if not SIS itself.

Fang *had* to be CIA.

'By all means do whatever you think right, Richard. Obey your rules. Of course your captors may wish to sell you on—or seek ransom for your release. The Syrians or the Iranians can be expected to pay handsomely for you. Or indeed the Soviets. I'm sure the Centre would love to get their hands on a newly-hatched SIS officer, especially one with your experience of Afghanistan and a recent graduate of Fort Monckton. Century House won't be pleased in any case, and if you come up with a bizarre tale of an East Asian woman who tried to recruit you, they'll think you're delusional or a very bad liar. You'll be damaged goods either way. The stain of doubt is permanent, regardless of official outcome; you know that much by now, surely, after your adventures in Afghanistan. Perhaps I should say *misadventures*. It really is up to you.'

How did she *know*?

Her source or sources must be SIS—or very close to the Service or perhaps the Joint Intelligence Committee—and whoever this Fang was, fragrant or otherwise, she'd done her research and prepared well for this so-called interview.

Fang rose from her chair, still holding her purse, and stepped back.

'I hope you enjoyed your breakfast, Richard. I hope it was some comfort to you. I'm sorry I couldn't be of more help. I wish you luck. You'll need it.'

She turned away, walked to the door, her shoes rapping again on the cement floor, and she used the palm of her free hand to bang twice on the metal grate.

"Fang" had the upper hand, at least for now.

Brodick was reminded of a German word for negotiations under duress: *machtpolitik.*

He had no choice, not a sensible one.

The grate slid open, a guard's eye looked in, withdrew and the key turned in the lock. The cell door began to move.

Brodick rose to his feet. He leaned forward, his hands on the table for support. The word he uttered sounded in his ears like a croak of submission.

'Wait.'

8

It might have been months ago, but Brodick still recalls the night out in vivid detail.

Two vans with passenger seats, windows painted over, are waiting, engines idling, in the parking area of Fort Monckton. The student officers' names are called. Everyone is present and on time; no one wants to miss this chance to drink at the Firm's expense. Brodick finds himself squeezed between the multilingual Paula Lubnaig and the bulk of Captain David Sadler. Behind him, in the back, are the classicist Cynthia Payne and mathematician Harry Wood. The mood is buoyant. An instructor, General Service Branch Officer Bob Hale, turns around in the front passenger seat and distributes envelopes. They're not sealed, and each contains ten one-pound notes. Ten quid seems generous, for Brodick has frequently had a night out on half that.

It's the equivalent of twelve pints of Tennent's, by Brodick's calculations, maybe more. A pint is priced somewhere between 72p and 80p depending on the establishment.

'Pay attention. You've a job to do.'

Sadler shakes his head, mutters just loud enough for Hale and the driver to hear. 'For fuck's sake.' Hale ignores him.

'By closing time you should have acquired five names, five telephone numbers and five addresses. That's the minimum. To which you should add whatever personal details you can obtain: work, family, interests and hobbies along with a description of each individual. You get a gold star if you can get hold of vehicle registrations or national insurance numbers. Unlikely but possible,

I'd say, without picking pockets or stealing the lady's purse. I strongly advise you not to get pissed because you'll be required to write up your reports first thing on returning to base. The money is for buying drinks for others, not to get plastered yourselves. Stick to tonic. Questions? No? Let's go.'

In The Royal Oak, named along with all the other similarly named public houses scattered across the British Isles after the legendary oak tree in which the fugitive Charles ll hid from Parliamentarians, UB40's *Red, Red Wine* is belting out at full volume. The place is heaving. Brodick loses sight of Paula, Cynthia and Harry almost immediately, but he uses Sadler's size and natural aggression, ducking in close behind in his slipstream as the ex-soldier—muttering to himself—shoulders his way to the bar, causing some annoyance in the process with his big feet and sharp elbows.

Brodick has taken the precaution of removing everything from his pockets except for a cheap biro. It's instinct. He has no passport, no bank card, no receipts, no labels on his clothing: nothing that could identify him by name or origin. No litter to give him away.

He looks down the bar and spots a group of youngsters, two men and three women. They look like students. Their glasses are empty. With apologies and reiterations of 'Excuse me, please', he reaches them and succeeds in bumping into one of the males.

'I'm so sorry. My apologies.' He has to shout to be heard over the racket. 'Please, let me buy you a round.' Brodick won't take no for an answer. Then he seems to notice the others in the group for the first time. 'What are your friends having?'

By the time the drinks arrive, he's already introduced himself as Roy. He gathers up their first names. Billy is the young sociology student he managed to jab with his left forearm, spilling his shandy. Bev is Billy's girlfriend, or at least partner for the evening. They're both at Exeter University. Then there's Mike. Apparently the self-deprecating Mike isn't doing anything at the moment except renovate old bangers. Cheryl, orange hair and much facial ironmongery, is completing her Master's in Fine Art in Portsmouth.

Her pal, Georgia, with the heavy mascara and black lipstick, is visiting from Belfast. She's a dental nurse. One gin and tonic, one shandy, one vodka and lime, and Mike drinks Carlsberg. Georgia's poison is a half pint of Tennent's.

He tells them he's in shipping. Brodick has no idea what it means to be "in shipping", but given the noise level, he's pretty confident no one is going to ask.

They're friendly but cautious, properly so, though they warm up a little when he offers to buy the next round, too. 'You guys are studying; I'm earning a wage so let me pay.' Fortunately they decline—otherwise his cash would run out too soon. He tears off a piece of the envelope that once held the money and writes his assumed name down with a fake phone number and an old London address. Brodick invites them to look him up in London should they visit the capital. He eventually manages to get their surnames, but only the phone numbers of Billy, Mike and Georgia.

It's time to move on.

He spots Paula surrounded by a group of male admirers.

Phil Collins's *You Can't Hurry Love* is thudding through the walls and floorboards.

It's corny, but it's all he can think of. 'Don't I know you?' A shake of the head and a half-smile. 'I'm sorry. I don't wish to intrude, but let me buy you a round to make amends.'

Brodick gets away with it. Jake and Saul are together, it seems, rather better dressed than most of the customers, or perhaps just better off and a little older, in their mid-thirties. Are they gay? Probably. Who cares? Not Brodick, who is careful not to pay one more attention than the other. Saul is an architect, Jake a management consultant. He plays his shipping card. They talk—more like a shouting match—about football about which Brodick knows next to nothing. Jake is happy to talk. He's a Chelsea fan. He's also the petrolhead of the pair and owns up to owning a Porsche Targa, and is shyly proud of his acquisition. Saul buys another round for the three of them. Carlsberg this time. So far, Brodick has been drinking tonic with ice and lemon but now, as the witching hour approaches, he relents, and accepts a gin and tonic.

By closing time they're friends, up to a point, including swapping names, addresses and numbers. Sadly only one address for Saul and Jake because they're living together.

Brodick wants to see the Porsche nicknamed Wolfie and goes outside with them and memorises the registration while praising Wolfie in British racing green. 'Oh, I'm so envious: she's a beauty.' They shake hands and depart, not before offering Brodick a lift.

Brodick turns to go back inside to find his fellow trainee intelligence officers.

'Sir. One moment if you please.'

Two men appear out of the gloom, having apparently been waiting in one of the half dozen cars parked outside the pub. They wear dark car coats or short raincoats. One holds up what looks like a warrant card under plastic.

'Mr Brodick? Richard Brodick?'

'Who wants to know?'

'Special Branch. Detective Sergeant Brody and Detective Constable Simpson. Come with us please, sir.'

Brodick doesn't budge.

'I can't see your ID. Do you mind coming closer or moving into the light?'

They do mind. They move apart, circling, as if expecting Brodick to resist.

Before he can say anything else to buy time, Brodick finds himself spun around, off-balance, an ankle hooked from under him, then spread-eagled over the bonnet of a dark coloured saloon, possibly maroon, a four-seat Rover, several years old with paintwork that's patched and scratched. Brodick is patted down, roughly and thoroughly, pockets turned out, his feet kicked apart, his hands stretched out. As his wrists are pulled together and he's handcuffed and dragged upright by his collar, he notices the concealed radio aerial, a wire laid out along the top edge of the front window. It's a surveillance vehicle. Brodick commits the registration number to memory, the second of the evening along with four telephone numbers. It's ridiculous and he knows it, but what he's worrying about is the lack of a fifth telephone number. He makes no effort to resist: the two coppers might conceivably be armed, one of whom is decidedly large. He decides it would be useless to make a run for it because even if he managed to evade his pursuers; he's not sure where he is, having failed to make a mental note of the van's movements after leaving the Fort.

'Am I under arrest?'

No answer.

'Aren't you going to read my rights?'

Again, neither copper replies.

He's manhandled into the rear of the saloon, an officer's hand on his head to stop him striking himself against the edge of the car door. The officers squeeze in on either side of him.

'Let's go.' The driver reverses, turns the car and as they move off, Brodick just has time to see Sadler stagger out from the pub and stand swaying on the gravel before bending over and throwing up his supper along, no doubt, with several pints of lager.

9

Once freed from whatever and wherever it was that he'd been held, Brodick found a nearby taxi rank. It was only a few yards along the street and served the needs of those arriving or leaving the Lebanese military intelligence facility, if that's what it was. There was a small shop, too, really only a shack, that sold snacks: no doubt this was the origin of his chicken sandwich and Turkish coffee. They must be doing good business, having a captive customer base, quite literally. He ignored the stares of the cab driver in the rear-view mirror and the latter's attempts to engage Brodick in bad French, asking—inevitably—where he was from and whether he was working for the Deuxieme Bureau as the taxi began its descent to the city.

'*Vous-etes Francais, monsieur*?'

No response.

The driver tried out his English. 'You soldier, mister?'

No response.

'Spy?'

No response.

'CIA yes?'

No response. Brodick wasn't the only spook to visit, obviously.

'You like Lebanon, yes?'

For heaven's sake.

'Lebanese Forces, good, no? Phalangists: you like?'

Yeah, sure. Who wouldn't? Israel's Phalangist proxies, responsible for the recent Sabra and Chatila massacre of Palestinian women and children. Lovely people indeed, with their origins in the 1936

Berlin Olympics. But let's not be too fastidious.

This time he joined the steady trickle of pedestrians moving through the Barbir crossing to reach the western sector, but thankfully the snipers on either side hadn't yet woken, or were too hungover or strung out on cocaine or heroin, both of which were known to be widely used by militiamen: Christian and Moslem, right-wing and left-wing. He tried not to hurry, though his skin prickled with danger. With twenty tons of pressure an inch, a bullet travels faster than sound and Brodick knew he would never hear the round that killed him. He had been shot at often enough to know what a miss sounded like—a whisper, a whine, a flutter, a crack or a hiss—depending on distance, velocity, calibre.

Someone had called him at the Commodore on three occasions the previous evening, according to the clerk at reception, but had given no name nor left a message. No doubt it was Hasan. Brodick showered, changed, packed up his belongings, paid his bill and checked out. Then once again he set out again for the embassy—taking greater care this time as he walked out of the hotel—crossing over to the eastern sector yet again via the Museum crossing point and using two taxis and a random *service* to reach the hillside compound surrounded by pines in the exclusive suburb of Rabiyeh.

He showed his Sullivan passport to a member of the embassy's Lebanese guard force, waited for them to inform the embassy he was on his way, then walked uphill to an inner security ring comprising cheerful British close protection officers cradling Heckler & Koch submachine guns. The communications officer, Angus Henderson, was waiting for him with an enciphered message which Brodick signed for and which Henderson then decoded in Brodick's presence. There was a ten-minute hiatus during which Brodick thumbed through a greasy, year-old copy of *Tatler* and learned that it was non-U to allow dogs onto the bed and even more non-U to pee in the bath. If that wasn't entertainment enough, there was a lovely picture of the twenty-two-year-old Princess of Wales wearing Saudi Arabian sapphires in Brisbane, Australia: more than enough to warm the cockles of royalist hearts. Wonderful stuff, indeed.

Brodick learned he was to travel to Larnaca by sea where he would meet his handler; the *treff* or meeting was scheduled for the coffee shop at the Bay Marina Hotel in two days' time, at 1030 hours. That translated into 1050, given standard operating procedure. Said contact would carry, or would be reading, a rolled-up copy of *The Times*. Brodick's passage had been booked under the name Sullivan, but he would need to buy his ticket himself before boarding.

There was no mention of Hasan or Buckley.

He spent another night in Beirut, but this time in the eastern sector, at a grim hotel with a severe, prison grey exterior. It looked like something from the wrong side of the Iron Curtain and had recently served as the headquarters of the Israeli occupation forces, and the Zionist hero—or notorious war criminal—General Ariel Sharon, now Israeli defence minister, had commandeered the place. Brodick had no difficulty getting a room; the Israelis had withdrawn further south, and the place seemed empty except for what he took to be a middle-aged prostitute lolling on a sofa in the foyer like the leavings of a retreating army and whom he managed to ignore without any regrets. Sex was about the last thing on Brodick's mind. And if there was fighting in the city, he was too exhausted to care and slept through it undisturbed.

10

Brodick had an hour to spare before the ferry's departure the next morning, but he resisted the temptation to indulge his curiosity by exploring Jounieh with its jewellery and clothing shops, its clubs and bars and casinos notorious for Soviet bloc and Asian "hostesses". He avoided the old stone market because there was still a Mossad presence somewhere in the vicinity: a combined headquarters of the Israeli Defence Force, their security service, Shin Bet, and Mossad operatives working alongside their Phalangist collaborators. The Israelis had a SIGINT centre in Jounieh, too, someplace, monitoring the signal traffic of the Syrians as well as embassies. So he kept away from the town and port until most passengers were already on board before darting along the quay and up the gangway with just ten minutes to spare, queuing to have his passport checked and stamped by Phalangist officials, then locking himself away in his cabin, peeking out of his porthole to watch his fellow travellers.

But not before witnessing a dozen Soviet-designed BTR-60 personnel carriers unloading from a roll-on, roll-off freighter on the far side of the port. The wheeled armour was in desert camouflage, so too the uniforms of accompanying troops sporting Saddam Hussein toothbrush moustaches. They were indeed Iraqis, and the equipment Baghdad was supplying to the Lebanese Army and the Phalangists was intended to assist them in their joint struggle against Damascus. My enemy's enemy is my friend: Syria and Iraq being ruled by rival wings of the Ba'ath Party and each claiming to be the vanguard of Arab nationalism. More to the point, Iraq had been at war with Syria's ally Iran for four years with no end to the slaughter in sight.

The Israelis would have a good view of the proceedings. Brodick watched the BTR-60s roll out of the port and onto the coastal highway, heading north.

The sea was calm, the sky a perfect blue. It was just after ten in the morning, but the sun was already high and hot; perfect weather for the swarms of package holidaymakers from Northern Europe intent on grilling themselves along the Mediterranean littoral over the forthcoming Easter weekend—Lebanon excepted. Once Brodick was sure the vessel had left Jounieh, he slipped outside, hurried aft and climbed to an upper deck occupied by emergency life rafts but which seemed otherwise deserted. He lay down on the planking, rolling up his lightweight jacket and using it as a pillow. He closed his eyes, comforted by the vibration of the ferry's engines as the elderly vessel—she was at least forty years old and had served several owners—sailed west at ten knots, leaving Lebanon behind and the destination of Larnaca just one-hundred-and-thirty-eight nautical miles ahead.

His last thoughts before falling asleep were of his rescuer, "Fang". Or possibly his antagonist. He wouldn't have called her pretty. Attractive? Most certainly. Had she simply taken advantage of his detention through some contact of hers with the Lebanese military? Or had she arranged the whole episode? The latter seemed likely, and it wasn't out of concern for his wellbeing, for fear that he would end up in the Basra Prison, that she had had him snatched in broad daylight in front of his hotel. It seemed to have been a straightforward and well-planned attempt at recruitment, displaying both her power over him and the extent of her resources, then expressing her apparent goodwill while demonstrating her superior knowledge: in this instance, inside knowledge of Brodick's true identity and Buckley's alleged transfer to the Republican Guards barracks in the Bekaa. And there was the hook, too, naturally enough: the offer to help Brodick climb the

SIS ranks to the top floor.

If the approach had been made during his Afghan phase, Brodick would have been appalled. It would have struck at the heart of all he what he wanted to be, at the hand-me-down values and ideals of the loyal Briton he held himself out to be in his quest for a career in the Service. Indignant, he would have rejected the overture, and reported it, and suffered the consequences.

Not anymore.

In all, it was nicely done, a well-rehearsed combination of force, threat, flattery and promise, displaying just the right amount of inside information to leave him shaken and uncertain. He wanted to believe the promise and he'd taken the lure: as she must have known he would.

"Fang"—whatever her real name—was all about control, and he was the rat running through a maze of her design.

A year previously Brodick was a very different man, or at least he had held very different views. The idea of being played by a rival service's spy, of going along with her game—if indeed Fang truly was a spy—would have horrified him as disloyal and a treasonous act. Every patriotic bone in his body would have objected. Then he had wanted to work for the Secret Intelligence Service out of misplaced idealism—as he saw it now— out of a determination to play his part in the Cold War, to "make a difference": all those embarrassing truisms he'd adopted in support of his vaulting ambition. And yes, he'd wanted so much to emulate the accomplishments of his father, now deceased, a legend in his own lifetime for his recruitment at the age of twenty-three of a German military intelligence, or Abwehr, officer in Lisbon during the course of 1943.

So what had changed? For a start, as Brodick saw it, he had grown up. Afghanistan and its cruelties had purged him of any illusions about the Firm's good intentions or those of the ministers who tasked the SIS with their requirements. He had certainly achieved his ambition; but now it seemed a Pyrrhic victory, reduced to little more than a means of making a living, and a cynical one at that. He was still determined to make a success of it, only he was far less choosy in how he did so. Cut corners to fast track his rise in the espionage establishment of the United Kingdom?

Well, sure, why the hell not?

There was no glory to be had. He was in this for himself.

Just so long as he could get away with it.

Played right, Fang represented a huge opportunity.

There were no tourists on the boat that he could see, but instead a handful of unsavoury looking 'businessmen' escaping Christian-held Jounieh by sea rather than risk the 12-mile overland journey via the mainly Moslem and leftist western sector of Beirut to the airport in the southern suburbs. Militia officers, arms dealers, smugglers and spies; people not altogether unlike Brodick aka Sullivan.

After an uneventful trip—and Brodick was grateful for the rest and solitary nature of the passage—the ferry docked under a new moon at 2215, alongside a floodlit pier shared by an equally vintage warship, a French Navy corvette, so small and so ancient it looked to Brodick as if should have been donated to a maritime museum. There were two lights showing on this little gunboat, one on what Brodick supposed was the bridge, the other in the bows, but no sign of movement.

After Cypriot immigration officers had come on board and checked the passengers' passports, Brodick followed the others as they disembarked, struggling down the gangway with their suitcases, bags, cardboard boxes, mattresses and rolls of blankets. All Brodick had was what the navy calls a pusser's bag, a tan canvas affair with a zip which he hoisted onto his shoulder.

The Bay Marina Hotel was a few minutes away by taxi.

11

'Sad news about Tommy Cooper.'

The stranger dropped the copy of *The Times* on the table.

The recognition signal was part of the protocol between case officer and operative at their first *treff.*

'I didn't know.' Brodick turned it around so he could see the front page headlines.

'Collapsed and died on stage, would you believe. Only sixty-three. And the Libyans are acting up again. Shot and killed a young woman police officer in London. Bastards. In broad daylight. Unbelievable.'

The bearer of bad news was referring to the late WPC Yvonne Fletcher.

Fenner was in his late thirties, plump and pink-cheeked, in a short-sleeved blue linen shirt, very creased with damp patches fore and aft, hanging loose over grubby white chinos, and espadrilles on his feet. The Englishman on holiday was the intended image, no doubt, and he had the right complexion for the boyish role: splashes of pink on cheeks and forehead. He was the type whose skin would never really tan: just redden and peel.

'Nick. Nick Fenner. Political First Secretary, Her Britannic Majesty's High Commission, Nicosia. At your service.' A theatrical bow, followed by a firm if moist handshake.

'Richard.' Brodick resisted the temptation to wipe his hand on his trousers.

According to the rules, the next step would be to establish the time available for the meeting, and then when and where they would next make contact.

'Had breakfast, Richard?'

'I did. The buffet finished at ten. I imagine we could order coffee, though.'

'Great! Wouldn't mind a cold beer to be perfectly honest.' Big toothy grin.

Nicholas Fenner's grey eyes strayed momentarily across the room to the only other people in the coffee shop. When Brodick turned in his chair and followed the glance, Fenner dropped his gaze at once: a sure giveaway.

Most folk staying at the hotel would be on their sun loungers, splashing around in one of the three pools or shopping in the arcades. This young couple were looking on as their—presumably their—children ran around the room shouting, the childish cries helping to blanket out whatever Fenner and Brodick had to say. The couple wore their holiday clothes, too: t-shirts and shorts, trainers in the case of the woman, flip-flops for the man. Fenner's clumsy response suggested they were part of his team, minders from the Nicosia Station watching Fenner's back, carrying out route surveillance detection. Cypriot ports of entry pullulated with spies of one kind or another, from Fatah to Mossad.

Families made good cover in this tourist paradise.

'So what was it that persuaded you do join our little outfit, eh, Richard? Couldn't have been the pay, now, could it? Or has it proved to be a horrible mistake after all, and you can't wait to get the hell out and back to a decent life on civvie street?'

He'd often asked himself the same question.

Coffee was brought. Fenner waited until the waiter had left.

'I've a lot to tell you, Richard, but perhaps you might start by describing your adventures in Beirut, if you would.' Fenner's intonation was very much public school.

Brodick recounted his checking in to Le Commodore, the head on his windowsill—Fenner manufactured appropriate expressions of surprise and disgust—the telephone call to Hasan, the meeting, the negotiation. Brodick was careful to add that Hasan had warned him that Buckley was likely to be moved out of the so-called Basra Prison in a matter of days. He mentioned the final price he'd agreed, and how he had decided to visit the embassy the next morning to send off a signal seeking authorisation. Only he never got there. He was abducted—and Brodick described his kidnapping in detail with a self-deprecating humour—and his incarceration in what he assumed to be a Deuxieme Bureau headquarters or detention centre in the hills to the east of the capital. He thought it might have been in the Baabda neighbourhood where the presidential palace was located. Perhaps Fenner would know who his kidnappers were. He said he blamed himself for being too lax when he'd left the hotel in the morning.

Fenner listened without interruption. He frowned into his coffee and played with the spoon. 'You weren't interrogated?'

Brodick was giving *The Times* front page his attention, or pretending to do so, feeling the blood pounding away in his chest, his temples. He felt hot. He told himself to watch his body language. He'd never been a good liar, but he thought he was improving with practice.

'No. I wasn't. It puzzled me, too.'

'You weren't abused in any way?'

'I was roughed up when I was thrown into the boot of the Volvo, and hooded on arrival. But not beaten or tortured, no.'

'Any idea why you were left alone in the cell?'

'None.'

'Were you entirely alone or was there another prisoner?'

'I was entirely alone.'

Liar.

'Were you asked your name?'

She knew my fuckan name. She knew far too much about me and the Firm.

'No. They took my Sullivan passport away along with my belt, laces, watch and the small amount of cash I had on me and it was all returned to me when I was released.'

'Were you asked to sign anything?'

'No.'

'Did you have to fill in a form of some kind?'

'No.' He shook his head. That might not have been the right answer, but at least he hadn't hesitated.

'Well. That is extraordinary. And lucky. You did well over the money, I must say, and you were absolutely right to seek authorisation. It would have been refused, I'm sure you realise that. I'm also pretty sure your suspicion was right: Hasan was setting you up for Islamic Jihad and would have pocketed the fee himself. A finder's fee. Your brief detention is intriguing; aside from being uncomfortable and rather worrying, as it must have been at the time. One might be forgiven for thinking that someone was trying to protect you from Hasan and what was clearly going to be a trap. Or prevent you from reaching our embassy at that particular juncture. Perhaps there might have been something going on at the time that they didn't want you to witness. Any thoughts?'

'I've thought of little else and have come to no conclusions, I'm afraid.'

'Hasan's tuned out to be a bad egg, obviously.'

'Do you want me to write this up as a contact report?'

'Don't see the need as things stand, though I'll consult. If anything changes and we need to revisit this, I'll let you know.'

'Sure.'

'You know that we have confirmed the presence in Beirut of at least twenty-three foreign intelligence and security agencies: and the real figure could exceed twice that. Some friendly, most of them hostile. It really is a spy swamp, not unlike Berlin's *agentsumpf*.'

Brodick nodded. He couldn't think of a response; not a sensible one, anyway.

'Hasan was right about Buckley being moved. He was taken to the Bekaa the very next morning after your meeting with Hasan, or so we understand from a reliable allied source. He's now a guest of the Iranian Revolutionary Guard special forces formation known as Al-Quds and he's been locked away in the Sheikh Abdullah base.

I don't rate Buckley's chances of survival very highly.'

'So my trip wasn't worth it. I'm sorry.'

'Oh, I wouldn't say that. We were seen trying to help our allies, that's the main thing. Call it public relations. You did it all by the book. We do keep tabs on Lebanon's so-called Deuxième Bureau, but we've heard nothing of a UK citizen named Sullivan being held. The French are pretty close to them, of course, and we've heard nothing from the DGSE, either. Seems your stint in prison was unofficial and went unrecorded.'

Fang had made sure of that.

Brodick struggled to make sense of his mission and its failure. At the start it had been presented as important enough for him to risk his life, to seek out the kidnappers; and now, well, it was just dropped, brushed aside, an incomplete file locked away to gather dust. Was it really as Fenner described it: merely a public relations exercise, a cosmetic effort to please their U.S. counterparts? He couldn't help but wonder whether SIS ever seriously contemplated finding Buckley. Was the life and wellbeing of a junior SIS officer so cheap? Or had the British lost all sense of their own national interest as distinct from Washington's? Most likely it was a combination of these.

'Now I must brief you, Richard. MacGregor has plans for you.'

'Go ahead.'

He had told the truth. Mostly. All he'd done was to omit all reference to Fang. He began to relax. It seemed he'd got away with it, at least for now. It wasn't going to be so bad after all. The rack and thumbscrew could wait.

Behind Brodick the three children were wrestling on the floor and managed to knock over a chair. Both parents shouted at them to stop it. It had little effect.

'Oh, I almost forgot. I'd like you to take a quick look at something.'

Fenner extracted a manila envelope from inside *The Times*. It contained a sheaf of A4-sized glossy photographic prints, which he laid face down on the table.

'Have you by chance seen this individual during your trip? I know it seems unlikely.' He picked up the first, turned it over and handed it to Brodick. 'Seen her on the off chance, perhaps, spoken to her, been approached by her?'

Fenner stared down at the photograph. 'We think she might have been in Beirut at the same time. Oh, I know. It's a large city. Of course. But maybe in the airport lounge?' Fenner handed Brodick the second. 'She might have been on the plane to Damascus. Maybe you spotted her at the Commodore bar or the reception desk but forgot and didn't give it any further thought. Why would you, after all? Or in the lift or corridor. Did she go for a swim in the hotel pool? Think back, Richard.' Fenner passed Brodick the third print. 'Maybe you bought her a drink. Natural enough: an attractive woman on her own. Or in the Wimpy, where you met Hasan? Take a good look. We're in no rush.'

Fuck.

'I think I'd remember buying a woman a drink. I'd certainly remember *her*. No. I'm sorry to disappoint you. I wish I'd known earlier and I'd have kept an eye open for her.'

Brodick was indeed getting better at lying, but even so he knew he was digging himself deeper into a hole without any visible escape route.

Was this some twisted trick, some game they were playing and they knew all about this Fang?

The first print was grainy, out of focus and greatly enlarged. So was the second. The subject was the same in both. Brodick made a show of studying all three, moving the coffee cup and saucer away, clearing a space and leaning on his forearms, head down to study them spread out in front of him. Head down to hide his expression.

There she was. Unmistakably a woman. Unmistakably an Asian woman, erect, slim and in dark clothing. Unmistakably Fang.

Striding along a pavement, a blur of movement. Emerging from a vehicle: the slim legs, the heels. She had the figure of a gymnast or long-distance runner: light and nimble on her feet.

The third showed the same woman in a doorway, stationary and wearing a long coat with a high collar, hair blowing in her face, what looked like a Prada bag slung on one shoulder. All but one of these muddy images displayed action, momentary motion caught by a photographer shooting from a vehicle or a static surveillance post.

Brodick felt himself blush; he knew his neck and ears had a tendency to go bright red when he was caught out lying and now he felt them burn: and it wasn't the sun from lying in the sun on the deck of the ferry. He sat back, held up the prints in both hands, looking at them in turn, in an effort to at least partially conceal the tell-tale signs that he'd been caught out.

Stay calm.

'Hmm. No, can't say I recognise her.' He shuffled the photographs together and handed them back. 'Sorry, Nick. Who is she?'

Of course he knew.

Jesus!

Fenner shrugged, but Brodick thought his case officer had failed to hide his disappointment.

12

Back to that infamous night out.

Shorty, aka DC Simpson, paces near the door of the interview room, cracking his knuckles and scowling at Brodick. Shorty is a small, dark man with black hair—no more than five-six and skinny—with a tattoo showing above his shirt collar. His skin is tight and creased in innumerable small lines. It resembles nothing so much as yellow parchment stretched across jaw and cheekbones. Shorty looks nasty, the kind of man on a short fuse who will throw a kick or a punch without warning. He has a strong Glasgow accent.

His companion sits—or rather slouches—opposite Brodick. Brody is stout, double-chinned, and seems almost amiable. His deep voice is West Yorkshire. He stretches his legs out, ankles crossed under the table.

'Now then, let's do this, shall we, and we can all go home to our beds.' The detective sergeant's tone is conciliatory, practical, world-weary.

Brodick says nothing. He faces the door and Brody, back straight and keeping hands in his lap. He does his best to stay calm, to look pleasant, agreeable as if he's the one in charge. He doesn't meet Shorty's eye. He doesn't want to provoke him. Instead, Brodick looks at the table.

DS Brody tries again. 'Name? Sir?'

'I'm so sorry about this.' Brodick frowns, shakes his head, still staring at the table. 'I'm sure it's just a mistake. Maybe I did something or said something…' Brodick's voice trails off.

'Name? Let's start with that, shall we.' The detective sergeant's tone is patient, his pen poised over a ruled A4 pad.

'It's clearly a mix-up. I do apologise to you both for wasting your time.'

'If I could just have your name and address, sir. It's a formality, see.'

Shorty's knuckles crack three times in rapid succession.

'Gie us your name, ya wee shite.' The detective constable has turned abruptly, lunges towards Brodick and leans over him, his hands on the table, expelling sour cigarette breath into Brodick's face. Shorty would have found his true calling in the East German security police, Brodick decides. How long before he brings out the knuckle duster and cosh?

'That's enough, Kev. Come away now.'

Brodick throws up his hands in mock surrender. 'I'm not trying to be difficult, gentlemen, really I'm not. Please.'

'If you could just let us have your name, your current address and your date of birth and we'll get this over with.'

'Look, detective sergeant, I'm sure someone will be along soon and sort all this out.' Brodick offers his inquisitors an exaggerated Gallic shrug. 'Sorry officers, there must have been a mix-up. I'm really sorry. A thousand apologies.'

'Mix-up, my arse.' Shorty is prowling and snarling again, pulling at his finger joints, baring his yellow teeth. A Glesca attack dog.

They don't hit him. They don't use a telephone directory; a common police method because it leaves no bruises if done with some skill.

There is a recording device to one side, but it isn't turned on. That's a sign that this isn't, after all, official. It's a performance, a *danse macabre*. Brodick persuades himself of it and immediately feels much better. They're play-acting. So is he. It's just a game.

The seconds and minutes tick by, though Brodick tries to avoid being seen to look up at the clock on the wall above the door. He keeps it up for forty-four minutes: silences, interspersed with grovelling apologies. Then they leave him, Shorty fumbling for his cigarettes, cursing under his breath, and calling Brodick a wee bawbag—this insult is intended to be heard—while his superior heaves himself up out of his chair.

They've already strip-searched him and found nothing.

They're both disgusted, disgusted with themselves for having got nothing at all out of Brodick, and disgusted with Brodick for his unrelenting litany of mock-humble apologies.

Shorty mutters a farewell full of menace, something along the lines of: 'Awa' tae fuck.'

His partner takes a more conciliatory approach. 'Can we get you a cuppa?'

'Thanks.' Brodick attempts a winning smile. Charm personified. 'That *would* be kind, detective sergeant—as long as you guarantee your colleague won't piss in it.'

The Yorkshireman smiles. 'It's been known to happen.'

13

At the Bay Marina's reception desk, Brodick hired a car, a grey-green Skoda Octavia, and the little convoy set out. Fenner led in a white Land Rover with Cypriot plates. Bringing up the rear was a dark blue Renault station wagon, spattered with dried mud, carrying the family from the coffee shop, kids rampaging in the back, proud parents in sunglasses up front seemingly oblivious of the civil strife behind them. Brodick was piggy in the middle. The journey took just over an hour and, according to Fenner, there were plans to build a proper, four-lane highway to the inland capital and that would cut the journey time in half. The convoy's progress was slowed somewhat by both the poor state of the double lane and Fenner's meticulous speeding up and slowing down to detect any tail.

There didn't appear to be one.

Fenner turned off into the Nicosia Hilton's parking lot. Brodick followed, but the blue Renault sped on past, the children waving and sticking out their tongues. Brodick registered as Drew Sullivan, handed over the Sullivan passport, dropped his bag and off they set out again, this time with Brodick in the front passenger seat of the Land Rover.

Fenner glanced repeatedly in his mirrors. 'Looks like a clear run today. Sometimes we have a procession of interested parties in our wake.'

Brodick didn't ask who the followers usually were, but Fenner told him anyway. Brodick was aware that SIS stations routinely used Automated Number Plate Recognition or ANPR—code name GOULASH—for identifying suspicious and potentially hostile vehicles.

'Mostly the Centre's hoods, and the GRU. The former often use local friends in the Cypriot Communist Party to burn rubber and wear out shoe leather. They like to ring the changes in the vain hope that we won't notice. Then there are the East Germans and Czechs. Mossad, of course. They're supposed to be our friends, but don't you believe it. They can be very aggressive. Give them a finger and they'll take your whole bloody arm, without anaesthetic. The PLO factions and Iranians tend to rely on static posts. The Americans bug the hell out of us, naturally, and we reciprocate the favour while proclaiming undying brotherhood, but they don't tag us as a rule because it's not polite between friends and allies, or so we're told.'

Fenner didn't mention the Chinese and Brodick didn't ask.

Behind chancery's bandit-proof doors and coded locks, Fenner laid out his wares.

'You're going back to Beirut, I'm afraid. Surprised? I hope it isn't too much of a shock, old man. But look on the bright side. Something's come up: or rather, someone has. This is your chance to shine. You're going up a pay grade. You'll be independent from the Beirut station with your own secure comms. You're going in as a TCI Section VCO. Does that mean anything to you?'

How SIS loved its acronyms.

'I think it means I'm to be a Visiting Case Officer as part of a Targeting and Counter-Intelligence section or TCI—that is, seeking to recruit hard target personnel. Who exactly is the target?'

'Non-official cover again, I'm afraid.'

NOC meant Brodick wouldn't have the protection of diplomatic cover if things went pear-shaped.

Brodick had some idea how this worked from his training. "Hard case" targets meant those people SIS would try to recruit outside their home countries for the simple reason that it was almost impossible to do so on their home ground. The CIA referred to such locations as "denied areas". A case officer had a tough job running an existing agent somewhere like Moscow without being expected to devote himself simultaneously to recruiting more prospects. So the target would be approached in a third country, recruited there, and run from the SIS station in the target's own country if and when he or she finally went home.

Brodick also understood that when a TCI section's VCO recruited an agent in a third country, the station in the capital of the recruiting territory was usually kept out of the loop. Compartmentalisation was an essential part of the process.

The Soviet Union, Eastern Europe, North Korea and China all qualified as "hard target" states.

So who was it?

Fenner was still talking. 'Not a target but targets, plural. Oh, and you'll be reporting to me, by the way, at least for now. I'm a member of the TCI Section. Beirut Station has enough on its plate: disrupting the local militias is a big enough task as it is. Same goes for Nicosia.' Big smile, Fenner patting down his stray blond hair in an oddly self-conscious gesture.

SIS had its own travel agency, Levant Travel, established twelve years before the Lebanon civil war erupted in April, 1975. Fenner explained that its main office was still in West Beirut, but that had to change: and sooner rather than later. Levant Travel washed its own face, and there was usually a very small annual profit—which had saved it from the savage SIS cuts of the 1970s—but clearly there was insufficient business in West Beirut to justify the payroll and high visibility, and the staff themselves were physically at risk simply commuting to and from work. There were four other branches: a foothold across the Green Line in the eastern sector of the Lebanese capital, one in Damascus, another in Amman and one in Nicosia. Fenner indicated this last branch might be worth expanding into the firm's new regional headquarters. Brodick should visit; it would help cement his cover as Chief Representative, East Mediterranean.

'Are any of Levant Travel's local staff aware of our ownership?'

'Only one and we want to keep it that way. You'll meet up in

West Beirut. He's an old soldier from the Arab Legion, believe it or not. He thinks we're just a branch of the Foreign Office and we try to keep it that way. He's very distinguished and favours pin-stripe suits and a tightly rolled umbrella. Loads of gravitas and a hopeless Anglophile. Name of Fawzi. A Sunni Moslem. He and the current ambassador are pals. Sir Christopher was a subaltern in the Trucial Oman Scouts and, like the Arab Legion, the Scouts are long since defunct. They're a pair of dinosaurs. Fawzi's your local manager for both Beirut offices: though he seldom travels across the Green Line to the eastern sector and then only to drink dry sherry with His Excellency. Fawzi reports to you. Speaks no language known to mankind, was how MacGregor described him to me. It's a scary mix of Arabic, French and English and all delivered at high speed. Don't worry: he won't be offended if you ask him to slow down and repeat himself. He's used to it.'

'He'll be indoctrinated as far as my role is concerned?'

'Already done, and only up to a point. He's not party to the specifics of your task. He was here last week for that very purpose.'

Brodick must have looked worried. 'Don't fret, Richard. He's completely trustworthy, though of course you won't be sharing product with him. Like everyone else he has to go through the positive vetting checks every couple of years, but not enhanced vetting. He'll be of practical help and you can ask him for advice. If you want a driver or someone to stake out a location, he'll find the people. Sometimes he uses his relatives because they find the cash comes in handy. I don't know how true it is, but he seems to have the ear of the president, the prime minister, the speaker of parliament and a dozen ministers. If you need introductions to anyone, ask him.'

'Maybe he should be doing my job.'

'You're not the first to suggest it. But no: he loves a gossip and, like so many of his compatriots, relishes all manner of conspiracy theory. Impartial truth is an alien concept where Fawzi is concerned. He's not cleared for secret classification and he's no head agent, I'm sorry to say; though he might drop a tasty morsel in your lap now and again. Sometimes it's worth following up, but mostly he's just trying to win your approval. All you have to do is be prepared to listen. He really wants to be appreciated. Don't we all? He'll be useful if you want to buy a car, book air tickets, keep an embassy under surveillance, figure out how to get somewhere safely, and change money.'

A late lunch at a local taverna followed, Fenner apologising for not inviting him home to meet his family. Brodick tried the pork dish known as *afelia* with yoghurt and halloumi, washed down with Keo lager. They didn't talk shop for obvious reasons. Fenner attacked his chicken with gusto and did his best to entertain his guest and subordinate with small talk, but the two spies seemed to have little in common and Brodick's head was in any case spinning with the day's news of his so-called promotion, the fact that his lie about Fang had gone unnoticed. They drank their coffee in silence and within the hour were back at work at the SIS Station: a suite of offices in chancery, suspended off the floor and lined in metal, a giant Faraday cage, in effect.

Fenner passed Brodick a sheet of paper.

'From the latest Red Book assessments.'

The Red Book—named as such for its distinctive red cover and being the weekly compilation of the latest Joint Intelligence Committee assessments—was issued every Friday morning.

It was followed by a typed list of Requirements for Lebanon.

'Bloody hell! Thirty-two items?'

'Memorise the first ten. Go on, do it now.'

Brodick read it through three times.

'Done?'

Brodick stared at the paper and reluctantly let it go, Fenner pulling it out of his hand and dropping it into the office shredder along with the Red Book excerpts. They would be bagged and burned, a twice daily routine in the Nicosia Station.

'Focus on your TCI targets. There are only two. The rest are background as far as you're concerned, in the event that you stub your toe on one or more of them.'

Brodick's voice sounded unnaturally thick in his own ears. 'This woman—the number one item here on your list—she's the same one in the pictures you showed me. Right?'

'Indeed she is.'

'And her name?'

'She calls herself Fang. It's her workname. Real name: Chen Meilin. I believe Chen is like Smith or Brown: commonplace. For our purposes she has a code name: DRAGON. But of course she must never know that.'

'What's so special about DRAGON?'

'She's a very busy, very active lady. She keeps turning up, the proverbial bad penny, trailing her coat in all manner of strange and dangerous places. Baghdad. Tehran. Damascus. Aden. Now Beirut. Officially, she's a so-called honourable correspondent accredited to the New China News Agency.'

'Xinhua.'

'And we know what that "honourable correspondent" means, don't we? Xinhua's effectively the PRC embassy in Hong Kong. Chen Meilin has to be *Guoanbu*. One of the new breed. She has plenty of freedom—autonomy—as her position would suggest, and she has to be pretty senior, too, for someone her age to be gallivanting around the cesspits on her own. She seems to be some sort of trouble-shooter.'

'You think she's 2nd Bureau, foreign intelligence?'

'Very likely. Or the 5th.'

'Counter-intelligence.'

'Right. And there's always special operations: the 7th. Any or all of the above. DRAGON may have links to several PRC intelligence organisations.

'We think she may be after someone called Li Zuanfei, a polymath. Brilliant maths brain. He's there: your second interest. The Israelis and probably the Centre are also rather keen to meet him. He's travelling on a Canadian passport and is believed to be headed for Beirut. We want anything and everything you can get on him. Don't make the pitch: leave that to us. For now you're our access agent. You're to look him over, that's all, and bring him to us if he seems receptive.'

'And what exactly are my orders with regard to DRAGON?'

'Find out what she's up to, along with her *modus operandi.* Try to locate her, discover where she's staying in Beirut and, if possible, make contact. Who is she seeing? What's she after? Is it Li? What makes her tick? Is she vulnerable to an approach? Did her family suffer during the Cultural Revolution? Does she have some axe to grind we haven't thought of? Is DRAGON a secret anti-communist? Maybe she's religious. I understand her English is pretty good.'

'And if I do manage to make contact?'

'There's only one thing *to* do in this game. Get alongside. Make friends. Recruit her, Richard. Take your time gaining her confidence, but recruit her. Make your pitch when you think the time is right. Little by little: until there's no way back. Turn her. Whatever it takes. However long it takes. You'll need either positive inducement or what our pals from Moscow Centre call *kompromat:* or both. Finally, when she's well and truly hooked and you have her bona fides tucked away and there's no way back, run her in place. Make MacGregor proud. Make us all proud.'

Of course. Silly of Brodick to ask. What else?

14

The Fort Monckton class that assembles that morning is glum and distinctly under the weather. The trainees are reluctant to learn. They're all late, and trickle in—stumbling in some cases—to their desks. Olcott is within minutes asleep and snoring, head on his arms. Payne also has her head down and her eyes closed. There's a further hiatus as Gill and Lubnaig head for the water cooler so they can swallow painkillers for what they say are crushing headaches. Someone else asks if they've any tablets to spare. They do. Pills are distributed, shared. It comes as no surprise to Brodick: the vans had returned the students to the Fort at around 5am, and they were invited to write up their reports immediately before being permitted to totter off to their beds. Most had grudgingly complied.

All three instructors are present, standing at intervals around the lecture room. They too look exhausted and hung-over: *peely-wally* would be the Scottish expression. An unshaven Hale is up front and yawns before reading aloud from a file, frowning with concentration.

'There were a couple of standouts in last night's exercise, I have to say. One of you—no names, no pack drill—managed to speak not a single word while they were a guest of Special Branch. Not one in more than two hours of being badgered and bullied. Not threats of beatings or indefinite incarceration: not even kindness in the shape of offers of chocolate bars and coffee broke the silence. That's pretty good self-control. I don't know if the same method would have succeeded in the face of direct physical coercion; and we hope we never find out. Though I should warn everyone that we will run an escape and evasion exercise specifically to test your ability to stand up to pain and physical discomfort in your final month.'

'You mean torture.' The comment is Wood's.

'If you prefer to use the term, Harry, then fine. Torture it is.

'If I may continue, thank you, a second trainee—again it would be unfair to single people out by name—set something of a precedent. I haven't seen this before. I don't think anyone has, actually, least of all the participating Special Branch officers. The student in question drove his or her inquisitors up the wall by constantly apologising, an unceasing stream of "sorry" and "surely there must be some mistake". One of the inquisitors—a man with a reputation as a ruffian—came very close to physically attacking the trainee in question. To that individual I say, well done. Outstanding. If there was a prize for this exercise, you'd win it by a mile, though I doubt whether the two gentlemen from Special Branch would agree. Each said to me—independently of the other—that they wouldn't be volunteering their services on the next course. I don't know what the KGB or HVA interrogators would have made of it, but it was certainly original.

'Let's have a round of applause for our two colleagues.'

There are a few scattered and half-hearted claps. Those still awake turn and peer at one another in an effort to discover the culprit's identity. To hide his blushes, Brodick puts his head down on his arms and pretends to sleep.

Reggie has his hand up. When the instructors take no notice of him, he calls out. 'Hey guys, where's Superspy Sadler this morning? Feeling under the weather, is he? I guess even our resident Rambo needs his beauty sleep.'

This raises an uneasy laugh.

Hale clears his throat. 'I was coming to that. Mr Sadler will not be joining us. Not today. Not at any time. It has been decided that his undoubted skills will be more fruitfully employed elsewhere.'

'Did he decide to drop out, or was he pushed?'

'I understand it was a decision taken jointly by Mr Sadler and the directing staff.'

'He misses his teddy, does he?'

It takes a few more days for the details to filter through to the trainees but eventually they do so. *Captain* Sadler, former company commander of the Duke of Edinburgh's Regiment, a rather undistinguished yet snobbish regiment of the line, spent most of the cash he'd been given on himself with inevitable results. And his efforts to seek names, telephone numbers and addresses from other customers had fared badly, especially as he seemed to those he approached to be drunk and aggressive. Frantic, with only minutes to go before the publican called time, he found a telephone directory behind the bar, tore out several pages—to the publican's fury—and copied down five names, addresses and numbers at random and, once he was dropped off at the Fort, he made up the descriptions himself. That was after having taken a swing at one Special Branch officer and having tried to bite off the other's ear, actions that failed to impress. Unfortunately for Sadler, the instructors checked his fiction by calling the numbers on his list. He was given twenty minutes to pack.

*

Nothing stays secret forever: not about Sadler, and not about Brodick, for that matter. Stuff will out eventually and at suppertime it does. There's always going to be someone with a big mouth, with a desire to show off what they know.

'Is it true you worked as a head agent under journalistic cover?' The questioner is Paula Lubnaig, sitting opposite him as they pass around the salad. 'Like, my sister's a reporter for BBC Bristol and she says there's a special place in hell for journalists who work as spies, or spies who pretend to be journalists.'

Brodick looks across at her, fork halfway between plate and mouth. 'I'm sure your sister is right, Paula. Though I'm not convinced BBC Bristol, for all its undoubted skills, has a great deal of experience in these matters; but you might ask those nice folks at Tass, Novosti and Pravda for their opinion. Or Xinhua, for that matter. I'm sure they'd have something interesting to say on the subject of journalistic cover.'

He sees the colour rise in her neck and face.

'Don't fucking patronise me, Brodick. I'm not asking them. I'm asking you. We hold ourselves to a higher standard, surely.'

The fork continues its journey and skewers a slice of tomato.

'Do we, Paula? Are you sure about that?'

'Fuck's sake, of course!'

'Is that why you're here? As patriotic defender of British exceptionalism? Doing your bit for the Empire? Standing up for democracy, are we? Are you aware of the role of the Firm in the history of Reuters, for example?'

The tomato slice is eaten. Brodick chews, watching her. He knows he shouldn't have said that, but he couldn't resist it. She really is angry now.

'Is this a private fight or can anyone join in?' Anna Kingarth looks from one to the other, smiling brightly.

Paula snorts and sits back, folds her arms and looks away. 'Be my guest. Richard's being a total arsehole today.'

'Only today?' Anna leans forward and drops her voice. 'Richard, please. I want to ask you something. There is one small matter you might confirm for us, if you don't awfully mind.' She speaks sweetly, with a strange, drawn-out emphasis on the word "awfully" and Brodick braces himself. 'We're told that while working as a contract labourer you—what's the word—*removed* a KGB asset. An asset who was actually your agent. Is that true?'

'Removed?' The question comes from Kevin Andrews at the end of the table.

'Terminated then,' says Anna. 'Rubbed out. Erased. Liquidated. Bumped off. Terminated with prejudice. Whichever Hollywood euphemism you prefer.'

'*Killed*, is what you mean,' Kevin adds helpfully. 'Assassinated. I don't know if there's any truth to any of it and I don't particularly care, but what bothers me isn't whether it's true or not, but that someone who should know better has clearly been talking out of turn on a matter which would almost certainly be highly classified.'

'Well, Richard?' Anna, undeterred by this sensible intervention, is still leaning forward, eyes still on Brodick. 'Did you? And did you pull the trigger yourself or did you pay someone else to do it? We all saw how much you seem to enjoy the firearms training and unarmed combat.'

It's true, he does. Brodick puts his knife and fork together. He forces himself to do so slowly, with great care. He picks his napkin up off his lap and dabs his mouth with it. Then he takes a sip of his Marks & Spencer Chablis. He looks up, returns the curious looks he's getting from those at the table. He calms his beating heart, and with sheer willpower somehow prevents his ears from turning crimson. He smiles at his interlocutor.

'I don't know what you're talking about, Anna. Sorry.'

15

Brodick couldn't sleep at all during his first night at the Nicosia Hilton. The hotel was more than adequate, the service was efficient and friendly, his room was spacious with a view of the gardens and pool, and the enormous bed was comfortable. He inspected the room with care, but found no signs that it was wired for sound or imaging. That wasn't the reason for his restlessness. It was the silence. There was no gunfire to rock him to sleep; there was nothing at all, not even a hum of traffic. The normality of the place shook him; it took three days and nights before he was used to it. No one stared at him. No one seemed to be following him. He was ignored. Pedestrians sauntered, not ran from one corner to the next. Folk smiled, strangers said good morning. They walked their dogs, went shopping and sat out on the pavements drinking coffee. No airstrikes, no artillery bombardment. If he was under surveillance, then it was extraordinarily sophisticated.

This is how people live. This is how life used to be, remember? It's called normality.

He took a taxi to Proteras on the southwest coast. In contrast to nearby Paphos, it wasn't yet colonised by foreign retirees or overrun by summer hordes of beer bellied, red faced, tattooed Brits, Swedes and Germans competing for a few inches of sand yet to be covered in concrete. He swam, ate seafood, drank wine, napped. He learned all over again how to do nothing of any importance. He enjoyed his idleness and solitude. He would have enjoyed female company more, but he told himself he couldn't have everything and a female companion would only mean complications and there were enough of those already.

He had two more days to himself before his return to Beirut.

Back in Nicosia, he visited the offices of Levant Travel, shook hands with everyone, drank coffee with the local manager and was on his way again within thirty minutes, walking back to the Hilton for yet another *tref* with Fenner, who was waiting under a pergola by the pool, dressed in a Hawaiian shirt decorated with pineapples, drinking not coffee but what looked like an enormous cocktail with an orange swizzle stick and miniature umbrella protruding from the top of the tall glass. On a chair next to him lay a document case partly obscured by *The Herald Tribune.*

It wasn't yet 11am.

'I take it that your shirt is all about hiding in plain sight.'

'Something like that, old chap.' The remark clearly nettled Fenner, but to his credit he did his best not to show it. 'Feeling rested, Richard?'

'Pretty much, thanks.'

'Hilton okay?'

'It's great. Many thanks.'

'Protaras is pleasant, isn't it?'

'Perfect for a short break.'

'You deserved it. Will you try one of these?'

'Sure.'

'Bit early in the day, but what the hell. A negroni is great for this weather. Dry London gin, Campari, Vermouth rosso and God knows what else.' He signalled to a waiter.

What did London have to do with it? And wasn't all gin dry? Fenner was showing off. Brodick knew his case officer was an Old Stoic, having been to Stowe School, which included the show-off William Branson among its more visible alumni.

'I bring news.'

Brodick felt his holiday slipping away, to be replaced by the dark mantle of SIS spy.

'Fawzi has been organising your Beirut pad. You don't have to take it, mind you. It's rather grand, or so I'm told. Haven't seen it myself, but it was occupied by your predecessor when we still had a sizeable presence. Penthouse, sea and city views. Lift, cameras, steel outer door and shutters. Marble everywhere with some decent furniture. Fawzi says he's managed to negotiate a forty percent discount on the rent. Landlords don't like their properties left empty, especially during a civil war.'

'You'd make a great estate agent, Nick, but I might not like the colour scheme.'

'I just said if you don't like it, don't take it.'

'I'm kidding, Nick.'

By inclination and choice, Fenner was a desk officer, not a field operative. Messing about in dangerous places wasn't part of his job description. The notion that he would personally service a dead drop in pouring rain and under fire along some blind alley, a *zoqaq*, in downtown Beirut was absurd. Fenner employed other people to do that. Brodick couldn't even imagine Fenner in the field, but maybe that was because of the pineapples. Nothing wrong with pen-pushers, of course, nothing whatsoever, and nothing wrong with pineapples. Fenner's path was the shortest to the fifth floor; and hence the smart way to the top. Brodick hadn't thought of it that way until now. The most danger Fenner was ever likely to face was placing his ergonomic desk and chair too close to his office air-conditioner. Or being hit by a ball on the fairway of Dulwich & Turnham Green Golf Club.

'Who's the landlord?'

'Landlady. Lebanese living in France. In finance, whatever that might mean. Banking. A euphemism for money laundering, I'm sure. Not to worry: you won't see anything of her. All she wants is the rent. Have a look at the place, tell Fawzi what you think. He'll deal with the contracts and payments and will liaise with the owner. She won't even know your workname. It's in Raouche: the bit on the map that sticks out with the lighthouse, and as a matter of fact it's just a minute or two on foot from Buckley's old pad.'

'That's encouraging.'

'Isn't it just?' Fenner gave Brodick what he must have imagined was a reassuring smile. 'But you're smarter than Buckley. Or perhaps you have a stronger sense of self-preservation. Either way, you'll change your routes, your times, your vehicles, your drivers. If they want to grab you they'll have to use a small army. That doesn't mean they won't try, mind. Labour's cheap. I gather the going rate for a hit is fifty U.S. Right?'

'Something like that.' Brodick had no idea, but it sounded about right.

'By the way, our cousins tell us,' Fenner was presumably referring to the CIA, 'that Buckley is still alive, but in a very bad way. Lots of physical stuff as well as all manner of drugs and apparently there are unconfirmed reports he's been shipped to Iran.'

Brodick breathed in slowly. 'No hope of rescue?'

'None. They'll get everything they can get out of him. Whatever's of no interest to the Iranians themselves they'll package and sell to others—the Soviets, the Chinese—in return for intelligence Tehran wants. Stuff from Buckley is already circulating on the market, apparently, for sale to all interested parties.'

The negroni arrived. It was cold, sweet and wonderfully strong.

'You're full of good cheer today, Nick.'

Fenner smiled, showing his perfect deskman's teeth. He extracted an official-looking document from the case.

'Aren't I just? I've got something else: some DIA intel on your Chinese lady. Open-source material, basically. It's mostly about DRAGON's old man who's a powerful star in the Chinese intelligence cosmos, and becoming more powerful by the day. Family is still so important in China.'

'Which explains why you want her so badly.'

'Uh-huh. But the lady's also gaining quite a reputation in her own right.'

SECRET
Source: US Defense Intelligence Agency
Subject: PRC national CHEN MEILIN workname FANG (see also CHEN AIGUO)

1. CHEN MEILIN workname FANG believed to be eldest child of CHEN AIGUO, latter appointed head of ILD in 1982, aged 56. See also International Liaison Department of CCP Central Committee or *Zhongyang Lianluobo* abbr. *Zhongkianbu* (political intel, liaison with foreign political parties). CHEN AIGUO has also recently taken control of the security committees: the ministries of Justice, State Security (*Guoanbu*) and Public Security (*Gonganbu*) as well as National Minorities.

2. CHEN AIGUO's *guanxi* (relationships) said to be extensive: his primary protector reported to be CHEN YUN, inventor of economic intel, as well as BO YIBU, app. deputy premier 1978, also father-in-law JIA CHUNWANG, rumoured to be in line to take over the *Guoanbu.*

3. CHEN AIGUO's wife JIA LIHWA (subject's mother) is currently a producer on the BBC's Chinese language service in Hong Kong. Intel role not known.

4. CHEN AIGUO led missions to Tehran, Algiers, Pyongyang. Visits of a technical nature, including arms and technology transfers. Proposed setting up paramilitary police force, People's Armed Police (PAP) (*renmin wuzhuang jincha*). Reportedly inspired by Royal Ulster Constabulary (RUC) handling of public disorder in Northern Ireland.

5. CHEN AIGUO has been associated with arms transfers to Syria, Iran, Iraq, Libya, N. Korea. Regarded as hard-line advocate of active PRC support for Khmer Rouge, Afghan resistance to Soviet occupation, counterinsurgency in Tibet, special ops against DALAI LAMA in exile.

6. CHEN AIGUO, of Hakka origin, widely seen in PRC as bastion of authoritarian old order but supporter of economic reform. His

CPC reputation is said to be 'firm yet flexible'.

7. CHEN AIGUO is reported to have three children. CHEN MEILIN is thought to be the eldest. The second, also a daughter, attends medical school in Baltimore. The youngest, a son, currently a pupil at a private Hong Kong high school, lives with his mother LIHWA.

8. CHEN MEILIN (birthdate unknown but thought to be 1956) attended Tsinghua University and Berkeley UC as postgrad. At the latter she is believed to have acted as ILD agent targeting overseas mainland Chinese and Taiwanese and reportedly succeeded in persuading an unknown number to join CCP and/or return. Monitored by FBI during this period. She then worked as a correspondent in Hong Kong accredited to Xinhua. Intel activities suspected but unsubstantiated. (See UK/HKG/Local Intelligence Committee).

9. CHEN MEILIN has carried out short-term, apparently solo missions throughout the Middle East, and is thought to have been a *Guoanbu* cadre since 1983 while maintaining links with ILD and Xinhua as 'honourable correspondent'. Handler(s) not identified. Rumoured to hold PLA2 (military intelligence) rank of colonel.

Brodick read it through twice. Then a third time, slowly.

So this wasn't bluff, some kind of exercise. This was serious.

'I'll need to bait the hook, Nick. Something really juicy.'

'I suppose you will, yes.'

Brodick thought he'd have to argue about it.

There was a pause. A light breeze ruffled the pool and brought welcome relief to Brodick. He should buy sunglasses. Fenner wore those tear-drop aviator shades much in fashion in the seventies. Fenner must know how this worked. Brodick surely wouldn't have to explain it: or maybe he would.

'I'm small fry in comparison. There's no reason at all why she'd agree to meet me, let alone listen to what I have to say, unless DRAGON can be persuaded to regard me as someone who could prove to be a useful source. In other words, a potential recruit.'

The positive aspect to all of this was that Fenner had no idea Brodick and Fang had already met, that they had the outline of an agreement already, and that now they could meet openly. DRAGON was recruiting him. He was recruiting her. It was all a matter of perception. It would be an elaborate courtship. It would thrive on the universal currency of deceit. It wasn't love that made the world go round, but lies. Brodick's people would have to be persuaded Fang could be recruited, and her people had to believe that Brodick was a good prospect, or maybe they'd already decided or she wouldn't have bothered springing him from his cell in the mountains.

What the end result would be was another matter.

'Go on.'

'It has to be something of real interest, Nick, and genuine, do you see? But not an item that could in any way jeopardise our people.' That much was obvious. Brodick had Fenner's full attention; he had removed his shades and was frowning at Brodick. Obviously, Brodick *was* going to have to explain it although he was sure Fenner was well ahead of him on this.

'Such as?'

'Let's take this month's U.S.-Israeli naval war games in the east Med. Maybe an MoD assessment which we could tweak and reclassify secret would be a tempting morsel. Perhaps, just for variety, add the Security Service manual "Security Advice for Visitors to China".'

'They probably have that. The latter. There must be dozens of copies floating around the Fragrant Harbour. Even I've read it and I have no interest whatsoever in China.'

'Doesn't matter, though, does it? The aim is to show willing. The Chinese play a long game. At the start it's all culture and expensive seats at the opera, proclamations of undying friendship, bunches of flowers, noodles at posh eateries and all that crap.'

Fenner tipped up his glass to seek out the last drops. The toy umbrella fell to the ground, but Fenner made no effort to retrieve it. He took something out of his briefcase: a Minox LX camera that fitted easily in the palm of one hand.

'She might find this useful once you've recruited her.' Fenner also had film and he handed over both. 'If she prefers a 35 mm reflex, there's a Minolta with automatic focusing in your office safe.'

Brodick would not be distracted. 'Maybe we could throw in that DIA report you just showed me. Sure she'd be tickled pink to read about herself in the imperialist enemy's files. Flatter the Communist ego. DRAGON might send it to her dad. Maybe we have something too on the listening devices being developed in Vladivostok by the Soviet Institute of Oceanography. Sonar. The Chinese have been trying to penetrate them for years, so I'm told. They're well behind on Soviet expertise and very keen to build up their anti-submarine warfare technology.'

Fenner put his shades back on and stared off into the distance at nothing in particular, though he was probably studying other tables under the pergola as well as the three swimmers in the pool. The place was surprisingly quiet, which was presumably why Fenner had chosen it for their meeting. Brodick was counting on Fenner thinking he could take credit for these ideas. If successful, he'd reckon on this making his career. Let him. Brodick needed Fenner on his side: even though he didn't trust him.

'An imaginative selection, Richard, and I take your point, but we don't want to be *too* generous at the outset, do we?'

'It's low-grade, Nick. Chickenfeed, let's face it, but promising enough to get her masters interested. We don't know how long she's going to be in Beirut. Or why. With a foot in *Xinhua*, PLA2 and *Guoanbu*, the lady's going places and we need to get her attention with something more than the merely titivating. It has to be solid, and valuable.'

PLA2 was military intelligence, but of course Fenner already knew that.

'Let's see what we can come upon with. It has to be material you could easily lay your hands on. It'll also have to be authorised by Century House and that means a stack of bureaucrats ticking lots of boxes. We're talking Security Branch. The Area Controllers, Middle East and Far East as well, because this is going to be a joint affair. That's a long way up the ladder. Don't expect quick decisions, Richard. We're talking about doubling you, in effect. It's a tricky business.'

Isn't it just?

'To be absolutely sure, maybe we could offer one more titbit into her welcoming party bag. Something on the dissidents in Hong Kong, courtesy of those lovely people on the Local Intelligence Committee in Kowloon.'

'Jesus, Richard, you really do have ice in your veins.'

'I take that as a professional compliment.'

'You know what they do to dissidents they manage to get hold of?'

'You're going to tell me anyway.' Brodick looked away, squinting in the brightness.

'They kill the young ones with lethal injections and cut them up for human transplants. They've a special treatment for the old and infirm officially known as "assisting production": they're forced to dig their own graves and then they're buried alive in them. The Communist Chinese killed three times as many Chinese as the Japanese ever did.'

But that was history and Brodick was irritated by Fenner's moralising. All that might very well be true, or it might not. Her Majesty's Government didn't seem to shrink from doing business with Beijing's corporate giants, after all. Several Tory cabinet ministers had stakes in Chinese companies, and Chinese investment in the UK was growing rapidly. Nobody seemed to object to all the cheap Chinese-made goods on the high streets of English cities. British politicians were always willing to cosy up to tyrants if there was cash involved. The list was long: the white South Africans, the Saudis, Chile's General Pinochet, the

Argentine military junta.

'Be that as it may, Nick. I'm not going back to Beirut empty-handed. If I'm going to play this game for you then I want to do it right, and that means I need some trump cards so I stand a decent chance of winning. I may need your approval to go to London so I can credibly beg, borrow or steal whatever it is we decide to offer.'

We. Not I. You're in this TCI Section, too, Nicholas Fenner.

Fenner said nothing. He seemed pensive, no doubt thinking about how he could benefit: and what would happen to his career if it all turned FUBAR. Deskmen didn't like to end up as midwives of failed operations. MacGregor certainly wouldn't tolerate failure. Fenner tapped the DIA report on the table so he could fit it neatly into his document case.

He came to an executive decision, the fruit no doubt of many years of private education and Whitehall experience. 'I think we could both do with another couple of negronis.'

16

The officers' training course devotes three months to the primary adversary, the *Komitet Gosudarstvennoi Bezopastnosti* or KGB and half that time to Soviet military intelligence, *Glavnoye Razvedyvatel'noye* Upravlenije or GRU: although in some respects the latter, though smaller, is regarded as the more formidable.

The lectures, sometimes involving guest speakers, begin with the history, from Lenin's Cheka to Stalin's OGPU. Their course reading list includes John Barron's *KGB: The Secret Work of Soviet Secret Agents,* Varlam Shalamov's *Kolyma Tales* and Aleksandr Solzhenitsyn's *Gulag Archipelago.* Brodick especially enjoys a series of talks by a retired Security Service officer on The Great Illegals, their long training and painstaking preparation of their bogus identities. Arnold Deutsch, cosmopolitan Austrian Jew and chief recruiter of Cambridge University students, is the outstanding example of an effective agent runner, along with Richard Sorge, who posed as a pro-Nazi journalist in Japan.

Brodick feels inspired: though he recognises that this is possibly *not* the object of the proceedings.

From an eminent Trinity College historian of intelligence, the trainees learn that successful codebreaking all too often requires agents' theft of diplomatic ciphers and highly classified code books rather than mathematical genius: a phenomenon mastered by the Tsarist *Ochrana* and on which Stalin's foreign policy was largely based and known as a "pinch" in SIS terminology. To their dismay, the course discovers how the constant flow of secret and top secret Foreign Office documents gave Stalin the edge at both Tehran and

Yalta conferences. The Soviet dictator knew more about Britain's nuclear weapons program than Prime Minister Clement Attlee's own cabinet. The trainees also pore over case studies of British "walks-ins" who supplied ciphers to the Soviets, motivated more by a thirst for hard cash than ideological rectitude.

In between lectures and discussions, the trainees are sent outside for fresh air. They practise tradecraft and agent-handling skills, pursuing one another on foot through the potholed streets of Portsmouth with varying degrees of success—Kingarth's rainbow socks are a notable standout—using department stores and telephone boxes to test their ability to track and observe their targets or identify their watchers, the latter role usually played by their instructors suitably disguised with false moustaches and peculiar hats.

They practice Soviet-style tradecraft: in the enemy's shoes, working in pairs, with one watching the other's back, often from a static position, a first floor shop window, a staircase or rooftop, a stationery car, a park bench.

Brodick learns something new, something he didn't practice in his Afghanistan incarnation. It's taken out of the CIA's playbook. Thirty seconds is all it takes to service a dead letter drop. Thirty seconds can be found in hostile territory, right under an adversary's nose, or gaze, even when followed by two or more cars as well as a team of watchers on foot.

Sometimes the Soviets will have two radio cars in front and two or three more behind. It's a matter of slowing down and then speeding up, of using the angles of street corners to evade watchers. It might involve turning two corners in rapid succession to drop a package in a doorway, unseen by watchers fore and aft. Speed, cunning, pluck: they all count in a "hard target" country. Brodick is amazed by what can be achieved with good planning, reconnaissance, and a bold, can-do approach. As for the all-important brush pass, handing over or receiving messages on the move can also be done while under close surveillance on enemy territory. It takes a little magic and plenty of practice, such as walking into a department store and shaking an umbrella, opening and closing it with the right hand to distract attention, while with the left dropping the item into question from a coat sleeve into a shopping bag held by someone approaching from the opposite direction: even while being observed by no fewer than five watchers. Or taking off a jacket or scarf, and again making something of a drama of shaking off the rain.

Deception works: again and again they prove it to one another. Brodick enjoys a sense of gleeful satisfaction at pulling off these stunts.

They learn that wheels offer a huge advantage because a car provides not only control—in the sense of speed and direction, such as a three-point turn—but a crucial 360-degree vision. An agent on foot is far more limited—and vulnerable. They practice the "car toss": exchanging material between two cars on the move, and they make up their own dummy passengers known as a Jack-In-The-Box, or JIB. The students are taught that route surveillance detection can take four hours or more, sometimes an entire day, and that's aside from the detailed planning and prior reconnaissance that must go into it. Spending ten hours on the move outside in the streets—in deep cold or extreme heat—is the norm, along with hunger and thirst, while every SIS station should ideally have a wall map that marks suitable routes, dangerous chokepoints and sensitive locations to be avoided such as permanent surveillance posts or security service headquarters and training centres, along with useful locations for dead drops.

The map is built up through trial and error over a considerable period of time with everyone contributing, including the partners of a succession SIS officers.

In a hostile environment such as Moscow, once a case officer's movements have been tagged by the KGB, the latter will send in several surveillance teams into the chase and as many as ten surveillance vehicles linked by radio. They have no shortage of resources and they'll throw everything they have at a target that interests them. And in contrast to the Centre's tradecraft, the

SIS officer must continue his mission even if he's under intense scrutiny.

Brodick learns about the U.S. use of disguises, of the employment of deep cover case officers, and he discovers how rare successful recruitment is. It's extraordinarily difficult to do. Most of the Agency's assets are walk-ins, people who have approached the Agency for one reason or another.

In bad weather—and there is no lack of it—Brodick and his colleagues polish their skills at photographing documents with ingenious cameras. In the indoor small arms range they practise with AK-47s, Makarovs and Tokarevs. And yes, it's true Brodick does find this therapeutic and even enjoys the stripping and cleaning of the weapons, so much so he volunteers to clean and reassemble those of his colleagues. And, after lunch, they perfect the techniques required to kill one another on the unarmed combat mats.

At weekends there are thirty-mile endurance hikes on Dartmoor and shorter, twelve-mile "social walks" on the South Downs.

Then, having dried out and changed, it's back to their desks with blistered feet and sore muscles and more discussions, this time on what the Centre—the KGB's First Chief Directorate—calls "The Five": Anthony Blunt, Guy Burgess, John Cairncross, Donald Maclean and Kim Philby. Briefings follow on Soviet Science and Technology intelligence (S&T) collection, both the KGB and GRU having had considerable success in stealing technology from the United States in World War Two, the most notable being penetration of the MANHATTAN nuclear project by scientists such as Britain's very own Klaus Fuchs.

The entire class suffers temporary depression when they learn—courtesy of an ancient ex-CIA lecturer—how the U.S. Communist Party actively helped the Centre penetrate every significant branch of the Roosevelt administration.

They cheer loudly, though, when they learn of Operation VENONA, the breakthrough in cryptography that revealed Soviet penetration of the OSS, forerunner of the CIA.

There's a sense of smug satisfaction when it's revealed that Philby was never trusted by his Soviet masters, not even when he defected. The Centre still suspected that the British spies they'd recruited were all part of some huge anti-Soviet conspiracy on the part of the wily imperialists. If only!

The class negotiates its way through a jungle of sinister acronyms: the Czech STB, the East German HVA and Stasi, the Hungarian AVH, the Polish SB, the Cuban DGI, the Bulgarian DS and Romanian DGSP.

They examine "friendly" agencies: West Germany's formidable BfV and BND, the French DGSE, the Portuguese DGS and PID. They don't forget the Yugoslav OZNA, either. Or Japan's NAICHO and South Africa's unlovely BOSS.

They tour Britain's GCHQ in Cheltenham and have a day out visiting the NSA's secret SIGINT station at Menwith Hill in Yorkshire with an agreeable pub lunch on the way back.

Through it all, Brodick keeps his own counsel. He watches and listens and he wonders how much he's going to remember. Not for a moment does he feel himself to be anything other than the odd-man-out, the outsider. He's used to it and it comes naturally to him.

One cold, rainy Wednesday afternoon, as the mud-spattered trainees gather for tea and chocolate cake after stumbling through the mire of the coastal path, Cynthia Payne has a question.

'What about the Chinese? Does anyone know *anything* about them?'

Indeed. No-one seems to know or care enough to answer, but one of the instructors mutters something all but inaudible about squeezing in a day or two 'later on' to address the issue.

17

'You see? Carrara marble. Beautiful, no? And down there, look, you see? Yes? You have the French and Swiss embassies—and on the other side of the penthouse, Mr Richard, the western side, *c'est incroyable*—an uninterrupted view of the Mediterranean. No one can see you on the 7th floor. Totally private, *mon ami.* What is the saying? An Englishman's home is a castle? This one is a beautiful castle in the sky.'

Fawzi flashed Brodick a dazzling smile.

They'd only just met that Monday morning. Brodick was a little taken aback by the breezy familiarity and he turned away to watch the guards patrolling the walls of the French and Swiss embassies below, bareheaded men in combat vests, carrying bullpup automatic weapons, spare magazines bulging in their vest pockets. On this seventh floor balcony—the smaller of the two—looking out in the direction of the city to the east, he almost tripped over a cluster of dead plants in terracotta and plastic tubs, no doubt the once carefully tended pride of the previous occupant and his wife before they were withdrawn at the outset of the Israeli invasion two years earlier. He didn't feel at all comfortable out here; standing upright he could be seen—or shot—from other windows, other balconies of tall buildings, mostly offices. It wasn't at all private. No, Brodick would make an excellent target for a bored sniper. He retreated indoors.

In the distance, somewhere in the foothills of Mount Lebanon, a roll of thunder. But wait a moment, it couldn't be. The sky was cloudless. It wasn't thunder but artillery. The Syrians were providing fire support to the PSP, Amal, the Lebanese Communist Party and the Syrian National Socialist Party in combined assaults on Lebanese Army positions on the ridges at the village of Souk al-Gharb southeast of the capital.

If successful, the attacks would effectively cut the capital off from the southern suburbs—and the airport—and strengthen the Syrian grip on Beirut.

Resplendent in double-breasted navy and chalk pinstripe, silver grey tie and matching pocket handkerchief, Fawzi led the way across the immense sitting room to the opposite, western side of the penthouse flat. It was wonderful in its way, of course it was, and Brodick had to accept he now belonged to a temporarily privileged—albeit greatly diminished—expatriate community with an unearned lifestyle far beyond its individual members' means or station in life. No doubt it had once been the same for British colonial officials lording it over the Empire's hapless millions, only to return at the end of their careers to a much reduced status, tending their roses in seedy, damp suburbia. This place was as big as an aircraft carrier's flight deck. Well, almost. Maybe a tennis court. The dining table could easily seat twenty. He stopped to admire an immense, inlaid Damascene chest of drawers in the hallway. On top of it stood a huge vase. Ming, if he wasn't mistaken.

And he had all this to himself.

If it wasn't for the war, and the fact that his accommodation costs were covered by Century House via Levant Travel, Brodick would probably have struggled to pay the rent for the maid's room out of his own pocket. It was, he reflected, the sort of property normally found advertised in the weekend *Financial Times* property supplement.

He helped Fawzi slide back the big glass doors—the entire wall of the western side of the penthouse was glass, double-glazed—and they stood out on the balcony that ran the length of the property. The view was sea and nothing but sea, a vast canvas of tranquil blue. He had to bend forward over the balustrade and look straight down to see the cliffs fall away to the coastal road and below it, the rocky seashore. This balcony wasn't overlooked at all. It was true: no one could see him. There were chairs and a table out there. All that was lacking was the Bollinger in the ice bucket.

Brodick toured the main bedroom with super king-size bed, its tiled floors and walls and the matching en-suite bathroom, not unlike a mausoleum without windows. It was the "safe" room, Fawzi explained. Best place to be when under attack. Brodick noted that the television and CD player were all set up; the television room's four-seat sofa—navy with red piping—was immaculate, and so were the Persian and Anatolian rugs.

Artillery boomed again in the hills.

As he strolled from room to room and back again, one part of Brodick's mind was feeding his appetite for encouragement and reassurance; another part anxiously added up the untruths he'd been piling up, like an accountant counting and recounting his debts on a pocket calculator. The lie of omission about his having already met Fang, the lie of pretending not to recognise DRAGON in the photographs by the pool, the lie of dissembling over who she was and what she represented, the lie about agreeing a plan to recruit her when in fact he'd already agreed to her deal. He'd already been bought and turned. Hadn't he? He knew he wasn't lying simply to Nick Fenner, his case officer, for if that had been the case none of it would have bothered him. No, Fenner was just a rather unimaginative extension of MacGregor, like an arm or a leg, the latter being the one man whose approval Brodick sought, rather as he had avidly sought his father's approval and had never been certain of getting it. By lying to Fenner, he had lied to MacGregor and by extension he had lied to Century House.

To the "Firm". To the Family.

Betrayal was all too easy; it seemed to be a natural part of his armour.

One lie begets another. Lies multiply effortlessly. So do the risks.

Once he would have cared. Now the only issue he cared about

was getting away with it, using his deception to climb the greasy pole to a CBE, maybe a KCMG and finally a civil service index-linked pension supplemented by a director's seven-figure corporate salary in the private security sector. Why not?

Fawzi showed him the closed circuit television cameras and the monitor, as well as the immense steel entrance that resembled a door protecting a bank vault.

Brodick retreated into that part of his mind that offered him the comforting notion that it wasn't all his fault, after all. Fenner had wanted to believe the lies, never questioned the inconsistencies. So did MacGregor. They believed him because they wanted to, obviously. It was their fault because they'd put their trust in him. Brodick had only told them what they wanted to believe and left out the awkward stuff they wouldn't have wanted to know. They were as guilty as he was: worse, really, drawing the lies out him because they so dearly wanted it all to be true. They had set him up to fulfil their wishes. All Brodick had done was obediently grant them their wayward desires, unconscious though they might have been.

He told himself he wasn't to blame, not really.

Brodick had offered them the reality they wanted and there was absolutely nothing wrong with that, surely. It was a reassuring thought even if it was untrue. What was true and untrue, after all? We always tend to believe what pleases us, he told himself, even when the evidence indicates otherwise. Imagination always trumps logic.

The penthouse was indeed very grand.

Would Fenner send in a team of sweepers before Brodick took up residence? Presumably they swept the embassy regularly, or at least the chancery, and they'd presumably check this place out too. He would ask.

'It's great, Fawzi, thank you so much. I'll take it.'

Fawzi beamed, pressed his palms together and executed a small bow. 'I'll make the arrangements, Mr Richard.'

*

The restaurant to one side of the old Crusader harbour at Byblos (or Jbeil) was built at a time when tourists still flocked to Lebanon in the summer. There weren't any now—not sane ones anyway—and the place was almost empty. It was built on a concrete platform that jutted out over the rocks, the sea on either side within arm's reach, rustling and burbling alongside the tables as the tide came in or went out. The heat of the day was offset by a pleasant breeze and a cheerful yellow and white striped awning shielded the diners from the sun. Brodick and Fang were at the far end for privacy's sake. Only one other table was occupied: by a family of seven Lebanese, including grandparents and children, talking and laughing and bouncing about in their chairs.

'Shall I order?'

Fang put her menu down. 'Sure. I recommend the *Sultan Ibrahim*.'

'You've been here before.'

'I have.'

She wore a plain red cotton dress with buttons down the front and short sleeves, no jewellery that he could see and what seemed to Brodick to be minimal makeup aside from mascara. From the intelligence viewpoint, she seemed too striking, altogether too memorable for her role, but Brodick personally thought she was outstanding, so much so she seemed unapproachable.

'What would you like to drink?'

'Dry white.'

Brodick ordered the bream for them both, along with *tahini* sauce and a bottle of *Kefraya* blanc de blanc.

'Do you have any idea why the fish are called *Sultan Ibrahim*?'

'It's a long story, Richard. A myth. Something about a well-travelled Afghan sultan who throws a needle into the sea and the fish leap into his lap. But never mind all that, let's get down to work. Did you mention me to your people?'

'No. But they mentioned you, Fang.'

She didn't react but waited. She sat very still, watching him.

'I was shown a Defence Intelligence Agency report on you, your mum and dad and your siblings. It identified you as Chen Meilin, an officer in the *Guoanbu* with the PLA2 rank of colonel. A Berkeley postgrad. Your father controls a number of very powerful government committees.'

The wine arrived, Fang tasted it, nodded and their glasses were filled, the bottle was then propped up in the ice. Brodick noted that she liked to be the one in charge and he told himself there was nothing wrong with that. After all, he was her junior. This was followed by a serving plate with an immense heap of the small fish, along with bowls of *tahini* and a big Lebanese salad that they were expected to share and serve themselves.

'Can you confirm it: your family details?'

'Do you want me to?'

'Of course I do.'

'Why did they show you the DIA profile?'

'Because they wanted to know if I'd seen you or met you in Beirut, and when I said I hadn't, I was told to try to seek you out and make contact. They had photographs, too. It's something of a priority. They know you use the workname Fang. They know you're here. You're apparently a high-flier and the Middle East is your oyster.'

She didn't seem in the least put out by the revelation that Century House had her in its sights. Had she already known?

'We're both high-fliers, Richard. Don't forget.'

'I think you're far more senior and fly at a somewhat higher altitude. And you have a lot more clout than I'll ever have. The Arabs call it *wasda* as if you didn't know. In Russian it's *blat*.'

They lifted their glasses in a silent toast to each other.

'Why, Richard? To what end? Why do they want you to make contact?'

'Century House wants me to find out what you're up to and to make a play for you. They want to know if you're vulnerable at some level. To recruit you.'

'And you said?'

'That I'd not seen you or met you but that I would try to locate you and that I thought I was rather junior to be fishing for someone so much more senior and obviously well-connected. Why on earth would you want to change sides?'

Fang watched him and said nothing in response.

Brodick started on the fish, using his fingers, dipping them into the *tahini* and popping them whole into his mouth.

'Delicious, aren't they?' Fang used a fork. Brodick couldn't answer because his mouth was full.

'What are your people offering?'

'Are you interested?'

'Are *you*, Richard?'

'My people want me to turn you and run you in place.'

'As would we. Of course.'

Brodick refilled their glasses. The little fish were disappearing rapidly.

'If we're going to meet each other and help each other on a regular basis, we have to follow some ground rules, or it won't work because it will be too dangerous for both of us.'

'What do you suggest? I do wish you'd call me Drew.'

'Okay. Listen. Drew. You will need to memorise the following. First, you can tell your handler that the DIA has confused matters. Their report is flawed. The Americans have got it all mixed up. It's a case of mistaken identity. You look surprised: these things happen. Of course they do. The workname Fang—a common name, as you know—does not refer to Chen Meilin. It refers to Zhang Pusheng. Got that? Yeah? Good. Now Zhang Pusheng is the eldest daughter of a senior intelligence official, Zhang Tsen Tsiang. Zhang Tsen Tsiang—my father—is sixty-two years old and is the head of the United Front Workers Department or UFWD, which, as again you know, is responsible for persuading Chinese and Taiwanese to join—or rejoin—the Party and return to the homeland. It's one of several intelligence organisations with a very specific role in targeting overseas Chinese. Am I going too quickly? You want me to repeat the names? Yes?'

'I'm keeping up. Just. Go on.'

The *Sultan Ibrahim* were almost all gone. Brodick left a modest pile for Fang to eat once she finished speaking.

'Zhang Pusheng's grandfather, Zhang Changren—my grandfather in other words—was a veteran of the Long March before his death a few years ago. He suffered greatly during the Cultural Revolution. Pusheng's elder brother, Zhang Chunquiao, is a senior *Guoanbu* officer, formerly of the *Gonganbu*, the security service. Many *Gonganbu* cadres have moved to the *Guoanbu* as part of the latter's recent reorganisation.

'Confused, Richard? Too many names? I can repeat it if helps.'

'No. I'm coping, but I might write all this down and check it with you.'

These layers of deception ran deep. Why was Fang so keen *not* to be Chen Meilin?

'Well, here's the last name for you to remember. Fan Jin is the mother of Zhang Pusheng. My mum, yes? She's an artist, a painter. She travels all over the world, from Perth to Penang. And yes, she too has intelligence links. Of course. It runs in the family. She works as cultural adviser at the International Studies Research Centre or *Zhongguo Guoji Wenti Yanjiu Zhongxin*. It's quite new so if you haven't heard of it, I'm not surprised. It was set up by Deng Xiaoping expressly to provide detailed analysis of foreign developments for the Party leadership as he opens China to foreign investment and technology. Its work is also very secret.'

'Am I supposed to believe this is your real identity?'

'You are, yes. Because it is.'

If so, why did she tell him?

Lies within lies, like one of those painted Russian dolls.

Fang sipped her wine and looked at the bream. 'Are those for me?'

'I was saving them for you because you were busy talking.'

'You are too kind.'

Brodick raised his hand and a waiter approached. Brodick asked for another bottle of the blanc de blanc. They might as well enjoy themselves on such a beautiful day.

'So. Let me understand this. You are not Chen Meilin but Zhang Pusheng, at least for the purposes of our association.' Not that Brodick believed it.

Fang didn't answer for a while; she was too busy eating.

The fish were gone, and she laid her fork aside. 'When you decide to inform your employers that you have located me and made contact, yes, that is so. That's who I am. They will do their homework and they will discover all these people—this Zhang family—do indeed exist and they do play the roles I've described. Oh, I should add that Zhang Pusheng gained her Master's from MIT in molecular engineering.'

'She's impressive, this lady.'

'Thank you so much. You know that I'm from Shanghai originally?'

'No. Why?'

'Shanghai men are trained to buy and cook food, do the housework and look after the kids. We women control the money.' She paused to watch his expression. 'The guys in my city have a slogan: *gen dang zou, ting taitai de hua*. It means "Walk with the Party, obey the wife."'

'Is that a message, Fang?'

She grinned at him. 'What do you think?'

'So you've developed this legend of Zhang Pusheng from Shanghai to divert attention away from you, to protect yourself and your family. It must have taken quite some preparation.'

The comment prompted a broad smile. 'Richard, you're being egotistical. You shouldn't imagine that you're so special that you are the only new "friend" I'm interested in. You're not unique and that sense of individualism of yours is such a common Western failing. I cast my net wide and, believe me, there are many deep sea fish to be swept up into my net. Some are queueing up to jump right in. Just like you.' She grinned at him. She seemed in a relaxed, cheerful mood.

'So that's your job. Recruiter. Have you mentioned me to your bosses back in Beijing as one of your new so-called friends you're trying to bring on board?'

'No.'

'Why not?

'I wanted to keep this off the books and see where it leads, but now I think the time has come for us both to make our initial contact reports under the terms we've discussed. Nothing more than the fact that we have made contact, and that the other party is showing some interest. It's to cover ourselves: if we're seen being in contact without reporting back to our respective employers, we'd be storing up a great deal of trouble which we'd be hard put to explain away. We can't assume our respective organisations have not been penetrated or compromised in some way. It's a matter of our survival. Agreed?'

It made sense.

'Agreed.'

'So. I made contact with you and you showed some interest in my offer, and I will recommend further contact.'

Was she lying?

'Well, if that's the case, Fang, then I will say in my contact report that I have located you and managed to have a brief conversation during which you exhibited curiosity and interest; and that this, in my view, is worth following up.'

'Excellent, Richard. I mean Drew. And we must tell each other immediately if the situation changes on either side. If you think there's an opportunity to do so, don't hesitate to correct their misleading version of my identity and furnish them with the details I've just given you.'

'No problem. But please stop calling me Richard, at least in public.'

They shook hands on it. Fang's grasp was firm and cool. For Brodick, it was just an opportunity to touch her, hold Fang's hand, if only for an instant.

'Where were you trained, Fang? Was it by any chance Jiangnan

Social University in Suzhou, Jiangsu?'

She smiled. 'How did you know? Or are you guessing?'

He waited. She knew he knew that was where many intelligence people were trained.

'I have something for you, Richard. Sorry, Drew. My little gift to mark the start of a long and mutually rewarding friendship'.

'How thoughtful of you. What is it?'

'I think you will like it. So will your case officer.'

They drank wine in companionable silence and listened to the sea. The sound of artillery firing in the hills south of Beirut was so far off it sounded like a distant summer thunderstorm that might well never reach them.

*

There was plenty of paper, by the look of it official forms in Arabic, both typed and hand-written, much of it carrying official stamps with the national symbol of the Lebanese cedar. As an uncomprehending Brodick turned the pages of the file, Fang identified them one by one.

'First. That's the bill of lading and copies of the ship's papers. The Star of Basra, Panamanian-flagged, displacement around 11,000 tons. The owner is a Maltese shell company which is, in turn, owned by the firm Andreas Vale, registered in Lichtenstein.'

Next:

'Port clearance certificate.'

'And this?'

'Customs inspection and clearance.'

'But the cargo hasn't even arrived yet.'

'It arrives next week, on Monday or Tuesday. With cash paid up front, and a cut for everyone involved, that's not a problem. They like the paperwork to be ready, and it is as you can see for yourself.'

'And this one?'

'Cargo inspection. Eight containers of agricultural machinery checked and confirmed.'

'It's not tractors; so what is it?'

'What does the Silkworm mean to you?'

'Well it obviously doesn't mean those smelly little creatures from China that spin silk and eat mulberry leaves. SILKWORM is the NATO designation for a type of Chinese anti-shipping missile. There are several variants.'

The colour of the sea and sky was changing, darkening and becoming more intense in the late afternoon as the sun began its descent. A stiff onshore breeze ruffled the surface of the Mediterranean. The overhead canopy started to shake and billow. It was cooler now. Restaurant staff were resetting the tables, casting the last two diners long looks, wishing they'd leave so they could change the tablecloth on their table and put out clean cutlery. Brodick had won the toss to pay the bill. He would get the receipt, too, which he would claim on expenses.

They shared the tip.

'And the scientist in charge of Silkworm's development was Tsien Hsue-shen. A brilliant, U.S. educated scientist, I'm told.'

Fang clapped silently, smiling.

'Not at all bad for a *ying gui*—British devil—and a novice, Richard, though your pronunciation needs further work. We call it SEA EAGLE by the way.'

'Thank you so much. Please call me Drew, not Richard.'

Fang seemed to enjoy teasing him.

'We've supplied variants of these anti-shipping missiles to both sides in the Iran-Iraq war.'

'Why?'

'We like to stay on good terms with everyone. We're Chinese. We like to have not one iron in every fire but two. Call it insurance. In any case, why don't you ask your friends the Israelis why they are servicing Iranian air force planes, why Washington provides Baghdad with the latest intelligence and why you British are happily supplying dual-use equipment to the Iraqis which they can use to make poison gas and nerve agents. Nothing whatsoever to do with oil reserves, of course.'

Touché.

Two irons in every fire or two *opposing* irons in every fire?

'I'm grateful for all this, Fang. Truly. But I need a source. I can't name you for reasons we've already discussed and agreed. So where did I get this little treasure trove of yours?'

Brodick was lying. He had every intention of naming Fang. He had every intention of not only naming her but taking the credit for recruiting a senior *Guoanbu* officer with influential family ties. But he wasn't about to tell Fang that, and he was going to feed it to Fenner and the rest of the TCI Section in UK Station bit by bit, by stealth, not all at once.

Fang was probably planning on doing something very similar.

'That's taken care of. I've got a name for you. He is the source. My source. That doesn't mean you should barge in and try to recruit him. I need to deflect the attention away from me, but that doesn't entitle you to muscle in on this contact. He's mine, okay?'

Brodick threw up his hands, a gesture of surrender. 'If you say so.'

'His name is Mouftaka. Sabri Mouftaka. He's deputy director of the Lebanese ports authority. Mouftaka is in his forties, well educated, a logistics specialist, but he needs hard currency to get his family out of the country. He has a wife and three kids. I think that's all you need to know if questioned. Oh, and this little bundle cost me just eight hundred Deutschmarks plus six hundred U.S. dollars. Cheap, wouldn't you say? You will reimburse me, of course.'

Well, she'd given away a source. That was something at least.

'And what's this?'

Brodick had to establish that she was his agent, not the other way around. It was a matter of self-preservation. *Sorry, Fang, but maybe you're lying to me, too. In fact, I have to assume that you are.*

'That's the outgoing cargo, down as construction materials, mostly cement. Payment, if you like. More of a reciprocal gesture, I guess. Same vessel, the Star of Basra.'

'What is it really?'

'You remember that Lebanon's National Museum was looted in the first years of the war? No? Well, there are a couple of Phalangist warehouses on the east side still stacked to the roof with stolen museum artefacts. Etruscan, Phoenician, Greek, you name it. Stuff from right here, where we are today. Including these: seventeen marble Roman torsos dated between CE100 and CE300. Plus half a dozen sarcophagi dated around 200 BCE along with some frescos and a ton of Phoenician and Greek amphoras.'

'That's the payment for the Silkworm?'

'I said it's a reciprocal gesture. Word is the Iraqis already have a buyer: a private American museum on the West Coast. Baghdad needs hard currency. But that's capitalist culture for you: no moral scruples at all.' Chen Meilin, aka Zhang Pusheng, aka Fang gave Brodick a wide smile and broke into a laugh.

*

They stood next to each other, looking out to sea. For how many generations had others done the same: colonists, traders, soldiers, sailors, spies, conquerors? To the west, at their feet, was a small, perfectly formed Roman amphitheatre, over to the right and further downhill the Crusader port buttressed by slabs of stone that had once formed part of a Norman fort. Behind them, further up the hill, squatted a Norman church, still in use by Greek Orthodox Lebanese. There was plenty of statuary around them on the promontory itself, much of it cracked or broken and some buried and only accessible by treading carefully down into subterranean caverns. Figures on horseback, armed with spears and bows: Etruscan, for the most part, or so Brodick believed, and certainly too big and too heavy for the criminals to carry away. Everything else had gone, and the so-called antique shops of Jounieh and Beirut exhibited scores of what the shopkeepers claimed were genuine artefacts. Small figurines and coins for the most part. Not that Brodick would know the genuine from the fake.

'Now tell me what you want.'

The breeze had dropped. Brodick could smell Fang; and yes, as her workname suggested, she was definitely fragrant. He resisted an impulse to take her hand in his and squeeze it. He told himself not to be so bloody stupid. A failure to control himself could wreck everything.

'I want you to find someone for me, Drew, and introduce him to me.'

She turned to Brodick.

'Please understand. It's what I need to persuade my people that you are indeed my agent, and that I have successfully recruited and turned a young, up-and-coming SIS officer at the very heart of imperialist circles. I'll only use it once we reach that stage in our relationship.'

He wasn't sure he believed her or anything she said.

'So who is it?'

'His name is Li Zuanfei. He's a Canadian national—or at least he travels on a genuine Canadian passport and has a registered home address in Toronto. He majored in mathematics at Shanghai University at the age of sixteen and he had his Harvard PhD by his twenty-second birthday. He's a brilliant polymath. He's best known by the public for his book on human consciousness, "*The Neuroscience of Being*", and he's due in Beirut any time if he's not already here. He's supposed to attend a small and closed academic conference at which he'll give the inaugural lecture—at the American University of Beirut—in the western sector.'

'So? China's not short of any number of brilliant mathematicians and scientists. You get many of them trained in the States and then bring them home and put them to work building your Communist paradise. Physics, aeronautics… you name it.'

'We think other parties may be involved and they're going to make him offer if they haven't done so already.'

'Maybe my people are interested, too.'

'In that case you'll have to be seen to try to recruit him, won't you?'

'Why him?'

Fang frowned, irritated. 'Because he's the world's leading authority on cryptanalysis, Richard. I mean Drew. He's a genius. And, to use your English expression, brilliant cryptanalysts don't grow on trees. Not even Chinese trees. Moscow used to help us with this work, but I have to admit we're still years behind the West when it comes to computerised encryption. It's a top priority and it's your job to help ensure that I succeed where the other parties fail, including your employers. In any case, he's one of ours.'

So that was the favour, a test of sorts. "Ours" being Chinese ethnicity.

Brodick pondered the request before asking another question. 'Why would the American University be so foolish to try to run such an event in the middle of a civil war?'

'I would imagine it's because they want to give the appearance of normality, that they're open for business. Otherwise they might have trouble with continued funding. When Americans start disappearing and dying, the dollars dry up. Haven't you noticed?'

'You could always approach him directly.'

'That wouldn't work.'

'Why not?'

'We tried talking. We made him an offer. He isn't interested.'

So this Li was to be the test of Brodick's loyalty to Fang, and his disloyalty to SIS.

They walked back towards the road, but Brodick stopped. He didn't want to accompany Fang to the parking lot above the port and the swimming club next to it. It was too open, too public.

'Something else. Before we split up.'

She turned to him.

Brodick felt tense, on edge. This was the point at which he must turn the screw.

'I need something more from you, too, Fang. I need your bona fides. My people will want proof of who and what you are. They'll need to know you're sincere and not what the Americans call a dangle. For a start, I need names and profiles of workmates or associates you think might be receptive to an approach from our people. Targets for recruitment. Not in China, almost certainly, but elsewhere. Singapore. Macau. Hong Kong. China's foreign missions in Europe or the States. Let's say five. Five prospects, preferably *Guoanbu.* Do you think you could manage that? Again, not for immediate use: only when we decide to take matters a step further. Or if you don't like the sound of that, you could instead start with a detailed graph showing the structure of the reformed *Guoanbu* along with all its bureaux and the names of the responsible ministers, directors and every bureau chief. Your order of battle, in other words.'

There. He'd set out his demands and now he waited for her response.

'I know what order of battle means.'

She gave him a long, cool look, eye to eye. He knew she was perfectly aware what he meant by bona fides. In the matter of espionage, it was universal.

Hers was a measuring look, Brodick decided, the look a woman gives a man when she's considering if he's someone she wants in her life in some form or other. It was a look Brodick had experienced before, a look that coolly assessed whether he was someone the woman in question wanted in her bed. He'd seen it before at parties, in bookshops, at railway stations: it could happen pretty much anywhere. Fang turned away without answering and made her way down to the car park. What had she decided?

'Would you like a camera? I suggest a 35mm Minolta XD-11—it's got an automatic focus—or the more easily concealed Minox LX. Whichever you prefer. I can supply the film for either. Better than taking out files and copying them and then having to put them back.'

He took the little Minox out of his pocket.

'I'll take that. The Minox.'

Brodick halted and watched her go, but he took a few steps back and to one side, changing his position. He did not want to be seen watching.

A car pulled out, a cream '71 Mercedes 280 SE, and the driver, features invisible behind the windshield, turned around in his or her brown leather seat, leaning over the backrest to open a rear door. A private hire? An embassy vehicle?

Brodick memorised the Lebanese registration, with both Arabic and Roman numerals.

To establish her bona fides Fang would have to offer a lot more than that. She would have to give up at least one network, or possibly identify an important agent buried in a Western government.

So would he. This was just the start.

Brodick was reminded of those games of chicken played out in school playgrounds.

Which of them would go first and shoulder most of the risk—and the agony of failure?

Fang got in the back, turning and sitting and then drawing in her legs, without glancing up to see if Brodick was still there, watching her. As the Mercedes climbed to the main road, another vehicle pulled out and followed, this time a black VW Golf, the brand of hatchback much sought after by fashion-conscious militia types like Hasan. So popular were they that they were usually acquired by threatening owner-drivers at the traffic lights at pistol-point. This one turned right, the same direction as the Mercedes. The driver seemed to make no effort to keep his distance. Backup or tail? There was no way of knowing.

18

At long last, a lecture on the subject of China.

'Ladies and gentlemen, my name is Len. Or, if you prefer, Lennie. That's what my friends call me. Lennie. And no, it's not my real name, but it will have to do. So sorry. As you can see, I'm of Chinese origin, and as you can hear, I learned my English in a Chinese language laboratory—in Chengdu, as it so happens—and hence the North American accent for which I can again only apologise. Sometimes I even pretend I'm a shopkeeper in Sacramento, California, to avoid accusations and anti-Chinese discrimination.'

Len—or Lennie—bows to his audience and puts his palms together as if he is not, after all, a senior intelligence analyst and simultaneously professor of Chinese studies at the Sorbonne and visiting professor at the University of Birmingham—but instead a very humble Buddhist monk and a joker.

Is he serious? Brodick can't decide.

Len or Lennie is entirely bald, his head shiny as if polished, his face smooth, tanned and oddly unlined. Of slight build, he wears a button-down, blue striped shirt, charcoal trousers and black loafers; he could be a City of London trader who's decided to dress down for the occasion. Brodick finds it impossible to estimate his age. His attitude—his demeanour—seems to be mocking and certainly mischievous.

'Folks, I'm your tail-end Charlie. I'm told you have been looking at dozens of intelligence and security agencies, the good, the bad and the hideous over the last several months. My commiserations.

That must have been quite an ordeal. Well, I'm bringing up the rear. I'm going to talk about China, and even if you're planning on having a nap during my talk, I would ask you to try to remember the three points I'm going to make in my opening remarks. Please stay awake for that. Just three.' He holds up three fingers. 'The rest won't matter that much and then you can snooze as much as you like.'

Lennie walks around the lecture room while continuing to talk. He pauses now and again and examines one or another student with evident curiosity.

Brodick notices he wears a gold watch on his left wrist. It looks expensive.

'I can hear what's going on in your heads right now. You don't believe me? Okay, let me tell you. One of you is saying to himself that he's going to be the very best in his chosen field and because he has his sights set on being top dog, he's going to build his career in Bonn and Moscow. No need for all this stuff about China. Who wants all that developing world shit? Not me, buddy. Who cares about the Chinese anyhow? He has no plans at all to end up in the Asia-Pacific region. Am I right? Yes? I think so. No chopsticks and noodles for me! Well, good luck with that, sir. I know you were a *brilliant* student at—where was it—Balliol College, Oxford?

'Now I hear another's mind working. I can hear the cogs clicking: this lady has her sights set on Havana and Caracas, and maybe Sao Paulo and Lisbon. She has an amazing knack for languages. Wonderful! I envy you your talent. And here's another: this guy's dream is to be chief of station in Washington, where the real power lies. Wow, just wow. There's nothing like secret power inside the Beltway. That's real Alpha male ambition. Right?'

They turn their heads to follow Lennie as he moves between their desks.

Len claps his hands, and some people jump.

'Still awake? Ten years ago all that would have been a perfectly respectable and sensible position. Not anymore. That's no longer the reality. Maybe none of you wants to go to China or anywhere near it. Trouble is, ladies and gentlemen, it doesn't matter because China is coming to *you*. No matter how hard you try, you won't be able to avoid China or the Chinese.

'They are already here, even if you don't want to see them.'

His tone isn't appreciated by everyone if their expressions are anything to go by.

He explains that the Chinese Communist Party or CPC has, after intense deliberations and analysis, concluded that the People's Republic will replace the United States as the world's most powerful economy by 2030.

'Don't believe me? Read your *Financial Times*. Look at Chinese growth figures. Study the exports. Track the investments. Assess at the *value* of the US Treasury bonds Beijing has bought and continues to buy. The World Bank had already sent out two teams of economists to advise Beijing on quadrupling economic growth.

'I said *quadruple*. That's right: you heard me.

'Point two. China intended to achieve military parity with the United States, its number two adversary after the Soviet Union, by the year 2020.'

There's much muttering about this and Len has to raise his voice.

'For some perspective, please note that in the last five years the Chinese have built the equivalent of the entire Royal Navy in both ships and naval infrastructure. And in another five years it will double again.

'So tell me: who is going to rule the waves, comrades?'

Chinese submarines were now regularly spotted in the Caribbean and they operated in both the South Atlantic and Indian Ocean. The PRC had SIGINT bases in both Africa and Latin America. Cambodia, of course, and Mongolia. They were talking to the Cubans about setting up their own SIGINT site right next door to the huge Soviet aerial farm at Lourdes on the island: right on the doorstep of the United States.

And the trainees shouldn't forget the joint US-Chinese SIGINT station spying on Soviet missile telemetry. The CIA had built it and trained the Chinese operators.

'Not heard of Operation PAMIR? No? It's still highly classified, that's why.'

The Americans had lost their base in Mashhad, thanks to the 1979 Iranian revolution. Instead, the Chinese cyber-warfare capability received a huge boost when the CIA Science & Technology Department built them two brand-new SIGINT bases at Qitai and Koria in Xinjiang, code named SAUGUS and SAUCEPAN. It was a joint operation. The technical supplies came from the CIA and National Security Agency or NSA.

Len smiles broadly. 'Oh, and the West German BND are also participating.

'You already know about China's satellite program and its growing strategic nuclear arsenal. Of course you do. All the British can manage to do is to *rent* an American satellite. It's a kind of timeshare. Or spy-in-the-sky timeshare.'

No one finds this in the least funny.

'Let me tell you a little joke now you're still awake. Mikhail Gorbachev arrives at his office in the Kremlin one morning and an aide says he has some good news and some bad news. Which does the Soviet leader want to hear first? The bad, says Gorbachev. Okay, the Chinese have reached the moon. Gorbachev looks worried. And the good news? The aide nods. Boss, they've all gone.'

There are a few smiles, and one chuckle.

'And my third fact for you to consider and remember, hopefully: PRC intelligence officers and their agents working in the United States are now more numerous than their KGB and GRU counterparts combined. Yes, that's true. And get this: around twenty percent of all Soviet diplomats stationed abroad are full-time KGB or GRU officers. The figure for Chinese intelligence officers—that's PLA2 and *Guoanbu* working under diplomatic cover—is between forty and sixty percent. Go figure, guys.'

Lennie has everyone's attention. No one is taking a nap just yet.

'Finally, ladies and gentlemen, let's dispel a Western myth; it used to be said of Chinese agents that they worked for love—for love of Marxism-Leninism Mao-style, for love of country—or for love of family. Or because they were blackmailed or forced to do so. And that they were never paid because Beijing couldn't afford to do so. It used to be said all you had to do to recruit a Chinese agent was to show him or her a fistful of dollar bills. Today China has oodles of cash and it does pay its operatives; and it pays them well and probably better than you.

'Thank you for listening. After lunch I will talk to you about the recent reorganisation of Chinese intelligence with the strategic aim of developing as a global superpower. As *the* global superpower. Thank you so much.'

Lennie bows.

19

"Housing" Fang was Brodick's next job. It meant finding out where DRAGON lived, what her routines and habits were.

'Do you know the driver?'

The young man perched on the edge of the office chair on the far side of Brodick's desk shook his head. He leaned forward, hands together between his knees, rocking back and forth like someone with a stomach ache. He didn't make eye contact. He was tall but slightly built, with narrow shoulders, a Van Dyke beard and a narrow face with a sallow complexion and enormous, dark brown eyes.

'Can you find out?'

'Sure.' Farid was the second of Fawzi's sons, an engineering student. They didn't seem much alike, at least in appearance. Farid wore faded blue jeans, a rumpled green t-shirt. He found it difficult to keep still: hence the knees pressing against his hands in an effort at self-restraint. It irritated Brodick; he wondered if the kid was on marching powder or something similar. There seemed to be only three desirable professions for the male offspring of middling to upper class Lebanese: engineering, medicine and the law in that order, and the law was a long way down because the profession was considered little better than criminal. Engineer Farid seemed to have plenty of free time on his hands, and he was certainly keen to use it to obtain the dollars Brodick had to offer.

'If he seems amenable, perhaps you could recruit him to log her movements. I'll give you the cash to pay him if he agrees.' Farid nodded, shrugged.

'Yeah. Okay.'

'And you're sure it's her?'

'Sure I'm sure. No question. They're not that many Chinese women in Beirut right now. Not young and pretty ones, anyhow.' Farid glanced up at Brodick and caught his eye, grinning as if he expected Brodick to appreciate the comment and share the male sentiment, but Brodick gave no sign that he did. Farid seemed to think that because his father worked with Brodick that somehow entitled him the right to a degree of easy familiarity, but it was not a view Brodick shared. The boy would have to earn his cash without favours. And Fang wouldn't appreciate being described as "pretty". Brodick found himself in the curious position of wanting to defend Fang, somehow.

'This is the registration, right?'

Farid leaned further forward to squint at the scrap of paper Brodick placed in front of him. 'Yeah, that's the one.'

'Cream Mercedes, a 280 SE?'

Farid nodded.

'It's a taxi?'

'Not sure. Don't think so. It doesn't have red taxi plates. Think it's a private hire.'

'Will you find out?'

'Okay.'

Brodick was thinking about installing a tracker to monitor her movements.

'So tell me about her routine.'

'She doesn't have a routine, that's the thing. She doesn't work to what you call a schedule. It's good security. She comes out of her place at different times; mostly she's early, sometimes she's late, okay? Sometimes it's lunchtime before she appears and occasionally she stays home all day, usually the weekends. Maybe she does this for safety reasons.' Farid shrugged as if to say, what do I care what she does or when she does it?

'So the driver doesn't sit there waiting for her. He comes when she calls him.'

'I guess so.' He paused. 'There are times when she makes him wait.'

'Where does she live, Farid?'

This is what he'd wanted to ask at the start, but had kept it back so it wouldn't seem to Farid that it mattered that much.

'On the east side. Up on the mountain. You can see the building from the streets here in the western sector. It overlooks the city. It overlooks everything. I can show you.'

'Does this place have a name?'

'Uh-huh. Bellevue.'

'How original. It's a hotel or what?'

'They're apartments. One bedroom. You know: bedroom, sitting room, bathroom, kitchenette in the living area—and a balcony. The place is new, maybe three or four years old. They're mostly for rent, but I think some are leaseholds.'

'You've been there, have you?'

'Yeah.'

'So tell me.'

'She lives in number forty-seven. She rents it. Three months' rent as a deposit up front. I talked to the guy downstairs at reception. He's the manager and he claims he's a partner in the business but maybe he was just trying to impress. He prefers French to Arabic. You know what I mean. A Maronite. Also kinda… you use the term gay, right?'

'We do. How do you know she's in forty-seven?'

'Because he talked about the tenants, and he said there was a Chinese lady in forty-seven. It's kinda like unusual, yeah.'

'Go on.'

'He's, um, effeminate. I pretended I need somewhere to rent so he showed me a vacant one. Tiles on the floor, walls recently painted pale yellow or beige. Modern furniture. Like Scandinavian, you know? Those whaddya-call-em flatpack chairs and beds. Very simple but clean and modern. He kept touching my arm.'

Farid was not without initiative.

Again, Brodick considered the possibility of wiring the flat.

'Direct lines or switchboard?'

'Switchboard operated by reception. No direct outside lines.'

'Okay. Well done. What else?'

'The balconies are amazing, yeah. Small, maybe two people could sit out there. It's like being right in the sky and sort of scary. Not a place to be if you're scared of heights. You can see everything from up there. Like you're a bird, know what I'm saying? You open your arms wide, like, and your left hand is where the airport and the southern suburbs are. The Green Line is kinda straight down there directly in front of you. Then Beirut port, and where your right hand is—Jounieh. Man, you can see it all. The whole friggin' war.'

'How much is the rent?'

'Don't know exactly, but I guess it's a couple of hundred bucks a month. Dollars. No one wants Lebanese pounds, right?'

'Did the manager say anything more about the Chinese woman?'

'No, and I didn't ask. I didn't think I should. I was pretending to be a possible client. I think he fancied me and I didn't want to let on that I prefer the ladies so I thought it best not to mention her.'

'Do you think you could go back and talk to the manager again? You could ask what the rent is and say you forgot to ask the last time because he was being so nice and helpful.'

'I guess. Sure. Why not? I don't like him hitting on me, though.'

'So you've said, but I'm sure you can handle it. Is there more than one entrance?

'You can get in or out from the basement. There's a small area of grass—a lawn, I guess you'd call it—where people hang up washing and there are steps around the side to the road.'

'You can do so without being seen from reception?'

'Anyone in reception will see or hear the lift, and of course anyone going up or down the stairs will be seen, too, unless the receptionist is distracted or watching TV.'

Perhaps the manager could be bribed to let Farid borrow the master key for thirty minutes.

'So when she does go out, where does she go?'

'I'm not watching her 24/7, Mr Drew. You know that, right?'

'You're not being paid for working round-the-clock.'

'Twice in the past five days I've seen her visit the Chinese embassy on Sursock. She didn't stay long: less than an hour each time. She also visited the Xinhua office, and stayed longer, all afternoon.'

'What else?'

Farid shrugged, made a face. 'Couple of restaurants, hotels.'

'Did she meet anyone?'

'Not that I saw.'

'Did she make you?'

'Did she what?'

'Did she spot you watching her or following her?'

'Can't tell to be honest. Don't think so.' He shrugged.

'Does she use the same driver to take her to the west?'

'Yeah. But not always. I saw her walk over once.'

'Where else does she go?'

'She visited Beit Mery. You know it, yeah? Always popular in summer because in the mountain it's always cool. She went to dinner at one of those fancy roadside restaurants. The kind of place people go to see and be seen. Wednesday, I think. Yes—Wednesday.'

'Who with?'

'Oh, yeah, I forgot. She did meet someone. Some Asian guy. Maybe Chinese, but I wouldn't know. He was already waiting for her. They ate, then they separated and she went home. They didn't kiss or hug: nothing like that. They looked kinda formal. Not laughing and smiling. Serious, okay? Business, not romance. He just got up and walked away and she stayed at the table for a few minutes and paid.'

It sounded to Brodick like standard fieldcraft: arriving and leaving separately.

Maybe he was her case officer, a Chinese version of Fenner.

'Does she have a place here, in the western sector?'

Farid looked confused. He shrugged, looked away.

Brodick explained what he meant. 'She spends time in the west but repeatedly moving across the Green Line isn't exactly safe. She must have a bolt hole on this side. A flat. A hotel room. A private house. Somewhere she can stay overnight. Maybe she stays with Chinese friends or diplomats.'

'I don't know, sorry.'

'Try to find out, will you?'

'Okay.' Farid looked unhappy, the corners of his mouth drooping. Maybe it was just his way. As if it was something he didn't believe in, or didn't want to do.

'You've done well, Farid. It would be really helpful if could find out if she has some sort of accommodation on this side of the Green Line. This is for you—thank you.' Brodick pulled a roll of dollars from his pocket, held in place with an elastic band. 'That's for the five days, plus a bonus for your good work.'

'Mister Drew, if you want me to cover 24/7 I have a friend who could help.'

'I'll think about it, Farid, and let you know.'

Farid must have some inkling of what Brodick's role was. He didn't ask Brodick about the Chinese woman or why Brodick needed the information; an indication that he had a pretty good idea about Brodick's true calling. His father, Fawzi, must have given him a few hints if not told him outright. Brodick would have to live with it, but what he wasn't going to do was make it worse by taking on some unknown quantity in the form of Farid's "friend" who would have no reason to show either loyalty or discretion.

20

Len is back, waiting for them in the Fort Monckton lecture room.

He begins his "lesson" at the dawn of the twentieth century with Shanghai, so-called Paris of the Orient and port city on the Huangpu river: one of the world's biggest cities undergoing rapid change and population growth. Some 30,000 *waiguo guiro,* or foreign devils, held sway over more than half of the city's population in the French Concession and Anglo-American International Settlement: that is, around two million Chinese.

The city's extremes of wealth and poverty were unequalled, yet Shanghai's rich and powerful were indistinguishable from the criminal underworld.

'They were joined at the hip. They needed one another,' is Len's view.

Both relied on extreme violence.

The head of the Green Gang or *Qing Bang* was Du Yuesheng, a man with a powerful ally in the form of Felix Bouvier, owner of the city's greyhound racing track as well as its legendary casino. Bouvier had close ties with the nationalist general, Chiang Kai-shek, as well as Etienne Fiori, former French intelligence officer and head of the French Concession's Special Police Bureau.

Fiori was involved in the Corsican mafia, allied to the Green Gang.

Du supplied Fiori with opium via Marseille, while Fiori played his part in a white slave ring, the Grande Combine, in which Corsican gangsters "recruited", that is to say abducted, French girls for the largest brothel in the world: in Shanghai.

In this milieu the Chinese Communist Party was formed in a series of secret meetings. Locations were repeatedly changed to evade Fiori's police. The delegates decided that it was essential the fledgeling communist party align itself with the Dr Sun Yat-Sen's nationalist Kuomintang or KMT. The CCP (*Gongshandang*) was based on the Soviet model and its aims were to establish a revolutionary army, overthrow the bourgeoisie and secure the rule of the working class. Private property and class differences would be abolished.

A young delegate to these undercover sessions, already enjoying a reputation for brilliance, would become known as Mao Zedong, or Red Sun.

On April 12, 1927, the CCP's former allies, the Nationalists, mounted a counter-revolutionary coup: thousands of communists were assassinated in Shanghai and other cities. The KMT called it "cleansing". The CCP's membership was annihilated, falling from 60,000 to 10,000. In response, the Red Army was formed, along with a clandestine service that would be named the Special Services Section or SSS. It carried out an underground war of car bomb attacks and assassinations of suspected collaborators.

'The Communists called the KMT "bandits" or *tu fei,* and the KMT called them "Communist bandits" or *gong fei*. You'll find many Chinese say that the two are *fen zang*: dividing up the treasure. During the Maoist period, the Communists practiced Red Terror or *hongse kongbu* on the mainland. In the 1950s and 1960s, the KMT practiced White Terror or *raise kongbu*.'

And this is Len's point:

'We see the origins of the modern Chinese state right here in colonial Shanghai: conspiracy, loyalty and betrayal, colonial bullying, corruption, foreign repression and revolution, alien invasion and a clandestine war of great savagery. Remember: espionage is the very soil in which Chinese communism was born. It's not simply a tool of the state. It *is* the state. The state's protection and its primary weapon. Remember also, if you would, that Communism—whether Chinese, Russian or Vietnamese—celebrates and romanticises the secret life, from codewords and tradecraft to spy satellites and strategic deception. True then, true now when it comes to the fourth and soon the fifth generation of Communist Chinese leaders, and that's because intelligence is seen by Beijing as an existential matter: not simply as a game of diplomats. To the Chinese, it's a life and death issue.

'By the way, they don't lock up the spies they catch: they shoot them, and if it's one of their own then they show the execution on video link—and it's compulsory watching for all *Guounbu* staff, *pour encourager les autres*.'

21

Brodick's office was more monk's cell than office. It had two doors, both with combination locks—one to the outer corridor and the other to the main office—the latter a large room with several white-topped tables pushed together, chairs around it and three of the new bulky computers with green screens. This was where the younger travel agents worked: two men, three women. Not that they had much work to do in the middle of a war zone. It was just a matter of clocking in and clocking out, and collecting the monthly pay checks. It must have been tedious, especially so with the value of their wages rapidly eroded by hyperinflation. But what choice did they have? Jobs were hard if not impossible to find, even for young graduates.

There were French doors—again protected by steel shutters painted white—and a balcony off the main room overlooking the street out front, but these doors were seldom opened unless it was during a prolonged lull in the fighting.

Brodick's desk was small and cheap: it was more a secretary's desk of stained wood with three drawers down one side. Of the two chairs, Brodick's was the larger "executive" type of chrome and fake leather with a high back and armrests. There was a small, single window over the street—more loophole than window—with steel shutters. Against the back wall stood a four-drawer metal filing cabinet in dull green, secured with a padlock. There were no pictures, only a calendar two years out of date.

Fawzi had expected Brodick to take up residence, as it were, in the executive offices at the far end of the corridor along with Fawzi himself and the other elderly staff members, who arrived for work every day on time in suits and ties and carrying empty briefcases. They spent their days reading the local papers, drinking coffee and sharing the latest gossip. There was nothing else for them to do, after all, and at 5pm they'd troop out, taking the newspapers with them, hurrying to avoid getting caught up in any street battles. But Brodick found the heavy curtains, the dark wood panelling, the carpets all rather depressing, and he didn't want to spend his time listening to the old-timers with their political speculation and wild conspiracy theories.

He didn't like being watched; he needed privacy.

What was important in his monk's cell lay behind the filing cabinet and partially hidden by it; only on closer inspection did it reveal itself as a storage cupboard with a metal door, padlocked and painted white to blend into the surrounding wall. A safe. Once Brodick had pushed the filing cabinet out of the way and unlocked it, there was a space big enough and deep enough to crawl into.

It contained Brodick's spy gear.

First was a large attaché case with a hard shell.

It contained Brodick's own radio station, in effect, a PRM-4150, codename TITHE.

Provided separately was the MA-4245 cipher unit. Voice or data could be transmitted at an impressive rate of six hundred groups a second. The set had been designed for covert Stay Behind Organisations, the Diplomatic Wireless Service as well as for special forces.

And for spies like Brodick, working as illegals without diplomatic cover. He would no longer have to make the hazardous trip to and from the embassy across the Green Line every time he wanted to send an encrypted message—or receive one.

His encrypted TITHE messages would be received, processed and routed to their destination by the Service's very own Automated Telegram Handling System, or ATHS.

Also in there was a tiny Nagra JBR covert recorder, something that could prove useful, as well as a clever and highly classified item courtesy of the CIA: a tiny radio that could scan several bands at once, the earpiece flesh-coloured and almost invisible, connected by wireless to a receiver the size of a pack of ten cigarettes that could be hung around Brodick's chest in a cotton harness. A wire connecting the two acted as the antenna. It had been developed by the Agency for detecting surveillance teams right in the heart of hostile territory, in central Moscow no less, which was always crawling with KGB radio cars and foot-soldiers, including watchers with telescopes stationed on rooftops or the upper floors of high-rise buildings, but that didn't mean it couldn't be used to monitor other parties here in Beirut, such as the *Guoanbu*.

And the Minolta XD-11 with the 35mm lens.

Brodick loved his gadgets. He would take them out and run his hands over them every day he came to work on his cover as a Levant Travel executive.

There was something else. He wriggled into the cupboard and regardless of dust and cobwebs discovered a peculiar item right at the back. No one had mentioned it and there seemed to be no record of its existence. It had been forgotten. Inside a very dusty shoebox he found an Astra 400, the ugliest semi-automatic pistol he'd ever seen, a Spanish military officer's sidearm used by both republican and insurgent nationalist forces in the 1930s—reliable, accurate and the action was clean and still in good working order—and it fired 9mm Largo rounds. It was heavy compared to modern pistols; in both weight and length he thought it similar to the Colt 1911 but a lot less attractive. There were two full spare clips with the handgun along with a cleaning brush and a bottle of 3-in-1 oil, all wrapped in oilskin.

Intelligence officers didn't usually carry arms and, although Brodick had been trained in their use, carrying a handgun on operational duty was disapproved of. It was considered counter-productive. Too risky, in effect. Perhaps it had been issued to an SIS officer attending what the Lebanese called the "spy school": the Arabic language training course run by the Middle East Centre for Arabic Studies (MECAS), established by the British Army in Jerusalem and then moved to Lebanon under civilian control where it ran uninterrupted for thirty years until 1978, three years after the country's civil war erupted.

Still, the handgun might come in useful, especially if it was off-the-books and untraceable. He just had to make sure it was never found in his possession. He decided he would take it home and keep it under his pillow. Just in case.

Brodick locked himself in: securing the outer door to his office as well as the internal one and then lifting the attaché case up onto the desk and opening it up. He would send off an encrypted signal to Fenner that he had made contact with Fang. That should please his case officer and buy more time. Brodick would make it short and sweet; he wouldn't go into detail. He would spin it out as long as he could. He had no intention of mentioning Fang's attempts to recruit him, not now, not ever. The details of Fang's elaborate denial of her identity as set out in the DIA document and her alternative "legend" could also wait. So would her report on the forthcoming Silkworm missile delivery, at least for a few more days.

From the window came the rumble of artillery fire.

So far so good, Fang, but can I trust you to do the same?

*

There were two of them.

The world had rolled over into night by the time Brodick left the office, but he spotted them almost immediately. One stood right across the street from Levant Travel, the second was over to the left, on the near side, around thirty paces away. When Brodick turned right and started to walk, they moved, too.

If they were surveillance, they weren't very good; but then, in Beirut and in the midst of internecine slaughter, they didn't need to be.

Maybe they were just thugs after his money. If so, they were in for a nasty surprise.

The Astra 400 was wedged into the small of his back, under his shirt, and he'd already jacked a round into the chamber.

There was light: huge sheets and waves of it flickering on and off, accompanied by continuous rumbling and growling. It wasn't lightning, though it looked like it. It wasn't thunder, though it sounded like it. It was gunfire. The sound of tearing cloth was small arms automatic fire, both short and long bursts. The tapping of single rounds provided punctuation. The sullen thuds of mortar rounds shook the street under Brodick's feet and set his teeth on edge. This orchestral din came from the south, or so it seemed to him. The flashes illuminated the street for a couple of seconds at a time, revealing the details of otherwise blank, dark, almost invisible buildings. There were parachute flares too, with their smoky trails and then their incandescence without shadow, drifting eerily across the southern sky and seeming to make the city dance, the buildings wobble and hop in the waves of extreme light and then total black.

Brodick felt a frisson of fear but a fear equalled by the sheer excitement of it all.

It was the war, that was all. It was really quite exhilarating. He told himself people will get used to practically anything provided they managed to survive.

*

At the top of the vertical leg of the Y—just before the road plunged down between the French and Swiss missions with the heavy sweet fragrance of honeysuckle—there was a solitary streetlight and Brodick turned to observe his followers strolling after him so he could get a better look at who they were. The first man was short and portly, his belly pressing against a rumpled shirt hanging outside baggy chinos. He kept his hands in his pockets. Late twenties or early thirties. Asian. Once he'd come on down, his companion entered the pool of light—it was impossible to avoid it—and Brodick made him out too as Asian; only taller, thinner, roughly the same age. He wore a floppy sunhat. He had on a light windbreaker of shiny, synthetic material.

So Fang had her own team.

Fortunately, the usual Kurdish lads—sporting red armbands and AK-47s—of the PSP didn't seem to be around that evening. Not that they ever troubled Brodick. Indeed, when their patrols passed or when they manned improvised checkpoints they usually recognised him, would call out to him, shake his hand, offer to escort him to his door or invited him to have a Turkish coffee. The kids no longer asked him for his papers.

Brodick kept going. He crossed the street, Yale key to the compound gate already in hand. He opened it quickly, stepped inside, and locked the gate behind him. He stood back a little and turned to watch. He felt safe. The short, rotund Chinese stopped on the edge of the pavement, looking left and right and left again as if trying to decide whether it was safe to cross. Of course it was; there was no traffic. His companion came on past him, crossing over and without hesitation strode right up to the iron fence.

'Good evening, Mr Sullivan.' He spoke in confident, accented English.

The man raised his right hand and two fingers appeared between the uprights, the first and middle finger holding a slip of paper.

'Please.'

He didn't appear to be armed with gun or knife and in any case he didn't seem in the least threatening. He didn't look the violent type, though Brodick had to admit he was by no means sure what the type was. He seemed to Brodick to be anxious to do whatever it was he'd been ordered to do - hand over a message of some kind.

How had he identified Brodick? Perhaps they had his picture. Perhaps they'd followed him to the office earlier and had been watching the entrance ever since, though he was sure he would have noticed these two for the amateurs they seemed to be. Possibly they simply had his physical description; and in any case, westerners were rare in Beirut in the wake of assassinations and kidnappings, so it wouldn't have been difficult.

Brodick took a step forward and snatched the paper from him and stepped back at once, just in case.

'Thanks.'

Before Brodick could think of what else to say, the tall Chinese had already retreated and turned away, heading towards his companion on the far side of the street. He'd done his job, delivered the message. It wasn't until Brodick had gone up in the lift and was stood outside the steel door of his flat that the movement sensors switched on the spotlights and he could read the message.

It was just one word and four digits.

A place and a time.

22

Len is in playful mood when his afternoon session gets underway.

'Remember this date if you please, ladies and gentlemen: June 6, 1983. Less than a year ago. It's the opening session of the sixth National People's Congress. Parliament, in other words. Shall I tell you a counter-revolutionary joke? Yes? Okay. In Beijing people have a nickname for this august body: "The three hands"– *wo shou, pai shou, ju shou*. That means: shake hands, clap hands and raise hands.

'Be careful who's listening if you repeat this on the mainland.

'So, at the NPC Chinese Prime Minister Zhao Ziyang announced a new Ministry of State Security or MSS. The name: *Guojia Anquanbu.* Most people use a short form, *Anquanbu* or *Guoanbu.*

'Make no mistake: it's going to be China's version of Moscow's KGB or Langley's CIA.

'It has started small—some 7,000 officers or around the twice the current number of SIS staff—the very best recruited from the Party's *Diaochabu,* responsible for intelligence in China's diplomatic missions around the world, as well as a larger number of counter-intelligence people from the ministry of public security, the *Gonganbu.*

'It's already grown quickly, by how much I don't know. The chief is Ling Yun. I don't know much about him or his new organisation either, to be honest. I do know it's expanding fast, and that Ling Yun was appointed by Deng Xiaoping himself and that its ambitions are global.

'I know where its headquarters are if that's any help, and I can tell you how to get there if you happen to be sightseeing in Beijing. Take a 322 bus. It's the stop before the Summer Palace and after the zoo. If you don't know the Summer Palace, it's an extensive royal park within the Imperial City.

'Go take a look, why don't you, huh? Sure they'd be happy to see you.

Kingarth raises a hand.

'Yes?'

'Just how much do we know about Chinese leaders? How accessible are they?'

Len paused, shook his head. 'We know almost nothing: their families, sexual preferences, sports and interests, dietary and drinking choices: how they relate to each other, nor how they agree or disagree over policy. They never display emotion in public. So the NPC sessions are Orwellian: 3,000 people with blank faces all reacting the same. This is the victory of Leninist party discipline!

'Mao said: *you ren de defang, jiu you maodun.* "When there are people, there are conflicts." So we know there are power struggles, but of details we know almost nothing. We pick up whispers of an assassination, rumours of a coup attempt—but that's all.'

Len walks around the room, looking at the student spies.

'After Mao's death, Deng Xiaoping did not want a repeat of the chaos, bankruptcy and death toll: fifty to sixty million Chinese died during the Maoist era. So he instituted time limits on the top leader, a maximum ten years. A wise move: after he left office, the leader could have a comfortable retirement.

'Anyway, let's get back on track to our Chinese spies.

'The *Guoanbu* is divided into departments, known as "Bureaux". I believe the 1st Bureau is responsible for internal security, *anquan*, in the provinces. It's also responsible for its own detention camps within China's very own Gulag, the infamous *laogai.* Captured spies are held there. All we know is that it's no holiday camp. Take a hint: that's a gigantic understatement.

'The 2nd Bureau is believed to be responsible for foreign

intelligence. Its agents are usually posted abroad under diplomatic cover as second secretaries or so-called advisers. Your Chinese counterparts, in other words.

'Not much is known about the 3rd, though it appears to be responsible for infiltrating Hong Kong, Macau and Taiwan, the territories Beijing plans to incorporate into the People's Republic—rather sooner than later would be my guess. When it comes to Taiwan, we should remember Sun Zi's motto: *win the war without fighting it.* That means persuading the Republic of China leadership and public that they would lose and so not to fight.

'The remainder of the bureaux, I'm sorry to say, are still a mystery. Some say the 7th Bureau is devoted to special operations, *tewu*. The 8th seems to be an open-source research organisation and has taken over control of the China Institutes of Contemporary International Relations or CICIR, an enormous network of thinktanks that presents itself as academic and thoroughly respectable, but is staffed and run by intelligence people. It casts a very wide net, trawling for people of influence in the West and penetrating Western research institutions. They don't just sit behind their desks, these professors and doctoral students, or amble around libraries and give lectures. They go into the field, too, and get their hands dirty. Afghanistan, for example, visiting the *mujehadeen.*

'The rest of it… Well, it's going to be your job and those of your colleagues to fill in the numerous blanks in our knowledge.

'And the best of luck with that, comrades.'

23

When a case officer and his or her agent meet, there are certain universal questions and answers that usually precede all other business. In this instance, Brodick wasn't sure who was agent and who was case officer. Ostensibly he was both, and so was Fang. Or, to put it another way, it wasn't yet clear to Brodick who would eventually take which role.

She was already waiting, having chosen a corner table near the windows on the far side, her back to the wall at the far end of the restaurant so she could see everyone else and, if she turned her head to the left, she had a view of the Mediterranean. In the dark, though, all that could be seen through the glass was the dense mass of water below a starlit sky and the rise and fall of white bars marking the waves as they rose and broke on the shore. Despite the chatter in the interior, the sea could still be heard through the panes of glass, a faint hiss.

On seeing her, Brodick ran through a range of feelings. Instinctively, his first glimpse of her pleased him, excited him. This was followed by a nervousness approaching on dread. He felt danger, a sense of the threat she posed. Not being someone who spent time analysing his instinctive responses to others, Brodick had little idea why he felt any of it.

The Spaghetteria Italia wasn't that busy. The tables nearest Fang were so far unoccupied and that would make conversation easier and safer. Whether or not the Spaghetteria was full depended on the state of the war outside: sometimes, during a prolonged lull in hostilities, lasting days or even as long as a fortnight, it was packed and clients had to book a table well ahead. When it was really bad, or the fighting was in the neighbourhood, it was empty or very nearly empty. Just occasionally, it had shut down.

'I'm sorry I'm late. Have you been here long?'

'My people found you, then.' She didn't answer his question. She didn't even look at him, but past him as if she wanted to see who took interest in his arrival at her table.

Brodick pulled out a chair.

'They followed me from my office. They didn't seem to mind the fireworks.'

'They're used to it. It seems to have stopped; did you notice?'

He took a seat on her left, his back to the windows. He would have liked to have had a view of the sea, but there was in any case little to see out there and he would have felt very uncomfortable with his back to the entrance as well as to other diners.

Now she looked him over. 'I hope they didn't alarm you.'

Brodick shook his head. There had been just the one word on the slip of paper: *Spaghetteria*. And the time: 21.30. It was now 21.55.

Brodick kicked off with the standard preliminaries of a *treff*. 'How long have you got?'

'I always have time for you.' Her mouth twitched in an almost-smile.

'But you live in the east, don't you? You don't want to cross back too late.'

Fang studied his face if trying to find some deeper meaning in the remark, almost as if she knew he'd been trying to find out where she lived.

'Don't worry about me. What about you?'

'I've also all the time in the world: for you.'

The smile broadened, dimpling her cheek. 'Such courtesy! Such a gentleman! Are all you British so nice? And when and where shall we meet next time?'

There it was. They were sharing the preliminaries fifty-fifty. What Brodick really wanted to know was whether she knew of his secret staircase. She was wearing the Chanel version of the People's Liberation Army uniform, or so it seemed. It was a figure-hugging pantsuit in olive green, with lots of loops, epaulettes and military style, rectangular, button-down pockets and a tightly synched waist that showed off her figure and modest bust to good effect. All that was missing from this sexy outfit—yes, it was definitely sexy—was a red star. The combination of sex and military gave off a vague hint of S&M. Was she into that? It seemed a suitable outfit for the woman who had arranged his kidnapping and then displayed her power over him with an ease of manner that seemed well practised. Perhaps she was into it but didn't know it, but then again she was no ingenue. Around her throat a necklace of what looked like obsidian gemstones caught the light as she moved.

'I don't mind. I could come to your side next time if it's easier for you.'

Brodick noted she wore a wristwatch this time, on her right wrist, the face turned inwards. It had a lot of knobs and dials. A diver's watch. Or a soldier's.

'As you wish.' She looked around the room again, at the other clients.

The waiter was hovering, so they picked up their menus. Fang barely glanced at hers before putting it down again; she had already decided. She asked for the calamari as a starter and osso buco for the main course. Brodick already knew what he wanted; this was one of his favourite eateries not least because it was so close to the flat and relatively safe. In fact, the place was known for its fish but he ignored that and chose instead insalate di rucola followed by one of his favourites: risotto al fungi porcini.

'Wine?'

'Sure. You choose.'

Brodick selected the Frascati. Fang didn't comment; she didn't seem to care one way or the other, though Brodick imagined that she preferred dry white, but he didn't really know because she'd never said. She was quite self-effacing in some ways—in the ways that didn't matter. It was her way, apparently; to give ground on trivia but hold out for the important stuff. Successful people were like that.

When they were alone again, they resumed where they'd left off.

Fang said, 'This time next week? It'll be after the missile delivery. We should have plenty to talk about.'

'Why don't we meet the same night of the delivery and watch the unloading from a suitable vantage point?'

Fang hesitated a moment, but apparently she couldn't see any objection.

'Fine. Good idea. Monday. We should agree signals.'

'Any suggestions?'

'You know the stone steps behind my flat?'

'I came down them to the restaurant this evening.'

So she did know. 'There are eighty-seven of them all told.'

'Okay.'

'I suggest the eleventh from the bottom. I'll leave an inverted "V" in yellow at knee height on the right-hand side going up and at least twenty-four hours before the meet. Meaning it goes ahead as planned. No signal, no meet. If either of us need to leave a date and a time then a note inserted on step twenty-one, right hand side, knee height. There's a useful gap between the stones right there.'

Brodick took his hand out of his pocket and showed her his yellow wax pencil.

'And I will mark your inverted "V" with a short horizontal line in white chalk to acknowledge at least twenty-four hours ahead. No acknowledgement, no meeting.'

'You'll do this yourself, Fang, not use your people.'

'And the same goes for me when I want to call a meet.' She frowned at him. She didn't need a lecture on tradecraft.

'And the location?'

'On reflection I think I'll meet you here in the west if it's easier for you.'

'Then how about my original suggestion, Fang: that we watch

the ship's cargo being brought ashore. Together. From a safe distance.'

'You have somewhere in mind?'

'On the east side, there's that old Ottoman villa in Kesrawan on the hill overlooking Jounieh port. It's a restaurant. They make pancakes—crêpes—both sweet and savoury, and we can sit outside. I'm told service is lousy but that doesn't matter.'

'I know it. It gets pretty crowded in the evening.'

'Then let's meet there earlier. They open at 1600, so let's say 1700. If it's too busy, we can go for a coffee elsewhere. Bring your own mosquito repellent.'

She hadn't pushed for a *treff* in the western sector, and Brodick hadn't asked if she had a place on his side of the Green Line. The case officer-agent-case officer preliminaries were completed by the time the wine arrived in an ice bucket with a crisp white napkin around it. One of the reasons Brodick liked the Spaghetteria was the way the staff managed to provide quality starched white tablecloths, napkins and shining glassware. Each table was untrammelled, a virgin snowfield: at least until the soup. He couldn't blame the management, not in wartime, for the tinned peas. So many items were unobtainable, even on the black market. Well, everything was black market now. Fang tasted the wine and they waited while the waiter filled their glasses. Fang watched the man leave the table, weaving his way back to the kitchen. He was very tall and hunched in his white jacket and he shuffled rather than walked as if lame. His old man's jowls were babyish, his mouth an overturned crescent of pain.

'Our waiter looks so terribly sad.'

'He is. He has good reason to be.'

'You know him?'

'I can't claim to know him, not really. Abbas is Palestinian. I was told he lost all his family in the camps during the Israeli invasion and occupation. Wife, kids, parents. He has no one left. He's only forty but he looks sixty. He never speaks. At least, I've never seen or heard him say a word.'

'At least sixty, I think. More like seventy. We'll leave him a good tip.'

As if that would make any difference.

'I always do, Fang.'

'You come here often, then.'

He didn't deny it. 'I like it and it's convenient.'

'Those people over there: the four on the far side. Who are they—do you know?'

She meant the four, well-fed middle-aged men in suits and leather jackets. They'd eaten and their plates had been taken away, the several wine glasses and empty bottles removed, the crumbs swept away with a small pan and brush. In their place a waiter brought brandy glasses and a bottle of cognac XO. They were leaning back, chatting and laughing and two of them were busy lighting up what looked like immense Havana cigars. They didn't bother removing the gold and red bands around them, something Brodick had been raised to consider vulgar. He thought he recognised two of their number.

'One is George Habash, leader of the PLFP: the Popular Front for the Liberation of Palestine. He's based in Damascus, mostly. He's a Christian and the PFLP—as you will know better than I—is Marxist-Leninist and close to Moscow. It's quite a surprise to see him in public.'

Don't patronise her. She probably knows more than you, you idiot.

'And the others?'

'I recognise one. Bassem Abu Sharif is one of his names. The guy with the missing fingers and the scarred face. You see him: on the left, in the black leather jacket? He's Fatah, one of the most senior officials and an aide to Yasser Arafat. Smart guy, likeable and decent by all accounts. By that I mean he's not corrupt. He's often involved in sensitive negotiations with foreign governments. He's a pragmatist.'

'How did he get his injuries?'

'Mossad sent a letter-bomb to him in Damascus.'

'Beirut isn't safe for them after the PLO withdrawal.'

'Beirut isn't safe for anyone at any time; but for them there's a constant risk of assassination wherever they are. London. Prague. Makes no difference.'

'The other two?'

'I don't know them.'

'They seem to be enjoying themselves.' Fang's tone sounded disapproving. Perhaps she thought all Palestinians should be in the front line, regardless of age, seniority or function.

Their starters arrived and Abbas topped up their glasses before limping away.

'Fang, talking of danger, aren't you taking a risk meeting me in such a public place?'

'Like those Palestinian officials, you mean? It's not quite the same, though, is it? As a matter of fact, it is a risk, but not quite what you have in mind—and it would be far riskier for me if we were to meet in private—in your home, for example. Or mine.'

'How so?'

She looked up at him. 'I'm at risk from my own people.'

'I don't understand.' Was this an appeal of some sort, an attempt to present herself as vulnerable, in need of a foreigner's protection?

'Okay.' She nodded, apparently weighing up whether or not it was a good idea to talk about it. 'I'll explain. The danger is one of contamination. Contamination by foreign and specifically western influence. A virus we call bourgeois liberalism. It's seen as a real threat, Richard. I know you must find that hard to grasp, but try. It's no joke. I need to get close to someone like you for professional reasons. But to get close to you is to attract the attention of my colleagues as someone who may be compromised by our association. In English you have this saying: damned if you do, damned if you don't. It's better for me to be seen talking to you here—openly—than for me to vanish behind a locked door where anything can happen and nothing is known but all kind of imaginings result.'

'Are we being watched by your associates?'

She gave an almost imperceptible nod. 'Just as I assume your people are watching, too.'

'But why this fear of foreign infection?'

'Why? First off, China is not a nation of immigrants. We never had wave upon wave of alien cultures, each one imposing its language and culture on the inhabitants. We're not used to that. We're pretty homogenous. We don't have a history of foreigners mingling with the Chinese. The Han are an overwhelming majority. In our history we didn't have a succession of invasions by Saxons, and Picts, Jutes and Normans, then later, large immigrant populations of Jews, French Huguenots, Indians and Pakistanis and so on.'

Brodick was listening, but he was also watching her, noting how slim she was, how pale her arms were, admiring her pianist's slender wrists and fingers, the way she used a forefinger to move her hair away from her face, looping it behind one ear so she could eat, and noting how small and neat that ear was before it vanished again behind the black silk of her hair. Brodick was powerfully attracted to her, no matter that Fang was a CPC member, and he was pretty sure by now that she wasn't a *meiren ji*: a honey trap, literally "beautiful person plan". She was far too senior for such an escapade. It was usually left to wannabe actresses and models, waitresses and hotel maids, surely: people who were vulnerable, who could be bribed or blackmailed into the humiliating role of offering sex to foreigners of interest to the authorities, mostly academics, diplomats and journalists. Suspected spies, in other words. She put down her fork and looked up at him.

'Now, Richard, you know this—how much we Chinese suffered under attacks from Westerners—the Opium Wars, the Boxer Rebellion, the humiliation and brutality of the colonial French, British and American so-called Concessions imposed on us at the start of the twentieth century. And then the Japanese invasion and occupation. You do see, don't you? World War Two started in 1931 for the Chinese and we lost fourteen million people.'

He waited while she ate again.

'We were very nearly crushed at the outset. The Party, I mean.

It was born in a time of great trouble, of violence, and it was deeply penetrated by our enemies. At one point the KMT—the Nationalists—came so close—' she put-up her right hand and showed Brodick her forefinger and thumb, almost touching, a fraction of an inch apart '—to totally destroying us. We were riddled with scores of their agents. We lost 50,000 out of our 60,000 Party cadres. But our very young intelligence service saved us from total extermination. Have you heard of the Dragon's Lair?'

'No.'

'I'll tell you the story. I won't forget; it's important that you should know. But the point, Richard, is that when it comes to foreign powers, even the Soviets—who did help us a lot in the beginning, training our cadres, our spies and providing us with military equipment right up to 1960—along with the Americans, you British, the French and the West Germans, you all pose what I think you call an existential threat: to my country, its government and above all, the Party. So on the one hand, to fight this intelligence war, I have to get close to our enemies, to people like yourself, because that's what you are, an enemy, but at the same time in the process of getting close, I raise the suspicions of the very people I'm working for that I might be compromised by this contact. Get it?'

'I think so, yes.'

'It's a contradiction, I know. I have to be careful. I have to follow procedure. There are rules, you do see that, don't you? I have to be correct in everything I do, or everything I'm seen to do. And I must have an unblemished record as a Party member. I can't step out of line. I guess it's hard for you to grasp, but this is the reality. In my country people don't ever mention the ministry of state security or the ministry of public security. Instead they talk carefully about the *youguan bumen* or "relevant department", and they never mention a security officer's name; instead, they write it down on a piece of paper and pass it to whoever they're talking to. You understand?'

'But you are already stepping out of line. With me.'

'Richard. Drew. If we are to make this relationship work—this professional relationship—we will have to know exactly how each of us stands. We do this together, or not at all.'

'You *are* a believer, though: a Communist.'

'Of course I am. I'm surprised you even question it. To me, and everyone in my organisation, Marxism isn't just an idea. It's a science. It's also our future, our way of life. In the same way that your people are Christian or at least of Judeo-Christian heritage.'

'You're telling me you don't want to defect.'

'Of course I don't. Never. Just look at my country's potential.' Yes, Brodick thought, and look at the lack of it in Britain's crumbling institutions, the insular delusions of what passed for his country's political class. She spoke with conviction, her voice rising. 'Never. No more than you would want to, I imagine.'

Little did she know how little he cared for it. That was his weakness.

Fang looked around, hoping no one had heard her outburst.

'Okay, Fang. Because if you do—if you change your mind, if things in your world become unbearable for whatever reason—please bear in mind that you need to tell me in good time so we can prepare for it. A lot of planning has to go into someone like you coming over to us. It would take weeks—not hours or days.'

She gave him a broad smile. 'You're very kind to show me your concern. But don't worry. It's not going to happen.'

'But this close monitoring of the Chinese population by police, security, local volunteers, party members, block neighbourhood leaders and so on—I think it's called the community grid system—it must feel pretty oppressive at times, this sense of being constantly watched, scrutinised, reported on. I'm told there will be, in a matter of another generation, around 600 million cameras on your streets and public buildings, almost one for every two people.' Brodick reasoned that a little probing would do no harm. 'Doesn't it get to you? Isn't it scary?'

'On the contrary, I feel safe. We call them *tian yan*, the eye of heaven—or the emperor.'

'An excellent name.'

'I think so. Safety and security are important to us Chinese because of everything we've been through. That hasn't occurred to you, has it? In terms of numbers, we have less than half the police officers in the United States for every thousand civilians. We're lightly policed compared to your so-called liberal democracies. And our history teaches us that we have to be constantly on alert for enemies within. We just see things differently, we do things differently and that's because we *are* different.'

'So 1949 still means a lot to you?'

'Of course. We call it *jiefang*, liberation.'

'Not everyone does, though. The Republic of China was the legitimate government at that time; your Communists were the rebels.'

Fang smiled. 'I know what you're getting at, Drew. Our KMT enemies refer to it as *lunxia*n, catastrophe. Just like the *Nakba*, the term used by Palestinians to describe how they were forcibly driven off their land by the Zionist colonists in '48. For Chinese counterrevolutionaries, the *shen zhou* or Chinese holy land, fell into the hands of *gongfei*: Communist thugs!'

*

Fang put her knife and fork together and dabbed at her mouth with the napkin.

'Are we done?'

She shook her head. 'I'm going to be reckless and order the tiramisu. I'll regret it when I step on the scales in the morning, but I don't want to think about that now.'

'I'm going to have a cappuccino.'

'Make it two.'

They waited in silence while their table was cleared of dishes and empty glasses.

'I've got something for you, Fang.' Brodick pulled a plastic folder out from under his shirt and t-shirt and pushed it over to her.

'I love surprises.' She pulled the file across the tabletop towards her but didn't open it.

'This probably isn't the place to read it now.'

'What is it?'

'First, a report on the recent Soviet naval exercise in the east Med. Operation OKEAN 84. They moved an AGI in from the Indian Ocean to join its sister ship from the Black Sea.'

'Circulation?'

'NATO navy chiefs, chiefs of staff, intelligence brass.'

'That's how many: three hundred?'

'Not a bad guess. Two hundred and thirty-four.'

'It'll be on Kremlin desks already, I should think. If not ours.'

'Probably; and before it reached its intended audience. But don't tell me you're not interested.'

'It's a start.' She shrugged. 'Classification?'

'Secret.'

'What else?'

'A Security Service briefing on developing a coherent British policy towards Hong Kong dissidents in the run-up to the handover, comments from other parties attached. Basically, how we should manage growing pro-democracy protests without unduly upsetting Beijing or provoking full-scale rebellion. I know there are talks underway this month.'

'British policy just isn't that important, or hadn't you noticed?' She grinned at him, but he didn't rise to it. 'You won't like this, but your precious United Kingdom is seen by our leadership at as a third rank country—and only because of the value we place on the research departments of your universities and your skills in media.'

'Our diplomatic and financial standing must count for something in Beijing, surely.'

Brodick can see amusement in her eyes. 'Maybe.'

'One country, two systems. Isn't that official policy on Hong Kong? As the report points out, our single battalion of Gurkhas could probably defend the British military headquarters there for all of fifteen minutes in the face of an all-out assault by the PLA.'

'If that, Drew. Five minutes seems more realistic.'

'Indeed.'

'You know our official line on Hong Kong, Macau and Taiwan, don't you? It's simply that the Chinese populations of these territories are very keen to be re-united with the People's Republic. Very enthusiastic. So enthusiastic they can barely wait. But it isn't true.'

'No?' What a surprise.

'They hate us. That's the truth. They like our money, but they hate us mainlanders. The Hong Kong people call us *qianggup ren*, the people of the strong country. It's not a compliment. They are mocking the man they call the Emperor for constantly saying we will be one of the world's strongest powers. That will be the problem, not your handful of colonial soldiers.'

Fang shifted, leaning towards him and dropping her voice. 'I need more, Richard. Sorry, Drew. To demonstrate to my people that you are genuine, by the next time we meet I will need a breakdown of the UK's order of battle in Cyprus: both GCHQ and SIS. Structure, procedures, names, personalities. Can you do that? And seeing that you know something about the Palestinian issue, would you be prepared to write around fifteen hundred to two thousand words on the future of Palestinian resistance? With a deadline in two weeks? You'll be paid for it.'

'Yes. I'll provide both, but I don't want payment.'

'I know that; it isn't the point, though, is it? My people will want to know you've taken the money and signed a receipt, so you'll have to take it. It's procedure. It will make them more comfortable knowing you've done so. It will help me, too.'

'No problem.'

'You've told your people that you've made contact with me, but no more than that?'

'As we agreed.' It was a lie, but Brodick thought it smoothly done.

'Did you pass on the report of the Iraqi missile delivery next week?'

'I did.'

'But not naming me as the source.'

'No. Just the port official. Again, we agreed to this.' Lie number two.

If the *Guoanbu* had an asset inside SIS he would soon know about it. It would be Brodick's version of a Barium meal.

'Now I have something far more important for you. I did say I would help you succeed in your career, didn't I?'

'You did.'

Fang had been sitting on a small manila envelope no bigger than a postcard and she shifted in her seat, pulled it out and placed it on the table alongside Brodick's offering.

'You wanted my bona fides. Here's the first part. It's the name of a senior intelligence officer of a NATO government who is working for us. Our mole. For *Guoanbu*. The Public Security Ministry as it was then turned him twelve years ago and we've run him in place ever since. I'm giving him to you. My gift to your SIS. I hope they appreciate what a prize you have for them. You'll deserve a promotion for this, surely. As you say in your country, with this you should go to the top of the class.'

Brodick tried and failed to keep the surprise and pleasure from showing. He didn't quite believe it. Nothing was ever that straightforward. He pulled the envelope towards him but stopped short of opening it. 'It's genuine? He's still in play?'

His heart was pounding away. This would bump him up the SIS ranks and no mistake.

'Oh, yes. Still working for us. Very much so. Would I lie to you?'

Fang was indeed ruthless, but at least they were on the same side.

Temporarily.

'Would you lie to me, Fang? You would, yes.'

Fang smiled and reached across the table and touched Brodick's hand. He was instantly aroused at the fleeting contact.

Brodick examined the contents of the envelope. 'There's just a piece of paper and a name. That's all.'

'What did you expect? A complete history? An encyclopaedia?'

'I'll need some background.'

'You can find that out yourself, Richard. Or your people can. They'll figure it out.'

'If you keep calling me Richard and not Drew I will start calling you Meilin or Pusheng instead of Fang and I know you wouldn't like that.'

Brodick was going to ask her to complete her bona fides by supplying a diagram of the *Guoanbu's* organisation, along with its bureaux and the names of all its senior officials, but it would have to wait. They'd both fallen silent because the tiramisu and the two coffees had arrived.

24

It is the last in Len's series of talks on Chinese intelligence.

He urges them to follow him outside. 'It's a beautiful day; let's not waste it. We could all do with some sun. Come on, guys…'

He suggests they should make themselves comfortable on the walls of Fort Monckton, massive structures built to withstand a naval bombardment and broken by embrasures for the big guns that had guarded the seaward approaches, but which have long since been removed. So the students sit on the edge in a row, feet dangling, hands raised to shield their eyes as they squint out at the shimmering estuary beyond.

'As Westerners, you probably make a sharp distinction, if only unconsciously, between gathering secret intelligence as intelligence professionals, and the collection of information from open sources. You may despise the latter, but that would be most unwise. The People's Republic of China makes no such distinction. It's all one and the same. You can view the Chinese intelligence effort as a vast, high powered state-sponsored vacuum cleaner scooping up everything it can get hold of and, believe me, it's a great deal and it's worth billions to the Chinese economy.'

Lennie squats down alongside his listeners, unwrapping a ham and cheese sandwich from Marks & Spencer. 'Forgive me—I haven't had breakfast and I can't wait for lunch.' It's already noon and warm as only an English summer day can be, but it doesn't seem to effect Len's appetite.

'So, if you take the 40,000 mainland Chinese students in the United States right now, you can imagine that a substantial number have been asked to do their patriotic duty. Nothing wrong with that, you say. Nothing wrong with taking photographs - photographs of power stations, nuclear reactors, naval shipyards, air force bases, research institutes as well as snapshots of their fellow Chinese students and their professors. It's not strictly illegal for the most part. What does break the law is so minor that in most cases U.S. officials don't want to know because to them it's just a nuisance. What you might not know is that this vast amount of apparently innocuous information—much of it in the form of images snapped by Chinese residents, tourists and students alike—finds its way back home and forms a gigantic crossword puzzle. It's examined, collated and analysed. To the *Gouanbo* and PLA2, everything is of potential use. Nothing goes to waste.

'Add to that scores of postgraduate Chinese who apply for permanent residence each year, the academics who gain access to western research institutes plus the activities of so-called diplomats and you have a truly massive intelligence effort. I have to say, though, that in all honesty Chinese intelligence is no better than the Chinese state itself. It is extremely bureaucratic. It is cumbersome. It is riddled with rules and tier upon tier of committees, often in competition with one another. Political commissars are very successful at stifling initiative and instilling fear. And yes, it is fractious. And yes, there is corruption.

'When I jumped into a taxi onetime in Beijing, the driver turned me and said: Line up one hundred policemen against a wall and machinegun them to death. You might—just might—kill one innocent man.

'Supermen and Wonderwomen they are not.

'Their intelligent services are far from perfect. But the *Guoanbu* is relatively de-politicised. Its intelligence chiefs are patient and professional and they take the long view. The number of operations is such that even if they do involve poor planning and poor operational security—and they do more often than not if you follow the large number of arrests by the FBI in the States—the sheer scale of it has to be overwhelming for our security services.

'My point is that our narrow, traditional categories of espionage don't really count for much when compared to China and its intelligence establishment. We have much to learn from them. A PRC dictionary defines intelligence or *qingbao* as: "investigative and other methods to collect confidential information on military, political, economic, scientific, and various aspects of the other side". Now that's pretty broad, I think you'll agree.

'If I had to invent a slogan for Chinese intelligence, it would be "everyone spies". Or maybe "the everyman spies".'

So ends the final talk on Chinese spooks.

25

Maha was beautiful. There was no other word for it. She was probably older than Brodick, exactly how old he had no idea, in her mid- to late forties possibly, and she had grey streaks in her dark hair; but none of that mattered. She had always been beautiful, that was obvious, and she would still be beautiful when very old. It was just the way she was. Brodick could see in his mind's eye what she must have been like as a child and what she would look like when frail. The beauty was herself, not her age or even her wonderful bone structure. She was no doubt born that way. It must have been in her genes. It was something in her smile, her eyes, her complexion, her warmth. She seemed to exude humanity, generosity. An inner sense of happiness that not even a low wage and a vicious sectarian war and foreign occupation could demolish; she was funny, talkative, sensuous, hospitable, curvaceous, informal and a great cook. Her laughter would start as a deep crackle like kindling, then roll out of her in great gusts of merriment while she rocked back and forth unabashed, unrestrained.

Greek Orthodox in origin, divorced and recently disappointed in a love affair with an Italian helicopter pilot working for the UN, who'd reportedly gone back to his family in Milan at the end of his Lebanon tour without even saying goodbye. Maha lived in a tiny flat—located in a partially bombed-out building in Mreisse, accessible across a couple of planks laid over the chasm of a bomb crater and across a pile of litter-strewn rubble and through a hole in the back wall—with her fifteen-year-old daughter.

Maha was senior travel agent at Levant, but that was just a means to an end, for Maha was an artist and the pittance she earned at Levant kept her—and her daughter—fed and clothed with just enough left over—it wouldn't suffice for much longer—for canvasses, stretchers and paint. Her abstracts were all over the walls.

She had won a national award as travel agent of the year; the year being 1975 when the war erupted, sparked that April by the slaughter of a busload of Palestinians, ambushed by Phalangist gunmen. Brodick gathered she was a leftist: a supporter of the small but intellectually vigorous and mostly Christian Syrian Nationalist Social Party or SNSP, which espoused a Greater Syria that would, if it had its way, incorporate Lebanon.

There was always food—and drink—and there were always guests.

Including Brodick, who was, technically at least, her boss; and that made for an awkwardness between them, but it couldn't be helped and Brodick wasn't sure if he could or should do something about it to make things easier between them. He felt he had to keep his distance. The urge he always had when they met to put his arm around her, to ask her out: that simply wasn't something he could allow himself. It would be an abuse of his authority, something Fawzi would pick up on immediately, and it would find its way to Fenner in Nicosia and thence to Century House in South London. At the very least, it would embarrass everyone involved, including Maha.

Brodick always brought food and wine when visiting and ensured that at least one of Maha's colleagues was present, in this instance Patrick, a bespectacled Maronite in his twenties whose two passions were photography and his communist faith.

'Did you notice anything on the way here?' Maha's question seemed directed at both men. 'Didn't you notice how quiet it is today? The guns are silent. It's eery. It makes me feel anxious. Even the Israelis aren't paying us their usual visit by flying over our heads.'

'We're so used to it,' Patrick said, turning to Brodick, 'that we feel uncomfortable when we don't hear gunfire. After nine years of it, we're all neurotic. If it's quiet we worry about whatever happens next instead of enjoying the few moments of peace.'

Brodick understood only too well. 'It wakes me up when I *don't* hear it.'

Maha turned to Brodick. 'I called, like you asked. The man you're interested in finding isn't registered as Li but as Lee, double e, same goes for his passport: Canadian as you said.'

'But you found him.'

'Li Zuanfei or Tony Lee is at the Summerland Hotel. Sorry if I didn't pronounce the name right. Room 428. Odd choice of hotel, but I guess it's safe as anywhere else in the city while Amal is still in control of its security.'

'Rather too close to the refugee camps, though.' Brodick meant the Sabra and Shatila camps as well as Bourj Barajneh. That was where the recent fighting had been, on the city's southern periphery. The Summerland was a sprawling, five-star hotel right on the coast and it was all but empty thanks to the war and its unfortunate location. Whoever had built it had decided sensibly enough that proximity to the airport and seashore would make good commercial sense. But few could have foreseen the war, the invasion, the Shi'ites pushing out the Christians from the southern suburbs, the fighting between right-wing Christians and leftist Palestinians, between Israelis and Palestinians, between Israelis and Shi'ites, between Shi'ites and Christians, between Shi'ites and Palestinians and between Shi'ites and Shi'ites and the Druze against pretty much everyone else. Especially the Maronites, a feud that went back to the 1860s thanks to the British and French.

It turned out to have been the worst possible place to build a hotel.

'You can call him.'

'I will. Many thanks, Maha. I'm grateful for all the effort.'

'We don't have much to do at work, so we're always happy to help out. Don't hesitate to ask if there's anything else I or Patrick can do.'

Brodick hadn't said why he wanted to find Li, and neither Maha nor Patrick had asked. Perhaps that should tell him something; that they knew, or suspected, that he was no ordinary travel executive and administrator, but something more and also a lot less. Brodick wondered how much Farid or his dad Fawzi had shared with the staff. Not that there was much Brodick could do about it.

They lounged or sat cross-legged on cushions scattered around the little sitting room. They'd taken their shoes off at the entrance. Despite the chaos outside and the crowded furnishings and paintings inside, the place was spotless. There was a low, light blue sofa, and the big cushions everywhere. It was a place for relaxation, for informal gatherings, for listening to music, for puffing on a water pipe, for avid conversation.

'I asked around,' added Patrick. 'He's here for some AUB academic conference. I think the university booked him in there. Li or Lee—however you spell it—likes Beirut nightlife, apparently. There's not much of that at the Summerland so he takes a taxi into the city.'

'What's he looking for? Female company?'

'How did you guess? He especially likes wine, women and song.' Maha laughed as she said it. She had a forgiving nature.

'Doesn't everyone?' Patrick glanced from Maha to Brodick.

'Speak for yourself.' Maha shook her head in mock disapproval.

They were sharing what Maha had called a light lunch, to which Brodick had contributed a bottle of Arak and the dessert. It had started around noon and would continue until sunset if not much later, until the food or the guests ran out. There were bowls of fattoush, hummus, falafel, tabbouleh, baba ghanoush, a pile of hot pitta bread. Brodick was already very partial to mezze: especially his own contribution in the form of the very sweet, sticky and rich dessert, baklava, from West Beirut's best patisserie.

If Brodick felt at home and relaxed anywhere, it was here. He wasn't being judged and nothing was expected of him. He could be himself.

'He's certainly into wine and women; I'm not so sure about the song,' Patrick said.

Maha turned to Patrick. 'The music at *Backstreet* is pretty good. At least I think so.'

'What's the *Backstreet*?'

'You don't know it, Drew?'

At least they were on first name terms now.

'No. Tell me.'

Patrick was the one with recent experience. 'It's a pub or nightclub. I go there once a week or so. It opens around 9pm, but only gets going late, after midnight, and it closes when the last customers leave, usually around three or four in the morning.'

'I like it,' Maha said. 'It's fun. They always have the latest hits. Not that I've been for ages and I don't have the stamina for these all-night venues.'

Patrick frowned at Brodick. 'I can't believe you haven't been there yet.'

'I go to bed at nine every night with a cup of hot milk.'

Maha chuckled. 'You don't really expect us to believe that, do you?'

Patrick shook his head. 'You sure don't go to bed with just hot milk, boss.'

'It's true. I'm too scared to go out after dark and I'm too old and jaded for nightclubs.'

Patrick was still shaking his head in disbelief or pity.

'You're not married.' Maha made it sound more like an accusation than question.

'No, I'm not. Not anymore.'

'Then you've no excuse,' Patrick added. Maha nodded. She agreed with Patrick.

Brodick did indeed go to bed early, very early, but he had trouble sleeping. He would drop off around eleven and then wake up again around three hours later, then doze at five or six. He tried going to bed much later. That didn't work, either. Either way, his nights left him feeling exhausted. It wasn't the gunfire. He didn't know what it was. Only the previous night he'd wandered around his cavernous flat in the dark, barefoot, in his boxer shorts and, unable to sleep, had discovered that day's copy of *L'Orient Le Jour*. So he'd put on the spotlights and at 3am sat down at the dining table and gone through it, struggling with his schoolboy French, and discovered that the *Basra Star* was expected to dock in Jounieh on Monday night at 20.00 hours.

'*Backstreet*'s close to where you live,' said Maha. 'Just beyond the end of Bliss Street.'

'You could walk it easily, ten or fifteen minutes, though I wouldn't advise it so late.'

'I'll find him there?'

'Most nights,' said Patrick. Or that jazz place…'

Maha shook her wavy hair away from her face. '*Blue Note*, you mean?'

'That's the one. I'm sure you must know it, Drew. The *Blue Note*. Small place, most of the customers are foreigners of the older type, lecturers from the AUB and guys from the UNHCR. And a few crazy Lebanese into jazz. That's also within walking distance.'

He'd never heard of it.

Patrick laughed in a way that said he didn't believe in Brodick's claim of a monastic lifestyle.

'Have you met Abrielle yet?'

'Who's Abrielle?'

'She goes to both places. She's a television reporter and books her flights through us. Abrielle is very sociable; she goes out almost every night to a party or club. I'm sure you two would get along.'

Maha raised her eyebrows, but it wasn't a question, more like giving Patrick what seemed to Brodick to be a warning look, as if to say "don't".

Patrick was undeterred. 'Petite, very chic. French-speaking. Her dad does business with Syria. You've not met? No?'

'No.'

Maha was shaking her head.

'Don't encourage the boss to walk anywhere day or night,'

Maha told Patrick. 'Or he'll spend the next five years in a basement chained to a radiator and I'll blame you if that happens. I'm not sure your friend Abrielle is worth it. I'm not sure anyone is worth it.'

As for Brodick, he felt he had Li Zuanfei almost in his sights.

26

'The Chinese lady's got a single room at the Mayfair. Small, quiet place; just a couple of minutes' walk from Hamra. Checked in a week ago but, according to reception, she's not there often. Comes and goes. Spends the night only occasionally and when she does, she arrives very late, after midnight, and leaves again really early without breakfast. Sometimes she uses her room simply to change her outfits.' Farid plucked at the cuffs of his long-sleeved shirt, perhaps irritated by it. He'd already loosened his tie and collar. He and Brodick were sitting in the otherwise deserted general office of Levant Travel, drinking coffee. Farid had come in to report to Brodick and to collect his week's payment.

'The Mayfair's not far from here. Thanks Farid.'

'She has these two Chinese guys with her when she's out and about. At least, I assume they're Chinese. I guess they're her bodyguards.'

Brodick waited.

'They take turns driving her. The one not driving sits up front and our Chinese lady sits in the back. The two of them seem to work out of the embassy, but I don't know where they live unless the embassy itself has rooms for staff. They don't stay with her at the Mayfair or at the Bellevue apartment. Sometimes they have two cars, and she changes from one to the other. They also seem change their routes pretty much every day.'

'Just as I do; as all foreigners should.'

'My dad says hi and hopes you like your apartment.'

'Thanks, Farid. Tell your dad I really love it. Are they armed?'

'Armed—as in carrying guns?'

'That's right, that's what I meant.'

'Not that I saw, but maybe… you know, tucked under the shirts or jackets.'

Farid was only part-time, and it was inevitable that his observation of Fang would be patchy and incomplete. Aside from that, he wasn't trained in surveillance and he wouldn't notice that carrying a firearm changed the way someone moves.

'They behave like guards, walking ahead and behind, you know, kinda checking out places she's going into.'

'Any unusual destinations?'

'She went to the north two days ago, taking both her people and the two cars.'

'And?'

'She saw Franjieh.'

'Did she indeed? Father or grandson?'

'The old man, yeah. At the family home in Zghorta. You know where it is, I think.'

'But you don't know what was discussed.'

'How could I? I just drove past a couple of times. The old man welcomed her in person with his grandson next to him. They stood out on the steps to welcome her. I saw them. The Chinese guys waited outside, and the staff brought them coffee and what looked biscuits or cake.'

'Did she stay in Zghorta or return the same day?'

'She came back. To the Bellevue.'

'Did she or her escort make you, do you think?'

'Make me?'

'Did they see you? Recognise you?'

'Don't think so, chief. I stayed well back. It wasn't necessary to keep them in view all the time.'

'And the cars?'

'A Merc—the same cream 280 SE—and a Volvo. Neither of them new.'

'Diplomatic plates?'

'Lebanese civilian registrations. They weren't taxis: they didn't have red plates.'

'She signed in at the Mayfair Hotel under what name?'

Farid shrugged.

'Can you find out? Maybe photograph it or copy it? I need the date. Slip one of the receptionists a few lira and ask him or her to do it for you—could you do that?'

*

By all accounts Zghorta was an attractive town surrounded by snow-capped mountains. Clean, crystal clear air, it was said; so different from the smog and heat of Beirut. The summers were warm but not unbearably muggy, and the winters cold but dry with frequent snowfall. It was on Brodick's wish list of places to visit. Maha had said in passing that the far north of the country was known for its great food, for being a beautiful landscape populated by hardy villagers; mostly Maronite Christians, highlanders who were fiercely independent, often violent and clannish but also hospitable and loyal.

She said motorists had to navigate their way through no fewer than eleven checkpoints en-route: Army, PSP, Phalangist, two more Army outposts, two more Phalange, two Syrian—though she wasn't certain about what she said was a growing Syrian military presence—and the remaining three manned by the Franjieh clan's Marada militia.

Suleiman Franjieh, born in 1910, personified the northern type, apparently.

Maha said his name meant "occidental". No doubt the family would have rejected the label "Arab" and insisted instead they were Phoenician. Nothing like an imagined ethnic identity to fire up the militant imagination and fuel sectarian bloodshed.

Suleiman had come to prominence—if it could be called that—in 1957 when implicated in the murders of clan rivals, and he'd fled to Syria and the protective embrace of President Hafez al-Assad.

Matters came to a head in 1976—a year after the civil war erupted—when Franjieh was reported to have invited Syrian troops into Lebanon in support of the Christian Maronites, the country's politically dominant community, against Palestinians and Lebanese leftists.

Maha was clearly no fan.

What could Fang have had to say to the white-haired old brigand in his Savile Row suit and handmade brogues? What interest could the elderly Franjieh senior have in a young but senior Chinese communist intelligence officer?

*

'Did you see this?'

Farid offered Brodick a copy of *an-Nahar*, but Brodick's Arabic wasn't up to it.

'Tell me.'

'As soon as there's a lull in fighting, the criminals and gangsters come out of the woodwork.'

'Really? I thought they were the ones running things these days. They're called politicians.'

Farid didn't find it funny.

'I'll translate, Mr Drew: the latest trick here in Beirut, the Western sector in particular, is that gunmen visit private homes, holding up bunches of flowers so the residents are persuaded it's a friendly visitor and safe to open their doors. Then the gangsters push their way in and take everything worth stealing: televisions, jewellery, cash. So far, police say, these gangs have netted the equivalent of millions of dollars, killing two and wounding seven other residents who made the mistake of resisting. They only target the wealthiest neighbourhoods.'

'I'm safe. I don't think anyone's going to bring me flowers any time soon.'

'Well, look on the bright side, Mr Drew. The airport opened

again today.'

Now that was news. Would Fenner fly in to meet him to discuss Brodick's imminent report of a mole inside a Western government? Brodick thought it unlikely. Fenner was not a man to put himself in harm's way.

*

After Farid left, with considerably more cash in his pocket than when he'd arrived, Brodick locked himself in his office and dragged out TITHE, setting it up on his little desk. There wasn't much for him to see and it hardly seemed worth the trouble. There were indeed the acknowledgements he had expected—all "signed" by Fenner's personal call sign: 037495NS—in response to Brodick's double encrypted signals. There was Brodick's very brief report of having made initial contact with Fang, then another, equally succinct report that Fang seemed receptive to further meetings and hadn't recoiled from a recruitment pitch. Again, Fenner had acknowledged receipt of the report by diplomatic bag on the impending supply by Iraq of anti-shipping missiles into the hands of the Lebanese Army and Phalange. No comments or questions, nothing to add. Just the acknowledgements—each of which involved hitting a single letter and which the Firm termed automated receipts—and it was all that Brodick expected at this juncture. At least the system was working. Now it was time to let Fenner know about the alleged mole. No name, of course, not yet. No identification of country or government. Simply that the source was DRAGON, that it was urgent and the message double-encrypted, for Fenner's eyes only.

URGENT PRELATE PRO 037495NS.
DRAGON reports identity of NATO member state's senior intel officer said to have worked for PRC for 12 years. Guoanbu mole allegedly still in place.

That should shake sleepy Nicosia Station out of its semi-permanent doze along with Brodick's negroni-loving, Hawaiian shirt-wearing case officer and possibly the duty officer at Century House in Southwark as well. Brodick could well imagine Fenner complaining with some bitterness that his weekend had been needlessly interrupted, and that Brodick could have done the decent thing and waited until Monday.

All done, Brodick locked everything away, checked he'd left nothing lying around and started to leave. He realised as he went down the stairs to the ground floor and out onto the street, nodding to the male receptionist, that he felt the pang of loneliness, the lack of company. He was indeed lonely, that empty sense of something or someone missing, a void. Not that he needed intimacy so much; he missed the company of other humans in general, the background chatter, the laughter and clink of glasses in mixed company, the relaxation of engaging in small talk with strangers. What he really wanted—as he climbed into the back of a *service* taxi—was to perch on a barstool in a crowded restaurant, bar or club with a double whisky in his fist, one forearm on the bar top keeping him steady as he drank. One of the gratifying aspects of going out in Lebanon in the evening—or indeed at any time—was the habit of the city's bar tenders to pour huge drams. Forget the measly British tot. In Beirut, they served doubles, even triples, as standard measures.

It was Saturday, after all. The lull in fighting seemed to be holding. There was no better opportunity to try out the nightclub mentioned by Maha.

Both women intrigued him. Maha was the loving, companionable sort, a good friend, someone of great warmth and generosity of spirit who would always make a man feel good about himself; affectionate, gregarious, kind and sensual yet with ample empathy and the sensitivity to accurately assess her lover's needs—or so he imagined. She would be smart enough to hold her own in any company, but it was her emotional intelligence and her ebullient sense of humour that attracted him most.

Maha would no doubt make a wonderful wife and mother.

Fang could not be more different. Like her predilection for red and black, she represented extreme danger: physical and emotional. An existential danger, then, and the danger of risky opportunity, too. She was as tough and disciplined as they came, obviously. She didn't show emotion if she could possibly help it, and she usually could. She was power. She was control. She liked to dominate. She was the female equivalent of an Alpha male. In fact, Brodick thought she seemed to embody the masculine traits of giving nothing away, of keeping emotions out of her work, of being rational and quite cold in her ruthless drive to achieve whatever it was she was pursuing: presumably one of the top jobs in the *Guoanbu*. Would the Chinese contemplate a female director-general or intelligence minister? Perhaps DRAGON would be the first woman to rise to the very top of Communist China's reformed intelligence apparatus. For his part, it would be all too easy to become hopelessly infatuated, as if drawn inexorably into the jaws of an Orinoco crocodile. Her bite would be more than fatal. She would swallow him whole. Brodick told himself he should never forget that she was an enemy intelligence officer.

A United Nations helicopter pilot might have left Maha, the shit, but no-one would be permitted to leave Fang without her say-so, at least not while still alive.

Brodick was fascinated when he knew he should be repelled.

He showered, shaved, pulled on a clean, lightly starched white shirt.

He was looking forward to seeing her; it was a powerful fascination that he knew could be addictive. Maybe she knew, too, and was counting on it.

27

All at once, the training is over and done with.

It seems such an anti-climax. There is no farewell dinner, not so much as a few jolly pints in the pub along with their instructors, sharing in the newly qualified officers' sense of accomplishment. Even Fort Monckton's commandant is absent - he's on an official visit to the Federal Republic, apparently. Brodick can't help feeling disappointed that after all their efforts, there are no speeches or certificates, no pat on the back. He reminds himself this isn't Sandhurst; there is no march-past, no ceremony, no medals, no presentation made to the best of them. After a shower and dressing for the final supper of cottage pie and two veg followed by a rather idiosyncratic variant of tiramisu, Brodick just happens to peer out of the window and sees, through drifting rain, one of the Fort's anonymous Ford saloons drive into the compound and stop right outside their building. The driver, a woman in a blue MoD uniform and peaked cap, gets out and opens an umbrella as two people dash out into the downpour and splash through the puddles with their suitcases.

As they struggle with the boot, Brodick recognises Paula Lubnaig, the Latin languages specialist, and Harry Wood, the maths whiz kid. He reckons they must have planes or trains to catch. They hadn't mentioned their early departures and said no goodbyes.

Three more slip away overnight, for next morning at breakfast, the very last meal, five chairs are empty.

Nobody speaks. The remaining officers eat quickly, glancing at one another without a word and without interest. Already they seem to be strangers. To Brodick, everyone seems to have wrapped himself or herself in a protective veil of anonymity. They have entered the secret world and now there's no going back.

28

Brodick set out shortly before midnight, keeping to pools of shadow like stepping stones thrown by the streetlights, weaving through a line of pollarded trees on the pavement. Brodick tried to be as inconspicuous as possible as he headed to the lights of Bliss Street. Close to the university, it was a late-night student hangout, mostly, with kids in t-shirts and jeans gathered around the juice bars and shops selling falafel and shwarma sandwiches.

Like everyone else, Brodick had heard the rumours: that Islamic Jihad was edging its way into West Beirut, street by street, block by block, pushing in from the southern suburbs and driving out the Shi'ite fighters of the rival Amal militia and, in the process, spoiling everyone's the fun by ordering pubs and clubs to shut. Those owners who refused to comply had their windows smashed, along with their stocks of liquor. Not unnaturally people with the means to do so were more determined than ever to make the most of these tranquil interludes before violence returned and Shariah was imposed on the neighbourhood by force. Many "westies" who could afford it spent their weekends in the eastern sector; and not just Christians, but Moslems too went across, because it was seen as safer, and the mostly Christian territory under Army and Phalangist control was far more extensive, with a greater choice of places to go to have fun. In the hot weather, the mountain resorts were especially attractive.

He slowed, paused, stopped, moved again, only more slowly, creeping along, head down, hands in pockets. He felt he was being watched. He didn't turn or make any obvious attempts to identify any tag he might have picked up, but it was an unmistakable sense that made the hair rise on the back of his neck.

It was just a feeling, albeit very strong, his in-built alarm screeching loudly.

He bent down, attended to a shoelace. A couple of minutes later he stopped to peer at his wristwatch. He stopped yet again a little further on as if searching his pockets.

He found himself in a quiet, dark and cobbled alley and he had to hold himself back from breaking into a run. It was scary and definitely not somewhere a foreigner should ever find himself alone and at night. For a moment Brodick thought he'd made a mistake and lost his way. Finally he saw what he was looking for. The Backstreet was almost invisible and it wasn't until he was right outside that he saw the small blue neon sign oddly lopsided above the door, which was ajar. He glimpsed the light and heard—or rather felt—the beat of the music.

An enormous man—both tall and immensely broad, with a full beard—stood in the entrance and smiled at Brodick, then stood to one side to let him squeeze past, watching him carefully as if sizing him up. Brodick expected to be searched, but it didn't happen. Maybe it was obvious to the bouncer that Brodick wasn't carrying, or maybe it was because he was so obviously a foreigner. Most of the time, when they weren't being kidnapped or assassinated, Westerners were given the benefit of the doubt.

The music was too loud for either of them to say anything.

The place seemed full, but it was not yet overcrowded. Almost immediately Brodick and Patrick spotted each other across the pub, raising hands in salute, Patrick in the far left-hand corner beckoning him over. Brodick nodded and smiled, but took his time navigating his way among the tables, looking about him, checking faces and careful not to bump into anyone. At this relatively early stage of the proceedings, the music was fairly low key. The Thompson Twins were finishing *"Hold Me Now"* and this was replaced by a Julio Inglesias and Willie Nelson duet *"To All the Girls I've Loved"*: if he wasn't mistaken, both of them current hits.

The bar was over on the right, where the pub's famous barman Habib held sway, not merely serving up his cocktails but keeping his customers amused with a stream of jokes in Arabic, French and English. Brodick knew they were jokes from the way those seated at the bar rocked back and forth, and exploded in salvoes of laughter.

'So you came, Mr Drew!' Patrick was on his feet, a broad grin on his stubbled face, clearly pleased to see Brodick. He had to shout to make himself heard.

Someone cleared a pile of bags off a chair for him, but he remained standing.

Patrick made the introductions. 'I'd like to introduce you to my friends. This is Zahla, AUB fine arts postgrad, her boyfriend Malek who's big in advertising, right Malek? And this is the person I was telling you about, remember? Mr Drew, this is Abrielle, an old friend of mine. She works in television. A famous reporter. Famous in Lebanon, anyway. Abrielle, this is Drew Sullivan, my brand-new boss.'

Brodick indicated he would head for the bar to buy a drink and asked—a flurry of hand signals, raised eyebrows, smiles and a pointed finger—whether he could get drinks for anyone else. Patrick's friends shook their heads or put up the palms of their hands; all except Abrielle, who stood up, nodded, and joined him.

'I'd like a drink; I'll come with you.'

She took his arm as they made their way over to Habib.

'You're new to Beirut, then. Are you British?'

He watched her out of the corner of his eye as they waited for their drinks. Abrielle was indeed petite: the top of her head was level with Brodick's chin. She wore her hair in a smart bob, there were gold bracelets on her right arm, a gold cross gleamed at her throat and gold earrings winked at him, all this finery set off by a closely fitting and backless black dress and glossy patent black heels with straps over the top of her small feet. On her right wrist there was a Cartier watch, no doubt genuine. She wore lots of mascara in a manner that reminded Brodick of the country's most famous singer, Fairuz.

'I'm not like other girls, Drew.' She sipped her martini, looking up at him. 'Are you married?'

Brodick shook his head.

'You know people have been talking about you; I've been looking forward to meeting you.'

Brodick felt uneasy. Why would anyone want to meet him or talk about him?

'Please, don't be offended. Patrick is glad to be able to show you off to his friends. Gossip is our chief amusement, Drew, especially when there's a new foreigner in town to talk about. There isn't much else to do. Don't worry. It won't last long, a few days at the most. Then you'll be yesterday's news like everyone else.'

'I'm glad I'm providing you with some distraction.'

He was rewarded with a smile, slightly mocking. 'Which hotel you stay?'

Another shake of the head from a puzzled Brodick.

'You have apartment already?

'I do, yes.'

'Wow. I'm surprised; that was fast. You've only just arrived, no? Two weeks ago, yes? That's very good.'

Good? In what sense?

'Alone? You live alone?'

'Yes.' This was some interrogation, but he wasn't really thinking about that or anything else. He was drowning in her scent, the sight of her pale and flawless skin, the silkiness of her hair, her shape, her lips, her hand on him, her movement.

Instead of heading back to her friends, Abrielle drew him away. 'Up there. Come. We can talk. If you don't mind.' There was a spiral iron staircase and an upper floor, which Brodick knew would be even hotter, and up there near the ceiling the cloud of cigarette smoke would be a dense fog. But he wasn't about to argue. He was intrigued. And she was right: it might be quiet enough to talk. He followed her, trying not to stare at her embonpoint figure.

They had no sooner settled at a vacant table at the edge of what amounted to a mezzanine platform, when Abrielle declared she wanted to dance right there, next to their table, to *"Here Comes the Rain Again"* by the Eurythmics. Her hands were light, her figure moving close. Abrielle excited Brodick, and she knew it. Her hips brushed against him.

When they sat again and picked up their drinks - Brodick had a very strong gin and tonic—it seemed to be all gin and only a splash of tonic—and he was trying to take it slowly, in small sips, because he could feel it kick in on his empty stomach.

'What did you mean when you said you weren't like other women?'

She smiled at him, leaning in closer so that he breathed in a lungful of her Opium. 'I don't do dates, Drew, so please, I beg you: don't ask me out. I don't like presents of flowers or chocolate. No presents at all. Really. I don't want a boyfriend or a husband. I don't want romance, or love, whatever you want to call it. I don't like games. I don't want to go with you or any other man to restaurants or to the cinema. It's so *boring*.'

'If you say so.' He was surprised, intrigued.

'I like my life, Drew, you understand? I like my freedom and I don't want to give it up. I like to control things and that freedom doesn't include being one half of a couple.'

She looked him in the face, watching his reaction. Brodick made sure there wasn't one.

'So you're happy in West Beirut?'

'Why not?' She shrugged. 'It's my home, not so? I have good job: a great job. My family is here. I have friends. Why would I want that to change?'

It was said defiantly, as if daring him to argue.

'What family do you have?'

Family was something he realised she didn't want to talk about, but Abrielle went along with it out of politeness, to humour him, as the Rolling Stones started up *"Undercover of the Night"*. It wasn't one of Brodick's favourites. 'My mum. My dad. My two sisters and my brother.'

'You're Christian, not Moslem.'

'Maronite Christian, Drew. Not everyone in West Beirut is Moslem or Greek Orthodox.'

'I get that. But why stay in a war zone?'

'Because it's our home. Maybe we will move soon—to France. If it gets worse. My mother is half French. We speak French at home, not Arabic, though I speak Arabic in my work. We have a house there, in a village on the edge of Paris. perhaps you know it: Verneuil l'Etang?'

'I don't, no. You should go; it would be so much safer.'

'But I like it here; in fact I love Beirut. There is nowhere like it. My work is here. Same with my dad. The war is a kind of freedom to some people. I guess you haven't heard that before; but then you haven't been here long enough to find out much, have you?'

He ignored the question. 'What does he do, your dad?'

She shrugged as if to say it was unimportant. Then she hesitated before answering, looking around as if she was worried about being overheard, though there was no chance of that. 'He is a financier.'

A Maronite banker in West Beirut? To Brodick that sounded odd, but it was probably best not to inquire further. Offshore funds accumulated from what - warlords and their illegal taxes, drugs, guns? Both? He shouldn't judge: the City of London was no better.

'You should go, Abrielle.'

'Really? Should I?' That's why I don't want boyfriend or husband telling me where I should live or how I should live.' Abrielle was quick to anger.

'Apologies. I didn't mean to—'

She smiled at him, not for the first time that evening, showing her very white, very even teeth. She squeezed his arm to let him know she wasn't serious, that she didn't mind his paternalist advice, not much anyway, and that she wasn't going to take it. She'd drawn a line, it seemed to Brodick, and all was fine so long as he didn't try to cross it. She'd told him her rules and it was up to him if he wanted to see her again.

They danced again, this time to a Bruce Springstein number.

Who was she really working for?

Not for one moment did he take her strong come-on at face value.

Abrielle drew Brodick's attention to Habib behind the bar on the ground floor. 'You see? He's smart, Habib, don't you think? He just gave away a bottle of champagne to that fat Lebanese guy and his X-ray girlfriend. Now all those other Lebanese are ordering champagne, too. Look at all the bottles. Oh, he's opening another. Krug this time. There's a kind of Lebanese male with money who likes to show off in front of his mistress, so Habib—look he's getting another bottle out of the cooler—Bollinger—and he will sell ten or fifteen bottles for each one he gives away. He picks the ones with money: bald, fat and insecure, with women who are not their wives. I think you have an expression: surgically enhanced in the company of men who can't get it up without pharmaceutical help. Habib picks them carefully, and their fat wallets and competitive spirit do the rest.'

'You're very cynical.'

'I'm not stupid, my dear. If one is not stupid, then one cannot be anything *but* cynical. I am Lebanese and my precious Lebanon is destroying itself and it makes me sick.'

The place was packed now, and heaving with dancers pressed together. It was also getting a lot hotter and smokier. Because it was so packed, some women had kicked off their shoes and had climbed onto the tables to dance. The music was louder, too.

Abrielle seemed to know what Brodick was thinking. She pulled his head down with one hand and spoke into his ear. 'You see, when there's a lot of shooting outside, Habib just turns the music up loud so we can't hear it. That's why people love to come here: they feel safer even if they're not. We all have our illusions that make us feel better, and making ourselves feel better and safer is the only game we have left to play here in Beirut. It's our game of pretence, and everyone likes to forget the risks at least for a few hours.'

She was dancing right up against him, her hips pushing into his groin with inevitable results.

'Can I get you another drink, Abrielle?'

'Not now.' This time when they sat down, she leaned her forearm on his thigh while reaching down for her cigarettes in her purse, and then, once she'd lit her cigarette, placed a hand on his upper thigh. Her fingers soon strayed lightly—unmistakably—fluttering over his trousers, feeling him erect. She pressed down and smiled into his face. She could reassure herself he would not need any pharmaceutical assistance, at least not in that department.

Mossad? The Agency? The Centre? She could be working for anyone. Given her French connection it could well be *la Piscine* as the DGSE was known, for the agency's headquarters on Boulevard Mortier and its proximity to the municipal swimming pool.

'Give me your phone number,' she said. It sounded like a command. 'And I will call you and ask if you would like to watch a video. You like films? Yes? You have video player? Then I will bring video cassette. Maybe in the afternoon. Early evening. Or very late. Sometimes in the morning. Okay? I will choose the film.'

Brodick found one of his Levant Travel business cards and gave it to her. As Duran Duran's *"The Reflex"* started up, he looked over Abrielle's shoulder and saw Patrick watching them from the floor below, a grin on his face. Patrick caught his eye and gave a thumbs up. Brodick reflected on the fact that Beirut's western sector was small, socially speaking. Everyone in what passed for the middle class knew everyone else. It wouldn't be long at all before his flirtation with Abrielle was all over Levant Travel and beyond. As long as she wasn't working for another intelligence service and was what she said she was: a local television reporter.

Her behaviour surely didn't seem conventional. He'd heard it said at one of Maha's lunches that the Lebanese lived as if every day might be their last, that there was something frenetic in their enjoyment of the moment. But it was also entirely possible Abrielle had another agenda, that it wasn't Brodick she was after at all, that she saw him merely as a way of gaining access to Li Zuanfei or even

Fang. Or maybe she simply wanted to know what Brodick himself was up to; but if this was so, on whose orders?

'I'm going back to my friends now, Drew. I will call you.'

She touched his shoulder, a farewell of sorts. Brodick watched her go, carefully negotiating the iron steps in her heels, one hand holding the rail, the other her purse. He waited a few minutes before following; he decided to get himself one more drink before heading home. It was already nearly 2am and he saw that some other customers were leaving. There was a vacant stool at the bar and he climbed onto it, ordering another G&T with ice and lemon. He wouldn't be able to drink more than one more of these without falling over.

He heard the door open behind him, felt a rush of cooler air and heard voices, and he turned to look; another couple were leaving, laughing arm in arm, the woman leaning heavily on her escort, but as they did so, they passed the man coming in from the street. They stood to one side and so did the newcomer. He was alone. In the momentary confusion he wore a slight and apologetic smile; Brodick thought it might be shyness or awkwardness or perhaps the stranger smiled in anticipation of the pleasures to be found at the Backstreet. He was broad with wide shoulders, a dark suit, very crumpled as if he'd slept in it, along with a white shirt open at the collar. His Asian eyes were hidden behind the thick lenses of a pair of heavy spectacles. He walked over to the bar, hands in his trouser pockets, and stood right next to Brodick without noticing him.

It was none other than Li Zuanfei, cryptanalyst extraordinary and person of interest to at least two rival intelligence agencies.

*

The late arrival was unprepossessing: unshaven, bad skin. Early thirties, possibly. He waited patiently enough, ordering a spritzer when Habib eventually extricated himself from his more ebullient and demanding customers.

'Cheers.' Brodick lifted his glass.

The Chinese nodded, lifted his own.

'You're American?'

'Canadian.' He didn't look at Brodick when he replied.

Brodick offered his hand. 'Drew Sullivan. I'm new in town.'

'That makes two of us. You're not American, though, are you? British? German?'

The hand was big, hard, dry and surprisingly strong—and it swallowed Brodick's.

Li didn't seem very pleased to make Brodick's acquaintance; he seemed bothered by it, as if Brodick was intruding in some way, but was being nevertheless civil, or trying to be.

'I didn't catch your name.'

'People call me Tony. Tony Lee. It's easier than Li Zuanfei, I guess.'

For several minutes they were silent, sipping their drinks, listening to the music, watching the people, the women especially in Li's case.

'What's your line of work, Tony?' Brodick was pushing his luck, but after the gin and given the late hour—or rather the very early hour—he wasn't going to even try being subtle or discreet.

'I'm an academic, okay.' Li's tone was defensive.

When Li turned, Brodick saw a mass of old acne scars on his jaw and neck.

'Just visiting?'

'Uh-huh. Right. I'm giving a talk. Conference at the American University.'

'There must be less risky places to hold a conference. Not that it's any of my business.'

'Same goes for you, my friend.'

The volume of the music had dropped and they could hear each other talk without having to shout, no doubt a signal from Habib equivalent to the English publican's call of 'Time gentlemen, please'.

'Let me tell you a Chinese joke, okay?'

'Sure.'

'Hijackers take over a plane at Beijing airport. A People's Liberation Army team attacks the plane and kills all the hijackers. They find a stack of passports which they must return to the passengers. The first man, who is black, steps forward. Who are you? I am Pele. Prove it! He takes two footballs from his bag, bounces them on his shoulders and knees without dropping them. Fine, you are Pele. The second is a fat white man with a beard. I am Pavarotti. Prove it! He starts to sing with a deep voice. The windows crack and the other passengers weep. Fine, you are Pavarotti. A Chinese in his sixties with gold-rimmed spectacles is next. Don't you know? I am Hu Yaobang, General Secretary of the People's Republic of China. Prove it then! The man trembles, looks to one side and the other. He starts to sweat. I cannot do anything! Fine, okay, you are Hu Yaobang!'

Brodick chuckles.

Patrick and his friends were among those leaving, collecting bags and jackets. People were kissing, hugging, calling out in Arabic, French, English, waving, laughing, the inebriated stumbling among tables and chairs. On her way out, Abrielle didn't look at Brodick or even glance in his direction, but chatted to Zahra, who was holding Malek's hand. Patrick brought up the rear. He smiled, winking at Brodick as they moved to the door.

Patrick called out to Brodick over his shoulder. 'See you later, chief.'

Li was watching. 'Friends of yours?'

'Colleagues. Local staff.'

'She's very pretty, that one.'

'Which one?' Brodick pretended not to know.

'The little one in front. In black. With all the gold. Gorgeous, yeah?'

'I guess you could say that.'

Brodick wondered how Abrielle would respond to Li's interest if she knew.

Li told Brodick he was an ardent admirer of Samantha Fox. He even had a Samantha Fox calendar on his wall back home. Doubtless along with countless millions of other horny, unattractive males, but Brodick kept the uncharitable thought to himself.

'And what do you do, Mr Sullivan?'

'Call me Drew. I'm in the travel business. I manage some of our branches in the region.'

'Not much travel in or out of Beirut nowadays, right?'

'That's exactly the problem, Tony.'

'They're probably scared stiff you're going to give them the sack and close shop.'

Brodick raised his eyebrows and smiled. 'May I give you my card? Maybe we can meet up sometime. Let's have a drink. Or maybe lunch if you have the time. I'll be around awhile yet.' Li took it, staring down at it, then pushed it into a jacket pocket.

'Where are you staying, Tony?'

'The Summerland. Do you know it?'

'I know of it, but I've never stayed there myself. It has a good reputation, or used to.'

'It's okay, I guess. And you, Drew? Where do you live?'

'My company rents a flat near here; a ten minute walk.' Brodick told himself he was giving up all this personal detail in an effort to make Li feel safe, at ease.

'You're British, right?'

They were the Backstreet's last customers. It was already Monday and presumably some people had to go to work in a matter of five or six hours, financiers and bankers excepted. The bouncer had come inside and exchanged words with Habib. They glanced over at the two remaining drinkers, the Chinese Canadian who called himself Tony and the Briton who called himself Drew. Habib came over to them.

'I'm sorry, gentlemen. We're closing. It's gone three-thirty.'

'Sure,' Brodick smiled. He liked Habib, he decided. 'No problem.'

'Can we get you a lift home? Hamza here can take you both as long as it's on this side.'

Li shook his head. 'Thanks, man, but I've got a car and driver waiting.'

'I'm all right,' Brodick told Habib, knowing full well he shouldn't walk home this late. He shouldn't walk anywhere at any time, come to that.

Li turned to him as if he'd heard his thoughts. 'I can give you a lift, buddy. It's really not safe to walk.'

'That's kind of you, Tony. Are you sure? I'm not far from here.'

'No worries, Drew.'

And that was that. Brodick slid off his barstool, feeling suddenly exhausted—and drunk. He nodded to Habib and Hamza. Hamza was helping clear the tables of the evening's debris of bottles and glasses. It was a start of sorts; Li Zuanfei wasn't that friendly, just cautiously sociable and helpful like so many citizens of his adopted country. He seemed more Canadian than Chinese. Would Brodick have offered a fellow drinker the same favour if he'd had a car complete with chauffeur on standby? Probably not. It didn't mean the Chinese Canadian wasn't suspicious, and who could blame him in a strange city tearing itself apart at the seams when spoken to by a complete stranger in a pub? He was probably used to it. Li was no doubt already aware that he was in possession of highly marketable skills sought after by governments the world over, and it was perfectly possible he'd already been approached more than once, by the Chinese, his own government in Ottawa as well as those folk at the U.S. National Security Agency, just for starters. He had no reason to think that Brodick or whoever it was that paid his salary would not make a similar overture—and of course he was right.

*

Brodick stank. He knew it when he entered the confined space of the lift up to the seventh floor of his apartment block. The cigarette and cigar smoke were on his clothing, his skin, in his hair. Add to that an unmistakable whiff of gin and his own body odour and a disgusted Brodick shucked off his shoes and started pulling off his clothes the moment the front door slammed shut behind him. He hopped first on one foot and then the other, shedding his socks, then walked through to his bedroom and the en-suite, dropping his clothing and switching on lights as he went until he stood naked under the hot water, lathering himself with shower gel.

He let the needles of hot water sting his face, pound head and back.

Disconnected thoughts drifted through his mind; his next meeting with Fenner and what he, Brodick, would and wouldn't say. What he would report about Fang, what he'd leave out, what he would say about the mole, about his contact with Li Zuanfei. He turned around, held out his arms, and this time he thought about Abrielle and her peculiar offer of trysts-by-video. His mind meandered on, to Fang this time and back again to Fenner.

That was when his front doorbell rang: long and loud.

He jumped, startled, then turned off the water. No, it wasn't a mistake: it was definitely his front doorbell. It was the first time he'd heard it and whoever it was had a finger pressed down and kept it there. Brodick's first thought was it must be the Sunni Moslem janitor who lived with his family on the ground floor in a small flat that opened onto the parking area. They had exchanged nods and smiles but so far hadn't exchanged a word. What could he possibly want at this hour? And why so insistent?

Out of the shower, now, almost falling, running—slipping on the tiled floor, putting a wet hand out for support—he skidded down the corridor, around a corner into the hall and to the front door, leaving a trail of soapy shower water, opened it, and peered through the peephole in the steel outer door. His heart was pumping, he was gushing sweat—out of fear, anxiety, anger, bemusement, resentment.

Mostly fear.

A bunch of flowers. That's all he could see through tears of shower water and sweat. Blink and look again. Flowers. Yellow, red, white with some green stuff and held so close he could see nothing of whoever it was that held them. Which was the intention, presumably.

What the *hell?*

He took a step back, turned and ran for the bedroom, leaped up on the bed, plunged his right hand under the pillows on the far side and found the Astra 400. He'd remembered the warning: Farid's tale of hooligans who used bouquets to gain entry to luxury flats and robbed the occupants at gunpoint, killing and maiming as they pillaged their way through what remained of Beirut's haute bourgeoisie. He loped back to the front door and as he did so he checked that a round was still in the chamber of the old handgun.

Brodick came to a halt, chest heaving, sucking in air. His eyes stung and he wiped his face with his left hand. He held the Astra with his right and slid off the safety with his thumb. His mouth moved; he was muttering instructions to himself. Okay. Steady. Breathe normally. Shoot first. Double tap the bastard. Or bastards. Do it fast. Feet apart, knees slightly bent, left foot forward, he leaned forward, reached out with his left hand and slid back the bolt holding the steel outer door in place.

Once again he squinted through the peephole. The flowers were still there.

The fuckan bell was still ringing.

He pushed hard, grunting with the effort.

As the door swung outwards with the medieval slowness of a drawbridge, Brodick jumped back and resumed his firing stance, a two-handed grip, raising the weapon to eye level, not aiming but looking across the top of the barrel the way he'd been taught; his target the bouquet and whoever was behind it. His forefinger curled around the trigger as the mingling of sweat and water ran down his flanks and belly and trickled on down his legs to form a pool around his feet.

The flowers fell away, petals scattered.

Fang froze, immobile, mouth open as if she was about to speak or scream, but she made no sound. They stood there, both of them, for what seemed an eternity.

29

Fang uttered something short and sharp, an explosive phrase that sounded, at least in its vehemence, like *hun dan*: the equivalent of "bastard" or "wretch". She looked Brodick up and down and, his manhood on display—the reproductive paraphernalia themselves somewhat shrunken by his agitated state—put her head back and followed the curse or whatever it was with a shriek of laughter, putting one hand to her mouth.

'So sorry.' She almost choked on the words before spluttering with laughter again, walking through the doorway into the hall, quite undeterred by the handgun still in her face.

'No, no—I am sorry.' Brodick's confusion was complete. What was she sorry for? For laughing at him? For swearing? For appearing at his door in the wee hours? For the flowers? No woman had ever brought him flowers before. And why should he abase himself? He had nothing to be apologetic about. The exchange struck him as absurd and at this point Brodick realised with an onrush of self-awareness that the absurdity did not end there; he was naked and dripping while still holding a loaded and cocked semi-automatic pistol, safety off and the muzzle pointed directly at Fang. As embarrassment took hold and sweat ran freely, he dropped his arms, both hands still holding the Astra, not as a weapon now but as an inadequate fig leaf.

'Wait. Please. Just a moment.'

He turned and fled, skipping away, sliding around the corner of the hall and into the bedroom, tossing the Astra onto the bed and on through to the bathroom and snatching up a towel, drying face, neck and chest with it, pulling it around himself and rushing back the way he'd come, realising too late that it wasn't a bath sheet but a skimpy hand towel that provided but minimal modesty. He was still bare-arsed.

Fang was still there, her composure restored.

'So this is where you live.'

She stepped past him and as Brodick pulled the outer door shut and followed it with the inner wooden door, bolting it top and bottom, she dropped what was left of the bedraggled flowers into the Ming vase.

'Show me, Drew. Give me the guided tour.'

'I'll get some clothes on; I won't be a second.'

'No. Do it later.' It was no request but a command. She moved closer and touched his shoulder. 'You have a good body. I like.' She grinned at him, eyes a-glitter.

Brodick felt a tentative stirring of the hitherto reticent appendage.

Down boy.

Fang marched on past him and took up position in the living room, feet apart, hand on hip. 'You're alone?'

'I am.'

She turned to her left. 'What's out there?'

Fang was dressed to kill, turned out in a black evening dress, off the right shoulder and exposing very pale skin, with what appeared to be a sapphire and diamond brooch pinned on one breast. A string of pearls, stockings, heels, glossy hair pulled back with the sheen of a crow's plumage completed the look. A million-dollar, Vogue cover look no less.

'A balcony with a sea view.'

'I want to see this famous view.'

He slid the glass door back and they stepped out, Fang first. Brodick could hear the unseen Mediterranean, a band of dense blackness even darker than the sky above. It seethed below on invisible rocks while above, stars tumbled down around them like dying sparks.

'I was passing and saw your lights. You didn't close your curtains.'

Presumably that meant that he was being watched.

Brodick didn't have curtains, only French-style metal blinds that could be lowered or raised by cranking a handle. And yes, when he'd left for the Backstreet, he had forgotten to lower them and he had left the living room and hall lights on—as he usually did, if only to give the impression that someone was home.

'I was at a diplomatic dinner, followed by a dance.'

He hadn't asked. Who had she danced and dined with? Not that he was jealous—no, not at all, just curious. He wondered where the dinner was and which embassy had hosted it. Yugoslav? West German? Pakistani? Beijing and Islamabad were close these days, with Beijing supplying arms to the anti-Soviet Afghan guerrillas and acting as a counter- weight to India with its close Soviet ties.

Fang turned to him and he breathed in a cloud of Arpege.

'You'll be pleased to know I met Li Zuanfei tonight.'

'You talked?'

'We did. We agreed to meet up.'

'Good.'

'He's staying at the Summerland Hotel.'

She didn't respond. In fact, Fang didn't seem to pay attention at all. She was looking closely at him, then put a hand—her right—on his stubbled cheek, moved it around to his neck and drew him to her. Her mouth was on his. Soft, inviting, then probing, pushing. Both arms were around his neck pressing against him and he reciprocated, embracing her.

What happened next was something of a muddle. To any observer they would probably have resembled two very inept partners in a confused tango, pulling and pushing, struggling through the door and back into the living room, the male now totally naked and the woman fast becoming so with his help, discarding her shoes and outer clothing as they made their wayward progress, stumbling into the dining chairs. Somehow they found their way in the midst of this close combat to the bedroom and fell together, still entwined, onto the bed. Brodick pushed the Astra away, back under the pillows. Fang drew him in and Brodick took the plunge. Still they wrestled, at one point tumbling off the bed onto the floor, tangled in the duvet. After a time she was on top of him, pressing him down, riding him with a ferocious energy. Quite how long this went on Brodick had no idea. It has been said, unkindly, that the average time of coitus for the male Briton is under three minutes, but this encounter must have lasted somewhat longer and anyway Brodick chose to see himself as a Scot: and that must guarantee him another minute or two of stamina, surely, thanks to Irn Bru, haggis and square sausage, to say nothing of the deep-fried Mars bar. Her obvious enjoyment spurred him on; she spoke, she shouted, she whispered, she muttered. Mandarin Chinese for the most part. Whatever it meant he had no idea, but she was noisy. None of it made sense to him, but she did seem to be enjoying herself and that loud enthusiasm spurred him on, and she did not hesitate to let him know what she liked best and how it was to be done, and he did his level best to please, delaying his own gratification until he estimated that he had done his duty, and then some.

A little later, she turned towards him and flung an arm across his chest.

'What do you think of China? The truth.'

Brodick, taken by surprise and still short of breath, thought quickly. 'I admire the history and culture, what little I know of it anyway. Its civilisation.'

Did they really have to do this now?

'And?'

'And I respect its amazing progress since 1949.'

He couldn't think of anything original to say. He thought it would be impolitic to mention the tens of millions who starved to death under the direction of the Great Leader. During the Great Famine of 1958-62, it was estimated that between thirty-five and forty-six million Chinese died, but how many young Chinese people today knew of it? It wasn't taught in schools and universities, obviously. It was taboo, and dangerous to mention in public. Fang would know of it presumably because of her privileged access to banned books and Party documents.

'What's your favourite Chinese novel?'

'Chi'n P'ing Mei. *The Plum in the Golden Vase.*'

'You like erotica?'

'It's not that erotic.'

'You're right, it isn't. I would have thought you would have preferred *The Romance of the Three Kingdoms*, by Luo Kuan-Chung. Lots of adventure and fighting. The kind of thing boys like. Overgrown boys like you.'

'I haven't read it.'

'You should have been a diplomat, dearest Richard.' She laughed, then pulled his hair, but not so hard that it hurt. 'What do you know about our leader, Deng Xiaoping?'

Brodick turned to face her, raising himself on one elbow.

A post-coital interrogation? Really?

'Not much. Sorry. Let's see. I do know he fought the Japanese for seven years, and then the Nationalists in the civil war. He's tough, smart, brave—physically and morally—and he's intellectually capable though he never had a chance to go to university, he's very determined, and he and his family suffered greatly during the Cultural Revolution, especially his kids. The Red Guards threw one of his sons out of a window, breaking his back. He's authoritarian and totally loyal to the Party. He unified the country, overcame his rivals and is largely responsible for opening it up to the outside world and for rapidly developing the economy and reducing poverty. He encouraged the Democracy Wall—for a time. His biggest failure—not that *you* would call it a failure—was his brief war with Vietnam. He used the Soviet threat to enable normalisation of ties with Washington. How's that for a quick summary? He is quoted for having said at some point, "I do not care if a cat is black or white, as long as it catches mice". Oh, and he must be eighty or thereabouts. Born 1904, I seem to remember. People say he's very short and that nowadays he has poor hearing.'

Fang patted him on the shoulder. 'Okay. Not too shabby for an imperialist foreign devil who knows next to nothing about my country. I shall make it my business to improve your socialist education.'

'Thank you kindly, comrade, from the bottom of my rotten bourgeois heart. I thought you were worried about us doing unauthorised things behind locked doors, about being infected by a foreigner, an enemy.'

'Maybe it's a risk I consider I can take now that you're supplying us with product, Richard. It's a kind of antidote to any Western plague, but it will require a regular supply to ensure continued immunisation.'

'Drew. It's Drew. I'm glad. Being a traitor has its upside, obviously.'

'I've got to go.' She jumped off the bed and ran to the bathroom. He realised as he lay there, waiting, that he'd been well and truly screwed. Royally fucked, and in more ways than one. Not that he hadn't enjoyed the experience—he had. Hugely. Come to think of it, he was actually *happy*. That was unusual. The pall of loneliness had evaporated. After a minute or two Fang re-emerged, bath towel around her and proceeded to collect her clothes, picking them up off the floor and dressing quickly. She didn't seem to mind him watching. Her underwear was black, like the dress. She didn't bother with her stockings, pushing them into her purse. Then she used the bathroom mirror to adjust hair and lipstick, leaving the door to the bedroom open.

She dropped her lipstick back in her purse and snapped it shut. 'They're waiting for me.'

'Who are?'

He sidled over to the bedroom's solitary window. The small gaps in the metal blind offered fractured glimpses of the street. Right below, near the entrance to the flats, he could make out the cream Mercedes parked partly up on the pavement, and her two Chinese minders stood there, talking. One was smoking, using the pinch and claw method, holding the cigarette with the burning end inwards, towards his palm, holding it with thumb and middle finger: the tell-tale sign of someone who works out of doors. His companion was gesticulating, waving his arms about as if describing the huge fish that got away. Or maybe it wasn't a fish at all, but an imperialist spy.

As she put on her shoes, she looked up at him. 'I'll see you soon.'

'I'll be there.'

Brodick dragged on his jeans and went ahead of her to the hall and opened both doors once again. He had to unlock the first, top and bottom, unbolt the second, push it open with his shoulder.

'Sleep well, Fang.'

She strode past him. She didn't turn to look as she waited, watching the lights marking the slow ascent of the lift, and said not another word until the doors opened and she vanished inside. She knew there was a security camera out there. Brodick locked up again, went back to bed and his last conscious thoughts as he turned onto his side were that espionage was a game like any other. Whatever people did for a living, whatever their game, whether it was soldiering, advertising or spying, there were really only two motives that counted for anything. Sex and money. Not sex or money, mind: sex *and* money. They were inseparable, and the more he had, the more he wanted.

Consequently it never ended well. How could it?

Fang represented promotion, professional success and yes, more money.

That was what he wanted, wasn't it?

He could smell her scent on the sheets and he was still smiling as he drifted off.

*

The air was still and the heat oppressive. At least up on the hill, overlooking the port of Jounieh, it was slightly cooler and there were fewer mosquitoes. As yet there were no other customers as yet and Brodick picked out a table against the fence—a simple four-strand wire affair partly covered with honeysuckle—so he had a clear view of both the sea approaches and the wharves where the *Basra Star* was expected to dock in a couple of hours. The restaurant staff ignored Brodick; he was far too early as far as they were concerned. A waiter had put his head out of the door and scowled at him and then vanished inside. He didn't need to speak; his expression said it all. Right below, perhaps three hundred yards away, stood the ferry that was due to leave later that night for Larnaca. There wasn't much activity; it was far too early for passengers to begin boarding. Looking further out beyond the port over to his left, Brodick picked out a small oil tanker at anchor and two freighters. One looked about the right size for the *Basra Star*. He could make out containers on her deck and she seemed quite low in the water, indicating a full load. A whisp of smoke escaped from her funnel.

'You're always early.' Fang looked different; her hair was drawn back in a ponytail, she wore blue jeans and a loose, long sleeved linen shirt of pale pink. She could have been a Lebanese undergraduate if it hadn't been for those bewitching east Asian eyes of hers. Brodick decided he preferred this casual Fang to the more formal version. She seemed more approachable like this.

Out of habit he stood up as she came up to his table.

She pulled out the chair opposite and sat.

'You went back to sleep?'

'I did. And you, Fang?'

'A couple of hours.'

'I'm flying to Nice tomorrow, by the way.'

'Why?'

'Meeting my boss.'

'Mister Fenner?'

'That's right.'

'Why doesn't he come here now the airport's open? Seems like a wasteful expenditure.'

'I'm sure he doesn't think so. I suspect he has a strong instinct for

go to a second career in industry or private security. I think you call it the "revolving door".'

Who was "they" and "we"?

'Thanks, Fang. Much appreciated.'

But Malry wouldn't have another five years. He wouldn't have three months.

'Drew, I hope this settles the matter of my bona fides.'

'I'm sure it will.' Brodick didn't really think so, but he felt he had to reassure her. If this was kosher—and Brodick had reason to think it wasn't—then the betrayal must have hurt, deeply. Malry's loss would be a savage blow. The detailed breakdown of the *Guoanbu* and its mysterious bureaux or departments could wait a while. It was pretty incredible that they'd given up such a prize: an agent who could go on to even greater things. Fenner would be chuffed.

He bloody well should be.

'I have to say this, Fang. I'm sorry about it, but hear me out if you would.'

She looked at him, surprised.

'It seems to me that there are three or four possible scenarios involving Malry.'

She was still watching him closely, holding eye contact.

'Scenario One. Someone—or perhaps a faction—inside your own organisation, has expressed doubts about Malry. They suspect his enormous intelligence contribution has been contaminated, may always have been, that he might well have been under DGSE control all this time, from the start, feeding you shit, tantalising shit, but shit all the same. Rightly or wrongly, this doubter or doubters suspect he never really was China's man. Now of course this may be more about a power struggle inside the *Guoanbu* rather than a serious question mark over of Malry's true allegiance. So, it's finally been decided to give him up: to see what happens. Will he fly off into the sunset and be awarded a gong by the President of the Fifth Republic himself in a private audience at the Élysée Palace, followed by a top job as a corporate executive? Or will he and his wife be detained on arrival in Paris and vanish off the face of the earth for the next two years: subject to hard interrogation, then held in solitary? You said yourself that Malry's time in China is almost done. So he served you well for 12 years; why not use him as a wrecking ball as his final act of treachery? Well? It's creative. It's ruthless. It has *Guoanbu* written all over it.'

'Drew. This is pure fantasy.'

Fantasy or no, she wasn't laughing.

'Scenario Two. This is a variant on Scenario One. He's being thrown to the wolves. It'll spare your people resettlement costs, especially now that he's providing much less quality material. Maybe the marriage has broken down. Who knows what the details are, but the point I'm making is that a judgement has been made that the operation is on its last legs and it would be best to salvage what's left. And you do that by revealing his betrayal in order to engineer a crippling attack—nothing short of a volcanic eruption—inside the DGSE, effectively paralysing it for many months. Maybe years. It will isolate the DGSE from its customers in government, and it will ensure that allied intelligence agencies keep their distance. The DGSE will go into deep freeze. A couple of dozen senior officers will take a redundancy package, a minister will resign. A splendid coup de grace to end a twelve-year-long penetration agent's career. I'd be proud to design such a cynical plan. Don't worry, I won't tell Fenner. What do you say?'

'Is there going to be much more of this?'

She was shaken, though, he could see that. He was warm, very warm.

'I'm almost done. Scenario Three. My money's on this one. I think you have gone rogue, Fang. Your ambition has got the better of you. Let's say you've known for some time that there's a senior Western intelligence officer working for the *Guoanbu*. It would be hard not to see the signs. A very special mole with all the protections and special handling that must involve, the secret allowances, the stream of secret material requiring special indoctrination, the safe houses, the security. As someone who is not cleared for the product or its originator, you nevertheless pay attention, you're professionally curious, even envious, and then someone, out of the blue, drops a remark and you see the light. Maybe you're having tea with your boss and he says to you in a pensive tone of voice that it must be hell being married to one's case officer for so many years.'

'Drew. Stop. *Now.*'

Brodick would not be deflected. 'So you troll through the diplomatic lists. Maybe you're more daring; you ask questions of the DGSE's relationship with, say, the Syrian *mouhabarat* or Lebanon's own military intelligence, and the ultra-secret source provides an answer. So you identify a French intelligence officer working under diplomatic cover with a Chinese wife. You weigh up the risks, and you decide that on balance you're outside the immediate target area of a *Guoanbu* witch-hunt. Weeding-out, to use your term. But they won't look at you, will they? You're out of the loop. You're a shithole-and-palmtree specialist like me, out in the cold and up to your neck in the complexities of the Middle East which no one really cares about except for the no-small-matter of energy supplies. It takes a while but you find a hook to hang this on—that's me—and you give me his name, and then, later, you add some background detail. Admit it, Fang, you've gone solo. It takes guts. It takes huge ambition. I'm really impressed.'

She was silent.

'I could add a fourth. I think you know what this scenario would be. Your Jean-Philippe Malry has done nothing, is no mole, and never was, but is instead a successful and highly effective French intelligence officer and this is nothing more than a *Guoanbu* smear to destroy his career and create havoc in the French intelligence services. '

Fang had turned away. She seemed to be cursing under her breath, in Mandarin.

'I'm right, aren't I? At least about one of the possibles. You see, Fang, it's what I would have done. Bravo.'

She wouldn't look at him.

'You're a bastard, Richard Brodick.'

'Drew, please. And what does this make you, Fang, or whatever your real name is?'

Silence.

'If you won't tell me the truth, at least tell me his codename. His *Guoanbu* codename.'

But she wouldn't. Of course not. Not yet anyway, no more than he would tell her his SIS monicker and Brodick didn't press it because he could see she was angrier than he'd ever seen her, and she was struggling to stop herself from lashing out and trying—heroically—to bring her feelings under some semblance of control.

Was he right?

30

It was getting dark, the cicadas were rasping away in the umbrella pines, a sonorous scraping, and the recalcitrant waiter had reappeared, this time with menus. The other tables were filling up.

Fang shook her hair away from her face like a dog emerging from water. 'Is that our ship?'

'The one on the right would be my guess. I think that's a tug heading out now with a pilot to help bring her in.'

Fang applied herself to the menu. The displacement activity seemed to be working, at least for her. She was calm again.

Brodick couldn't stop thinking about the French mole. He wondered what it was that had succeeded in turning Malry at the start. Was it the wife: love or sexual passion? Was it money? Ideology? Perhaps a little of everything? He'd had a good run for sure, these past twelve years, but now it was about to end, unless of course the French didn't want the embarrassment of a trial and could turn their man, and do so convincingly, without the wife finding out. That way he might keep his job and salary a while longer and retire on full pension with the usual honours, whatever they might be. Pulling off such a stunt would be tricky, of course, and it went without saying they'd never really be able to trust him again, especially with his wife looking over his shoulder and reporting back to Beijing on her husband's behaviour. But twelve years was exceptional.

Brodick's feelings about Malry were ambivalent. On the one hand he admired his pluck and skill, his ability to get away with his treason for so long. On the other, Brodick's stomach lurched with a queasy thought: such a man as Malry would have had a massive amount of highly classified material cross his desk, stuff from the NSA and CIA, from the British and West Germans to name but a few, to say nothing about the high-grade intel flowing in from other French overseas stations.

How many circuits had he compromised? How many agents had been shot, and worse?

'What are you going to have, Drew?'

'The lemon and whatever it is. Lemon and cinnamon. And you?'

He really wasn't in the least hungry so he'd chosen at random, not caring what he pretended to eat.

'I'll have the chocolate.' She looked up and smiled at him. It was a reflex, an automatic smile, more a matter of courtesy, of polite reassurance. No one would have thought, watching them closely, that they'd spent a torrid hour—or however long it was—bonking with such abandon in his bed that very morning or that they were both deeply involved in a game of treason and that they'd just had the spy's equivalent of their first marital tiff.

'Shall we order something to drink?'

'Not for me, Fang. I drank rather too much last night…' He left the rest unsaid.

The thought of agents being tortured and executed had put him off eating and drinking.

'We can have coffee later then.'

Having given their orders to the reluctant waiter, they turned their attention to what was happening out in the bay. The cluster of red and green lights in the darkening sea and sky suggested the *Basra Sta*r was approaching, closely assisted by the tug. The two intelligence officers would have a ringside view of the arrival of the Silkworm missiles.

'You were going to tell me something.'

'What?'

'Something about a dragon's lair. You said it was important, and that we'd find the time for it. Looks like we have a while yet before our ship docks.'

'I'd almost forgotten.' She glanced out at the ships as if calculating the time of the *Basra Star's* arrival. 'I'll give you the short version, all right?'

'Go ahead.'

She seemed relieved to talk about something that had nothing to do with Malry.

'My tale starts off in Canton, in 1924, at the Huangpu Military Academy, established by Sun Yat-sen and the Soviets, to train officers to fight the warlords of northern China. Mikhail Borodin, the Comintern's permanent representative in China, was in charge.

'In October '26, Borodin sent his bodyguard, Gu Shunzhang, to Vladivostok, for training in clandestine, revolutionary methods.

'Gu, born in 1902, was a tough character. He came from the wrong side of the tracks in Shanghai. A street kid, yes? A punk. As a teenager he got to know the bars, opium dens, the tarts. He had affairs, and he survived by cunning and brute force. He joined the infamous Green Gang. He became a secret member of the CCP. He led a double life. With a public persona as Hua Guangqi, he performed as a magician—an illusionist—in top nightclubs and casinos. Today they'd call him a celebrity.

'Back from the Soviet Union, he and the notorious Fang Sheng formed a special unit to defend communists from the Kuomintang. In 1927, Chiang Kai-shek formed his Kuomintang army and government base in Nanjing. Just as the CCP was preparing for an insurrection, the nationalists struck—Green Gang thugs slaughtered thousands of Communists.'

Fang had to pause for a minute or two as the waiter brought their food.

'This was when?'

'March, 1927.'

'Go on.' They both glanced out to sea. There was still time; the *Basra Star's* progress seemed very slow. Brodick picked up a fork and tried to slice off a piece of his lemon crepe.

'Well, Gu—along with other Party leaders—found refuge in

the French Concession. In Hunan, Mao Zedong's insurrection was crushed, while the Canton Uprising of December 1927 was defeated with around 15,000 comrades killed. It was a terrible time…'

'Perhaps we should eat now, Fang. The ship's about to come in.'

People in military uniform—disrupted pattern camouflage—were gathered on the wharves, waiting, some of them armed, and a crane had moved along rails to the berth where Brodick expected the freighter to dock. He took another mouthful of food. He didn't think much of it; he decided it was like eating cardboard soused in weak lemon juice with a powdering of cinnamon. He put his fork down.

'How's yours, Fang?'

She shrugged. 'We didn't come here for the food, did we?'

'It's disappointing.' It certainly wouldn't make the grade at *La Chandeleur*: the day each Spring that the French set aside for eating crepes.

Arc lights along the quay were switched on abruptly.

'My history lesson will have to wait, Drew. Sorry.'

Whatever was happening in the port had their full attention.

The Larnaca-bound ferry was all lit up too, and passengers were starting to board.

'Those are Lebanese army troops?'

'Phalangists would be my guess, with maybe a few soldiers among them.'

There were trucks, four-tonners in olive green and black camouflage; a dozen or so of them drawn up nose-to-tail, partly obscured by a warehouse, along with two huge tank transporters. Brodick looked back over his shoulder. The other diners in the restaurant garden were busy talking, eating and drinking, oblivious of events in the port area.

Something—a flash of light—made both Brodick and Fang turn their heads to the right. A lightning strike was Brodick's first thought. The light preceded the sound. It was no more than a flickering, the way a car's headlights can be seen rising and falling as it approaches at night, rising up the uneven gradient while still out of sight. In this case, the flickering was behind the eastern hills overlooking the coast. The ripple of light pulsed and died, stopping altogether, then started again, only more strongly.

The flashes of light were followed by a rumbling.

The rumbling became a roar.

In a second or two the roar became a rushing, like a train at high speed somewhere above them in the night sky, a fiendish whoosh of sound, now a multitude, a cacophony of continuous screaming from the mouths of a hundred devils, louder and louder.

Brodick reached for Fang, but she didn't need his help or want it. She was staring fixedly, the lips of her wide mouth slightly parted, the light flickering on those wide, high cheekbones. She didn't seem afraid, at all, in fact she seemed to be smiling, totally engrossed.

Instinctively Brodick tried to make himself a smaller target. He slid off his chair and onto his knees and knelt by the fence, fingers clinging to the wire, his face against the strands. They should take cover, of course, but he just had to see this. He couldn't tear himself away. He sensed what this was: 122mm Katyusha rockets streaming overheard in volleys, one salvo after another, several in the air at once, heading for the freighter and the wharf.

They seemed to rip the very night sky apart.

When they hit, the ground shook again and again. The detonations sent up columns of fire. The explosions marched along the wharf in quick succession, consuming the trucks, the warehouse, catching the dockers and the military personnel in the open, then marching onto the freighter and its cargo of containers.

Brodick discovered that he wasn't afraid at all.

Like Fang, he was fascinated.

The Syrians must have a spotter nearby, directing the gunners.

Each detonation was marked by a ball of flame, one linked to the next in a chain of fire.

He could feel the heat of each blast.

Brodick knew something about these weapons. Nicknamed

Stalin's Organs and resembling a stack of organ pipes set up on the back of trucks, they were designed to break up infantry attacks. The salvoes of rockets fired in rapid succession were effective against troops and soft-skinned vehicles in the open, but they were—generally speaking—ineffective against those able to dig in properly.

Brodick sensed he and Fang along with the other diners weren't in the direct line of fire, so he reasoned that they really had no cause for alarm, but then he glanced back to see that all the diners and staff had fled indoors, leaving food and glassware on the tables, jackets and handbags dumped among the pine needles on the flagstones.

For Brodick hadn't reckoned on the cargo of missiles, their warheads, or the solid propellant they contained.

Fang, also mesmerised by the fireworks, put out a hand and gripped Brodick's shoulder, fingers digging into his flesh. She wasn't seeking reassurance, but urging him to stay put, to watch what was about to occur.

An immense fountain of fire marked the freighter's death throes.

As the propellant and warheads exploded, the old rust-bucket seemed to rise from the sea, its back broken, and then collapsed back again into the oily waters, on its side. Its stern went down first, the bows briefly silhouetted against the flames. Black smoke billowed up in a thick column from the dying ship, blown apart by immense explosions and for several metres around the Basra Star the sea itself was on fire and seemed to be boiling.

The blasts singed Brodick's hair, stinging face and hands. Instant tan.

His nostrils and mouth filled with the stench of burning bunker fuel.

Debris fell around them. Something jagged whined overhead. The table next to theirs spun around and turned over.

Tiles from the restaurant roof clattered to the ground.

Down below, body parts littered the quayside.

Brodick pulled himself up and settled his backside on the chair.

The lull in Lebanon's civil war was over.

31

Brodick hated Fenner. It wasn't merely contempt or loathing. It was that pure flame that scalds hater and hated alike. Brodick hated his case officer because—despite himself—Brodick admired him, couldn't help himself doing so, and worse still, would really have liked to *be* him. Indeed, not so long ago, before his Afghan caper, Brodick had tried to be very much like him and the memory of it grated.

Hatred is recognition of a kind, a grudging respect.

It was partly envy and partly shame. Fenner was so English in that he couldn't imagine being anything else. Fenner could never be mistaken for a German or a Frenchman, for example. He couldn't mistake himself for one, either. It wasn't just his appearance, his shambling gate, his careless manner of dressing, his messy hair, his hand gestures—he flapped his hands and wiggled his fingers—or his limited range of facial expressions. That constipated grin, for example. Fenner seemed to embody Englishness—whatever that might be, and Brodick would have been the first to admit not to being able to express the notion with any clarity—and in this case it was a very middle-class Englishness, a smug self-satisfaction, from the eighteen-carat gold signet ring with the family crest on the pinkie of his left hand and the public school drawl to the Victorian walnut barometer in the hallway of his home. Not that Brodick had ever stepped inside Fenner's home—though Brodick would have been willing to take a large bet on its being located in the Home Counties—and had never seen whether Fenner had such an utterly useless device on his wall, but he would be very surprised if he hadn't.

Fenner was secure in who he was, so completely and disgustingly pleased with what he was or thought himself to be. He had his place in the world and had been born into it. He hadn't had to plough his own furrow. He was a man devoid of spontaneity or even the possibility of change; he was stamped and moulded like one of those red-jacketed lead soldiers Brodick had played with as a child, rigid and utterly predictable. Obviously, his loyalty to the Crown was unshakable as it was unthinking in the way that a Labrador retriever didn't really have to think a great deal about picking up a wounded pheasant on one of Fenner's driven shoots back in Sussex or Surrey. Fenner was also the kind of Englishman for whom it was inconceivable to vote for anything other than Conservative and Unionist Party candidates even if they were corrupt or as thick as two short planks, or both. Which—by Brodick's reckoning—they invariably were. Policy had nothing to do with it; it was all about the myth of Churchillian grit, a historical fantasy of greatness that never was, unless slavery was tantamount to greatness.

To be English was to be British, to be British was to be English.

Brodick being Labour or perhaps Liberal, depending on his mood.

In short, Fenner was two-dimensional and loyal to obsolete institutions, loyal also to a state of being that Brodick both despised and, to his shame, envied. By contrast, Brodick was a mongrel of foreign origin and he knew it; born in Beirut, carried off within weeks by sea to Cape Town and never quite belonging anywhere, yet at home everywhere, the product of a foreign mother with psychological issues and an absent father with a drink problem and given to violent rages. His sense of identity and his values constantly shifted but always with the sense of being less than his fellow countrymen, for he felt himself a colonial and hence inferior in some way. The imposter syndrome. A political chameleon and a professional foreigner, Brodick envied the narrow, simple gaze of Fenner's, untroubled by anything approaching intelligent self-awareness.

Yet Fenner's values and outlook were precisely those that Brodick had adopted to secure his own entry to the Service as a head agent on contract on the Afghan frontier. He'd been just one of the many "contract labourers" recruited with Mrs Thatcher's approval in an effort to make up for the decline and neglect in SIS coverage. In Fenner, Brodick saw himself as he used to be at the start of that first SIS adventure: naively patriotic, unquestionably loyal, desperate to be accepted by what passed for the Anglo-British establishment. He'd wanted to *belong*. He wanted to be accepted. It hadn't lasted very long, however. The price had been too high.

And here Fenner was in the flesh, strolling slowly towards Brodick along the *Promenade des Anglais*, striped shirt hanging out of his long, baggy shorts, hands in pockets, whistling tunelessly, smiling to himself in the sunshine, squinting out at the pleasure boats on the bluest of blue *Baie des Anges,* a battered brown leather briefcase hanging by a strap from one shoulder. Route surveillance detection didn't get more casual than this.

The Englishman abroad. *Fuck*.

The city of Nice was in some ways the obvious choice for a *treff* between case officer and operative. Brodick could see the advantages. There were daily direct flights from both Beirut and Larnaca and the flights took little more than an hour.

Fenner dragged out a chair, plonked himself down on it, puffed out his cheeks, threw down his briefcase on another, scratched his ear and looked around him then up at the solitary palm tree towering above their table. It offered little in the way of shade.

'Good flight?' He didn't look at Brodick as he asked.

'Not bad.' It wasn't bad at all, Brodick thought, if the traveller wasn't too dismayed by the alarming scowl of a black turbaned, beetle-browed Ayatollah Khomeini on a massive billboard on the coast road just outside the entrance to Beirut airport. No doubt the ferocious glare was seen by some as reassurance, a welcome home. For others, it was both a shock and a warning, and Brodick was glad to get away from it and all that it implied.

The two men went through the impersonal procedure of their

trade: they had an hour for their discussion, they agreed to meet again in Larnaca in ten days' time. Yes, at the coffee shop at the Marina Bay; Fenner was nothing if not a creature of habit and Brodick didn't even bother to suggest to his superior officer that he might consider a visit to Beirut because he knew he never would, not while there was a civil war raging. Fenner asked the standard stuff about Brodick's security, his cover, his Levant Travel colleagues, the situation in the city and yes, the lull in the fighting was indeed over as of the previous evening, and now Brodick in turn summarised—leaving out Fang's presence and the proximity of the events—the delivery and destruction of the Iraqi Silkworm missiles and the *Basra Star* in Jounieh port.

It was all correct and proper routine: textbook stuff.

Fenner wasn't really paying much attention to any of it.

'And DRAGON?'

Brodick knew what Fenner was after. 'I have the name and a short biography.'

A waitress appeared with a welcoming smile. Brodick didn't fail to note that she had very short hair, freckles, an oddly old-fashioned black uniform, frilly white apron and matching cap. He asked for coffee, Fenner smiled up at her—it was more gloat than smile—and in execrable French ordered a beer and a *pain perdu*.

Brodick produced the slip of paper with the Frenchman's name on it and placed it in Fenner's plump and sweaty paw.

'Why didn't you include the name in your last signal?'

'I'm never sure the extent to which our encrypted signals might be compromised.'

'Trust me, Richard. They're not.'

'I'm sure you know better, Nick, but I don't share your confidence. Sorry. I preferred to give it to you in person as I knew we would be meeting.'

Fenner looked down at the paper. 'Who and what is this M. Jean-Philippe Malry when he's at home? French, presumably. Or Belgian.'

'It says right there that Malry is currently DGSE chief of station in Beijing.'

He handed over the summary and the negatives provided by Fang.

'Is he by God?' Fenner sat back and stared at Brodick, mouth agape.

'He's listed in the French diplomatic directory as a political counsellor in their Beijing mission and specialising in cultural exchanges.'

'And?'

'I'm told Malry produces such an abundance of material he has two handlers to cope with it. His wife is a Chinese national and she's in on it; they work as a team, according to Fang. The wife helps service his DLBs when he's otherwise engaged. Whether she recruited him at the start I don't know, but it's quite possible. They met during his first junior posting to the consulate in Hong Kong, and recruitment followed during his first posting to the mainland. Shanghai, I believe. This is his final Chinese tour. He's coming up for a promotion in the next few months and is heading for a desk job in Paris, possibly Director Asia-Pacific. Allegedly he's only a couple of years away from a deputy directorship. He's worked for the Chinese for twelve years.'

'DRAGON gave him up quite easily?'

'She did, yes.'

'It must have hurt, or it will soon do so.' Fenner said it with satisfaction, and followed it with a delighted chuckle. 'You can never trust the bloody French.'

All very well, Brodick thought, but how much UK material had been leaked by Malry?

The coffee and beer arrived.

When the waitress had gone, Fenner took out a handkerchief and wiped his face with it. A patch of damp spread slowly across his shirtfront. That morning's sea breeze had long since died.

'So you think DRAGON's on the level, do you? About this fellow Malry? Twelve years as a Chinese mole is quite an achievement.'

'I'm not entirely sure about her; not yet anyway. I need more.

We need more. She's also handed over a breakdown of the *Guoanbu* and its bureaux, a decent diagram of the structure, what each bureau does and the names of their departmental chiefs. It's a start. This name alone doesn't amount to bona fides—not yet.'

Fenner waved the paper. 'But if this is genuine, it's a game changer. You've hooked her, Richard. You should be over the moon. Why do you look so glum, old chap? She's your agent and if you really still have doubts, I need to know. London will need to know.'

Brodick sipped his coffee. It was very strong and very hot: just the way he liked it.

'She's using number stations. One on the east side, one on the west.'

Brodick nodded. He knew about these short-wave voice transmissions. A deadpan voice would read out a word as a recognition signal, then a series of numbers. Usually, it was based on letter substitution, taken from a book, maybe more than one book, then transposed a couple of times. What made it virtually unbreakable was that it was based on the classic one-time pad or OTP. Unless one got hold of the key…

'We have to ensure this is all valid, Nick, that it checks out. And she's a lot more senior and experienced than I am.'

'So?'

'Doesn't it strike you as just a little strange that DRAGON allows herself to be recruited by a Brit very much her junior and relatively untested and then drops this in our laps? You said yourself she's a highflier.'

Fenner took half his beer in one long swallow, then wiped his mouth with the back of his hand and burped. 'That feels much better.'

The *pain perdu* arrived and there was another pause.

'As far as she's concerned, you're a ranking British intelligence officer. You've your professional life still ahead of you. That's all that matters. You've got the mileage they want from you for the long term.' Fenner flipped his napkin over his lap, picked up his knife and fork, eager to begin.

It made sense, of course, given that Fang had recruited Brodick, and that she would help him progress, push him up the slippery SIS pole into the right jobs and places to serve her interests and those of the *Guoanbu*. If that was the plan then it was only natural that Fang or her masters would select someone young and at the start of a promising career in British intelligence. They would want to make him totally dependent on them, bend him to their will. Didn't Fenner see that: or was he hiding it?

'Okay, I take your point. But if I was jumping ship I'd want someone with a certain authority and experience to do the job properly. Defection's a tricky business. Didn't you tell me that? I'm still not entirely sure I fully understand her motives.'

Fenner shrugged. He was more interested in eating than the possibility that Fang was a dangle, a very sophisticated one. He didn't seem to share Brodick's concerns about Fang's motives, or lack of them.

'By the way, Fang went north a few days ago. To Zghorta and the home of Suleiman Franjieh. Apparently they met and it occurred to me later that perhaps she used Franjieh as a conduit to Damascus and tip off the Syrians about the missile shipment.'

'Why would she?'

'Two birds, one stone, Nick. China sweetens its links with the Assad regime while at same time keeping in with the Iraqis and their Phalangist and the Lebanese Army pals.'

'Sounds all a bit complicated to me, but I'll look into it.' Fenner spoke out of the corner of his mouth, still chewing. He didn't like complications.

Was Fenner really the simpleton he seemed?

'Maybe we—and not the Chinese—tipped them off.'

Fenner almost choked. 'What? You think *we* told the Syrians? I very much doubt it.'

Fenner liked everything simple. Playing a double game didn't seem to have occurred to him, or if it had, it wasn't something he wanted to contemplate. So much the better. Brodick decided it was time to change the subject. Or perhaps it wasn't a change; it might indeed offer a clue to her motivation. 'Have you heard of something called the Dragon's Lair? Fang was telling me some story about it, but we were interrupted. She seemed to think it important. Something to do with the early years of the CCP when it was still very clandestine and at war with the nationalists.'

'Can't say I have. Chinese history's not my thing, I'm afraid. When's your flight back?' Fenner glanced at his wristwatch for the fourth or fifth time.

'Six sharp.'

'Well, I think I'd better find an earlier flight myself and let our people know about your M. Malry as soon as possible. I was planning on spending a night at the wonderful Hotel Negresco right behind us, but I don't think I can now. This is too important. I'll have to cancel and they'll probably charge me a cancellation fee. Next time, maybe.' Fenner then repeated himself. 'This is a really big deal, Richard, you know that, don't you? We'll have to verify it, of course, and decide how to manage the intel.'

'So you've said. You'll inform the French.'

'The DGSE? Of course we must, absolutely, once we've asked Beijing Station for an assessment: without spelling out why.'

'Do you have something for me to give DRAGON?'

'I do indeed.' Fenner reached for his briefcase.

The booklet's cover was plain beige, other than a tiny HM coat of arms in one corner and Top Secret in large, black capital letters splashed diagonally across the front. The cover was badly creased and carried the stain of at least one coffee mug.

Fenner passed it over to Brodick with a triumphant grin. 'She'll love that. She'll probably get a medal.'

'Christ, are you serious?' Brodick was shocked despite himself.

'Second tier diplomatic codes, Richard. Nothing to worry about. No cause for alarm. Not used for our Office traffic, of course. Only the older machines left in the region are still using it, and they're going to be phased out. Diplomatic ciphers are due for routine replacement in the summer anyway, and the last of the older machines will go soon after. It's all been thoroughly thought through, I assure you. We worked very hard to get this. I thought you'd be pleased, old chap. I hope so, because the Foreign Office put up one hell of a rear-guard action. In the light of your latest information, it seems more than justified.'

Fenner leaned forward and spoke in a confiding tone. 'The Foreign Sec was overruled by you-know-who.'

He meant Number Ten.

'Still—'

'No still about it, old man. We've taken the trouble of preparing to seed our diplomatic signals with enough disinformation in the coming days and weeks to give Beijing a severe case of misdirection. We're not giving it away for nothing; we have to get some use out of it. We're doing this for you, remember. You're right—you've got to seem to be the real thing, a genuine *Guoanbu* recruit. We've gone to a lot of trouble to find ways of keeping Fang interested. Okay? She'll lap this up and so will her masters. They're not terribly good at computerised encryption, let alone decryption, and so this will be something of a bonanza. We've set up your special sub-committee to source what DRAGON is going to need from different departments. You're going to have a veritable industry of deception at your exclusive disposal. You should be chuffed, old boy.'

For just a moment—sitting there with Fenner on a gorgeous day, having handed over the name of the French mole—Brodick almost believed it himself: that Fang really was *his* agent and not the other way around, and it was of course up to him to maintain the illusion. Fenner was right: this was big, and it was all down to him. He was on his way. He was already building his own empire within SIS.

Thank you, Fang.

'And I'm expected to take this through customs?' Brodick held up the code book and flicked through its pages with his thumb. It resembled a small, thick telephone directory or railway timetable complete with cheap paper covered with columns of numbers in very small print, but the classification on the cover could be seen from quite a distance.

'Put it under your shirt, hide it in a copy of Playboy. Give it a new cover from a Tom Clancy airport thriller. Use your imagination, Richard: that's why we pay you such a big salary. Only joking. Are we done here? I enjoyed that, though I could have done with another beer. Oh, I almost forgot in my excitement. Any progress with our favourite mathematician, Li Zuanfei?'

32

The bar was an immense cavern and dark. It smelled musty. It had the dead air of a tomb unopened for centuries, though in this instance the oxygen-starved atmosphere was tinged with the sour stink of stale booze. Heavy curtains covered floor to ceiling windows that would have offered a fine view of the sea had they been pulled back. There were some low lights on the long bar and the tables. To Brodick it looked like an Edward Hopper painting, only gloomier. If the intention had been to create a cosy, romantic space, it had failed horribly. But it was the perfect place for a meeting.

Only one customer sat at the bar, right in the centre, leaning on the polished top with his forearms and nursing a glass beer mug that looked tiny in his immense hands. When Brodick's eyes became accustomed to the murk, he recognised the hunched figure; it was Li Zuanfei, otherwise known at Tony Lee, maths boffin extraordinary.

Lee or Li didn't turn to see who it was but spoke as Brodick approached; he seemed to know who it was already.

'The barman will be along in a moment.'

Brodick climbed on to a bar stool, leaving one vacant stool between them.

'Thanks for agreeing to meet me.'

'Thank you for coming all this way south.'

'That's okay, Tony. I'm glad to have this chance to talk."

'I want her phone number, Drew.'

'I'm sorry…?'

'I want her phone number, man.'

Li turned on his stool to face Brodick.

'Whose number?'

'That gorgeous lady in black with gold jewellery, of course. Who else? Don't say you don't know who I'm talking about. I saw you talking to her earlier. I'm talking about the sexy little woman at the Backstreet.'

'I think I know who you mean.'

'Of course you do, I know. Please give me her phone number. Are you seeing her?'

The man was a lech, that much was clear; though there were lechers and there were lechers. Weren't all men lechers of one sort or another? Wasn't Brodick? There were charming, suave lechers, there were polite lechers, there were sophisticated men who leched in an acceptable if not entirely attractive way, and there were objectionable, salacious lechers, lechers who were gauche, bad mannered, even violent. And there were the criminal lechers and just occasionally, Brodick supposed, there were men who progressed through several of these categories until they ended up either behind bars or as hopeless and helpless old gropers without the wherewithal to continue to do whatever it was that they used to get away with.

At any rate, Brodick wasn't keen on giving Abrielle access to Li or vice versa.

'That's not what I came here to talk about.'

'It's what *I* want to talk about, though. Do we have a deal?'

'Sorry, no phone number.'

'You don't have her phone number, or you won't give it to me?'

Clearly this wasn't some of kind of joke. Li or Lee was serious, even a little threatening.

'Does it make any difference?'

'I guess not, but then we have nothing more to say to each other.' Li turned away from Brodick and stared straight ahead at the ranks of bottles.

The barman's arrival interrupted this bizarre exchange. Brodick ordered an ice-cold Heineken. At least the Summerland was still serving alcohol, though how long that would continue would depend on the power struggle between Amal and Islamic Jihad.

The lager arrived with a decent head on it.

They both raised their glasses and drank, but nobody said anything. Brodick had a chance to look over his companion. He noted the Chinese academic's brawn, his immense shoulders and arms, the massive hands. So many Chinese were slim, slightly built. Not Li. He wasn't tall, but he looked as if he might have pulled a rickshaw on the streets of Shanghai, or dug coal out of a mountain for a living. He looked strong enough to have been a junior weightlifting champion, about to burst the seams of his summer shirt. His hair was thick and wiry, his complexion blebby. His muscular forearms and the back of his big hands were hairy, too, the fingers like sausages.

He was anything but handsome. Powerful, masculine, forceful—very much so.

'My conference is over and I'm leaving in a few days.'

'You're flying out?'

Li shook his head. 'I'm told the airport is likely to close again, so I'm going by ferry—from Jounieh—just to be on the safe side. I'll catch a flight home in Larnaca via London. Maybe you know this ferry yourself.'

'I do. I've taken the boat myself and will do so again next week. It's not too bad—it's just takes a lot longer, that's all, but it's a chance to catch up on sleep.'

'Uh-huh. In the meantime I'm staying put because I'm being followed.'

'By whom?'

'No friggin' idea. Couple of cars always behind my taxi wherever I go.'

'It's to do with your work?'

'What else? That's why you're talking to me here today, right?'

'What makes you say that?'

'Let me save you some time, Drew. I know you're British,

though you could be working for just about anyone, I guess. But you're going to make me an offer, or someone you work for is going to do so. I don't believe that stuff about working for a travel company.'

Li turned his head and Brodick saw that his eyes were like two small restless currants moving incessantly. They looked as if they were struggling to escape the massive cheeks and forehead squeezing them. A lifetime's endeavour by the look of it. Right now the small black currants were still and fixed on Brodick.

'Man, I don't mean to offend you, but I never believed your bull about being a manager of a travel company visiting Beirut in the middle of a shitstorm. So let me be frank. I won't work for the Canadian or American governments. I've turned down an offer to return to Shanghai. The PRC has been after me for years, ever since my first degree, and I'm not going back there. They made all sorts of promises, assurances, but I know they like to have leverage, but aside from a grandmother I haven't seen for fifteen years, I have no close living relatives in China. So there's no leverage in it for them except for the usual appeals to my patriotism and ethnicity.

'You don't know what it's like. The Communists said the revolution was to free the peasants, workers and soldiers. Right? But nowadays Chinese society resembles what it was before 1949. It has a ruling class of businesspeople, professionals and Party nomenklatura, then the middle class, and below them the low paid, working terrible hours.

'But now the Soviets are after me, too—but if you're going to make me an offer to work in Great Britain then you can tell your pals right now—I'm interested. Okay? If the terms are right. *If.* Otherwise it's going to be Australia. I like the Australians I've met, and they seem to have a really great country with some first-rate research centres.'

Brodick held up his hands, showing the palms. 'I don't have an offer for you, Tony. Sorry. It's not my line of work. But I do know someone in the UK embassy in Nicosia with the right contacts. I'm sure he'd want to meet you and discuss whatever it is you want to do. Maybe you could meet up in Larnaca before your flight home, or perhaps in London. I can arrange it if you want.'

'First things first. Give me Abrielle's phone number.'

'You're not serious.'

'You bet I am.' Li grinned at Brodick's surprised and disapproving expression.

Brodick's obsession—and it was an obsession—with Fang, both professional and personal, was by now complete. He recognised that Li was developing something similar towards Abrielle; the latter was sexy, unconventional, even fascinating. Her appeal was undeniable. But he had his suspicions about Abrielle's objectives, and helping Li and Abrielle get together didn't seem like a good idea at all. At the *Backstreet* she'd behaved very much like a *meiren ji* and that had put him on his guard. At first he thought she'd wanted to get into his flat to plant a recording device of some kind. But thinking about it, he'd come to the conclusion he wasn't her real target at all: he was just a stepping stone on Abrielle's path to her real goal, and that could be either Fang or indeed, Li himself. She'd have no difficulty in getting Li to agree to watching a video with her. She could be working for anyone, from the Iraqis and Saudis to the Israelis or the French. Whoever her handlers were, Brodick wasn't interested in a daytime tryst with Abrielle, not anymore, and he wanted to try to put Li off for as long as he could because he was afraid of what would happen if Li did succumb to Abrielle's undoubted charms.

'Okay. I don't have it on me.'

'But you will get me the number: that's a promise, right?'

'You have my word.' Brodick almost choked on the words.

'Okay. You call me with the number. Today. Then you can set up a meeting with your embassy contact in Larnaca.'

'Sure.'

'Let me tell you something about love.'

'Love?' Brodick was a little alarmed.

'The Chinese word for love is *ai*. It's a traditional character and it contains another character within it, *xin*, the heart. In

Communist China, many characters in Mandarin have been simplified—crudely stripped down, you might say—and in this case, the *xin* has been taken out of *ai*. What does that tell us about the Communists?'

It was a rhetorical question, clearly.

Li nodded, drank from his beer glass.

'Know what?'

'What?

'In the early years of the PRC, the main slogan was *wei renmin fuwu*: serve the people. Now it has been replaced by the very popular *wei renminbi fuwu*: serve the renminbi. That's our currency, if you didn't know.'

Brodick managed a smile. He was too wound up to find anything amusing.

'Look. Drew. You tell your friends or whoever they are that these are my terms. I'm not going to work full time for any intelligence organisation. I just wouldn't fit in: I'm no civil servant, okay? I hate all that nine-to-five crap and wearing a suit. And I'd make a very bad spy because I have never been able to keep secrets. I'm happy to be consulted by whoever it is on a fee basis from time to time and be paid well for it, of course, but I must have tenure as an associate or assistant professor of mathematics if I'm going to settle there. And the university has got to be the best in the field of pure and applied mathematics research. So in the UK that would mean Oxford, Cambridge, Imperial College, Bristol and St Andrews. Got that?'

'Forgive my ignorance, Tony, but there's no shortage of good mathematicians in China or anywhere else. What makes you think you're so special?'

'I haven't finished setting out my terms. You want another beer?'

Brodick shook his head.

'I must have the equivalent of $100k a year minimum, guaranteed, all relocation expenses, including temporary accommodation for three months, and a one-off, tax-free payment of $200k so I can buy somewhere decent to live. We're talking

US dollars. That's really important. I'm not going to stay in some rented shithole in the suburbs. Can you remember all that?'

'I'm listening.'

'You think I'm greedy? That my demands are excessive?'

'You've done your own research on costs and salaries, obviously, and presumably you have an accurate idea of what you're worth professionally. I really couldn't say whether you're greedy or otherwise. I'll pass it on. It's all I can do.'

'You can bet your British ass I've checked it out. What I'm asking for is realistic, believe me, because I want it to work. Now I'll deal with your question. I specialise in algorithms.'

'It doesn't mean much to me, I'm afraid.'

'Why am I not surprised? Like, there will come a time within a few years when everything we do is governed by them. It's a field that's advancing by leaps and bounds. You really don't know what I'm talking about, do you? So let's put it this way: maybe you want to know which offenders are likely to re-offend on release from prison, or which offenders are most likely to skip bail. An algorithm can provide the answer in seconds and achieve more than ninety-seven percent accuracy: a task that would otherwise take weeks or months to research. Or maybe you want to know how to drive up your computer sales in a given territory. Or how to get your novel onto the best seller lists in the United States. Maybe you want to encrypt your satellite communications so they're quite literally unbreakable. Or assess the number of serviceable, front-line aircraft are available on any one day in a foreign air force. That's what I do. Or at least, I build the algorithms to solve some of these issues.'

'You've told me what these things to do, but not what it is.'

'An algorithm is a process, a mathematical process. Like a complicated sieve. You feed in your input—it's processed by the algorithm—and then you have your output, the result. Now I'm getting algorithms to talk to each other, to exchange data and even exchange processes. I have algorithms within algorithms, like houses in a neighbourhood, all communicating with one another.'

'I don't think I'm any the wiser, Tony. Sorry. Is that why you think the Soviets are pursuing you? What makes you think they're on your tail?'

'Because two Russkies came here and invited me to lunch at the Soviet embassy. One of them was at the conference. They were polite, respectful: not at all what I'd expected. They told me I was a distinguished academic and my published work was greatly admired in their country. The usual bull. They said their colleagues at the embassy were interested in inviting me as an official guest of Moscow University to visit the USSR and give a series of talks and they would like to arrange the details of the trip and my remuneration over the lunch.'

'Talks on what?'

'Algorithms, of course.'

'Of course. And you said?'

'That I was grateful, flattered. That I would love to accept, like later this year.'

'Did you go to the lunch?'

'No, of course not. I didn't buy it, buddy. I said I was frightened by all the violence in Lebanon and didn't want to leave the hotel. Which is true. What I didn't say was that I really have no wish to end up working for the KGB or GRU.'

'What were their names?'

'Does it matter? They won't have been using their real names, anyway. At least, I don't think so.'

'When did this conversation take place?

'On Saturday. I think they had people watching me to ensure I was around when they came by. I'm sure they'll be back again.'

'They gave you their cards?'

'Sure. You want them?'

'It might help.'

Li plucked a wallet from his back pockets, extracted the cards; he seemed to have a large number, no doubt from the conference at the American University.

'And since then? Nothing?'

'No. But I'm sure they're the guys tagging me wherever I go. Not that I go anywhere much, not once the fighting started up again. I'm too fucking scared. I stay in my room or come in here for a drink. That's about it. It seems to have started all over again; something about a ship sunk by the Syrian military as it docked in Jounieh. You heard? Yes? Well, that's what the local media say, but who the hell knows the truth of what happened? I'm no longer sure whether it's safer to leave Lebanon by boat or by plane. To be honest, there doesn't seem to be much in it either way.'

Brodick realised at this point that he had something of a problem on his hands. Yes, he'd not only made contact with Li but encouraged the mathematician to confide in him.

The problem was indeed his success. Brodick's employers, in the form of Nick Fenner, wanted to get their hands on Li: but so did his supposed agent, Fang. They both wanted to snatch, bribe, employ or otherwise exploit Li and his skills.

How was Brodick to satisfy both master and mistress?

But then he was only acting as the access agent for both parties which meant he made the introductions—nothing more.

One thing was certain. It wouldn't be left to Li to decide his own fate.

*

The sunlight was so bright as they walked out of the hotel that both men shielded their eyes with their hands, and it took a moment or two before Brodick could make out anything at all in the glare. There was another shock: the bark of the big guns on Mount Lebanon.

Li had asked if he could join Brodick in his return by taxi to West Beirut. He said he could do with the company and he'd already checked out. All he had was the one bag and maybe Brodick could drop him off somewhere close to the Mayfair Hotel where he'd booked a room. It was poor tradecraft, but Brodick had agreed.

But now Li turned and ran back inside.

It was odd the way young men—and no doubt young women too—were afraid of the wrong things and unafraid about stuff that should scare them out of their wits. Both outgoing artillery fire and the incoming rounds were—as far as Brodick could tell—too far off to pose any real danger. On the other hand the two men sitting in the powder blue Chevvy and watching Brodick and his companion certainly posed a threat.

When Brodick's taxi turned up he asked the driver to pop the boot and dropped in his pusser's bag and was about to climb in the back when Li emerged once again and hurried over, carrying his own suitcase.

'Sorry, man, that scared the shit out of me.'

They sat next to each other on the rear seat, Li still very nervous. He sat directly behind the driver, slouching down as low as he could, biting his thumbnail and hiding behind the elderly man with abundant grey hair growing over his frayed collar. The driver crossed himself in the Greek orthodox fashion, then leaned forward and touched a crucifix on his dashboard.

'Where to, chief?'

'The Commodore.'

'Why?' Li was bothered by this apparent change in plan.

'It's safer than the Mayfair, Tony. Believe me. A little more expensive but safer.'

That was true, but the real reason was that Brodick didn't want Li rubbing shoulders with Fang. He didn't want them to bump into each other on the stairs or in the bar. Fang might make another approach on behalf of the PRC, and Li would run a mile. If there was to be another Chinese effort to recruit him, Brodick wanted it done differently: without scaring him off. Anyhow, he wanted Fenner to have a decent chance at this one.

The driver turned in his seat to look at Brodick.

'Too much shooting. Airport road very bad.'

Brodick wasn't interested in the driver's excuses.

He hit the back of the driver's seat with his fist. 'Let's go!'

Everything went well until they left the airport behind and were heading north along the coastal highway towards the city centre. Li was curled up in his seat, instinctively trying to make himself as small a target as he could, sliding down so that his head was below the edge of the window. He wrapped his arms around himself, his legs folded in a foetus-like position.

Maybe he didn't realise that were only two ways to take effective shelter: to huddle down directly behind the engine block, or crouch behind the wheels. But artillery? Nowhere was safe from those big guns except a well-dug slit trench and three feet of overhead cover of logs and sandbags.

The firing was regular: a steady series of deep barks in rapid succession, Brodick guessing it must be an entire battery of Soviet-built guns brought into action, and the impacts were all over on the left, between the highway and the sea. Brodick knew artillery shells had a tendency to throw forward on impact, and that the danger lay in an arc just beyond the point of the shell burst, which was why infantry, properly trained, could "walk up" behind a moving barrage onto the enemy positions. So he wasn't unduly bothered by the pall of smoke and dust slowly drifting away to the left. The taxi itself wasn't in the line of fire. It wasn't in the killing zone. Not yet.

But that all changed, and it changed fast. Probably the first thing that happened—that Brodick saw happen, which was not the same thing—was that the blue Chevvy pulled out and started to overtake. It moved right over into the outside lane despite the oncoming traffic, its wheels on the far side kicking up stones and dust. The Russians or whatever they were in the front seats didn't look at Brodick and his companions but stared straight ahead like soldiers on parade as they rapidly overhauled the taxi. One—the guy in the passenger seat—had a shaved head. The driver was bearded and wore glasses.

Less than a second later Brodick heard the unmistakable sound of an artillery round pass overhead. It was close. The sound wa very distinctive and couldn't be mistaken for anything else. I sounded a bit like a large metal tray whizzing over their heads, metallic screeching and flapping as it tore through the air.

Brodick tensed; his scrotum seemed to retract and his pulse raced. Everything around him seemed to slow right down, the colours and shapes were more vivid than ever.

It was no doubt the effect of adrenalin pumping into his veins.

The incoming artillery shell sounded so close Brodick thought that perhaps he could raise an arm and touch it were it not for the roof of the taxi.

The driver panicked. He stamped on the accelerator and the car lurched forward, but the driver also started weaving, throwing the steering wheel violently right and left as the taxi's speed increased, almost as if he was trying to catch up to the Russians ahead of them while at the same time trying to perform some kind of zigzag evasion like a WW2 destroyer trying to dodge a U-boat's torpedoes. He struck the horn repeatedly, though there was no point as everyone else was doing something similar, setting up a general howl of outrage and panic. The taxi rocked from side to side. Li was shouting: no, screaming, mouth open, his face contorted, eyes squeezed shut, the little black currants vanished in folds of flesh, hands clamped over his ears.

Brodick tried to use his arms and legs to steady himself and avoid being thrown around by the driver's manoeuvres so he could watch what was happening.

Brodick felt super alert, super aware. His senses seemed heightened, the colours and sounds seemed especially intense.

The next round fluttered and flapped over their heads and detonated just ahead, perhaps twenty metres or so, a huge column of dust and smoke and falling debris. It was swiftly followed by another—maybe half a second—and the latter exploded in a burst of smoke and flame to the right of the highway, this time a little further away but no more than ten metres ahead and Brodick knew that as this one "threw forward", their own taxi would be right in the cone-shaped zone of splinters and blast. It did indeed shake the taxi as if a gigantic animal had reached out and smacked it with its paw, and then they tore through the drifting smoke back into bright sunshine, only sideways this time, still apparently, amazingly, incredibly intact.

Except for the windscreen, which had vanished. Some of the glass was in his lap.

How did that happen?

Brodick sensed where the next shell would impact. The road had been neatly straddled by the two earlier rounds and he was not wrong. Unfortunately. For it struck the highway on the centre island, a juddering crash, an explosion he felt through his feet, his legs, his gut. Brodick flinched instinctively, hunching his shoulders, and the flash of light was followed by darkness as the taxi sped into the epicentre of the detonation.

He saw Li on the floor between the seats, rolled up like a ball.

The light of day again. Only this time the Chevvy and the two Russians were no more.

Where they had been, where they should be still, the road was clear.

As the taxi rocked and shook at speed on through another column of smoke and dust, Brodick saw pieces of the Russians' car: a blue door, a blackened and twisted part of the undercarriage, lots of smoking upholstery and rubber that looked like lumps of kelp washed up on a beach, along with the limbs of one man, or maybe both of them, smouldering in the debris but clearly human because of the torn clothing, the blue jeans on what had been a thigh.

It was all too much for the driver.

He turned the steering wheel hard over, and the car followed in a sluggish skid, nearly rolling over before straightening out and bouncing over the kerb and down an incline into a dusty side street to their left, towards the sea, between the kind of crude, unfinished concrete buildings typical of the southern suburbs, the stronghold of Islamic Jihad and the neighbourhood where foreigners were likely held captive.

Brodick yelled at the driver. He wasn't sure what he was shouting, other than that he should get out of there. It had been a stupid move. They couldn't move forward or back because other drivers had all the same idea and were trying to escape, to get as far from the coastal highway as they could. They were jammed tight in a queue of cars, bumper to bumper, and now they were a sitting duck for those guns. Surely the artillery spotters up there in the hills could see the sun reflected on the metallic river of traffic and its tributaries. Brodick thought that all they had to do was direct the gunners' fire to turn that same river of panic into a colossal inferno.

Li was struggling to open the door, sobbing and kicking at it.

Brodick grabbed him by the shoulders, pulled him away from the door to stop him killing himself and tried to calm him down, holding him in a bear hug. 'It's going to be okay, Tony. It's going to be okay.' Not that he believed it himself. The man wasn't just frightened. He was petrified. Brodick didn't despise him for it; he sympathised. It seemed extraordinary that he himself had been amazed, transfixed by what had just occurred as if he'd been watching a particularly tense and dramatic movie, seeing every move, every detail, not wanting to miss anything. He had been oddly calm. He knew he shouldn't have been; he had every reason to be scared out of his wits, too. What on earth was wrong with him? It wasn't natural. It wasn't human. It would have been entirely normal for him to have lost control of himself, to have soiled his pants, just like Li—who was now sitting in a puddle of his own urine—but instead he had remained a spectator. Would he have retained this peculiar sense of the observer if wounded, perhaps maimed? Would he have felt agonising pain and, shrieking with the shock of it, watched with some curiosity as he bled out, as he saw his own guts strewn across the back seat of the taxi, as he felt the light fade for the last time?

'You're going to be fine, Tony.'

In the circumstances, there wasn't much else he could do or say.

*

It was nearly midnight.

'Is this for me?'

'It is.'

'A present?'

'Something of the sort.'

'What is it?'

'A book.'

'That's very sweet of you.'

'I do hope you like it.'

'It's an odd kind of wrapping paper.'

'It's too late for Christmas. Nothing wrong with newspaper, anyhow. It's yesterday's *Cyprus Mail*.'

'I'm deeply touched.'

Fang unwrapped the parcel with care as if it might be dangerous, sitting cross-legged on her hotel bed and wearing nothing but her lacy black pants and a t-shirt. The bed was a small double, not really big enough for two people to sprawl across comfortably but in their relaxed, post-coitus mood, the lumpy mattress and noisy bedsprings didn't seem to matter. Fang had already sent her minders home long before Brodick's arrival.

'I love it, Richard.'

'Good. I'm glad. It's Drew, remember. For someone with so many aliases, you seem to find it hard to remember mine.'

She picked it up, riffled the pages and even sniffed it. 'It's current?'

'Oh, yes.'

'You're a star, Drew.'

'Thanks.'

'No, really. You stole it?'

'I did.'

'From Nicosia Station, from under the nose of your boss, Mr Fenner, right?'

'Uh-huh. It was lying on a desk and I took it while he was using the bathroom.'

'Careless. Of them, not you.'

'It was, yes.'

'They didn't search you when you left?'

'They never do.'

'In China, and our embassies abroad, we're all searched. In and out. Our bags, our clothing. They pat us down every time, run those machines over us. We're scanned. Security is very thorough.'

'Useful to know.'

'You don't use the same codes as this, do you?'

'My signals are separate from diplomatic traffic.'

'You have your own system, then, and your own encryption machine.'

'I do, yes.'

'Like me. I use the one-time pad and it's unbreakable as you know.'

'Unless someone steals it, too.'

She laughed at this, moved closer, pushed him back and straddled him, leaning forward so that her hair hung around his face like a curtain. Fang put her mouth next to his ear.

'My clever, clever English thief. I just love your bona fides. They're *so* sexy.'

'What book are you using for your one-time pad?'

'Oh, wouldn't you just like to know?'

'Bet you it's poetry. Or a novel.'

'If you're very nice to me, exceptionally nice, I just might tell you.'

It had been a long day, but at least Brodick was managing to do something right.

33

'I can't sleep. It's getting bad out there.'

Fang's bedside clock showed the time as 03.24.

Brodick turned to her. 'Neither can I.'

Despite the curtains, flashes of light splashed and rippled across walls and ceiling like one of those old black-and-white reels of film that would flicker constantly on the screen.

'That was close.'

'It's impossible to tell how close it is in a built-up area.'

'The building's shaking.'

Brodick slid out of bed, walked naked to the window and peeked out.

'Get back here. The window's not safe.'

He ignored her. 'It's a duel. Mortars, mostly. They're also using a lot of flares. Both sides. Or perhaps I should say all sides.'

'How can you tell?'

'Mortar bombs and artillery shells sound different.'

'So you're an expert now, after what: three weeks?'

'That's right. I am. They all sound different, in flight and when they detonate. I'm beginning to distinguish the different calibres, too.' Brodick turned away from the window and walked to the bathroom and, leaving the door open, lifted the seat and peed. Then he washed his hands and splashed water in his face.

'Come back to bed, *ying yi*, and tell me about yourself.'

'You just called me an English barbarian.' This triggered a peal of laughter from Fang.

He obeyed, not because he particularly wanted to but because he couldn't think of anything better to do, and he wasn't going to protest at being labelled English. He plumped up the pillow, pulled the sheet over his legs and groin, and sat up. He took her hand in his.

'What do you want to know?'

'Why aren't you scared? You should be scared.'

'I don't know. It's mostly exciting, to be honest.'

'You're weird.'

'Thank you.'

'Tell me about your mother and father.'

'Is this for your files? My *Guoanbu* psychological profile?'

She smiled. 'Maybe. I want to know.'

'My mother was not a well woman.'

Fang raised herself on one elbow and watched him. 'How do you mean?'

'She was diagnosed as manic depressive. Huge, uncontrollable mood swings. My father just said she was crazy. The psychiatrists gave her electric shock treatment. It was awful. Lots of drugs. Back then they didn't have a clue.'

'She was violent?'

'Sometimes. Nowadays it's called bipolar because it sounds less awful, apparently.'

Brodick had never spoken of it to anyone else and he didn't know why he was doing so now, opening up to—of all people—a Communist Chinese intelligence officer.

'She was violent: towards you?'

'Not generally. A few times, yes.'

He remembered being taken to hospital after one outburst in a restaurant because she'd thrown him out of his highchair across the dining room and the staff had called an ambulance, suspecting that he'd cracked a couple of his ribs.

'But you loved her, didn't you?'

'Very much. I always tried to stand up for her. She loved me, too. But I learned to keep my distance, not to get too close. She was so unpredictable. She wasn't in control of herself some of the time. I was ashamed of the way she was, and I blamed myself though it really isn't my fault. My family tried not to talk about it. Everyone was ashamed.'

'And your famous father? The great spy?'

'He found peacetime difficult. He couldn't adapt to it, I think, couldn't find a role that meant anything even though he was seen as a success. He was a secret drinker, and when he drank he used to beat my mother. It left bruises and sometimes a black eye. I used to hear them screaming at one another at night, the sound of the blows.'

Brodick remembered now that he used to lie in bed while the fights were going on and think to himself that things couldn't get any worse—and that had made him feel better. Not that they did get better, though, not for a long time.

'How did he treat you?'

'My dad? I always wanted his approval, like all children do, but he left us when I was around five. At least, I think I was five. I was sent to boarding school, so I guess I never got it. Approval, I mean.'

'Did he beat you?'

'Only for being naughty.'

'Much the same in China. What did he use to hit you?'

'His leather belt.'

'The English are so cruel to their own children.'

'I'm inclined to agree.'

'You were born where?'

'In Beirut. But we went to South Africa soon afterwards.'

Why was he confiding in her? It was so unprofessional.

'You were a colonial. You didn't belong in England or your precious Scotland and that hurt, too.'

'How did you know?'

'I know how it feels to be on the outside looking in, wanting to be accepted and loved, and maybe one day I'll tell you why.'

Their exchange was broken by a series of loud detonations.

'We'd be safer in the basement, Drew.'

'No, we wouldn't. We might *feel* safer, but it's not the same thing.'

'Meaning what?'

'A round from one of those bunker-busting mortars—they're Soviet 240mm mortars, huge beasts from World War 2, and both Syrians and Phalangists have them—went through the roof of a twelve-story apartment block just two days ago, and it went down vertically through all the floors and finally detonated in the basement. Forty-three people died. Dozens were badly injured. Maimed. Women, kids, entire families.'

Fang said nothing. Brodick reflected that most people would react: curse, cover their faces with their hands, mutter a prayer, moan or cry. Not Fang. She lay on her back again, both eyes open and made no sound at all.

She turned to him. 'Don't you feel scared—ever?'

'Of course I do. Often.'

'Really, Drew? You don't show it.'

'It's like an alarm bell ringing. It's there constantly, only with the sound level turned right down. It only gets loud when it's really very bad.'

'It's just a bell ringing in your head?'

'Something like that. It tells me to stop, to be still, to take cover, not to turn a particular corner, not to get in a particular taxi, or not to go out. It's instinct, I suppose.'

Fang frowned, thinking about what he'd said. 'Do your people expect you to seduce me?'

Brodick was surprised. 'I've no idea. I don't think so.'

'My people expect me to sleep with you to cement the relationship, to make you my agent. Isn't it the same for your people?'

Brodick thought for a moment. 'They might be concerned that if we slept together I wouldn't be able to stay objective, that my loyalties could be…'

He hesitated, searching for the word.

'Compromised.' Fang finished the sentence for him.

'Yes.'

'Whereas my boss would want me to be the one on top, literally and figuratively.'

'I like it when you're on top and I think you also like having a sex slave.'

'I know you do, British traitor—and pervert.'

They smiled at each other.

'We're enemies.'

'That's a harsh word, Drew. I would say we were adversaries.'

'Adversaries who like fucking each other. You've forgotten but you used the term enemy yourself the other evening.'

'You're so crude. I would say adversaries who have a soft spot for each other.'

'Really, Fang. I'm overcome. You have a soft spot for me? Really?'

She punched his arm and muttered something incomprehensible in Mandarin.

The room shook.

She was right: it wasn't safe in the hotel room. By hand gestures and a raising of his eyebrows he questioned Fang, wanting to know if she really would prefer to go down to the basement, but now that he'd taken her concern seriously, she waved it aside.

'Your embassy people will make Li an offer. You've already told them what his demands are. The equivalent of at least 100,000 US dollars a year, a 200,000-dollar tax-free lump sum, all relocation expenses paid and London has approved the deal. He's to be offered an assistant professorship at Imperial College, which I believe is in London. He will find a number of Chinese postgraduate students there, I'm sure.'

Were some of them *Guoanbu* assets? How did she know all this?

She seemed to know what he was thinking, and not for the first time. 'He told our people the same thing, Drew. And the French and Americans. Probably others, too. He's up for sale and wants everyone to know it.'

A particularly loud explosion shook the bed, so much so it felt as if it was airborne for a split second and the hotel room was lit up, so bright that there were no shadows. Even Brodick would have had to admit that *was* close, far too close. Fang grabbed his hand again and squeezed it hard.

Was that a new crack in the ceiling, or had it been there before?

She spoke with the calm tone that is only possible with immense self-control. 'Maybe that was one of your monster mortar bombs. If we died here they'd find us both naked in bed. It wouldn't look good.'

What would that matter how it would look if they were dead? It was more likely they'd have to scrape bits of them both off the rubble of whatever was left of the hotel with a shovel. Whatever gobs of flesh and splinters of bone were left would be inextricably mixed. They'd be beyond recognition, if it came to that. Appearances certainly wouldn't matter, not even to a senior *Guoanbu* officer. There were too many dead and dying in the city to bother with autopsies and DNA samples. The entire country was a crime scene.

The artillery bombardment—or duel—seemed to have stopped.

It truly was a deafening silence. Brodick's ears were buzzing: whether from the bombardment or the stressful nature of their discussion, he didn't know.

Brodick decided it was time to change the subject.

'You were telling me about the Dragon's Lair, you remember? A magician and Communist agent called Gu, a tough guy. But we were interrupted by the arrival of *Basra Star* in Jounieh. Maybe you could tell me now before we try to get some more sleep.'

Fang jumped off the bed, pulling one sheet around her and went over to the minibar and opened it.

'I'm thirsty. What would you like? I think we should have a drink first and then I'll tell you the rest of it. There's whisky and gin and some vodka...'

*

'You remember the man I was telling you about? As far as my people are concerned, indeed, the entire People's Republic, Gu is seen as evil: a traitor of the worst kind. A drug fiend, a womaniser, gambler, a liar: every crime and vice known in China is attributed to him in our history books.

'In 1931, Gu was head of the Shanghai Special Services Section, a crucial and senior role in the Party's intelligence apparatus. Despite his talent as a professional illusionist, Gu was recognised in Wuhan by a nationalist—a KMT agent—just as Gu emerged from a cinema or theatre. Or so the story goes. He was quickly set upon and overpowered.

'Remember, the split between the CCP and KMT had happened four years earlier, in 1927. General Chiang Kai-shek had taken us by surprise and launched a massacre of our members, setting himself up at his army headquarters in Nanjing. Two years later, after tremendous efforts, we succeeded in planting a trio of our best agents inside the Nationalist headquarters, in fact, one of them right inside the offices of the Generalissimo himself.

'Li Kenong, a journalist, was the leader. They are known as the Three Heroes of the Dragon's Lair. The others were Qian Zhuangfei and Hu Di. All our people have to study this episode. The Heroes' task was to serve as an early warning, a tripwire, to sound the alarm and inform the Party immediately of any major KMT penetrations of the Party or defections by our people. We were in a bad way, with surviving cadres having to flee the cities. We were isolated, and on the verge of total defeat, even annihilation.

'So Gu faced a grim choice. He could tell his captors what he knew, which was a lot—names and addresses, safe houses, organisational structure, communications and more—or be slowly tortured to death with the certain knowledge that his wife and children would also be murdered. What could he do? I don't imagine he ran laughing into the KMT's embrace. But he did give in. He had to. He agreed to defect, he even agreed to head up a new anti-communist investigations unit and to write a special manual on how to track down Communist cadres. I suspect—

and you won't find this is in any official document—that he was playing for time. Most of us would agree to anything to escape the exquisite pain of being tortured to death. To be honest, I can't blame him for trying to survive.

'It is said that he demanded a meeting with Chiang Kai-shek, who agreed to meet him after an interval of a few days. No doubt Gu wanted to appeal for the lives of his family. His captors in the form of a local BIS officer—'

'BIS?'

'National Bureau of Investigations and Statistics. The KMT intelligence service.'

'So innocuous, in name anyway.'

'This BIS official sent off half a dozen signals to Nanjing reporting Gu's capture. Gu was the KMT's most formidable opponent in Shanghai at that time. It was a huge stroke of good fortune for our Nationalist enemies. A great victory for them!

'But the head of the BIS, Xu Enzeng, had left his office to go dancing. One of the Three Heroes I mentioned—Qian Zhuangfei—was head of KMT encryption and his boss's absence gave him time to alert Li Kenong, who was working in the Shanghai Central Telegraph Bureau. Li in turn alerted others—and they managed to organise safe houses for around five hundred activists.

'I think Gu would have betrayed local cadres first. But there were soon roundups in several cities, multiple arrests, and clearly Gu was finally compelled to give them everything he had; probably rationing it as best he could to ensure he could stay alive and secure his family's safety. Or perhaps not. I don't know this for sure, Drew, but it's what I would do. It's the only intelligent, professional thing one could have done, don't you think?'

'And Gu's family?'

'Oh, Zhou Enlai ordered their execution: as a deterrent, you understand.'

'Oh, no. How many?'

'Ten family members were killed.'

'All of them?'

'The assassins left an infant alive. A girl. I don't think they left her alive on purpose. Maybe they just didn't see her. A professional accident on their part. It's said the slaughter took place when Gu was actually meeting the Generalissimo. A poetic touch, don't you think? The victims' bodies were buried quickly under a patio and it was only the stink of their decomposing corpses that led to their eventual discovery.'

Fang's tone was bitter. She looked upset, as if she was holding back tears.

'What happened to the child, the little girl?'

Fang shrugged, turned away as if distancing herself from the tale. 'No one knows.'

'What was her name? Was it Gu?'

It must have been. Brodick didn't know how Chinese surnames worked, whether they were inherited, passed down.

But what did it mean? What was this Gu and his murdered family to Fang?

There was something here, Brodick could feel it. Something about this was far more important than Fang was letting on, a coded message of some kind. He could sense the tension in her—or was he imagining it?

Fang put her head back and drank sparkling mineral water from a plastic bottle.

'If she's still alive she would be what, 49? 50?'

'Something like that, I suppose, yes. Maybe.'

Fang wasn't sharing the drama of the Dragon's Lair for Brodick's entertainment. There had to be a purpose. Brodick thought whatever it was it must be vital, at least to Fang. She'd clearly departed from the Party line. Why? What was he missing? Was this her story, in effect, though DRAGON couldn't or wouldn't admit it?

34

There was no one in the gloomy reception; the only sound was the ticking of a wall clock. Brodick made his way outside in the first, grey, flinty light and found himself standing on what looked at first like sea ice: silvery-grey stuff that crunched and cracked loudly under his shoes and stretched from one side of the street to the other, carpeting the road all the way downhill towards the Corniche and the sea. Only it wasn't ice but shattered glass from scores of windows and shop fronts shattered in the overnight artillery exchanges. The cars parked nose to tail on either side had also been hit. Two blackened hulks were still smouldering, glowing in the pre-dawn murk, and most of those Brodick passed had lost windscreens and the bodywork of several had been riddled with steel fragments.

The stench of burning caught in his throat: rubber, metal, paint, wood, all the toxic detritus of urban conflagration.

There was no one about.

Further downhill a large white stucco building, probably built around the turn of the century, had taken a direct hit and caught fire. It was a ruin now, a corpse of brick and plaster still burning, flames licking the French-style windows and wooden shutters, the blackened roof beams still alight, fizzing and crackling in the heat. The gracious palms that had stood sentinel outside in the garden had been reduced to blackened stumps.

Other streets—and it seemed quite arbitrary—appeared entirely untouched.

By instinct rather than design, Brodick made his way to the

penthouse, heading in the general direction rather as a horse might find its way home. Unlike a horse, however, Brodick was deep in thought. He was keenly aware that for the first time in Beirut he'd felt entirely at ease the previous night, relaxed and at ease in Fang's company and she—if he wasn't very much mistaken—had behaved as if she too felt the same way. The intimacy they enjoyed had blunted the obvious risks of staying in the room during the onslaught. Stupid though it was, somehow they'd felt themselves immune, or at least Brodick had. In fact, the external danger seemed to enhance the pleasure of their encounter.

They were still rivals. Neither could forget that, not for a moment, yet somehow Brodick had felt safe in her embrace, even happy. Happiness! Now that was a rare sensation. Consciously, he knew DRAGON was dangerous, dangerous to him, to his Service. And she, with all her talk of the danger of possible contamination by Westerners, must have sensed the contradiction even more keenly. He was her enemy, too. Perhaps being in the very presence of the foreign contagion had only added to their hunger for each other.

It wasn't love, surely, yet it was undoubtedly more than just physical desire.

Brodick went through what could only be called an accounting procedure. How much had he given her? What had DRAGON given him? Had he given away—betrayed—more than she? Or had Fang perhaps given him—and betrayed her service—more?

Was a soon-to-be obsolete diplomatic signal codebook worth so much more than her latest contribution: a diagram and list of Guoanbu bureaux and their senior staff along with a list of five names of Guoanbu operatives working outside mainland China who might be susceptible to recruitment by SIS? Would the five all turn out to have been dangles, deliberately offered as bait? Those papers detailing the Guoanbu's Order of Battle were now in his pocket—along with negatives of the documents—and he could feel the outline of them against his body. He had no idea of their real worth as yet because the tables and names and annotated diagrams were in Chinese characters and would have to be translated by the Far East Controllerate back in Century House.

What would MacGregor make of it?

Brodick had given Fang a diplomatic codebook; she had given up a senior French intelligence officer ostensibly working for the Guoanbu, a mole of twelve years' standing.

He had given DRAGON the breakdown of the SIS and GCHQ structure in Cyprus; she had given him details of an Iraqi arms shipment of anti-ship missiles to Lebanon's Phalange and Maronite-led forces and the organisation of a reformed *Guoanbu* and its bureaux.

Was this a rough equivalence in betrayal?

Brodick wasn't sure if it was safer to walk down the pavements, hugging the buildings on one side or the other, or better to keep to the centre of the street. He was always frightened when out on the streets, but it was a fear that was he was used to; it was manageable. He walked past a deli—one of the upmarket places favoured by well-off Lebanese and the few remaining foreigners—and a favourite pit-stop on his way home from Levant Travel where he could buy an entire, thee-course meal as a takeaway along with a decent bottle of wine, keeping his ride waiting while he dashed in to collect and pay for his telephone order.

He wouldn't be able to do that any longer.

The red awning had been ripped to shreds: only the metal frame that had held it in place was visible, and that too was twisted and blackened. As for the shop itself, all that was left was a scorched hole in the wall. The plate glass display window, the door, the wonderful cakes and desserts stacked up for all passers-by to see—all gone.

Even the big red sign above the shop displaying the name—*Chez Arabe*—had been torn away. The pavement outside was littered with rubble and glass and what had been, until yesterday, the contents of the shop: shelves and tables, cabinets, a huge oven, fryers, freezers, whole chickens.

He would shower, change and call one of the office drivers to take him to Levant Travel. He had signals to send, calls to make. He told himself he must remember to call Abrielle and ask her—as a courtesy—if he could give her number to "Tony Lee". She might well object. So far, she hadn't called Brodick to suggest they watch a film together, apparently her coded phrase for sex in the afternoon. Or morning. Not that he minded or especially sought out the experience; but he had to admit he was curious.

Thinking of having sex with Abrielle was arousing, picturing her naked on the couch in the television room: and all at once made him feel guilty. How peculiar! Why would he, a single man, feel guilty about a hard-on and a little flirtation with a stranger in a bar who'd felt him up and then promised him an assignation while everyone else was at work? Unconsciously he must be feeling a sexual loyalty to Fang, the very woman who posed the greatest danger to him, the woman who had recruited him, and whom he had recruited. Their love making was part of their arsenal of deception, a shared tool kit, yet here he was, on the streets of Beirut, feeling a perverse loyalty to Fang. To his Chinese target. To DRAGON, the woman who had set him up and bested him in prison. How weird was that?

He chuckled out loud at the absurdity of Richard Brodick, the man he knew himself to be and sometimes didn't know at all.

It was with that thought that he found himself almost home.

And it was also with that thought that whatever it was happened.

Brodick felt a terrible, blinding pain, a gigantic whiplash, to his head, as if some gigantic beast had crept up on him from behind, grabbed his skull in its claws and shaken him violently, striking his head with a hammer and, if that wasn't enough, ripping out the flesh and hair.

Brodick gasped with the shock of it as if he'd been plunged into a sub-zero sea.

There must have been a detonation, but he'd heard nothing.

He felt he had been scalped.

Fuckan hell.

In effect, that was exactly what had happened, only he didn' yet know it.

This something—this same mythical beast, presumably—threw him off his feet, punching him hard, simultaneously lifting and tossing him forward, and he saw with some curiosity the ground pass beneath him until he was dropped back to earth on his hands and knees in the broken glass.

As if in a dream he studied the gem-like fragments glittering below him, the grit and dirt, a strange world a few inches from his eyes. The universe of ant-sized creatures, of creepy-crawlies. How odd! The light seemed to pulse dark and light, a rippling, the world slowing down and Brodick floating, or felt himself to be. He was strangely relaxed, and he was being carried off somewhere—quietly, softly, and yes, almost happily and at peace. There was a serenity in dying, he thought. A comfort, even.

No pain now. Nothing more in this world to be afraid of.

He didn't resist because he couldn't.

Brodick seemed to have left, then returned, and now was conscious again, but his world had gone dark. His eyes were open but he couldn't see. He really was blind, yet his eyes flickered open and shut like an old movie reel. This puzzled him more than the cuts to his head, hands and knees, for the wounds were numb, and for what might have been for several of those same moments he stayed still, ears ringing, breathing through his mouth—he could hear his stertorous rasping—trying to work it out, until he realised it was his own warm blood that ran down his face and into his eye sockets, the corners of his mouth and off his chin, drenched his shirt and formed a glossy pool in the dirt under his cheek. He could taste it.

*

'You're lucky.'

'So I can go home?'

'I don't see why not. If you suffer a lot of pain or have any difficulty with your eyesight or speech, please come back as quickly as possible. Same goes for any severe headaches you may experience. Take these with you. They'll help with the pain. One before meals should keep it manageable and help you sleep. I advise you rest as much as possible over the next few days.'

'Sure. Thanks.' Brodick slipped the pills into his shirt pocket. Rest was out of the question. There was simply far too much to do.

The papers and film he carried were safe, though the envelope and one sheet carried his bloody fingerprints.

'In normal circumstances we'd like to keep you here for a day or two under observation and give you a scan just to make sure, but as you see…' The doctor shrugged, gesturing with a sweep of one hand to their surroundings.

Brodick could see for himself that circumstances were anything but "normal". The hospital was packed with patients—on gurneys lining the corridors, on stretchers on the floor, a floor slippery with body fluids despite the best efforts of the staff to repeatedly swab down the linoleum with disinfectant. Blood and piss, mostly. More patients were arriving all the time, and clearly the hospital needed to process people as quickly as possible to make room for the newcomers being carried in by paramedics.

There was much shouting, crying and sobbing as relatives tried to push their way in to find their injured family members. Police and paramilitary types were trying to restore order, but their heavy-handed efforts only seemed to make the chaos worse with scuffles erupting in both foyer and overcrowded wards.

Dr Rafiq—tall and broad in blood spattered scrubs—found the time to explain to Brodick that they were employing triage: attending to the wounded with the best chances of survival first. Rafiq spoke as he personally stitched Brodick's scalp back together—thirty-four stitches in all, he informed Brodick—and then watched as the long, crooked wound was bandaged by one of the nurses. The same nurse had then cleaned and bandaged his left hand, picking out fragments of glass and street filth, and had also cleaned the cuts of both his knees and shins. The patient realised with a pang of guilt that he was getting special treatment as a Westerner: not that it was deserved. They were kind to him, talking to him, reassuring him and he was using up their precious time.

The Lebanese surgeon offered Brodick a hand to get up off the gurney and he accompanied Brodick to the front door, stopping outside to light a cigarette.

'I was a cosmetic surgeon when the war started, you see. I went to Belfast to study battlefield surgery in '76 and that's what I've been doing ever since. I sometimes wonder whether I'll ever get back to cosmetic work—I guess it depends on whether this war will ever end. In my worst moments I fear it never will. This—today—is nothing. The Israeli invasions was much worse, believe me. This was just one incident, but an invasion means a continuous stream of the badly wounded.'

Dr Rafiq said that he and one of his colleagues had conducted a study of how Lebanese wounded in the so-called civil war had a sixty percent higher chance of survival than American troops wounded in Vietnam and eighty-four percent better chance than those injured in the Korean War.

'It's all about the time it takes for the wounded to reach the operating table before they go into shock. In Vietnam, thanks to the military's helicopters, U.S. soldiers were treated at a field surgery within an average of forty minutes of being hit. Here in Beirut, it's down to thirty minutes or less. Take a look at the map: the city is squeezed into a narrow shelf between mountain and sea. It's very compact. There's no other place for it to go. Second, we have a very high number of hospitals—many small and private like this one—in relation to the local population. That's because Beirut was the go-to destination for overseas patients. Medical tourism, they call it. Gulf Arabs used to choose to come here before the war for cosmetic surgery of all kinds, including restoration of the hymen, as well as specialised dental work.

'It means that in Beirut you're never far away from a hospital.'

'But you don't have helicopters. How do ambulances manage to get through to the wounded so quickly and get them back out to a hospital?'

'Good questions for a man who literally almost lost his head. When a car bomb goes off or there's an artillery or air attack, people don't wait for the ambulance. They just throw the wounded on the back seats of civilian cars and off they go, sometimes firing their guns into the air to clear a path for the injured…'

'So that's what happened to me?'

'Sure. Some PSP guys saw you hit—they said it was a single mortar round from Phalangist positions—and they commandeered a taxi and drove you here at speed. They fired their AKs in the air. It's become our equivalent of an ambulance siren. They didn't know how bad you were because of all the blood. That's the trouble with head wounds, there's always a lot of blood and the injury can look much worse than it really is.'

'I was lucky.'

'You were extremely lucky, Mr Sullivan, not just thanks to the PSP gunmen but because your skull and brain were undamaged: at least as far as we can tell. Whatever it was, it just sliced open your scalp. Probably a small, jagged splinter from a mortar bomb. It wasn't aimed at you—you were just in the wrong place at the wrong time. Pure chance. The cut was ragged, irregular. Another eighth of an inch and it would have penetrated both skull and brain tissue and you probably wouldn't have made it. By the way, you'll need to come back and have the bandages changed the day after tomorrow. Hopefully things will have quietened down by then…'

Dr Rafiq dropped what was left of the cigarette. He smiled at Brodick, shook his hand and turned away. Brodick had been treated with great courtesy and given an attention he didn't really deserve, or so it seemed to Brodick, but now he was forgotten as if he'd never been there. There were scores of people just like him urgently needing treatment, after all, and many were in far worse shape.

35

Brodick knew he looked terrible—and also ridiculous.

The bandage resembled an immense, off-white turban and it was starting to list to one side, giving him an absurdly rakish air. That wasn't all. His face was badly bruised and swollen down one side, as if he had a black eye, and Brodick wasn't sure if that was caused by the wound or whether he'd just smacked his face on the ground when the blast of the mortar bomb had tossed him into the air. His left hand was still wrapped up like a boxer's mitt. His eyes seemed unnaturally large, and somehow the right seemed bigger than the left, or was he imagining it? He stared at this gaunt and misshapen fellow in the mirror as he tried to shave without moving his head more than was absolutely necessary.

To his chagrin, Fang displayed no sign of sympathy. She put a hand up to her mouth in an instinctive gesture to hide her grin as he climbed in the back of the cream Merc without hitting his bandaged head on the edge of the door, sitting gingerly on the seat, keeping his back straight, like a damaged dowager trying to sit in a horse-drawn carriage without upsetting her tiara and losing her precious dignity. It would have been hilarious if he wasn't still in pain and bruised all over. Oddly, his hand stung more than his scalp.

For a rolling car meet, as this was known, it seemed to be in slow motion because of the dressing.

'You're not going to leave Beirut like that, are you?'

'It will be smaller by then—hopefully a lot smaller.'

'Did they shave your head?'

'Where the cut is, yes they did. Of course. They had to.'

Fang muttered something in Chinese. It sounded like the equivalent of "bloody hell" or some such.

'I'll wear a hat once they take this off until my hair has grown back.'

'You'd better,' and she couldn't stop herself this time, but snorted with laughter.

'Okay, okay. Very funny.'

'I'm sorry, Drew. Really I am.'

'No, you're not. You're not sorry at all, damn you.'

On the seat between them was a print-out in English from the China News Service (CNS), an outfit controlled by a spy outfit called the United Front Work Department. Brodick was of the opinion that the CNS seemed to have been designed by the *Guoanbu*'s top boffins as a weapon of mass destruction capable of killing foreigners by sheer tedium. This particular headline read *"Giant Panda Enjoys Leisure Time in Chengdu"*.

He didn't ask the obvious: why Fang had been reading it.

Perhaps it belonged not to her but to the two Chinese minders up front, who might be using it to practice their English. One of them was probably her communications officer when he wasn't being her minder or driver. Right now they were pretending not to see or hear anything, trying to be invisible, the one behind the wheel manoeuvring slowly through the streets of the western sector, stopping and starting and occasionally pulling into the kerb, circling back, reversing. Their version of route surveillance was thorough if somewhat obvious.

'So when do you leave?'

'Four days.'

'You'll have the stitches out by then?'

'Not necessary. They disintegrate by themselves, apparently.'

'You're travelling by ferry?'

'Yes, on Thursday night. Departure time 2200 hours.'

'And you're taking Li with you.'

'Only as far as Larnaca. There'll be a handover. Someone from the high commission will come down from Nicosia to meet us.'

The first *treff* between someone like Li and the handler making the formal recruitment pitch was known as the bump.

'Fenner?'

'Fenner, yes. He'll be there. But he'll be bringing along the cultural attaché, someone named Henderson as well as a woman, Olivia—Olivia Cheetham—from the British Council.'

Henderson would make the pitch.

'What happens then?'

Brodick shrugged. 'They'll make a fuss of him, make the offer, tell him what a brilliant man he is, praise his decision to come over to us, how wonderful that he has chosen the UK and what a thrilling place he's going to be working etcetera etcetera, buy him breakfast, maybe brief him on the university offer and relocation details, give him some brochures to read and then put him on a plane for London. They won't want him in Cyprus for any longer than is strictly necessary—if only for security reasons, I imagine. They'll want to move him on quickly. There'll probably have someone on the plane with him. Given that everyone seems to want to get hold of him, it seems a wise move.'

'And you?'

'Fenner hasn't said. He will no doubt give me my orders.'

'How are you feeling, Drew?'

'Kind of you to ask. As you'd expect with three dozen stitches and having been hurled through the air and dropped flat on my face. Aside from a splitting headache whenever I move and the bruises, I'm feeling bloody marvellous. I must count myself lucky I'm still around at all.'

'You'll be with Li on the boat, then. You're escorting him.'

'I'm only there so I can make the introductions and hear Fenner's instructions.'

'Is Li excited?'

'I don't think so. He doesn't show much emotion, but I think he's very, very glad to be leaving Beirut. He doesn't enjoy being shot at. It makes him nervous.'

'But I guess he's happy to be going to teach at a top UK university, right?'

'I imagine so, but nothing has been settled as far as I know.'

'You'll share a cabin?'

'Of course not. Why do you ask?' Brodick frowned and shot her a quick glance that only made his headache worse.

'I haven't been on the ferry, so I don't know what it's like.'

What was DRAGON planning?

'The cabins are small with double bunks, but single travellers can book one without having to share.'

'You'll be coming back to Beirut afterwards; I mean, after you've delivered Li to your embassy friends?'

'Maybe I'll have to go to London first. It all depends on what they think of your recruitment and what they expect of me. I really don't know; and they're not my friends. Are you finished with the questions, Fang?'

'Will the reception committee meet the ferry?'

'Too early. We'll gather initially at the Marina Bay Hotel in Larnaca.'

'Well, don't worry. I'll find you wherever you are, never fear.'

'I've got some papers for you.'

'So have I.'

They swapped packages: brown envelopes of supposedly stolen classified documents plus a couple of rolls of film from Fang.

Nothing else was said. Brodick had expected Fang to discuss their future and consider how they would manage their professional relationship, but perhaps she couldn't, given the presence of her minders. He asked to be dropped near the Commodore and, when they stopped, Brodick gingerly exited the Merc, taking his time, legs first, and then arse, torso and his lopsided, turbaned head last of all for fear of striking it on the car roof. He was worried about the bandage falling off and rolling under the car. That bothered him more than the possibility of being shot or blown up.

*

Brodick packed up his clothing and books, just in case they would have to be sent on after he'd left, a job that would no doubt be left to the capable Fawzi. At Levant Travel, long after his colleagues had left for home, he packed up the TITHE gear, and remembered to return the Astra 400 handgun to its shoebox, locking everything away in the "secret" cupboard, checking the desk drawers were empty and that he'd left nothing lying around.

The big event was the removal of Brodick's embarrassing turban, and its replacement with a much smaller gauze dressing—not unlike a skull cap—which now covered the very tender and pink wound running down the centre of his shaved scalp like a forest firebreak - or maybe a punk Mohican hairstyle in reverse. He went shopping for a hat and found a straw fedora that he thought concealed his bald patch; and he seemed to appear sufficiently normal for him to feel confident enough to say goodbye also to Maha and friends without spooking them or giving them grounds for ridicule. He told everyone that his assignment as Levant Travel manager was over and that he did not expect to return. They made all the right noises, naturally. Maha kissed him carefully on the cheek and hugged him, murmuring her concern and sympathy after his "incident".

Brodick was not at all sorry to be leaving, but of course he didn't say so.

But he would miss the penthouse and the west-facing balcony with the wondrous view of the Mediterranean. On his last night in Beirut—the Wednesday—he sat outside in splendid isolation with a bottle of Veuve Clicquot all to himself to celebrate his imminent departure—and as he toasted himself and refilled his flute again and again he pondered his professional relationship with Fang, aka DRAGON.

The normal course of events, in so far as he was her case officer and she his agent, would mean that he would be posted to the British embassy in Singapore or consulate in Bangkok and under diplomatic cover would run her from there. Or, if she was *his* case officer and he were *her* agent, then she would move to London to work under diplomatic cover in the PRC embassy to run him as her mole inside SIS. The contradiction was obvious, but how would they finesse it? It had to be a solution jointly agreed and undertaken; above all it would have to seem entirely natural and acceptable to both her employers and his, without raising any suspicion. A third country, perhaps, but which? Not only did they need a mutually agreed solution but the means to engineer it. But, as the level fell in the champagne bottle and the pink and violet sunset turned midnight blue and the stars appeared along with increasing numbers of mosquitoes, Brodick felt himself unequal to the task of working it out.

*

'Did you call her? Abrielle?'

'Yeah, I did. Thanks for the number, by the way.'

'Anything come of it?'

Li—or Lee—paused before answering. 'She said she was too busy right now.'

Now that was surprising. Maybe he'd got Abrielle all wrong from the start. Maybe she was just an independent young woman in a deeply patriarchal society who chose to fulfil her needs in her own way with whoever took her fancy. Beirut's own Clytemnestra.

'Really? You'd think a television reporter would want to meet a maths genius.'

'Fuck off, Sullivan.'

Apologies, Abrielle. I had you all wrong. You're no one's honey-trap, just someone who lives her life to the full on her own terms, and who could possibly object to that?

They stood side by side, Li/Lee big and bulky in comparison with Brodick, drinking Budweiser straight from the bottle and looking out over the stern rail, watching the final preparations to sail under the powerful port lights along the wharf. Just across the sheen of oily seawater was the blackened wreck of the warehouse on the opposite wharf and the twisted girders of cranes damaged by the salvoes of rocket fire that had sunk the *Basra Star* and detonated its cargo of missiles.

Li turned to Brodick. 'So you and Abrielle got together?'

'No. I've been really busy, too. In fact, I didn't hear from her again though she had my number. I don't think I was her type.'

'You didn't call her?'

'My impression was that she likes to make the first move.'

Brodick felt the engines of the ferry thudding through the soles of his feet like the heartbeat of some huge animal. Even the rail he was leaning against vibrated like a living thing. The dock workers were taking the gangway away now, wheeling it out of the way, and stevedores in orange high-visibility jackets and enormous gloves stood by fore and aft, waiting for the command to release the lines.

'I'm going to get my head down.' Brodick had finished his beer.

'Okay. I'm going to stay here on deck for a while. It's my first time. On board a ship, I mean.'

'It'll be a calm run, I think. Good night, Tony.' Brodick turned away.

'Night, man. Oh, Drew, by the way, what's your cabin number?'

'Seventeen. You?'

'Twenty-three.'

But Brodick already knew that.

*

His wristwatch showed the time as 3.40am.

Lying on his back in his bunk, Brodick realised the light shining through the tiny curtain across his solitary porthole was far too bright to be moonlight. A second realisation: the ferry had not reached its destination and was still at sea but was no longer moving, at least, she wasn't making any forward progress.

He heard muffled shouts, then hurried footsteps thudded overhead.

Brodick was up off the bed, pulling on his trousers and shirt, hurriedly buttoning both, grabbing his rucksack containing passports—both Brodick's and Sullivan's—along with Lebanese, Cypriot and British currency, keys and most precious of all, Fang's latest gift of secret documents and film secreted into the lining. He pushed his feet into his shoes, pulled his hat carefully yet firmly down on his head and glanced around the cabin, and went out into the narrow, dimly lit corridor.

He pushed his way through a crowd of anxious passengers, heading both ways in a confused melee while a disembodied Greek Cypriot voice crackled repeatedly over a loudspeaker in English and Greek, ordering passengers and crew to muster immediately in the saloon.

Brodick ignored the instruction, pushing his way out on deck and hurrying forward. He noted the steady though light breeze, the roll of the ferry. He was brought to an abrupt halt by a surprising sight; what appeared to be a modern fishing vessel lay not more than one-hundred-and-fifty metres or thereabouts off the port quarter, searchlights on the bridge continuously sweeping the ferry from bow to stern and back again. The strange ship—two-tone grey camouflage—was probably classed as an AGI, a converted trawler and intelligence ship displacing perhaps 3,000 tons; but there were no identification marks that Brodick could see, no discernible numbers on the bow, no ensign at the stern. His first thought was that she must be Israeli, but then again this was no fast patrol boat but an ocean-going ship more substantial. There was what looked like a 4.5-inch gun forward and a helicopter pad amidships. She bristled with antennae and the usual booms and cranes one might expect of a trawler.

Men in dark clothing were gathered opposite, some manning what looked like a 30mm twin barrelled Oerlikon cannon, its muzzles pointed at the ferry.

On tiptoe, he leaned as far as he could over the rail and peered down the side of the ferry to the waterline. There was at least one boarding ladder and at the bottom of it a rigid raider tethered alongside; it seemed that whoever they were, they'd already boarded and must have taken control.

'Hey!'

Brodick was pulled violently back, away from the railing, then turned and frog-marched back along the deck, so forcefully and quickly he was in danger of losing his footing. His arms were pinned behind his back by two men, both in black, faces obscured by black balaclavas and both armed with submachine guns or machine pistols, by the look of them of the universally popular Heckler & Koch type.

'Saloon! You go to saloon!'

They didn't sound like Russians.

When they reached the hatch they gave him a final push.

Brodick knew better than to try to resist.

The saloon was packed: frightened men, weeping women and wailing children as well as crew members. The bearded captain was there, standing slightly apart, his naval cap on the back of his head, scowling at his captors, arms akimbo.

The invaders were checking the passenger manifest and one crew member—a junior officer, probably—was calling out names. Those identified were told to step forward and show their passports. They were then told to return to their cabins.

Brodick spotted Li and waved to him. Li waved back.

'Lee, Tony.'

Li stepped out of the crowd, Canadian passport in hand. He stood patiently, smiling with polite deference, as they checked his passport with the name on the passenger list. Only he wasn't allowed to leave. Two of the boarders took him out on deck, holding him by the arms. He made no effort to resist, although he seemed so much bulkier than his escort. Brodick couldn't reach him, but instead turned and cupped his hands against the glass of one of the saloon portholes and tried to make out what was happening. Members of the boarding party had surrounded Li. They seemed to be talking or arguing.

They took Li to the head of the ladder.

They were going to take him with them.

This had to be DRAGON's doing. She had asked so many questions and, as far as Brodick knew, only she knew the details of Li's travel plans.

Brodick pushed his way forward to the front of the crowd and raised his voice, addressing himself to one of the "visitors" who seemed to be in charge. 'Mr Lee is a friend of mine. We're travelling together. Why are you abducting him? What's he done?'

'Passport.'

Brodick had it ready.

'Step back, Mr Sullivan. Wait here until your name is called.'

'Where are you taking my friend? He's an academic. Why are you doing this?'

Even to his own ears, Brodick's shrill complaints sounded pathetic, but he was mindful of the documents he was carrying and he wasn't about to push matters too far. A thorough search of his bag was the last thing he needed. This was no time for heroism.

The man—presumably someone of rank—placed a hand on Brodick's chest and shoved him firmly backwards into the crowd. 'You stay. We will call your name. Your friend okay.'

Brodick was sure of it: by the eyes just inches away from his own, and by the accent, the officer or whatever he was who'd just pushed him was unmistakably east Asian.

He had to be Chinese.

When Brodick looked again, Li had vanished.

*

Brodick ran.

He had no plan, no objective.

It was instinct that drove him out on deck, skidding aft, ducking out of the light and into shadow, leaping up, two steps at a time, up, up onto the lifeboat deck, the same deck where he'd slept on a previous daytime journey to Larnaca.

He took a deep breath of sea air, steadied himself, tried to think.

There was no way he was going to wait passively until his name was called.

He edged along the deck, looking back, watching out for armed pursuers.

Brodick knew only one thing: this was Fang's handiwork. It had to be.

He'd told her—foolishly—how, when and where Li would be tonight, and there had been just enough time for the Chinese to intercept the ferry and abduct Li.

Fang: one, Brodick: nil.

Shouted commands followed on the deck below, along with the crash of boots coming up the gangway behind him: several armed men, by the sound of it.

The documents were what mattered: Fang's secret files and undeveloped film.

If he was caught with them in his possession it was tantamount to a confession; and not just his freedom was at stake, but quite possibly Fang's life also.

For a second he thought of throwing himself overboard, but he sensed they'd pick him up eventually and, in any case, the intelligence he had would be ruined.

Brodick ran past two white cannisters containing life rafts. They were of no use.

Ahead were two partially enclosed lifeboats on their davits below the level of the deck. He ran past the first and on to the second. With moments to spare, he told himself he had no option but to try to find a way inside. He climbed the railing, stepped over and—trying to balance himself against the roll of the ferry, chest heaving, heart pounding—placed one foot onto the gunwale of the lifeboat and then the other foot, transferring his weight over and working his way around to the outside so that he was provided with at least some cover from anyone approaching. He couldn't stay there, though. He kept moving until he found a small, covered entrance protected by what appeared to be a flap of stiff canvas.

He almost fell over backwards at this point, but kneeling on the lifeboat, his weight on his hands, he managed to push the flap aside and squeezed his head and shoulders into the interior, wriggling furiously, kicking with his legs and feet.

He and his secret documents were out of sight in utter darkness.

Had they seen him?

There was an almost overpowering stink of fresh paint and seawater.

Brodick breathed through his open mouth and tried to still his heart.

Low male voices approached, the clink of what sounded like a rifle sling.

They were just feet away. Brodick, squatting in a puddle of rainwater or seawater, tried to hold his breath as if diving underwater.

More muffled shouts from below. They sounded like commands—in Mandarin.

A bosun's whistle wailed.

At last—as if another lifetime had passed—the voices and footsteps retreated.

The ferry's engines rumbled into life, vibrating through the lifeboat's hull.

36

London might be perpetually changing, and by no means always for the better, yet one thing stayed the same, at least for Brodick: the illusory sense of being at the centre of everything that mattered. The city's obsession with itself might help make the English political class hopelessly self-important and introspective, but for Brodick it was a homecoming of a special kind. It felt as if he was being plugged back in to the world, recharged. Call it what you will—the heart of Anglo-American culture, the centre of neoliberal global finance—it didn't matter. The transport system might be broken, the housing market a disgrace, the cost of just about everything prohibitively and absurdly expensive, violent crime at a new peak thanks to economic cutbacks in public services and education, and the corrupt politicians of Westminster might be quite shameless, yet for all that the sheer vibrancy of this billionaires' playground was always invigorating.

Just being back, pounding the streets, lifted Brodick's spirits. His first task was to replace the straw hat with something more durable and rain resistant, and he eventually found a brown trilby in Jermyn Street that would do the job.

There was nothing quite as satisfying as celebrating his return with an unfashionably traditional *treff* with the boss at Rules in Maiden Lane WC2 over the famed steak-and-kidney pie, washed down with a bottle of the house claret, followed by apple pie and custard and all of it on the Firm. Both the maitre d' and the barman recognised MacGregor, or pretended to do so, welcoming him back like an old friend. Even Brodick's host, in green tweed, seemed to have caught something of Brodick's relaxed and celebratory mood.

'I said you'd do well, laddie, and you have.'

'Thank you.' It was no small praise coming from MacGregor.

'How's the head?'

'Better. Thanks.' The wound was still tender—and ugly—but the hair was growing back and the stitches had all but vanished.

'We're all very impressed with DRAGON's latest material.' MacGregory paused. 'That paper by the PLA Navy chief—'

'Admiral Liu Huaqing.'

'Yes. Admiral Liu. His paper on the future role of China's nuclear submarines has the Americans very excited. They say they've never had such a clear description of Chinese strategic nuclear planning. It's unprecedented, or so they claim. Same goes for the submarine radiation leaks and their problem of the high noise levels of their boats.'

'I'm glad.' What else could Brodick say?

Other than it might help offset his failure to obtain Li Zuanfei's services.

MacGregor would have seen for himself all that DRAGON had supplied, and all that Brodick had provided to the *Guoanbu*. Presumably he'd formed a judgement, but he gave no sign of what he really thought.

'But there's a cost to your success as I'm sure you'll be aware.'

MacGregor's praise was rarely given and never unqualified.

He spoke quietly, his voice so low that Brodick had to lean forward to hear him. 'There'll be questions. Tomorrow before the committee—and forever thereafter, I don't doubt. Primarily they'll be asking you if she is really yours, or if you are really hers. They won't put it quite so baldly as that. No, don't answer now. I want you to think this over. Your success in someone so junior, relatively speaking, will raise suspicion and no little envy. In some ways you have been proven too successful too early on in your career for your own good. I have your back, but the questions remain. They won't go away.

'My own feeling, Richard, is that there's never a satisfactory answer. It can't be proven one way or the other, I'm afraid. It's in the nature of the beast. I'm not saying you should be evasive. I *am* suggesting that you listen attentively, that you take your time and frame your replies carefully, with some thought. Treat them all, no matter how idiotic or insulting, with due solemnity: yes, solemnity. My advice is not to show irritation or impatience. Someone may try to provoke you into an outburst or saying something silly that you'll later regret. You don't suffer fools gladly and neither do I. We have our share of idiots and charlatans, and trying to trip you up is something at least one person present will try in all likelihood. It becomes a habit after a while among Whitehall pen-pushers.'

The coffee arrived.

'There's something I feel I should tell you.' Brodick began hesitantly. 'As long as it's off the record and there will be nothing in writing now or later—'

'Go on, then, if you must.'

'DRAGON told me a story that goes all the way back to 1927. I'd like to summarise it if I may. I'll keep it as short as possible.' Without waiting for a further reaction, he related the events surrounding the Dragon's Lair, the three communist penetration agents in the heart of the Nationalist movement in Shanghai, the capture by the Nationalists of the famous illusionist and Communist agent Gu Shunzhang, his betrayal under threat of death by torture of Communist cadres, safe houses and networks, his "politically correct" posthumous demonisation in the Party history, and the slaughter of ten members of Gu's family with the exception of an anonymous female infant, and finally Fang's surprisingly open-minded if not sympathetic view of Gu: surprising in an in intelligence officer still paying lip service to the Chinese variant of Marxism-Leninism.

'Your point is?'

'You'll maybe remember that DRAGON contested the DIA version of her family history. She told us she wasn't Chen Meilin but Zhang Pusheng, that her mother wasn't Jia Lihwa as previously thought but Fan Jin, and that her father, a very senior figure in the

PRC intelligence community, wasn't Chen Aiguo after all, but one Zhang Tsen Tsiang. And neither we nor our American friends have since been able to confirm or refute any of it.'

'Does this matter?'

'I suggest—and I admit I have no firm evidence—that DRAGON's mother is that little girl who survived the massacre of Gu's family. The dates fit. I also suggest that DRAGON's mother's real name was Gu, but that it was changed—hidden—when she was adopted or fostered.'

'This is just a theory.'

'Yes, that's all it is.'

'I don't see the relevance.'

Of course he did.

'Imagine, if this were true, what exposure of the mother's true identity would do to DRAGON's father, indeed, to DRAGON's own career in the *Guoanbu*; in fact, to all her family.'

'Are you suggesting this is leverage we might use?'

'I suppose so—as a last resort—but that's not what I had in mind. What I'm really looking for here is motive, her real reason for collaborating. However she might rationalise it, we have to look deeper. At least, I feel I must. I believe Fang aka Chen Meilin aka Zhang Pusheng knows perfectly well who she is, given how important families are to the Chinese. If I'm right, it means that while mainland China is her home and always will be, she'll never feel safe. Insecurity is hard-wired into her from childhood. She can't bury the past, even under a patio, no matter how hard the Chinese Communist Party might try.

'They do a pretty good job of rewriting it.'

Brodick nodded his acknowledgement of the truth of MacGregor's remark, but he was not going to be diverted. Nor would he blurt out what was on the tip-of his tongue: that the British were pretty adept at it, too.

'She once lectured me on how the Chinese people were willing to give up freedoms we Westerners take for granted in return for a degree of stability and security.

'She'll always be looking over her shoulder, waiting for the 3am knock on the door. Security, safety: that's something she'll never have, no matter how high she climbs, or how powerful she becomes. She believes herself to be an imposter, to be somehow inferior to her peers, and she fears that the deception she inherited will one day be discovered. I know that feeling. That's why she's reached out. DRAGON needs friends, allies, a bolthole if things turn pear-shaped, even though she presents herself as iron-clad and indestructible. It's an emotional need.'

Not unlike his own.

Did MacGregor buy it?

He didn't look particularly convinced one way or the other, in fact his expression showed nothing at all, but really all Brodick had wanted was that MacGregor would hear him out.

'I have to ask you this, Richard, if only because others will. Don't take offence.'

Brodick waited. He tried not to show just how apprehensive he was.

'Have you slept with her?'

For once, Brodick answered quickly and truthfully. 'Yes.'

MacGregor nodded but said nothing more.

What did it matter? Sex was sex.

*

MacGregor dealt with the bill and they shared the tip.

'Are you ready for the meeting tomorrow?'

'It sounds a wee bit scary, to be honest.'

MacGregor held up his pale hands, palms towards Brodick. 'Oh, no, it will be all very civilised. Everyone will be charming. They'll flatter you, say all the right things to put you at your ease. Watch out for that: they mean to disarm you. Watch out for questions about your private life, too. They'll pretend to be interested in you. They're not. Just don't answer would be my advice. Better that than show emotion. Pretend you haven't heard if they ask you about hobbies or your sex life. No war stories, mind. Never do personal if you can avoid it: not in our line of work, not even with colleagues.'

'You'll be there, won't you?'

'Aye. I'll introduce you.'

'Thanks.'

'And don't forget: the TCI sub-committee is specifically set up to support you and for no other reason. You are the spear point in this operation, the officer who's making it all happen. Tomorrow's meeting has been called to offer you further support and to explore how we can achieve greater productivity while safeguarding the security of the agent and the agent's handler. *You*. You're not being interrogated, Richard, at least not officially.'

But that was precisely what he was being warned about.

Brodick put on his humble expression. 'I'm sorry about Li Zuanfei, aka Tony Lee.'

'There was nothing anyone could have done short of firing an Exocet at the bastards, and quite frankly preserving your relationship with DRAGON had to take precedence.'

'Any idea where he is, or who took him?'

'Not yet. I suspect the Chinese have him on the mainland by now. I doubt whether you'll be asked about it tomorrow. It probably won't even rate a mention. You never discussed Li with DRAGON, did you?'

'No. And she never raised the issue.'

The lies were coming easily now.

Brodick was well aware that it wasn't every thirty-something-year-old intelligence officer on the lower rungs of the career ladder who was rewarded with his own ad hoc Target and Counter-Intelligence subcommittee, in this instance a TCI subcommittee codenamed CARAPACE and running a senior Chinese intelligence officer, codename DRAGON.

Chip off the old block, they'd say behind his back.

'There'll be someone you haven't yet met: Derek Simpson, from Requirements. I don't think you know one Mavis Hyland, either. She'll represent Production and last, but by no means least, TCI

CARAPACE has its own Security Branch Officer, Harry Drygate, formerly a Special Branch detective inspector: and quite unrelated to the Glasgow craft beer of the same name.'

'Six of us in all.'

'I'm not a CARAPACE member, strictly speaking: just the supervising Controller.'

'But you're the boss.'

'If you put it like that, yes I am. I suggest you drop by my office around nine and I'll take you into the meeting.'

'Fine. Thanks.'

Even Max Weber had had trouble explaining the peculiarities of British bureaucracy, arguing unconvincingly that it was amateurish, honorific and collegial. As for SIS, its structure was both vertical and horizontal, and yes, it did manage to be collegial. It was one of its organisational strengths, apparently.

'What are your plans for this evening, Richard?'

'A good book and an early night.'

'You're at the George?'

'I am, yes.'

'Popular with Americans, I'm told. The rooms are a bit small.'

'It's fine. Water's hot and plentiful and the beds are clean and comfortable and that's all I care about.'

They collected their coats. Brodick put on his new hat. They went out into a thin, cold curtain of drizzle sweeping along the Ferraris and Porsches parked illegally in the lane.

'So you'll be on your best behaviour tomorrow.'

'I'll do my best.'

'You'd better, laddie.'

Brodick thanked MacGregor for the lunch and they were about to separate when McGregor halted, turned to face him and held Brodick's arm. He glanced over Brodick's shoulder before speaking in a low voice.

'Something you should know, Richard. It concerns our French friend, M. Malry.'

MacGregor looked into Brodick's face.

'The DGSE know. They have known for quite some time: for years.'

It took a second to sink in.

'You mean…?' Brodick grappled with the implications, couldn't find the words.

'Paris tripled their man, and have run Malry in place, along with his partner, and they started to do so before he could cause significant damage. He didn't have much choice. My view is that the Chinese have guessed, or at the very least Beijing have their suspicions and threw you a bone to see what would happen. Maybe DRAGON knows, maybe she doesn't. I would suggest that the *Guoanbu* want to see if he'll run, or if he'll be arrested. It's a test. You were the delivery boy, using Beirut as a somewhat circuitous route.'

'Does the TCI know?'

'Aye, they do. They're sure to ask you about it, seek your view.'

With that, MacGregor let go of Brodick's arm and walked away, leaving Brodick rocking on his heels, blinking in the drizzle.

Inwardly, Brodick was shaking as if he had a fever.

That's what this was, then, and had been, right from the start. From Brodick's detention and his recruitment—or Fang's recruitment—along with her promises to help his career, the romantic meals by the sea—well, not *that* romantic—the enthusiastic if clumsy lovemaking, the exchanges of secret documents, the Minox film: it was all about Malry, a man he'd never met, never even seen, and his equally mysterious Chinese wife. It had never been just about DRAGON and it had never been just about Brodick, either.

He would surely never see her again. He'd served his purpose.

And if they did meet and she asked him, what would he say? What could he say?

Fang could never know that he knew.

He would say nothing because he knew nothing.

37

Just around the corner, as Brodick was about to cross the street, a black cab rattled past, forcing him back onto the pavement and drenching his socks with filthy rainwater, and he caught a fleeting sight of the sole passenger in the back. He thought he saw long dark hair, Asian eyes, the distinctive cheekbones. Or he thought he did. Whoever it was had turned and looked right at him.

Did he imagine it, or did she smile?

Brodick's pulse beat a rapid tattoo.

Surely not… She can't be here… Can she?

He told himself not to be stupid; he was seeing things. He was seeing what he wanted to see, not what was actually there in front of his face. If MacGregor was right, Brodick was of no further use to Beijing, or to Fang for that matter. He'd been led quite a dance, and MacGregor knew it but had been too kind to say so. The rain stopped and Brodick's aimless perambulations around the West End continued as he worked off the lunch and the shock of MacGregor's news. So much for Fang's bona fides.

Would DRAGON want to continue their relationship? Almost certainly not.

Did he? Did the Firm?

The committee would ask, too, and he would say—suggest—that the DGSE might be encouraged by their SIS friends and allies to be *seen* to check all Malry's work, going back years, all his intelligence assessments and reports since arriving in Beijing. Hopefully, that would leak to the *Guoanbu*. Then he should be quietly flown back to France with his wife, officially on holiday or perhaps medical leave. He should seem to take this in his stride, suspecting nothing. The reason given would just have to seem plausible. He should then disappear for weeks, vanishing from view. Again, word would have to leak out—perhaps via a third party such as SIS, indeed from Brodick himself—that Malry and his good wife were being interrogated—separately—in considerable depth. Finally, the Malrys should return to work as if nothing had happened along with snaps of their family beach holiday and a tan to prove it. Cleared of all suspicion, naturally. Beijing's anxieties could be assuaged and Malry and his wife would be able to resume their deception.

So could he.

What was the alternative?

He stopped outside a coffee shop, its windows decorated with Italianate script in gold. Very chic. It was closed, the fragile gilt chairs hugging one another upside down on the tables inside. In Dover Street, he halted again to peer into the window of an art gallery specialising in the eighteenth century and admired a florid and no doubt priceless Fragonard landscape, and to one side what appeared to be a voluptuous Boucher nude in pencil. His back was clear as far as he could tell. In surveillance terms he was pretty sure he was *in obscura:* both in the clear and unobserved. Brodick absently slipped his right hand in his coat pocket and his fingers encountered a rectangular scrap of stiff paper, folded in half, which he was absolutely sure hadn't been there that morning or, for that matter, before lunch. He pulled it out with shaking fingers, opened it.

In blunt capital letters with a red, felt tip pen was a single staccato line:

'Churchill Hyatt, Portman Sq, room 217. 10 pm.'

Underneath, not unlike a signature, were Chinese characters which Brodick recognised as the ideogram for dragon, symbolising force, strength, power:

龍

Elation and apprehension struggled for the upper hand.

So much for the next chapter of "*War and Peace*" and an early night.

Did You Enjoy This Book?

If so, you can make a HUGE difference

For any author, the single most important way we have of getting our books noticed is a really simple one—and one which you can help with.

Yes, you.

Us indie authors and publishers don't have the financial muscle of the big guys to take out full-page ads in the newspaper or put posters on the subway.

But we do have something much more powerful and effective than that, and it's something that those big publishers would kill to get their hands on.

A committed and loyal bunch of readers.

Honest reviews of our books help bring them to the attention of other readers.

If you've enjoyed this book I would be really grateful if you could spend just a couple of minutes leaving a review (it can be as short as you like) on this book's page on your favourite store and website.

https://burningchairpublishing.com/product/spy-dragon/

Acknowledgements

My thanks to Peter Oxley and Simon Finnie at Burning Chair for their professionalism and enthusiastic commitment in publishing Spy Game and Spy Dragon.

A friend has gone out of his way to help, given his extensive knowledge of China and his fluency in Chinese. Because he lives in the shadow of the 'relevant department', he does not wish to be identified by name. I also relied on the following and would like to thank the authors and publishers for work that has helped plug innumerable gaps in my knowledge. That said, any errors are entirely mine.

Aldrich, Richard J., GCHQ, The Uncensored Story of Britain's Most Secret Intelligence Agency, Harper Press, London, 2010;

Andrew, Christopher, The Secret World, A History of Intelligence, Allen Lane, 2018;

Brown, Kerry, The World According to XI, L.B. Tauris, London, 2018;

Davies, Philip H.J., MI6 and the machinery of spying, Frank Cass, London, 2005;

Clissold, Tim, Mr. China, Constable, London, 2004;

Chang, Iris, Thread of the Silkworm, Basic Books, New York, 1995;

Faligot, Roger, Chinese Spies from Chairman Mao to Xi Jinping, Scribe, Victoria, 2019;

Hoffman, David E., The Billion Dollar Spy, A True Story of Cold War Espionage and Betrayal, Icon Books, London, 2018;

Jaber, Hala, Hezbollah: Born With A Vengeance, Colombia University Press, New York, 1997;

Mattis, Peter & Brazil, Matthew, Chinese Communist Espionage: An Intelligence Primer, Naval Institute Press, Annapolis, 2019;

Piper, Fred & Murphy, Sean, Cryptography, A Very Short Introduction, OUP, New York, 2002;

Smith, Michael, New Cloak, Old Dagger, How Britain's Spies Came In From The Cold, Victor Gollancz, London, 1996;

Vogel, Ezra F., Deng Xiiaoping and the Transformation of China, Harvard University Press, 2013;

West, Nigel, Spycraft Secrets: An Espionage A-Z, The History Press, Gloucestershire, 2017;

Yang Jisheng, *Tombstone, The Untold Story of Mao's Great Famine,* Allen Lane, London, 2012.

Coming Soon

The following is the first chapter from John Fullerton's next and third Richard Brodick novel, provisionally entitled Spy Hunt:

Shadows come alive, murmuring at her approach, breaking up and moving aside in the corridor, shuffling out of her way.

Cops, technicians, chambermaids, cleaners, curious guests, idlers.

Lishi. Left this world.

Siwang. Died.

Zou le. Gone.

Dao Tiantang. Gone to heaven.

Qu jian Ma-ke-si. Gone to meet Marx.

The comedian who mumbles this last, anti-Communist remark sniggers and falls silent.

She smells fear and sweat, the musty, unwashed bodies of winter, halitosis, cheap hotel soap, apple-scented shampoo and coal dust.

The Englishman is indeed already cold.

The woman whose work name is Fang knows it the moment she sees him, stretched out on his back on the Beijing hotel bed, his head resting on the pillows as if taking a nap. A big man, dressed in a suit, white shirt, no tie, shoes off, no sign of a struggle, no blood, yet she sees he is already absent from himself and this world.

An immaculate corpse ready for the undertaker. Even his sparse hair looks combed.

zou! zou! Move! Get out!

It isn't polite, but it is effective.

The uniformed police officer, the detective in his padded coat, two hotel security men and the duty manager troop out like scared children, the idlers in the corridor retreat. None objects. None questions the order. Only the detective hesitates, glancing back at her and opening his mouth as if he wants to say something only to think better of it. There is nothing for him to see; the intelligence officer's face yields nothing, her expression impassive, a mask of authority she wears for such occasions and there have been plenty of those. Her iron mask.

She moves fast. She slams the room door in the faces of the forensics team waiting outside and hurries around the bed to the far side, near the window, and takes from her jacket pocket a tin box the size of a spectacle case, which she places on the bedside table. She opens it, removes a syringe, inserts a needle, leans over the foreigner and plunges it into the carotid artery in his neck, drawing out just over five milligrams of viscous blood, removes the needle, caps the syringe and returns both to the container.

She notes cyanosis on the dead man's lips and fingers.

From her pocket she takes a pair of scissors and snips a lock of the man's greying hair. She holds his right hand firmly in her left and with her right, cuts off a slice of thumbnail. These are added to the tin, which she snaps shut and returns to her pocket.

Rigor mortis has started to take hold, starting with a stiffening of head and hands, and that suggests death has occurred within the previous two or three hours, though the heating of the room will have had some impact on its progress.

She makes two local calls from the bedside phone that together last less two minutes and twenty seconds, during which she gives orders for the body to be removed to the mortuary and within an hour of its arrival it is to be cremated. There is to be no autopsy. The services of neither police forensics nor the pathologist are required. There is to be no police investigation, no photographs and no witnesses. All existing paperwork will be destroyed and nothing more is to be recorded in any form.

The woman has seen bodies before. As a child doing the Cultural Revolution, she saw people throw themselves into a river to drown, death being preferable to what awaited them in life, and she'd seen that the dead women lay face up in the water, the men face down.

The audio and video tapes have already been confiscated along with the visitor's passport and briefcase and placed in the intelligence officer's custody: the back seat of her official car, a boxy Red Flag limo with brown curtains over the windows, watched over by her Peoples Liberation Army driver. Distinctions of gender seem to vanish on Beijing streets in winter because everyone looks similar; most wear long, cotton, padded coats and many women either cut their hair short or tuck it out of sight. Today it's twenty below.

The tapes and videos are not limited to the room itself but include the corridor, the lifts, the lobby, the bar, the coffee shop, the restaurant and the parking lot, the drive out front all the way to the gates and the street beyond. Everything from midnight until now: ten hours and forty-three minutes' worth of state surveillance.

All record of the *waibin*'s stay at the front desk has been destroyed or deleted, along with his credit card details on registration along with digital invoices.

Scrubbed clean, all of it.

Mr Peacock was never there, warm or cold, alive or dead.

It is a matter of national security. It takes precedence over everything and anyone.

The staff of the Friendship Hotel in Haidian district, northwest of Beijing, have never seen him. They will remember nothing and they will not talk, not so much as another whisper or murmur, on pain of unemployment and a compulsory vacation at the state's expense in the *laogai* or camps.

By the time the colonel of the People's Liberation Army's intelligence service—known as PLA2 and more importantly, the deputy controller of the *Guoanbu*'s 5th Bureau, responsible for counterintelligence—reaches her own office, a copy of the brief foreign ministry statement she dictated over the telephone lies on her desk.

A foreign businessman, Roger Atwood Herbert Peacock, aged 54, was found dead in his Beijing hotel room this morning by one of the cleaning staff. Mr Peacock, a UK national from Essex in England, died of heart failure, believed to have been triggered by excessive drinking. No foul play is suspected. The British consulate in Beijing has been informed.

*

You can find out more about this and other books by signing up to the author's website for the occasional blog post and news at https://www.johnfullertonauthor.scot

About the Author

During the Cold War John Fullerton was, for a time, a "contract labourer" for the British Secret Intelligence Service, in the role of head agent on the Afghan-Pakistan frontier. This experience forms the basis of the first Brodick novel, *Spy Game*. The events and characters of the second novel, *Spy Dragon*, were also informed by John's time as Reuters bureau chief in Beirut during part of the Lebanon civil war.

All told, he's lived or worked in 40 countries as a journalist and covered a dozen wars. For 20 years he was employed by Reuters as a correspondent and editor with postings in Hong Kong, Delhi, Beirut, Nicosia, Cairo, and London.

His home is in Scotland.

About Burning Chair

Burning Chair is an independent publishing company based in the UK, but covering readers and authors around the globe. We are passionate about both writing and reading books and, at our core, we just want to get great books out to the world.

Our aim is to offer something exciting; something innovative; something that puts the author and their book first. From first class editing to cutting edge marketing and promotion, we provide the care and attention that makes sure every book fulfils its potential.

We are:

Different

Passionate

Nimble and cutting edge

Invested in our authors' success

If you're an author and would like to know more about our submissions requirements and receive our free guide to book publishing, visit:

www.burningchairpublishing.com

If you're a reader and are interested in hearing more about our books, being the first to hear about our new releases or great offers, or becoming a beta reader for us, again please visit:

www.burningchairpublishing.com

Other Books by Burning Chair Publishing

Point of Contact, by Richard Ayre

Spy Game, by John Fullerton

The Curse of Becton Manor, by Patricia Ayling

Near Death, by Richard Wall

Blue Bird, by Trish Finnegan

The Tom Novak series, by Neil Lancaster
Going Dark
Going Rogue
Going Back

10:59, by N R Baker

Love Is Dead(ly), by Gene Kendall

A Life Eternal, by Richard Ayre

Haven Wakes, by Fi Phillips

Beyond, by Georgia Springate

Burning, An Anthology of Short Thrillers, edited by Simon Finnie and Peter Oxley

The Infernal Aether series, by Peter Oxley
The Infernal Aether
A Christmas Aether
The Demon Inside
Beyond the Aether
The Old Lady of the Skies: 1: Plague

The Wedding Speech Manual: The Complete Guide to Preparing, Writing and Performing Your Wedding Speech, by Peter Oxley

www.burningchairpublishing.com

Printed in Great Britain
by Amazon